Fake It

till
you # Make It

Fake It till you Make It

SIERA LONDON

FOREVER

New York Boston

Copyright © 2024 by Siera London

Cover design by Yoly Cortez. Cover images © iStock, Depositphotos.
Cover copyright © 2024 by Hachette Book Group, Inc.

Forever
Hachette Book Group
1290 Avenue of the Americas, New York, NY 10104
read-forever.com
@readforeverpub

First Edition: April 2024

Forever is an imprint of Grand Central Publishing. The Forever name and logo are trademarks of Hachette Book Group, Inc.

The publisher is not responsible for websites (or their content) that are not owned by the publisher.

The Hachette Speakers Bureau provides a wide range of authors for speaking events. To find out more, go to hachettespeakersbureau.com or email HachetteSpeakers@hbgusa.com.

Forever books may be purchased in bulk for business, educational, or promotional use. For information, please contact your local bookseller or the Hachette Book Group Special Markets Department at special.markets@hbgusa.com.

ISBNs: 9781538739389 (mass market), 9781538739396 (ebook)

Printed in the United States of America

OPM

10 9 8 7 6 5 4 3 2 1

To all my family and friends, this one is for us.
I love you more than words can ever express.

"As long as we are not ourselves, we will try to be what other people are."
                                    —Malidoma Patrice Somé

"Go confidently in the direction of your dreams. Live the life you've imagined."
                                    —Thoreau

Fake It *till you* Make It

Chapter One

FLEEING THE SCENE of a breakup should come with a check-list, and jumper cables. Amarie Walker sat frozen in the passenger seat of her best friend's new Toyota Prius, her life stuffed into three Louis Vuitton Damier travel bags with gold-embossed initials—his, not hers—in the back seat. Vali, her ride-or-die since freshman year of college, stared at her from behind the wheel.

"You ready to tell me why I drove five hours from the District to pick you up at the edge of nowhere?"

Ignoring the blatant dig about their current location, Amarie averted her gaze from Vali's face, a flawless mask of patience perfected by a nude color palette on her lips and round cheeks, with brows sharp enough to cut the national debt in half. How did she manage a Lizzo-worthy look at seven o'clock in the morning?

"I've ruined my life," Amarie hiccuped, wiping away the dampness trickling down her full cheeks. "I stayed too long and left too early—in the morning, obviously. Either way, I've ruined my engagement and my life."

And the foreseeable future, intentionally, according to

her mother. Who, in hindsight, Amarie should have called *after* she'd formulated a plan. As it was, she lacked a rebuttal to her parents' ridiculous accusation. What reasonable twenty-eight-year-old woman would choose homelessness, joblessness, and pennilessness at the same time? Certainly not Amarie. In fact, she rarely took one step without ensuring she had a safety net. Preferably, in the shape of another carbon-based life form. But not Russell. She was done with his excuses and her own; their love story was officially reduced to a forgettable paragraph in her dating history.

"Aw, my sweet friend with horrible taste in men," Vali soothed, pulling her in for a brief one-armed hug. "Who did slut-nuts do this time?"

"His future baby mama," she sobbed. "Take a left turn to go up the mountain, please." Tears plus Amarie always equaled the same equation—Russell inserting his thermometer in another woman's hot spot.

"Whoa," Vali mouthed, following Amarie's directions. They found themselves in a charming small town of bungalow houses, big yards, and American-made steel under detached tin-roof car porches. Like the homegrown establishments they drove past—Black Bear Barbecue and Things, the Yogurt and Yoga Place, and Dog-Eared Page Books—the town's landscape possessed an unconventional beauty of a bygone era repurposed. As the Prius's tires bumped and jostled over a weathered creek bridge lined with sleek chocolate cattail plants, champagne diamond–colored water spilled down an evergreen mountainside, crashing into cotton-tipped waves before disappearing beneath rough planks. The scent of damp earth and wildflowers wafted through the car's ventilation, the moisture settling on her skin.

"I love him, but I was stupid to trust him again."

"No, Mari. You're human."

"A stupid human."

"Trusting the man you love isn't dumb, girlfriend."

"Then why do I feel foolish?"

Vali shifted the car into a lower gear, her grip on the gearshift tight and prolonged. Her lips thinned, the angles sharpening to a needlepoint. "Because his lies fooled your heart. That's on him."

"What about me?"

"You'll heal," she whispered, as the odometer added another bumpy mile between an unknown future and heartbreak.

"You sure?" Amarie gulped down the ripple of anxiety swelling, threatening to capsize her confidence. She had expected an exhilarating rush of freedom after walking away from her fiancé of six years. Instead, she felt adrift, a broken fragment tossed into an unforeseeable future.

"Of course. I'm a nurse." Vali smiled.

"Instead of love, I settled for lies." A humorless laugh escaped her mouth. "After the first one...I knew." Amarie remembered the clawing pain in her chest the moment she'd overheard his sex-hazed voice and the phlebotomist's giggles through his office door. A guttural urge to rush in and jab Russell and that needle-wielding bloodsucker until she stopped seeing red had gripped her, but she'd battled the instinct. *Explosive* described their confrontation when he'd arrived home after *working late*.

"I come home to you," he'd explained. *"You live in my house. Work in my practice. We are partners who love and respect one another,"* he went on. *"That girl was a one-time mistake,"* he lied *through his perfect teeth.*

Amarie had convinced herself that because she shared Russell's granite bathroom counter space and slept, rather uncomfortably, in his queen-sized bed that crowded her generous curves, he respected the fidelity of their relationship. Of course, she'd heard his mutterings about her fashion sense. Trained herself to forgive his February 14 memory lapses. Had she morphed into a fiancéezilla? Nope. If she extended basic decency, respect, and love to this self-absorbed man, her commitment would pay it forward, right? She would give her best. In return, her man would reserve the number one place in his life for her.

"You should've called me," Vali fumed. "I would've helped you grand slam his tennis balls, Venus-and-Serena-style."

Amarie snorted, followed by a sudden peal of laughter. "Your bail would have been beyond my account balance at the moment," she sighed, breaking eye contact before Vali asked for more details. "Besides, a dollar menu is ten times his value."

Vali nodded. "No lies detected."

Which hurt even more to acknowledge. Back when they'd first met, Amarie had appreciated Russell's Ivy League style of classic white button-downs, V-neck sweaters, and khaki trousers. Closing her eyes, she envisioned that too-curly hair with the gelled side part, his studious expression behind wire-framed glasses. Then her favorite image, the day he'd spoken to her, a cheery Red Cross volunteer delivering free books to new mothers. His boyish smile had captured her naive heart in a made-for-daytime television soap opera. She had been completely smitten with his attention, and his status—shameful, but true. Nine months to the day, she'd practically skipped into her parents' Florida home, gushing to tell them that she, their late bloomer only child, had moved in with her doctor boyfriend. She'd been proud of herself. Her father had, too. That had been a first.

Amarie gave her friend's shoulder a playful shove. "Be glad I called after Prince quit spewing his guts. Tragic to witness. Kleenex worthy." Unfortunately, her 2005 purple BMW 328i sedan was ill-equipped for a successful getaway.

Hours before, Amarie had sat behind the wheel, peering into the darkness as billowy clouds of white smoke rose from beneath Prince's hood. A trio of judgmental goats had looked on as unshed tears stung her eyes. The check engine icon was a glowing red signal of how stupid she was to try to save herself or manage the basics of everyday existence. Alone and disappointed at her current predicament more than the breakup, she'd Facetimed Vali, sob-splaining how she was stuck in a *Blair Witch Project* reboot with unsavory onlookers, that being the goat trio.

"I know how much you love that car. I would've led the resuscitation efforts." Vali grinned. "And, not to be salty, but I would've stormed Russell's ivy tower last night, too."

"You're the best, Vali."

"No lies detected."

"Trust me." Amarie sniffed. "I spared you the slings and arrows of Russell's brutal verbal assault."

Amarie, ever the amenable girlfriend, had traveled a circuitous route to maintain peace, to avoid his temper, but she was sane enough to know her former fiancé would've lashed out at Vali to hurt her. Twelve months into their relationship, and she applied the term loosely with his tomcat tendencies, she and Russell were not the pining couple whose hands were always pawing at the other like she'd dreamed of. Sharing her misgivings with her mother had led to a prompt dismissal of her feelings and an accusation that Amarie's mental hyperactivity would lead to a bad decision that would sabotage her future. Sure enough, her mother had praised a cautiously optimistic Amarie on her engagement the following year. Even her father had foregone *working late* to join the two of them for a celebratory dinner.

The Prius crested a mountain into a Norman Rockwell utopia. Lush grasslands on the right, a serene lake beckoning gingham blankets and romance novels from the passenger window. A soaring kaleidoscope of trees waved to all who entered this untouched paradise. On her left stood a lone house, majestic and proud. This had to be the place.

"Stop the car."

"Okay." Vali slammed a hammer foot on the Prius's brakes. The abrupt action fishtailed the car's rear end. Gravel pelted the under-chassis. Inside the vehicle both passengers and the back seat contents jostled against the door panels. When the momentum released its hold on their churning stomachs, she and Vali exhaled in a rush.

"Sorry." Amarie winced.

"More warning next time or I'm calling you an Uber."

Pausing, Vali angled her head for a view of the house on the hill. The quiet serenity surrounding the stately home with its gabled roof and open-gallery veranda was a stark contrast to D.C.'s Georgia Avenue congestion. She cut the engine at the curb of a majestic country farmhouse complete with a storybook white picket fence. Lavender-tipped wildflowers blanketed a meadow wider than a city block as a breeze, soft and fleeting, bent the tiny blossoms into a subtle bow. Amarie couldn't afford to break, either. Life had twisted and bent her hopes beyond any semblance of her vision board. She could blossom where planted.

"Where are we again? Is this a low-budget surveillance stakeout of Russell's baby mama?"

"No." Amarie choked on her own laughter. "We're in Service, West Virginia." She motioned to the rural town they had driven through with its quaint cobblestone streets. "And don't make me laugh. This reality TV show is my life."

"It's a very lovely house and vet practice—in West Virginia," Vali emphasized. "Just saying, leaving your no-account fiancé is making you act loopy."

Amarie let her forehead fall onto her friend's shoulder, a steady support for the weight of this life-altering flight of fancy she'd undertaken. "I'm laughing, Vali."

No doubt her decision to dump the charming gynecologist— her mother's words—and his *zirconia* diamond ring in the trash can had disappointed her parents, but she was the one who had endured years of office gossip. She was the one who had held her head high under the pitying side glances of his friends' unsolicited prep talks: *You hang in there, girl. He'll get better.*

Angling her head, Vali gave her a wide grin. "I know you're hurting, girlfriend. But would you rather cry or laugh over Russell?"

Amarie shrugged, not sure how to feel. Six years of wasted time deserved a full-on sensory meltdown, right?

"He had Stacia in our bed... total lack of originality."

Vali's brows shot up, registering her surprise. "The divorcée who brings Panera Bread pecan braids every Friday?"

"That's her. It's brilliant, really. Stuffing me with pastries while Russell spread her jam in the back office." The fact that Amarie had been easily distracted with mouth-watering sweet bread while another woman stole her man should have led to crippling embarrassment. But after walking in on a naked Russell and the receptionist she'd hired four months ago, then having to make the emergency call to her best friend from the hood of her broken-down vehicle, recounting the story was low on her twenty-four-hour humiliation list. The fairy tale faded long before last night's final page was written. Amarie's prince charming never slayed her dragons. No, Russell's sword apparently was attached to an automatic drawstring that lowered his boxers and spread fair maiden's thighs. Strangely enough, she couldn't pinpoint when the relationship had entered a death spiral. Somewhere between her juggling to open the clinic every morning, the frantic dash to afternoon classes, or the late-night library study sessions, they'd drifted into toxic complacency.

"How much longer till the tow truck arrives for Prince?" asked Vali.

A fresh wave of anxiety squeezed her lungs at having abandoned her beloved safe haven on a coarse gravel shoulder behind the town's marquee. Working in the D.C. metropolitan area, with the sprawl-and-crawl traffic of five million people, Amarie spent more time in her car than at a physical address. Prince was a home away from home.

"No money for that." Amarie shook her head, truly dismayed at the swiftness of Russell's financial reprisal. "After accusing me of shattering his heart, Russell apparently removed my access to our credit card."

"No way," Vali gasped in outrage. "It…it hasn't even been twelve hours."

Amarie nodded in agreement. "The ATM debit PIN has been changed, too."

"You earned every dollar in that account. Butt wipe," Vali snapped, narrowing her eyes. "I hope you tagged him back."

A slow smile raised the corners of Amarie's mouth.

Vali's smile widened with wicked delight. "What did you do, naughty girl?"

Amarie counted off on her un-manicured fingers. "Hid

the clinic's website. Deleted the YouTube page. And because I'm that girl, I closed his LinkedIn, Instagram, and Facebook business accounts."

"Dang, a full-on social media massacre. Dr. Feldman is ex-communicado." She beamed. "I'm here for it, girlfriend. He should've been paying for your services. Seriously, you saved and earned that man a fortune. He wouldn't be on the top one hundred doctors in the D.C. area list without your social media genius."

"Thank you." She had accomplished something noteworthy, though unacknowledged. Her pounding heart slowed to a fast jog for the first time since she'd walked in on Russell's funfest. Amarie had created and maintained the online presence for Russell's practice for years. He'd never bothered himself with the logins or passwords. During their time together, she'd worked forty hours a week, off the payroll, to maintain his online visibility. She'd created press kits, written publicity pieces, and uploaded client testimonials for him and his colleagues. His patients had doubled in the first eighteen months of their *partnership*, as he'd called it. Instead of a paycheck, he'd surprised her with her very own prepaid Mastercard. He'd presented it in a wooden carved box with a giant purple ribbon, her favorite color. With a long sigh, Amarie acknowledged the comfort she'd settled into with Russell's periodic conciliatory prizes. Repeating her mother's mistake, she had numbed her heart to the stab of Russell's infidelity, finding the strength to refocus on completing her Bachelor in Nursing degree while cauterizing her wounds with the knowledge that she held a secure place in his life. After all, they lived and worked together—she had his faux-diamond engagement ring on her finger. Stacia's pregnancy had snatched Amarie's blinders by the pubic hairs and ripped them off.

"Whew, girl," Vali said, glancing at her watch. "I'll call AAA to load the Princester and grab some Starbucks for the road. We should hit Pennsylvania Avenue just shy of afternoon rush hour."

Vali grinned, Amarie didn't. Not sure how to broach the next topic, she stalled. "This town has literally one stoplight and zero Starbucks coffee shops. I checked. The caffeine withdrawal and the consumption of my last stress-eating snack has me on the struggle bus, for real."

Before Vali had shown up, she'd ventured away from three bleating protests to wander past the barn-style coffee and pastry shop, before tripping over a raised brick in front of a swing-door saloon, the Bear something or other. The entertainment district ended exactly three storefronts later with the bookstore, Dog-Eared Pages and Cinema. The real beauty beyond the single-storied simple architecture was the oasis of delicate white azalea blooms with green pointy leaves and pink rhododendron funnels with the largest leaves she'd ever seen splitting Main Street into two idyllic postcard snapshots. She'd inhaled the sweetened air, her mouth salivating at the possibility of a fresh start, fresh soil to nourish and protect the tiniest grain of hope buried within.

"It's all good," Vali reassured, her voice level and resolute. "I'm so excited for your life minus Russell the man baby. No offense, but he didn't deserve all your Black girl magic."

Amarie nodded in solidarity, but she felt untethered, her stomach looping in on itself forming a jumbled mass of nerves. "I...I know, it's just..." She shrugged. "No matter how hard I tried...I was never his 'one.' He screwed around, but I'm the one who's screwed. Why does life have to be so hard?" It's a question she'd asked since childhood, but the answer never came. Just more heartache and betrayal.

Vali gave her hand a gentle pat. "That's officially too hard to answer without caffeine."

All Amarie wanted was a do-over away from her parents' watchful eyes, Russell's lies, and her friends' successful adulting. Everyone seemed to rush forward with living their best life while she stumbled one step forward, only to twist an ankle and fall two steps behind. She'd never quite mastered soaring above the crash zone. The maternal warning instilled since childhood echoed in her head: *Don't be foolish and stupid. Keep yourself a man, Amarie.* The oppressive message scorched like the July heat pouring through the windshield, baking her brown skin to pure cacao.

Vali gave one of Amarie's shoulder-length locs a tug. "Stop that."

"What?" She jerked her arm off the lackluster gray door panel, fanning her toasty forearm in front of the tiny, not-quite-rectangular air conditioner vent. Bizarre how the unique held her attention, but her unique personality traits lacked the same appeal to others. Was that the reason Russell cheated? His women looked so different from her—petite and slim with stereotypical face paint, spidery false lashes, and skimpy thongs. Honestly, Amarie detested the clutter of overt femininity, the endless array of bottles, spray cans, tubes, and containers. Another reason why she maintained a primp-free style. The more effort she asserted with hair, makeup, life, the more tragic the outcome.

"I know your mom's mantra is trending or viral in that busy brain." Vali reached across the dust-free center console. "Your parents are wrong, Mari. You can have everything you want...without a man bankrolling your life."

"Of course they are. Look at how successful I've been since vacating my well-appointed junior suite in their waterfront estate. My magic, Black or otherwise, is underwhelming."

Amarie dangled Prince's key to emphasize her point. Her biggest fear was they were correct to not trust her on her own. She'd walked away from Russell, a man who didn't deserve her very lovable heart, determined that she could take care of herself, and her car had blown up—literally—on her first attempt at independence.

"They love you, but their marriage...the way Mrs. B tolerates your dad's disrespect...their advice on love is misguided. It's wrong of them to expect you to marry some douche who cheats on you because he has a cushy bank account."

"I know." Amarie swallowed the lump in her throat because fundamentally she agreed, but she had zero history as a soloist. What would she do without Russell at her back? Vali was funny, smart, and engaging. She could walk into a room and command attention. Amarie needed a plus-one. "I'm not you, Vali. A nursing degree without a registered state license is worthless."

"You'll pass next time."

"I've already failed the exam twice. Russell said it's too late to lie to myself. I'm not good enough at anything."

Vali bared her teeth at the mention of him. "Stop repeating his garbage. You two were like the FBI and the CIA, incompatible. You know your stuff, Mari. When you weren't caught up in his drama, you were busy being too scared to try."

Fear had always plagued her. Unreasonable, she knew, but she couldn't help the internal paralysis invading like a killer virus through her every thought. Her very existence as an adult woman teetered on the precipice of failure. The word applied to entirely too many areas of her life.

A twenty-eight-year-old woman with the professional resume of a sixteen-year-old.

Failure.

Six years in a four-year degree program.

Failure.

Five bad years holding on to a broken relationship, most of them in a bogus engagement.

Failure.

Somewhere in the years as Russell's fiancée, she'd lost the self-confidence that had buoyed her to travel from the safety of home to Howard University's campus.

"Your lovable, adorable self is enough," her friend teased. "We'll get back to the city and figure out your next step."

She couldn't stall anymore, so she just blurted out the decision she'd made while waiting for Vali to arrive. "I'm not going back."

Silence spread like a small, but deadly, mushroom cloud. Amarie turned to face the driver's seat. Vali's facial expression had slipped from elation to a low-browed concern.

"Okay," Vali drawled. "I might have spoken too soon on the coffee."

Amarie began to make her case. "I can't afford the city without a job. And before you interrupt, I don't want to be in the same city with Russell and his soon-to-be family. I'm done being ashamed of myself because of that man. It's one thing to know he's cheating, but...I can't unsee what I saw..." she trailed off, her breathing unsteady. After she regained her composure, she looked up to see Vali's tear-filled eyes watching her.

"I'm so sorry, Mari." She coughed to disguise the swelling emotion. "He's making you leave me, too? I-if this move is about money, you can slum it with me and Sunday until you find a place."

Amarie loved her best friend's youngest sister, but her

behavior ventured more into a drunken Friday night than her name led one to believe. Not counting the cost of surrendering to her parents' desires had landed her with Russell for six years. Amarie had to make her own decisions moving forward.

"Shh." Amarie gripped Vali's too-still fingers, stroking life back into them. "I have to do something different, Vali. There's nothing holding me in the city. Maybe Mother Universe will remodel my life into something spectacular."

Vali nodded wordlessly, dabbing away her tears. "Yeah... yeah, that heifer owes you big-time. Now," Vali cleared her throat, all business again, "how do you plan to make money in tiny town West Virginia?"

"This." Amarie pulled the Service county bulletin from her purse, the one she'd grabbed from a sidewalk newsstand, smoothing out the wrinkles before handing it over. Vali studied the handsome soldier in full dress uniform on the front page. His hunter-green eyes had snagged Amarie's attention, too, but the veterinary clinic job announcement had made her heart flutter.

"The head shape is better than Russell's, but that doesn't say much about the brain matter."

"Argh," Amarie rebuked. "Ignore the man. Read the employment listing below his photo." Yep, singular. There was only one business hiring in the entire town.

Vali's eyes drifted lower, then she started reading.

"Help wanted at Calvary Family Veterinary Clinic." She looked from the announcement to the majestic house on the hill with the posted sign. "Oh, now it all makes sense." Amarie sighed in relief, not having to spell it out anymore. "You've been stalling trying to drum up the right words to tell me you're staying here."

"Yes. No. Wait." Amarie jerked. "How did you know?"

Before Amarie could explain her decision, which was totally unnecessary, her friend was in action.

"How long have we been friends?" Vali planted her right hand atop Amarie's headrest, angled her head until she had a clear view over the luggage, and rolled the car backward toward the parking area.

"Is this a trick question because I'm really vulnerable right now?"

"You are so adorable when you're nervous," Vali laughed, turning the wheel.

"That transparent, huh?"

"Just a little, but it's cool. I'll walk you to the door, bestie."

Amarie was a curvy balloon of emotions looking for a sharpened pinpoint. Beneath her, she felt the hybrid's silent vibration against her full bottom as Vali shifted the car in reverse, parallel parking next to a vintage American-made car filling one of the spots marked FOR PATIENTS ONLY. What sense did that make for a veterinary clinic? The patients didn't drive themselves. Someone in this house had a sense of humor. Good, she'd be the perfect addition.

"Thanks." Amarie swallowed. Vali pocketed the keys. With the added seconds, Amarie used the time to focus on the task ahead: radiating confidence and making a stunning first impression.

"Since you are refusing to return home and this is the only gig in town, they'll have to tell us the job is taken and to get gone to our faces."

And just that quickly, her surety in her ability faded. She sucked her lower lip between her teeth as her stomach looped into a new knot. Beads of sweat heated her top lip and she quickly licked the salty-tasting droplets away. "What if the job's gone—"

One squeeze to her sweaty hand stopped the negative thought. "Girlfriend, you're going to get this job."

"You think so?" Maybe this was another mistake.

"Is my name Vali with an 'Ali'?" A reference to the best heavyweight boxer ever, Muhammad Ali.

"But—but I'm not formally trained for anything."

Vali raised a finger. "Hush, puppy." She grinned. "Your best friend is going to walk your scared butt to the first day of school."

"Work." Amarie rolled her eyes. "And kiss my booty."

"After your first paycheck, look up that soldier boy from the bulletin for a booty call," Vali laughed.

"Nope. The dating pool is full of pee." Amarie swallowed.

Vali gave her a look of horror. "Ew…that is a powerful visual. It's funny, nasty even for a nurse, but powerful."

"It's also true." Her best friend, having experienced the messy side of relationships, couldn't refute the facts.

"Relationships are simple, Mari. We women have to decide which men need to get gone from our lives, then we focus on the one who is ready for the altar. Simple."

"Save your quick tips. As of today, I'm keeping my mouth and legs closed. I want a job. I'm saving money to fix Prince, studying daily to pass the licensure exam, and focusing on the sorority of one, me-phi-me. That's the promise to myself."

"Go 'head with the game plan, Miss Former Hopeless Romantic."

"I gladly relinquish my title," Amarie laughed. "Now, do I look okay?" Reaching forward, she lowered the sun visor, flipping the cover for the tiny mirror. A tribal print scarf twisted into a front knot held her thick tresses in an inky waterfall hiding at least one of her red-rimmed eyes. Grabbing her handbag from the floorboard, she slipped Stacia's

1950s starlet oversized sunglasses over her ears and smiled at her reflection. At least she'd left her lying, cheating, pitiful excuse for a fiancé in a dramatic flair. That had not been the intention when she'd crammed six years of broken promises into commandeered luggage and donned the other woman's stylish eyewear. But the fun pettiness suited her fresh perspective.

"Fabulous as always." Vali snapped a quick two thumbs-up. They exited the car. The click of the door locks engaging had Amarie squaring her shoulders, totally ignoring her racing heart and sweaty palms. Looking heavenward, she inhaled deeply, allowing the sweet mountain air to fill her lungs until her ragged breathing slowed to a rhythmic in and out. She could do this.

"I'm ready."

Vali grabbed her hand, marching them up the seven steps—yes, she was counting—to an elaborate screen door, white scrolled edges in four corners. Behind it, a soft lavender–painted, dual-paneled door with canary trim stood ajar, like someone expected her arrival. Maybe it was a sign that this was the right decision. One that she could be proud of.

"Go handle your business while I test one of these chairs with the rocker bottom."

Amarie took in the six chairs placed equidistant on the wooden porch. "They're called rocking chairs."

"That's what I said. Now, scoot," she cajoled. "Show the good folks of Calvary Veterinary Clinic how much they need a sister like you on the payroll."

Amarie had perfected dependence on others. Low expectations had become synonymous with her picture, but no more. Starting today, she would strive for excellence and self-reliance. With the decision to remain behind her, the next step meant grabbing hold of the destiny that lay on the other side of this door. Only four weeks until the next licensure exam. That was ample time on the job to fix Prince and study like a lunatic. She pulled up her mental big girl sexy panties, because she hated thongs, lifted one shaky finger, and pressed the vintage doorbell.

Chapter Two

IF IT WASN'T for the family relations, Eli Calvary would fire his mother. But frankly, he didn't have the time or money to train another pet groomer. Sure, her pay had dwindled to a morning hug and a fresh-cut lawn, but as her employer he expected adherence to company policy. She'd breached the "no interference clause," which required the boss's—his—immediate attention. Add to it the receipt of three—yes, three—unwanted and disturbingly provocative text messages from local single women dinging him awake before his crack-of-dawn alarm, and he had two mom-generated distractions to address. Staving off the bank's foreclosure on every piece of property bearing his last name required considerable concentration. His momma's marriage-mart shenanigans, though well-intentioned, siphoned too much of Eli's brain power. He would solve the family's money problems without his remaining parent wholesaling him off to a mountain woman with a hefty bank balance and a penchant for dog collars and electric fencing. Yep, pure caged misery leashed to love.

Stomping up the back steps of his childhood home, Eli

knocked the mud off his boots, but the guilt of possibly losing the five-bedroom house—his mother's safe haven, the
only home his two younger brothers had ever known, and
his final link to his father—clung like cement. He'd caused
this and all because of a woman. Removing his ball cap, he
did a one-two windshield-wiper maneuver through a swarm
of buzzing gnats guarding the rear screen door.

"Momma," Eli bellowed, a fair warning that, like the
weather, his mood leaned toward overheated. July had ushered in West Virginia's hot and rainy season. Even with the
short half-mile walk across the back fields, the steady supply of Monday morning humidity had his T-shirt clinging
and his jeans damp. His casual combination of a dark shirt,
jeans, boots, and his headgear pulled double duty as office
attire and small-town formal dinner dress.

"Door's open," came Leah Calvary's comforting reply.

Eli looked down at his side. He gave his seventy-pound
golden retriever, Hiccup, a generous head rub. Throwing in
a good-natured scratch behind the ears earned him three
rapid thuds to the calf from the dog's dancing tail.

"Stay," he said to his constant companion. He'd keep the
visit brief. After four months back in his hometown, he'd
discovered being the only veterinarian operating a mixed-
animal practice within one hundred miles of the northwest
Virginia border kept him hopping faster than a one-legged
rooster in a chicken shack. How had his father met the
demand for forty years? Only six months after his death, Eli
felt capsized, sinking deeper underwater.

Entering the kitchen, he froze mid-stride, inhaling.
Was it his imagination or did he smell maple syrup and
baked bread? He did a quick survey of all the surfaces. Sure
enough, a plate of six fluffy homemade biscuits with crisp
buttered tops stuffed with thick-cut bacon sat in a faded

aluminum pie pan on the stove. Eli narrowed his gaze. Oh, she'd stacked the deck—aka hot buttered bribe biscuits—in her favor.

His mom sat at the oak table, her long sienna coils gathered in a single braid, her readers perched, her makeup subtle. As the Calvary family matriarch, she was always prepared, always put together. As a kid, he'd thought his mother was the prettiest woman in Service. With her flawless toasted brown skin, gemstone-green eyes, and natural grace, she'd commanded attention at those parent-teacher conferences.

And she still did. Her smile could brighten the cloudiest of days. And her heart...well, it beat to make the world better for others. Especially her family.

Like her, the home of his youth was a mix of classic style and modern design. The vaulted ceilings made the space seem cavernous, a feeling he still appreciated at his six-foot height. The left wall held gray Dutch door cabinets with natural stone counters and a huge farmhouse white enamel sink. The polished timber floors showed signs of a home well used and well loved.

"Good morning," his momma chimed, slowly lifting her gaze to regard him. She did that once-over thing that all mothers do with their kids—one head, ten fingers, no blood. He must have passed inspection because she moved to the next step on the checklist.

Seeing as this impromptu summons started before his workday, it would probably focus on his mom's two favorite topics: the bottom line and the opposite sex—money he desperately needed, the other he avoided at all costs. He got straight to the point.

"Three women ruined my sleep," he groused, depositing his cap on the arm of a kitchen chair.

Leah's brows dipped in a furrow. "Oh dear, sounds like a discussion for your brothers." She grinned at her joke.

Eli scowled. Crossing to the sink, he used the bar soap to wash his hands, then dried them on a cloth dangling from the under-sink cabinet knob.

"Rosa Mae Perkins sent me a selfie. Apparently, she's got a twenty-five-dollar donation with my name on it for the exorbitant price of watching her model lingerie," he said, jabbing imaginary daggers at his eyeballs.

His mother's face lit faster than a firecracker. "Nice." She chuckled. "You two went to high school together, right?"

"She was my history teacher, Momma... ancient history." He angled his head, gesturing to the scribbled office policy suspended by two Georgia peach magnets on the refrigerator. "Whatever fool notion is going on with that woman's mind, you started it," he accused. "That counts as two for one under interference violations. Unnecessary distractions. And matchmaking."

A big smile broke out on her face. "A woman that goes for what she wants should be applauded." She grinned. "Back in our heyday, Rosa Mae was Founder's Day queen. I ain't mad at her for pulling out the lace."

"Mad?" He chuckled but stopped himself. "Try traumatized. Why do they have a queen at the festival anyways? We build a stage every year for her majesty. Where's the king?"

"This may be a man's world, but it would be nothing without a woman, dear."

"You went there?" His mom winked, adjusting her glasses. She was actually enjoying this conversation. That made it worse than embarrassing.

"What?" She shrugged. "That was funny."

"Not even a little."

"Maybe Rosa Mae will put a smile back on your face."

Eli saw the concern before his momma quickly masked it. There was nothing wrong with his face or disposition. Trusted advice had been the hallmark of his relationship with his parents, but Eli relied on his own judgment in the female department. The last thing he needed was a woman softening him up so love could rip another chunk out of his hide. Once upon a time he dreamt of having a wife and children, but love, that cagey beast, had a vicious bite. Eli's wounds infected him beyond cure.

"Your meddling has to stop, Momma. These women booking needless appointments." He shook his head. "Jessie McGillacutty tried to French-kiss me last week after I gave her a Kitty Kibbles sampler. I had to racehorse hurdle over the exam table, and her acrylic nails drew blood."

"But that's just one woman."

"Doesn't matter. I'm telling you, women are a distraction I don't want or need."

"The right partner will change your mind."

"It won't. My focus is on getting money flowing into the business, nothing else." That statement seemed to redirect her attention away from his single status.

"Pendleton Community Bank turned us down," she stated matter-of-factly, with no question or judgment in her tone. "Have you told your brothers about the half payments on the mortgage for the last three months?"

"Not yet."

"Why not, Eli?" His mother studied him, concern in her eyes.

"'Cause I already know I messed up. Seeing that truth in their eyes, well…" He swallowed, unable to say more.

"They're your brothers, not a jury."

Didn't matter. Eli had judged and convicted his failures long ago. "Doesn't make it any easier."

"I know, son. Just lay out the facts."

The mortgage refinance denial letter burned in his jeans pocket, a lump of hot coal threatening to torch his father's legacy. Twenty-eight years this location between the mountains, this house, and the adjoining veterinary practice had belonged to the Calvarys. His father, Levi, had taught him and his brothers that a man protected and provided for those he loved. His family had planted roots, labored, and loved the ground he walked every morning. At thirty-three, Eli hadn't achieved a quarter of his father's successes at the same age. He fell below the measuring tape, but nevertheless, he would keep fighting. He'd figure the whole mess out before worrying Tobias and Noah.

"This month's payment was applied before the late fees. I know what I'm doing." He didn't have a clue, but he worked overtime to find the winning combination.

Each disastrous attempt to increase revenue, like the physical exam with a fifty percent off grooming package, had netted him two unpaid bills instead of one. Then there'd been the free hot dogs and popcorn that had morphed into a backyard barbecue keg party without a single pet appointment booked by close of business. Folks from two counties over had shown up for that dollar dump. Oddly enough, for those few hours he'd forgotten the severity of his missteps, how he'd been hemorrhaging money for months.

"All of us are in this together—"

"Not their problem or yours," he interrupted. "I resigned my commission to come home. Dad trusted me to handle it." As the eldest son, the responsibility to hold the family together fell on his shoulders, an imbalanced weight he wasn't sure he deserved to carry. How could he stand tall when his choices, bad choices, had dragged his family to the edge of ruin?

"Not alone," she chided. "We're a family."

During his four years as a U.S. Army veterinarian, he'd led commissioned officers and enlisted personnel under his command, ensured the health of military service animals, and participated in animal health clinical research both at home and abroad. He knew how to strategize and execute, and was no stranger to hard labor. He alone needed to fix this wrong. After all, their father had mortgaged the property so that Eli would have the down payment on his first home with his new wife. The wife who'd abandoned him before they'd spent one night in their custom-designed forever home. So, if anyone had to put in more hours and lie awake at night staring at the ceiling, gut churning over his choices, it had to be him. Maybe, if he got things right again, fate would grant him the redemption he desperately wanted. But how to save their homestead remained a scattered puzzle with missing pieces and no visual guide. Unwilling to admit defeat, even to his brothers, Eli drew on the strength of his military training. Quell the storm and bring the thunder. But first, he had to race relentless rain while navigating the floodwaters. He couldn't allow his failure to pull them all under the deluge.

His momma would accuse him of being bullheaded. He'd toss in a couple of *you're pretty stubborn yourself*s, and the whole day would sour faster than old milk on a hot day. The truth lay closer to shame than male ego. But the lie flowed sweet compared to bitter reality.

"Here we go again," he muttered under his breath, knowing how this conversation would begin and end. "I don't need another 'we are family' pep rally."

"Eli Calvary." His mother's voice held a note of warning as her gaze angled up at him. "You'd best get yourself a cup of coffee before you say another word. I'm in a good mood.

You best not jeopardize that. The pot is fresh brewed, go ahead now."

Chagrined, he resisted the urge to drop his head. He led the business now, but this was his mother. Leah Calvary kept a dough rolling pin within reach. She was known to swat a backside or three if he or his brothers usurped her maternal authority.

"Yes, ma'am." Snagging the mugs from the counter, he poured two cups of freshly ground dark roast, black, no sugar, placing one on the kitchen table in front of an unusually fidgety Leah. He thought back to the bribe biscuits. What was she up to?

As she relaxed in her chair, her shoulders fell away from her ears. "Any calls on the job posting in the bulletin?"

Eli tried not to deepen his scowl and failed. "Nope."

Praying for a miracle hadn't produced a single applicant or improved the red in his ledger. Six weeks ago, he'd paid eighty bucks to place a weekly help wanted ad in the tri-county bulletin. With his twelve-hour workdays, he needed more than a groomer on staff. He'd settle for a front desk receptionist/veterinary assistant/kennel technician who'd share in his fantasy that the clinic's floating pay scale was a financial adventure rather than a sign of imminent collapse.

"The right person will come along." She smiled at him. "You'll see."

"Yeah" was all he said, because he had his doubts—and an ever-increasing mountain of *Payment Overdue* notices.

"Where's your pup?" Leah asked, shifting from a hopeless proposition to his retired military pooch. Count on his momma to shield her son from experiencing more disappointment.

"Out back," he replied. "The sun will bake him before too

long." One look and he knew his momma suspected his exit strategy.

She chuckled, removing her glasses, nimble fingers folding the wings, one then the other, before setting them aside. "You think leaving Hiccup outside will make this a quick visit, huh?"

Despite his irritation at the conversation to come, he smiled. "Why'd you call a meeting?"

"Eat your breakfast before your brothers get here. You'll need fast reflexes for Mrs. Kline's feline, Adele."

A mixed practice like his, daily work with large and small animals, required stamina for ornery horses and cattle and a layer of protective padding for the household companions.

"You're stalling." Glancing down at the stack of pink papers beside his momma, Eli recalled the "add ink" symbol flashing on the office printer.

What has she done this time?

He imagined his face on a poster with the words FREE TO RICH WOMAN printed above his head.

"Hmm," she sighed, after a sip, not divulging her latest scheme. "That's good. It's a new blend I ordered from the computer."

For her birthday, Tobias had gifted their momma a laptop computer. Every item regardless of the retailer came from the ever-present computer. Eli detested the ease in which technology invaded everyday living, monopolized countless hours. For what? Likes and smiley faces from strangers? No thanks.

"Momma, spill it," he grumbled, ready to hear the mission impossible, reject it, and then get on with his morning. "Whoever she is...I'm going to pack up her juggling act and send her back to the carnival." He'd suffered enough humiliation for love's sake. "We can find our own women."

He watched as Leah struggled to hide her amusement.

"Name one woman you've entertained in the past four months, Eli Calvary. Who are you bringing to Gracie Lou and Caleb's wedding in three weeks?"

She had him there. In fact, the only woman to enter his mountain-view cabin on the west end of the property had been...no one.

"I don't want a woman or a date. I tried both, Momma," he huffed. He'd loved Cara with everything he had inside his heart. Shared his dreams of a family, passing on his share of the Calvary land to their children. "Didn't work." Consistency and loyalty were valued in his hometown. But in the world beyond this rural community, they'd been his weakness. Coming home to Service had restored some semblance of order in his life. He had a purpose, but no way to pay a debt on a life he never owned. A four-figure mortgage on an empty house.

She reached over and patted his hand. "Cara wasn't the one. She was a selfish, conniving—"

"Momma," he exclaimed, squeezing her hand, "I'm over it."

"And Vanessa Williams is my twin sister," she said in quick retort, her cheeks flushing red with irritation.

"Once the house sells, it'll free up some cash." That's if the property sold. According to his realtor, most growing families valued bedrooms over Cara's indoor serenity garden. "And please give Auntie Vanessa my best when you speak to her."

"Don't be flip, Eli. You're about to violate a momma policy and unlike yours, I have the power to exact punishment. That awful woman hurt my baby," she muttered. "I won't say any more about your ex-wife, but...I'm thinking aplenty."

"I hear you, Momma Bear, but beauty felled this beast." He'd been so taken with Cara's appearance and attention that he'd missed how different they were. Four years and one divorce decree later, he'd seen more than he'd ever wanted to witness regarding the ugly side of trusting the wrong woman. He was done. Cooked. Burned. Scarred.

"Beauty, huh...not the b-word I'd choose," she groused. "Keep living. You'll discern the difference between a woman's makeup and her make up. You're a man who trusts people at their word, Eli."

"Right." Scrubbing one hand over his scruff, Eli choked down old resentment with now-lukewarm coffee. Trusting people, especially women, led to disaster. He'd be like his father, self-reliant. Self-made.

Just then, Tobias, dressed in his emergency medical technician uniform, appeared with a grinning Noah on his heels. According to Leah, he and his brothers resembled their late father—warm beige skin, midnight hair, long legs, broad shoulders. The only difference was their eyes. Eli had inherited his mom's green eyes, piercing and assessing. Tobias's intense blue-gray eyes, like his personality, were a balance between a rising storm and breaking dawn. And Noah, his hazel gaze accentuated his big cat magnetism and trapped more women in the tri-county region than a possum cage coated with smooth peanut butter. His baby brother had never met a lady who garnered a "No, thank you" from him to a *closed-door* conversation.

"You alright, Mom?" Tobias bent and placed a kiss on their momma's offered cheek.

"Hey, baby. Everything is fine." His mother smiled up at her middle son, the worrywart of the pack.

Even as kids, Tobias had cataloged their injuries and checked the medicine bottles for expiration dates.

"I smell food." Noah grabbed two biscuits, biting into one before acknowledging anyone in the room.

"Hey," Eli protested. "Save one for me."

With his mouth full, Noah shrugged. "You had first dibs. Always go for the win, big brother."

His mom grinned. "Told you. No kiss for your momma, Noah Calvary?"

"Ugh, sorry Mom," Noah said, his big boots scraping across the wood floor as he wrapped their momma in a bear hug before stealing a kiss.

"I have a plan to save the practice and the house," she bubbled. "Take one." She flipped over the pink stack and passed a single sheet to him and Tobias. Noah had his hands full with their breakfast.

Eli did a quick scan, pausing on his Army commissioning photo from five years earlier. That was a lifetime ago when he'd been a different man. "Mom, what is this?" he growled.

Tobias read aloud. "Silent Bachelor Auction Fundraiser."

"Let me see that," Noah said, stuffing his mouth with the second biscuit.

Younger than him by four years, Noah had not endured as much matchmaking crazy as he and Tobias. Apparently, that was about to change.

Silent Bachelor Auction Fundraiser: Save the Calvary Family Veterinary Clinic & Homestead. Place your private bid to win a romantic dinner for two with a Calvary brother. All 3 are available!

As a bonus, the winner gets 50% off our 12-month pet grooming package!

Tobias crushed the paper, beer can–style. "Count me out. I had to replace two tires and my windshield after declining a second groping from Dixie Ball, your last recommendation."

"Disco Dixie. She's a handsy one." Noah winked, until their momma narrowed her eyes in warning. Before his baby brother could add more heat to the hot water pooling around his wildland fire boots, he changed the subject. "What I meant to say was, I saw these pink pimp posters tacked to every tree between here and Matt Johnson's farm."

"That's a half mile up the mountainside," Eli rasped. "How many of these blasted flyers have you posted?"

"Enough" was all she offered. "Plus, the paid ad in the county bulletin with your old Army picture."

"This—this is a violation of policy. You're matchmaking on company time," Eli stammered, disbelieving the start to his week. Talk about a fresh day in green hell. "Rosa Mae Perkins is sane compared to the crazies in these hills. This auction is a dog whistle."

Tobias nodded. "You ain't never lied."

"Rosa Mae power walks past the fire station. Might be worth a conversation or two." Noah winked.

Not-so-clever sexual innuendo metaphors were Noah's gift.

"You're stupid." Eli glared at his youngest brother before shifting his gaze to face off with his mother. "Some of the women in town, their bite is worse than their bark. How do we shut down the portal website thing?"

"You can't." Leah beamed. "That's the genius behind the computer. I have a password. With the cute pictures I chose of you boys, this will succeed. The women, I mean the bidders, place a dollar amount under a bachelor's name. That's you three, by the way. They can also donate directly to the fundraiser. If they place the winning bid, they'll have the pleasure of a romantic dinner with one of my handsome sons and a chance at happily ever after. All the bids are blind. That means you three won't know the bidders' identity or which of you is earning the most money. It's a win-win-win. Oh, and your dating profiles are hanging in the post office, too."

"You mean WANTED posters," Tobias groused, pacing the length of the floor, red spreading up from his collar the more he talked.

His momma pulled out the chair closest to her. "Tobias, don't worry. This is my best dummy-proof, money-making idea ever."

She practically squealed in delight, while Eli's blood chilled in his veins. More senior citizens sexting was in his future.

Eli ran a hand through his dense waves, staring at his momma. "Shut down the site. Cancel the ad today. I'll torch as many of the flyers as I can before the looney tunes start—"

The chime alerting them to someone at the front door ended his tirade. Because he had absolutely no idea what he could say to convince his mother to cease and leave the rescuing to him, he bellowed, "Come in."

The screen door slammed. Footsteps, small and light, could be heard in the formal living room, before a disembodied feminine voice called out.

"Ah, can you say something else? This house is even bigger on the inside." She paused, and then said, "I'm a little turned around."

"Who's that?" Tobias whispered. Noah shrugged.

Eli straightened. "We're in the kitchen. Back and left."

Laughter sounded cheery, but still distant, before she asked. "Your left or mine?"

With his long-legged stride Eli set off in the direction of their unknown visitor. "I'm coming."

"No," she snapped. "Don't move. I'll find you on my own."

Eli stopped in his tracks, not by direction but in

irritation. Who was this woman giving him instruction in his own house? "You hear this?" he accused Leah, pointing to the pink flyer as if it had conjured up a harbinger of doom. "She's one of them."

His mother snorted, pushing her chair back from the table. "This is a woman I want to meet."

He snapped out of his paralysis, moving through the parlor his mother used as a reading room. Tobias and Noah fell in step.

In strode a woman, skin the color of autumn leaves, five feet, eight inches tall, curvy, and smiling—unnaturally, in his opinion—for seven thirty in the morning. There was lots of hair, swept to one side by some fancy celebrity-style headwrap, and tons of purple. Her flowy shirt, the pants, and her painted toenails, which peeped at Eli from girly sandals with silver studs, were all purple.

"Who are you?" Eli stared in open curiosity—and irritation. She slipped a pair of jumbo sunglasses off her face revealing large brown eyes beneath fanning dark lashes. He paused, maybe even stared, taking in the details. A beautiful woman with obsessive tendencies. This was a bad combination.

"Ah…good morning, I'm Amarie Walker," she sputtered, then popped the county bulletin from under her arm. Half of his face from five years earlier stared back at him. The folded crease split his forehead into two sections like the separation between his former life and current day. Obviously, his momma's tomfoolery had brought the crazies a-calling. Eli was just about to haul her to the door when she announced, "I'm here for the job."

"Aw…really?" came Tobias's cautious, but optimistic, reply.

"Gotta be new in town," Noah said, more than a hint of interest in his timbre.

Eli shifted into business mode. "You didn't schedule an interview."

"Well, no, but I'm here now. Efficiency is a plus, right?"

"Wrong," he said dryly. "Following proper procedure is." Eyes wide, she looked past him to the rest of his family as if they might back up her statement.

"Huh...okay," she responded with a tilt of her head, causing all those curls to brush her exposed brown shoulder.

"Okay?" he quizzed. "Anything else you care to add?"

Service had grown to a little over one thousand residents in his thirty-three years. Still considered a small town, the meadow between the Appalachian Mountains had doubled in size. Folks tended to spread the word about newcomers in the community. Eli didn't know everybody, but he would've remembered her. This rogue candidate would inject an unexpected excitement into the daily routine.

Her skin looked soft and velvety like the suede coat he wrapped himself in during the winter months. In fact, all of Amarie Walker looked soft and warm. The more Eli studied her spiraled curls and cushy contours, the more he lost the flow of conversation, choosing to think on more intimate things he'd foregone.

"Well, I could step outside, and then call you, Mr...." she paused, waiting.

Clearing his throat and his brain of soft shoulders, he grumbled, "Calvary, Eli. The veterinarian and owner of Calvary Vet."

"Yes, of course you are." She sighed, the smile tacked in place with superglue. "I could call you, Mr. Calvary, and schedule an appointment for...now?"

She'd made her point. It would be ridiculous of him to send her away, his first and only party interested in filling the position. He could flex for a qualified candidate.

"No need," he said, in his take-charge voice. "Let's see your resume."

"Ugh, I—I don't have one."

"Not with you or not at all?" Oh boy, he was right to be suspicious. This woman with her disarming smile and sunny disposition hadn't prepared for the interview at all. She probably would be late every morning and leave early every evening.

She blinked. "Is an answer required for employment?"

Against his better judgment, he'd thought to give her a chance. He should have known better.

"You walk in for a job interview without a scheduled appointment or your job history?"

"I could just tell you," she mused, that wide grin of hers aimed at him, not the least bit perturbed that she wasn't meeting the boss's expectations.

Eli scowled. "No, you can't." He had procedures in place to mitigate these types of shenanigans. His future employee, whoever it was, would appreciate the structure he provided. This Amarie person, with her disarming purple haze, had antiestablishment vibes. "Come back when you have—"

His momma chimed in, and Eli gritted his teeth at the intrusion in company business. "I'm Leah Calvary, Eli's mother. I was just about to eat my breakfast. Would you care for a cup of coffee, Amarie?"

Her face split into a wide grin like she'd been offered a winning lottery ticket. "That would be divine. Thank you."

Not to be outdone, Noah added his two non-cents. "We have one homemade biscuit left."

"One... wait a darn minute," Eli protested. Now they'd offered up his meal to an unqualified applicant.

Tobias started to cough, a fluffy biscuit suspended inches from his full mouth. "Can't eat just one."

"Coffee and biscuits. You're speaking my love language," she rasped, accepting Noah's hand and doing what could only be described as a sashay. She smiled when she passed his stony form, her crisp scent of fresh apples and summer honey teasing his nostrils. "I like your benefits package already."

No, this couldn't be his Monday. This woman, this stranger who'd walked into his home, unprepared, and stayed for breakfast—an epic violation of policy. Whether his or the company's, it was unclear, but Amarie Walker was the absolute wrong person for the job.

Chapter Three

AMARIE MAY HAVE done herself a disservice by agreeing to breakfast…and basking in Eli's sour mood while consuming an obscene amount of crisped-to-perfection bacon. In her defense, it would have been rude to refuse her future employer's mother—and the smell of fresh-baked bread that filled the air had left her salivating. She attributed the momentary lapse in professionalism to sleep deprivation, Eli harping on her unpreparedness, and straight-up hunger. The Calvarys—except for Eli—had peppered her with conversation about the nearby waterfall, the locally grown fresh market in the town mall, and the Coffee Bean Barn, which was good but not better than Leah's supplier from the computer. As if the gateway to the World Wide Web was a physical place. How fun was that? Social media was Amarie's happy space, too.

The rapid fire of kitchen table conversation among the family over a shared meal was like a championship tennis match. Amarie devoured every lob and volley with increasing delight. Their open affection for one another stirred painful reminders of how her childhood home life had fractured all

those years ago. Self-expression. Acceptance. Family. The
things Amarie wanted but had never received were visibly
important to the Calvary family. Noah had won her over
with his boyish charm and those hypnotic kaleidoscope
peepers. But she wasn't fooled by his playboy façade—he'd
experienced heartbreak of the highest order. Tobias, with
his summer storm–blue eyes and slow smile, was watchful
but engaging, and harder to read with her social barome-
ter. The real jewel in the lot, her new insta-bestie, was Leah
Calvary, a sage beauty imbued with a mother's comforting
presence.

And then there was Eli. A brooding menace and crusher
of high hopes.

He stood in the bay window overlooking the kitchen
table, glaring at her like a stone-face Greek warrior, sunlight
painting his raven mane and full beard to a lustrous sheen
before fading against his tan skin. Amarie ignored him, or
rather pretended to, but his damp black T-shirt clung to his
broad shoulders, hugging his biceps tighter than a rock band
groupie. And the jeans—whew—gripped his tight butt and
long legs like a male stripper costume. He disappeared out
a back door off the kitchen, returning moments later with a
dark golden retriever, which was dancing, playful energy in
abundance, around his feet.

"Here, boy," Eli said, scratching the dog behind the ears
before giving his dense coat a gentle rub. Amarie watched
the brute of a man soften, the brackets around his mouth
vanishing as he led his pet to an aluminum water bowl.
Maybe there was an actual human being she could work
with cocooned beneath his steely exterior.

Without a word, he resumed his post, arms crossed under
impressive pecs and an equally impressive scowl twisting his too-gorgeous features. Or maybe not. Obnoxious

really, on his part, to parade that face and those muscles in front of an unemployed woman with a wounded heart. Though she couldn't see his rippled abdomen, she knew it was there, lurking beneath the surface to blindside her. All of it—the shirt, the jeans, the large feet hidden in scuffed leather boots—was a desperate plea for attention. But Amarie couldn't afford to be distracted by a well-toned body. Her interest in Eli Calvary stopped at employment. He could save his Magic Mike quick-pull Velcro seams for a high-wage earner who had the time to fall victim to overt masculine attractiveness. She was immune to handsome men—happy dogs who nudged her thigh, not so much.

"Aw," she crooned, blowing air kisses at the canine pawing her shoes. "Your pup is so cute. What's the name?"

The question seemed to further irritate Eli. How could it possibly be annoying to compliment his pet? She would be working with animals—in his clinic—and he should be impressed rather than agitated.

"His name is Hiccup," Noah answered, placing his cup in the sink. "He likes pretty ladies as much as I do," he teased.

Noah, the obvious flirt, Amarie already adored. Though she didn't feel a spark of attraction, she believed he could be a really good friend. "You're leaving?" she asked.

"Duty calls, darling."

He winked before walking toward a hallway adjacent to the refrigerator that Amarie hadn't noticed. She wasn't sure where it led, but it was closest to the veterinary practice. Perhaps it was the breezeway she'd noticed from the house's exterior.

Lifting her free hand, Amarie waved goodbye, having enjoyed the youngest Calvary brother's company. "Talk with you later."

The firefighter stopped mid-stride. Slowly he pivoted on

his heel, facing her, a devilish grin crossing his full lips. "I'd be happy to strike up a conversation with you—"

"Noah," Eli rumbled, the sound rough and jagged.

Red bloomed on Eli's neck, spreading like wildfire to consume his face. Huh, that couldn't be good. His tone had dropped several octaves, and Amarie swore she heard an undercurrent of menace.

"The gentleman doth protest too much." Noah laughed.

Eli's green eyes darkened in color, the fine lines bracketing them deepened. The air seemed to spark with territorial energy. Tobias's eyes were fixed on his brothers as if ready to intervene—and Leah had an odd sparkle in her gaze. Maybe talking had a different meaning in Service.

As fast as the flame ignited, it cooled, and Eli's lips twisted into a lopsided grin. "Shut up, stupid."

"I said what I said," came Noah's reply, before he sauntered off without looking back.

Huh, she must have misinterpreted the brotherly ribbing as a mountain instead of a molehill.

"Okay," she whispered, a bit baffled, and anxious to close the deal on her reason for being there in the first place. "We—we should negotiate the terms of my contract."

"You don't have the job," Eli snapped. "There is no contract."

Amarie inhaled through her nose, trying to slow the sudden increase in her heart rate. Don't panic. He was tossing hard balls, testing her mettle. She knew from talking with Noah that she was the first and only applicant in weeks. So, she didn't have any competition. Perhaps Eli's grumpiness was more physical than a permanent emotional state she'd have to coax into tranquility. Her nursing brain shot into caregiver mode. He hadn't eaten or drank anything since her arrival. The poor man probably had low blood sugar or some other chronic condition and because he looked strong and virile, she'd stereotyped him as a rigid ogre with bad manners.

Without thinking more on her approach, she blurted out, "Would you like a bite of my biscuit?"

Leah sputtered, "Dear Lord," at the same time as Tobias chuckled, "I doubt it will help."

"What...no," a slack-jawed Eli stammered. "I do not want to bite your biscuit, Amarie."

"Fine. I'm trying to be nice," she fired back, feeling as if she'd been chastised for exercising a basic courtesy.

"Aw, you're a sweetheart." Leah patted the hand Amarie rested on the table. "I tucked two biscuits in the oven for Eli."

"Wow." Amarie touched a hand to her heart. "What an awesome mom thing to do." Her mother likely would do the same, well, if her father didn't object. Because of her father's insistence that Amarie tough it out with Russell, she'd chosen not to retreat home. She was pretty sure—eighty-five percent—her mom would eventually support her decision to end the engagement. Not openly, of course. That would've shaken the tightrope on which her parents' marriage teetered. Her father controlled his wife by limiting her funds and friendships. Amarie might not appear to be alone in the world, but she was stag in this quest for independence.

"Eat up, dear." Leah beamed at the comment. "We have a busy clinic day ahead of us. Adele's stay is an overnighter."

From her seat at the table, Amarie raised her cup to her lips and looked directly at Eli. "Of course, I'm almost done."

Eli grunted at her response.

Amarie adjusted the now-empty stoneware plate in front of her. "I'm ready." She smiled, but inside she screamed into the pillow she wanted to aim at Eli's head. Leah gave

Amarie's shoulder a squeeze, a gentle nudge of reassurance that she appreciated. Every time the older woman patted Amarie's hand, showed the tiniest gesture of support, or fussed over her sons, Amarie felt a Hallmark movie *aw, that's so nice* moment.

She upended her coffee mug for the final swallow, declining a refill and adoring the Calvary family—well, as much as one could safely appreciate the kindness of complete strangers who offered food to a weary woman.

Facing Eli, she ignored the churning ball in her stomach growing in size the more he seemed determined to thwart her destiny.

"I know you're uncomfortable with my missing paperwork. Unfortunately, I haven't had an opportunity to compile an updated resume. You know, with me being new to Service. I read the job listing and jumped at the chance to get to work. But I can assure you, I have great people skills, which I believe will translate well to the animal kingdom. If you like, I can provide excellent references." The first being her best friend waiting on his porch. Like Amarie's path, the truth required a bit of bending. Russell had confiscated the new laptop he'd purchased for her.

"Jumped at the chance, huh?" Eli walked straight to the table, grabbing a chair, the scrape of the wood on wood jarring her as he turned it backward before straddling the seat. "What experience do you have in veterinary medicine, Miss Walker?"

Outside of dating a wolf in a white lab coat? Nada. That wasn't exactly true. Her mother had gifted her a caramel-and-white beagle puppy for her tenth birthday, deeming her old enough for the added responsibility. Amarie had run home after school every day for six months to roll on the floor with Princess.

"Well," she began, tightening her grip on the coffee mug, "there's an Italian restaurant with outdoor seating in Key West where my parents used to live. The three cockatoos there poop on everyone, but not me. And my best friend, Vali, has a cat who's never scratched my furniture during an overnight stay."

"None," he said, deadpan.

No time for fear, Amarie. Charming the boss man was all that separated her from the other pretty girls with the WILL TWERK FOR TACOS sign.

"In addition to social media marketing, I'm proficient with Microsoft Office 365."

"Don't need it. We haven't upgraded."

She heard a seed of rejection in his tone and her mind magnified her anxiety, wedging a hole in her chest for a boulder of doubt to settle. He didn't want her. A character role she seemed doomed to replay no matter how hard she tried to make herself useful.

"From Word?" she quickly recovered, refusing to allow grumpy pants to trample his very large boots on her usefulness.

"Try pen and paper," he said. "I've been animal handling since I was a boy. This job requires experience. An understanding of animal behavior. Physical strength and stamina." He went on, but Amarie tuned out.

His bullet point list of highly defined duties blasted holes in her employable attributes, each entry wound heightening her anxiety until sticky perspiration coated her palms. As a graduate of higher education, she should be more confident in her abilities. Her mother had insisted that Amarie earn her degree. Perhaps it was because a young Bethany Harris had married Dr. Reid Walker during her sophomore year of college, and then withdrew because of her pregnancy a year later. But after two additional years at the institution,

Amarie's genuine desire to serve and heal seemed minuscule in real-world application.

"Oh…" she whispered, her dignity Apollo Creed cornered against the ropes. She would not beg. "On my last job I worked with drug formularies. And I speak fluent insurance and medical billing lingo."

He paused for a second, his eyes narrowing. "Give me the name and phone number of your previous employer. After I verify your skills, I might reconsider."

Russell would never write her a job recommendation. So she quickly moved on, tripping over her words in the process. "I-I completed a four-year nursing degree program last December." His scowl deepened.

"You talk faster when you're anxious." His stare was assessing, disassembling her every utterance for details she wouldn't reveal. Slowly, his stunning gaze crawled up her stiff torso until it came to linger on her mouth. Tingles of awareness danced across her skin, following the path his eyes had taken. Oh, the reaction, a body betrayal she pretended did not occur.

"I'm not anxious," she lied.

"Hmm," he said, brows raised in obvious disbelief. "The number," he repeated.

Amarie jutted her chin forward in defiance. "I prefer not to disclose that information at this time. Now, are you really going to not hire me when I literally have no competition?"

Eli's eyes softened for a second, but then he crossed those sinewy arms on the chair back. Those arms would have had her swooning if they were on another human. Eli operated in perpetual beast mode, even when she presented the ideal solution. Which didn't make a lick of sense from Amarie's perspective. It was more important that she arrived ready to be a productive member of Team Calvary. She just had to convince him to see reason.

"I can help you," she said, her voice not quite as confident. She needed this job, but she hated the suffocating feeling of vulnerability. She knew firsthand how the world preyed upon the unwanted. Mentally, Amarie regressed to a child-hood memory, really a nightmare. Her mother, Bethany, rocking a sobbing Amarie as the ache of hunger burned her empty belly. That day, Amarie had made a vow. She would never give up, never beg, never quit, even if she failed.

Russell's stunt with the credit card had delivered a crip-pling blow, but she met Eli's eyes dead-on; she would not surrender to a metaphysical death today. Eli Calvary looked formidable and unyielding. He wasn't going to bend. She saw the truth reflected in his emerald eyes, but just then a high-pitched squeal came from the direction of the clinic.

"Adele! No. Stop. Come back," a woman's tinny voice called.

"She's loose." Leah jolted, clearly distressed, taking a few steps backward.

Amarie shot to her feet. "What is it? A bear. A moose? No—no, that's Alaska. A buck?"

Hiccup answered with a series of short, throaty barks and a sideways two-step. Whatever was heading their way, neither the Calvarys nor their dancing pooch wanted the smoke of the approaching fire.

"I'll grab the safety gear," Tobias called, before his fast footfalls carried him toward the front of the house.

She released a strangled gasp, there was nothing protect-ing her vital organs. "Oh God, it's a mountain lion. Isn't it?"

Eli jumped in front of her and Leah. "Noah, the con-versationalist, must have left the clinic door open. Stay behind me."

Startled by the demand, Amarie complied. Clearly a dangerous animal had broken free of its cage, and they were in imminent danger. Her heart began to pound as she listened for a throat-ripping snarl, a feeble scream, or a ferocious bark. When nothing happened, Amarie ducked around Eli's wide back to see a flash of white-and-black fur dash into the kitchen.

"Oh, that's—it's a kitty," she said, relaxing.

"Don't move," Eli snapped. "I'll contain her."

"Contain her? Like in *Jurassic Park*?" Amarie laughed.

"Adele hates people. Especially breathing ones," he whispered, edging forward.

Who was he to judge? Amarie thought. Eli Calvary was the most ill-tempered caregiver she'd ever met. It was vexing, really. Pediatricians, veterinarians, and older people should be friendly types. Not bossy, rule-followers, demanding official documents and such. Behind the safety of Eli's back, she lowered herself to her haunches.

"Tsk, tsk…come here, pretty kitty." Amarie stretched forward her hand, letting Adele come to her.

"Don't," Eli hissed. "She will bite."

"You, I'm sure. No way would a cute little kitty with a famous name harm her new friend, Amarie."

"I recognize crazy talk when it hits my ears." Eli balked. "Now quit fooling around with that cat before we all need eye patches."

"Don't be afraid, Eli. I'll rescue you." Amarie snickered.

Slowly, Adele lowered her head, making a cursory prowl in Amarie's direction. When she was in reach, Amarie held still until the tuxedo cat, not kitten, rubbed her fine whiskers against the back side of her knuckles. She placed a hand, a light touch at first, on the cat's nape, then she administered long strokes down the length of Adele's spine until she heard a soft purr.

"Whoa," Tobias said, entering the room to hand Eli a pair of long-armed gloves, "she's a pet whisperer."

Eli stared down at her, slipping his large hands into the protective gear. "I told you not to move."

Amarie looked up at him, smiled, scooped up a floppy Adele, and draped her over her shoulder. "My apologies. I thought my animal-handling skills took priority considering your health and safety were at risk, boss. Now, about the job."

Leah laughed out loud. Eli may have cursed, but she couldn't swear to it.

"You're hired...for today," he grumbled.

Amarie's breath hitched. She'd done it. Though an unconventional start to the interview, she had applied her unique talent, with the boss and ball of fur, and gotten the job. "Yes!" she cheered.

"Pay's eleven dollars an hour. Work starts now with Kitty Scissor Claws you're cuddling."

"But—" She stopped her happy dance. In D.C. she'd need three roommates, an EBT card, and a second job to survive on so few dollars.

"Final offer," Eli interjected.

"Okay," she acquiesced, but she still needed to fix Prince, find a place to live, and afford coffee.

"Welcome aboard, Amarie." Leah opened her thin arms wide.

"Ah," she said, a bit sheepishly, going in for a hug, "does the job include breakfast?"

"And lunch," Leah offered, closing Amarie in a warm embrace.

Eli threw up his hands at his mother. "Since when are meals and hugging a part of our hiring practice?"

"Since I'm the momma." Leah grinned.

He glared directly at Amarie. "Enough already. Time for work."

Not wanting to repeat the mistakes she'd made with Russell, she piped up. "I'm going to need everything in writing." She paused. "Oh, and a fifteen-minute break."

"A break?" Eli sputtered, his face awash in crimson again. "You haven't started work yet."

"Oh, you're right." Amarie beamed. "I don't need your permission."

Beyond satisfied with her performance, Amarie didn't wait for a response. She deposited a purring Adele into her boss's hands and headed for the veranda to tell Vali the good news. She could practically hear Eli's muscles harden to stone. His curse rang out, puncturing the air with spearing force. Greek warrior, indeed.

Chapter Four

To Eli's surprise, Amarie had volunteered to share in monitoring Adele's overnight recovery. She'd slept on his office couch in between vital sign assessments and surgical site checks without complaint. This morning she'd washed up in the house, joined in the Calvary family breakfast conversation, and then waltzed into the clinic exactly fifteen minutes before it opened without so much as a glance in his vicinity. He didn't have to tell her tardiness was not a rule he would flex on. There had to be an angle to Amarie Walker. No employee mustered her level of dedication on day one. He needed to uncover her playbook before he took a curve ball to the gonads.

His momma sidled up next to him, slipping her waterproof apron over her head. "You look well rested."

"Yep," he nodded.

"Having Amarie around to share the load is nice, huh?"

Refusing the bait, Eli kept quiet. The added hours of sleep he appreciated, but he'd withhold his praise till further notice.

Mrs. Kline arrived, hands wringing after a night of

separation from her emotional support feline. Amarie greeted Lois with a smile, depositing a purring Adele, the traitorous chameleon, into her owner's outstretched arms.

"She was a perfect houseguest. You trained her well," Amarie added.

Overjoyed, the retired seamstress babbled a string of baby gibberish into Adele's perked-up ear.

"Thank you for everything, Amarie." Their longtime customer embraced his new hire, patting a fragile hand, fingers twisted with arthritis, in genuine gratitude on Amarie's back for taming her normally ferocious feline into a sublime state.

"Wow," Eli muttered. "I actually removed the growth and stitched her up."

His momma nudged him with her elbow. "Play nice."

"Is that an order?" Kitty Scissor Claws released a noisy purr that grated like cheap wool on Eli's vexed nerves.

"Absolutely. Look at how happy Lois is... for a change."

Though he hated to admit it, Amarie had remained calm while the rest of the family had scrambled for cover yesterday. He had to laugh at her comfort with his family, too. His mom seemed to enjoy having another woman around the table, something Cara, his ex, never warmed to. And the curveball that hit before he realized he needed protective padding: Amarie had offered him a bite of her biscuit. Honest to goodness, he about choked on his spit at the bare skin images that prowled around in his dirty mind. All in all, the entire scenario, from the biscuits to Amarie's soap-bubble glee, had manipulated him into a false desperation, leading him to act out of character. Hiring a woman he wanted nowhere near him. Pretty women smelled of trouble and Amarie's crisp apple scent fish-hooked his nose. Baited, but not reeled in. No sir.

"How long are you going to watch her?"

Technically, he could justify his behavior as helicopter bossing. In all of ten minutes, he'd led Amarie through the five-room clinic. Muted shades of blue and green, colors found in nature, covered the walls in the grooming area and utility room that banked the hallway leading from the main house into the clinic's waiting room. Complimentary tones continued into the reception area, where a counter hid his office and the staff break room from spying eyes. Not that he had any secrets, but on the mornings he visited the large animal farms, he often changed out of dusty jeans and donned a fresh T-shirt before afternoon appointments. The women around town weren't above posting a pic of him in his skivvies on the internet for kicks. Amarie hadn't batted those long lashes at his non-techie patient management system or the clutter spread between his desk and the one she now occupied. Cara would have nagged until he put every slip of paper in its place to restore the room's energy balance.

"Not watching. I'm tracking an unknown entity." Especially since man's best friend had abandoned his post to flop on the interloper's sparkly toes. In another surprise move, she'd whispered what a good boy he was to keep her company.

"Right," his mom drawled, with a slow grin dripped in mischief. "Next time, try stealth mode. She knows you're looking."

He still didn't trust pretty smiles. Especially dimpled ones like Amarie's that lit up a room, competing with the warm rays of a summer sun. He especially didn't trust smiles that refused to produce a resume. Unless she'd totally wrecked her last employer's bottom line, why the reluctance to prove her knowledge, skills, and abilities? In his experience, women like her, with big city–style oozing off her, loved to broadcast their credentials. So, what was she hiding? A false identity? An alter ego who preferred naked bookkeeping by candlelight? He was well aware of how ridiculous his train of thought was, yet he couldn't stop himself from relaxing against his desk to watch her work. Maybe he'd catch her red-handed five-fingering the cash drawer.

"She's already making improvements. The money from the auction will make things even better."

"Stop while you have a win under your belt, Momma. She has a trial week," he said, gesturing to Amarie. "I'm not pinning a number on my chest to parade around for a bunch of crazed women."

Leah sighed. "Okay, but you have to admit. It's the best Tuesday we've had in a while."

"How's that? I'd hardly call subduing one pussycat a successful day in the office."

His momma shook her head. "You haven't snapped at anybody since she arrived."

"Coincidence," he groused.

"I think Amarie is a lovely addition to the Calvary family business. With her personality and your skills, imagine what you two could accomplish with the bachelor auction money."

"Never am I going to shake my butt for a bunch of horny women."

His momma's smile dropped, her lips drawn thin. Great, he'd said something wrong, but didn't have a clue what it was. Cara said as much. He just didn't get women, but he felt like a heel for hurting his mom.

"Everything isn't about physical needs, Eli. Sometimes a woman just appreciates the company of a decent man."

Longing pitched his mom's usual upbeat voice low, a melancholy tune of love forever departed. He was a heel for not realizing how callous his offhanded comment was, and how it would remind a grieving wife that she'd lost her soulmate.

"Momma, I—I'm sorry. I just can't seem to do anything right these days."

His mom placed a hand on his forearm. "Stop beating yourself up. You're doing your best. And that's enough."

Seems as if fate had a more stringent measuring stick than his mom. Either way, Eli's knuckles were bruised and his kneecaps sore from the recent knockouts surrounding the business. But he'd keep the faith. Keep fighting.

"I should've thought before I opened my big mouth." That was the story of his life when women were involved.

She chuckled. "True enough, but I'm your momma. You never have to be perfect or play the tough soldier. I know who you are on the inside, generous and kind."

"It's not that simple—"

"Don't be afraid to show the world who you are," she whispered.

Before he could ask for clarification, Mrs. Kline approached. "Eli, I'm sorry for taking Adele out of her cage yesterday. She just hates to be confined."

Now that, he understood. "The signs are posted to keep us all safe, including your pet."

She flashed him a blinding white denture smile. "I know, but Adele made a new friend with the front desk girl."

Friends? Eli barely had time for family. The sooner Amarie learned that completed transactions and fees for services were what he wanted, the better. The trickle-down payments he made to the mortgage since returning to Service four months ago chafed worse than a leather dog collar.

"Amarie is a saint, a true saint I tell ya. Did you see the way Adele cozied up to her?"

"I noticed," he deadpanned.

"Good thing you brought her on, Eli. She'll help you right the ship. Make Levi proud."

"Yep." Eli ground his molars at the subtle dig. "Saint Amarie is heaven sent."

"And all the way from Washington, D.C., to boot," she hooted. "Can't imagine leaving the big city to work with you. No offense, Eli."

"None taken." Plenty taken. He frowned, having learned more about his new receptionist/veterinary technician from his customer rather than personal disclosure.

"Well," she laughed, lifting her pet carriage from the floor to place it on the counter, "business must be on the rebound. I was a bit worried when I saw you and your brothers were hiring yourselves out as gigolos."

"What in the—"

"Lois!" His mom rushed forward, taking the soft pet carrier from the top shelf. "Let's get Adele's nails trimmed, so you can get home before *The Price Is Right*."

Service may be a small town, but rumors ran faster than a stray through an open door. He had to find reasons to hold his head high these days. These bachelor auction shenanigans added another weight to his load.

"Oh my," she said, looking at the faded *Army Strong* clock he'd gifted his father five years ago. "Look at the time."

Eli pushed away from the wall. "What you read in the bulletin was a misprint. Dad will be proud of all the improvements I have planned for Calvary Vet and the house. Don't you worry none. We'll be here when you need us."

"That's right. I'll be sure to tell those downtown gossips to mind their own beeswax."

The townsfolk referred to those higher up the mountainside like the Calvarys as uptowners. Main Street and the largest of the homesteads were across Cattail Creek closer to the holler.

"You do that, Mrs. Kline." Eli nodded, shuffling her along as fast as her orthopedic inserts would allow.

"Welcome to Service, Amarie," she called over her shoulder.

"Thanks, Mrs. K." His receptionist waved, her smooth arm extended high above her head.

Twenty-four hours on the job, and she was unduly familiar with the clientele. Strike one, day two. Eli didn't like seeing that much skin on the job, either. The woman was a smiling, waving safety hazard. *Painted toes and velvet soft arms*, he scoffed. A laundry list of company policy addendums would have to be added. Drats, Amarie's mere presence added more work to his, well, workload.

"Oh, I just love your posh accent," Mrs. Kline chattered on. "So Rodeo Drive."

Should Eli remind her Washington, D.C., was on the East Coast?

"Hate to disappoint you, Mrs. K. I'm not that fancy." Amarie laughed.

"That ain't what the purple BMW and the Louis Vuitton luggage says. I knew it had to be yours. All us mountain folks know better than to try to take these inclines in a luxury whip."

What BMW? He hadn't seen any designer suitcases. Amarie's smile faltered. It was barely perceptible unless you were watching, and Eli was...vigilant.

"How long are you gonna be here in town?"

"As long as I need to be," she said.

"I'd love to have you over for a glass of fresh-squeezed lemonade. My homemade peach pie is the best in the county. Ask anybody."

"I'll let you know."

Eli didn't like that answer. He didn't like uncertainty. He didn't like change. Life required predictable patterns and hard facts. And Amarie had a bunch of question marks after her name. Like, what was she doing ringing his doorbell before eight o'clock in the morning and accepting a job that paid a dollar above minimum wage?

Crossing the room, he kept his eyes trained on Amarie as if she'd disappear. He split the aluminum blinds, the thin metal releasing a distinctive pop. Mrs. Kline's 1976 gold Chevrolet Impala with matching carpet on the dash and his Ford pickup were in the parking lot. No purple beamer.

Eli turned and walked right up to the counter. The stranger he'd welcomed into their lives looked up at him, face drawn in trepidation.

"Where's your car, Amarie?"

Plenty of questions stirred in his head, but he'd start here. Like what led a city girl from the big D.C. to West Virginia, deep country?

While she'd scarfed down the last strip of bacon and the biscuit with his name on it, she'd conveniently revealed little about herself. His life and that of his family's wouldn't teeter off the edge because he let his guard down over a gorgeous smile. Or smooth arms the color of pure hot chocolate. Or—blast, he chided himself for focusing on the wrong details.

"What's that, boss?" She blinked rapidly, using her fluid soprano to lull him, a siren's song that would thwack like a rock against his hard head. Darn it. He loved and hated his situation.

Eli looked her square in the eyes, not the least bit humored by the stall tactic. She could save the angel of mercy act for some fast-talking city slicker. The more he

FAKE IT TILL YOU MAKE IT   57

thought about it, he decided Saint Amarie had skeletons and he planned to uncover them before his family got too attached. He tried not to think about how much he'd enjoyed bantering with her across the breakfast table.

"You heard me." Eli pointed to the parking lot, devoid of foreign automobiles. "Your car. Where is it?"

"In town."

"Where, exactly?"

Eli had lost too much—his heart, his father, his marriage—not to protect those who relied on him most. A charming woman had derailed his life once. After the divorce, he'd vowed he would reclaim his future one day at a time, one problem at a time. He caught a flash of his cute little kitten of a receptionist transforming from happy feline to cat on a hot tin roof. And Eli planned to turn up the heat. This would be Amarie Walker's last day on his payroll.

Chapter Five

WHOA, TALK ABOUT the perils of small-town life. Mrs. Kline had toppled Amarie's blissful existence faster than Oprah's Harry and Meghan interview. To make matters worse, she'd painted a Cristal-and-caviar level of luxury by spilling the tea on Prince and the designer luggage of unmentionable origin. Not that her private affairs, or how she came to be in West Virginia, required a security clearance, but what would Eli think if he saw proof that her past swerved into the unprepared lane most days? Three words summed up Eli: exact, ordered, and immovable. Would his military mindset demand immediate termination?

How unfair because she really could help him run the practice with improved efficiency.

Already Amarie had tidied her small desk twice, no, three times. Once had been plenty, but Eli watching her every move with his all-seeing eyes had ratcheted up her stomach acid production to gastric Chernobyl levels. She was one hairy eyeball away from a bathroom blowout of epic magnitude. To her credit, she'd sought expert advice, not on the gas bubbles arm wrestling her sphincter, but rather

on a best practices blueprint from the American Veterinary
Medical Association. The website had too many words and
not enough pictures for her taste. In the end, she'd resorted
to YouTube videos less than ten minutes in length explaining the day-to-day operations of a small veterinary practice.
Today she planned to peck out a to-do list in the notes sec-
tion of her smartphone, prioritize the action items from one
to ten, and implement the top three. Small, yet monumental, baby steps.

In actuality, animals and humans needed much the
same. There were medical consultations, physical examina-
tions, vaccinations, acute care, laboratory studies that could
be billed without actually seeing a doctor, and of course,
grooming services. Basically, she was a nurse in training for
quadrupeds.

But all her investigative work would be wasted if she got
canned.

Maybe Leah could help. Well, she already had.

The Calvary family matriarch had followed Amarie
onto the porch yesterday, where they had discovered Vali
slumped in a rocking chair, a one-hundred-and-eighty-
pound snoring toddler stewing in her own juices, literally.

Amarie quickly apologized a dozen times. Vali, being
Vali, had laughed off her mountain adventure, stating the
trip was worth it to meet Amarie's goat trio, who she'd
named Billie, Jean, and Diana. Leah had sprung into super-
mom mode. She'd tucked the luggage into the sewing room,
batting away Amarie's protests. Within minutes, Vali'd had
a travel mug of Leah's special blend cradled to her lips and
what Amarie considered the best baked dough north of the
Mississippi in her tummy.

Now Eli wanted answers. But she'd rather not divulge
the details before she had time to sort things out. Like

transportation, housing, and the rest of Maslow's hierarchy of needs.

"Amarie," Eli barked.

"What, you big bully?" She ignored the flash of warning in his eyes. "I'm thinking."

Even with his lush midnight beard, Amarie saw the muscle in his jaw tick. "Don't think. Talk," he demanded.

"Stop rushing me," she mused. Not that she wanted to be difficult, but what if Eli condemned her decisions? Like her father, would he use it as an excuse to remind her of how inadequate she was at…everything? Just like Russell, she would be giving him the ammunition to extinguish this little flame of success she'd ignited.

"I'm not a patient man."

She rolled her eyes heavenward. "As if that wasn't obvious."

"Talk," he ordered.

At a crossroads on day two. She'd hoped to avoid questions. Particularly those of interest to Eli "Doberman Pinscher" Calvary, whose very presence dizzied her wits, which was hard to do, while simultaneously curling her toes. Instead of socializing, something she worked hard at, she chose to power her productivity with positive vibes. She'd jumped at the chance to apply her nursing knowledge during Adele's surgery. Sterile technique, hydration status, urine output, she'd done it all without him directing her to assist. Up next, implementing her baby steps to success, which would benefit him even if she received a different kind of pink slip.

So, here she was. Tell him the truth. Get fired.

Delay the truth. Get fired. But at the end of the day, she'd be two hundred and twenty-four dollars richer.

"I'm not a patient man," she repeated, buying herself two

measly seconds. "I think that's a line from the *Forrest Gump* movie. You a fan?"

"No. And it's not."

"Okay. Okay." Maybe she could negotiate a settlement like those cheesy injury lawyer commercials. "You have to promise not to fire me, first. No matter what you hear."

"Not gonna happen."

"Have you never negotiated? There are trade-offs involved. Quid pro quo."

"Keep dragging this out and firing is what you're gonna get."

They were both healthcare providers, trained to be empathetic. He would understand, maybe even agree with her. She ventured a look up at those jeweled eyes that no print media could capture. Nope. No agreement in his stony features. Eli Calvary had a warring, avenger, dark-lord vibe. For now, she was under his command.

"So, Prince and I had a rough Monday," she began.

"Why? Did something bad happen?" He waited for her to continue and explain who and where her Prince had disappeared to. Eyes intent, focused on the words as they hung, unspoken, behind her lips. Lips he traced with his gaze.

"In a manner of speaking," she cleared her throat, "yes."

"Forget a manner of speaking." Their glares locked. "Tell me the matter-of-facts."

"Now see here, Eli Calvary. I still have a right to my privacy. Since when is my commute your business?"

No one had ever been interested in her comings and goings. That had bothered her for years. Then she'd found comfort in others not having any expectations of her. When no one cared, it didn't matter what your choices were, good, bad, or indifferent.

"You're hiding something."

"I'm a woman. I'm allowed secrets. A lady should possess a certain amount of intrigue. Just accept that I'm a mythical creature. As such, I can never be fully understood. Just move on."

"Ah, that's rich. You're rambling and BS-ing again."

Of course, he was right. It was one of her telltale signs whenever she got overwhelmed. She could do this. Amarie Walker failed at many things, actually most things, but no matter the circumstances, she finished what she started.

She sighed, not seeing any way around spilling the details Mrs. Kline missed.

"So, here's the deal—"

The bell above the door dinged. Eli turned just as Amarie looked up. In walked a colorful caravan of ladies waving pink flyers.

"Oh no you don't," Eli started, but Amarie seized the opportunity of distraction.

"Excuse me, boss. Customers before conflict."

"Howdy, Eli." A rail-thin woman with gray roots and blonde-frosted tips grinned. "Mrs. Kline said the new girl has livened up the place and to git here quick as lightning. I got questions about you and your brothers being up for grabs, too. Which one of you is into feet?"

"Noah," Leah and Eli yelled in unison.

Amarie so forgave Mrs. K for gossiping right now. She used the interruption to focus on her job. Eli's inquisition averted. "Happy Tuesday, ladies, step right up and I'll get you checked in. I'm Amarie, the new girl-slash-receptionist. I have a new intake form with our payment options for each of you to complete and then you can see the doctor."

Eli swung around so fast, Amarie took a step back.

"They don't even have pets." His voice practically boomed in the small space.

"Then I'll book them as walk-in consultations," she hissed, leaning in. "Let me handle this, please."

"You," he sputtered, "are not off the hook." Eli tapped the side of his temple, threatening her with his one-track mind. "Come on, Hiccup."

The canine resting at her feet lifted a brow in response but stayed put.

"Traitor," Eli barked.

Hiccup barked back and that was that.

* * *

For the next several hours, Eli had to stop his eagle eye routine and actually attend to his clientele.

Problem was, Calvary Vet had more females than felines filling the reception area. Well, that wasn't actually true, there were definitely some cougars with their claws ready to swipe at the only masculine prey. The exam room door opened, and an impatient Eli escorted the last of the ladies out the door.

It was the end of the day and Amarie had used the time to make herself invaluable—un-fireable.

"Why is my phone pinging with tomorrow's appointment reminder?"

"Because I wanted to remind you about tomorrow's farm appointment today," she said slowly, as if he had trouble understanding her.

"First off, I don't need reminders in my own clinic. Who told you to take the appointments online?"

"You did."

"Now, that there is a fib. Lying to me will get you booted out the door."

"You said the front desk is my problem."

"Yeah."

"So, that makes me management."

"That's not in the policy."

"I read your single-sheet policy manual. It's not expressly prohibited. I took creative liberties."

"Well don't. Post-it notes did the job."

"For you. All the YouTubers recommended this free cloud-based software for the practice."

"Anybody ever tell you the internet's not real? I'm running a business. Not an entertainment profile."

Amarie was quick to defend her process improvements. Social media had been her constant companion. With tens of thousands of people tuning in for her PerkyLateBloomer InstaG reels and TikTok videos, she'd found a safe place to share her authentic self.

"Leveraging social media is a great way to get your brand message in front of potential customers," she defended.

"And how'd you get my cell phone number?"

"From the employee roster."

"Momma," he bellowed. "What in—you gave her—that's confidential information."

His mom peeked her head out. "You said it was for employees only. That's me and Amarie."

"Thank you, Leah." Amarie gave a mock high-five. "As the office manager, we have transitioned to an online patient management system that allows our pet owners to schedule appointments via our web-based portal twenty-four hours a day. That means they don't have to wait for one of us to answer the phone. And then there are Zelle payments."

"Don't need it. Cashbox worked for my father. Nothing was wrong with the way it was," Eli said through clenched teeth.

"Trust me, you're too impatient for my dissertation on the

high cost of operational inefficiency. So, in addition to old-school cash and checks—ew, can you say dirty money?—we now accept contactless online payments. The money is deposited directly to the clinic's account for immediate availability."

Eli brows pitched low, his expression thunderous. He glared at his mother. "Tell me you didn't give our financials to a complete stranger."

"She's a part of the team, Eli."

"Fine," he spat. "Come tomorrow, I want you to teach me everything you've changed."

"Really?" she asked. Russell had never been interested in anything she did as long as it was done.

"This is still my business."

"I know," she said, her tone gentling.

Leah chimed in. "Wow, did you see how excited the women are about the bachelor auction? They booked out the afternoon schedule."

"Yeah, it's kind of weird to make this much money for the clinic from bachelor auction–generated consultations." Amarie offered a half smile, trying to envision Eli as gallant as the women described the man in the photo. "I still can't believe you looked that good in your military uniform."

"You made that point yesterday," Eli grumbled.

"The picture doesn't look like you up close nor at a distance," Amarie chirped.

"Whatever, you." He rolled his eyes, before dragging the conversation in a different direction. Though Amarie could stay right here, with the focus off her.

"So, they actually paid the consultation fee?" His tone was disbelieving.

"Yes." Amarie nodded. "Your time is money. Count on me to collect every penny owed."

"Imagine that. Asking your customers to pay for services rendered." Leah smiled, a little more than vindication in her voice. There was a large dose of *I told you so.*

Amarie fisted the dollar bills from the cash box and paraded the small booty in front of Eli's wide eyes. "Six hundred and seventy-eight big ones."

"Give me that," he said, pocketing today's revenue.

"Way to go, Amarie," Leah cheered. "Let's celebrate your second day with dinner at the Black Bear."

"Ah, I'll stay and lock up." She'd dodged the question about her car, but she didn't think the same tactic would work twice if he asked where she stayed in town.

"This is Service. We don't lock doors. Now go on." Eli pointed to the door.

Where could she go? She didn't have the money for lavish restaurant food. Anxiety gripped her stomach. Panic ripped through her chest. Breathing against the clawing pinch of her airway heightened her discomfort. Fear of discovery spread, biting into her until she felt genuine pain seize her limbs. Her nostrils started to burn, first inside, then moving higher until tears swelled and her head spun. She pushed back against the rushing tide. It had been many years since she'd slept in the back of a car. But she'd survived it once. And this time it would be her choice.

"Please, come." Leah hooked her arm through Amarie's elbow. "It's my treat."

Amarie wavered on now-trembling legs. With one hand she gripped her desk, her world slowed. Waters receded. Rotation ceased.

"Yes." She exhaled a shaky breath. "Thank you." She gripped Leah's hand tighter than called for. "Thank you so much."

"Pick up the mail while you're in town, office manager," Eli called from his office. "Momma's got the box key."

"Yeah. Okay." Amarie sniffed, grabbing her purse from the desk drawer before relocking it. "I'm ready."

"Amarie."

She stiffened at the stern timbre in Eli's voice. She'd almost made it. She envisioned the champagne waterfall on the way into town—plunging down, like her; crashing, like her; swept up, like her—until the current scattered the last of her pummeled remains. Turning, she braced herself the impending rejection.

"Yes?" That sounded too shaky, but at least it was just her voice.

"You earned another day on the job."

Amarie followed Leah out the front door, but not before saying to Eli, "Thanks...boss." She smiled so big, her jaw hurt. He actually wanted her to stay. Nothing could ruin her day. The thing about being wrong was that she rarely saw it coming before it hit her in the face.

Chapter Six

AMARIE DIDN'T TRUST him. Was it funny that neither of them trusted the other? Eli contemplated the question while Hiccup ran around the backyard, his tail a proud banner waving in high praise of his athletic ability. Familiar with his routine, Eli started on his pal's dinner bowl.

Only twenty minutes had passed since the women had departed, so he took his time reviewing Amarie's text updates regarding Calvary Clinic. She'd ended each message with a different glowing, round-faced emoji. During his years in the Army, not one of his many tasks ended with a happy face. Eli shook his head. "Women."

He took the shortcut across the Cattail Creek foot bridge into downtown Service. There wasn't much to Main Street, just enough to have everything he needed after a hard day's work—a cold beer, a hot meal, and fast music, the genre varied with his mood. Country to cool a hot head. Rhythm and blues to warm an empty bed. Hard rock to wake the dead for another day. The Black Bear provided all three. Didn't matter if you lived uptown or downtown, when the work ended, family and friends gathered here Monday through Saturday.

Sundays were reserved for the faith center. The owner, Gracie Lou, and her fiancé, Caleb, had an arrangement with the local minister. To facilitate the pews were full at the faith center, the pub opened after noon on the one day the community reserved for rest…and fishing.

Gracie Lou called to him from behind the bar where she filled glasses and mugs from the tap. "Eli, I hear you got yourself another fancy city girl. This one with a BMW."

Like most folks native to these mountains, she elongated the last letter: *B-M-dub-be-yay*.

"You heard wrong," he deadpanned, stepping up to the counter. All of five foot three in her signature red cowgirl boots, Gracie Lou Tyler had a skyscraper personality with a barn-red pixie cut visible in dense fog.

"Riiight," she drawled. "You bringing her to see me and Caleb jump the broom?"

"Nope." He grabbed the larger of the two from her hand, tipping his mug in thanks.

In Service, a wedding drew more people than a political rally from either party. Everyone pitched in to make the newlyweds' day memorable. Cara had pooh-poohed the idea, opting for a country club wedding on the military base.

"She's pretty. Nice, too. One of these other fellas is gonna lift his leg around your doorstep. Remember, snoozers are losers."

Eli waved a hand acknowledging he'd heard the warning. But Eli didn't consider Amarie his. With the bar at his back, the chatter increased in volume above the country music spewing from the vintage jukebox in the far corner. The center dance floor was empty for now, but the closer it got to sundown, the more freely the beer flowed and the faster the feet moved. He'd be home by then.

Prudence, the cashier at the General Trading Post and campground rental center, stepped in his path. Eli stopped on a dime, but his beer sloshed over the rim. Sudsy foam from the icy liquid flowed between his fingers to drip onto the floor.

"Dang it." He frowned, switching the mug to his free hand, rubbing the excess on his jeans, a wearable sponge for on and off the job. Couldn't say the same for the Army's service uniform. "Prudence, didn't see you there."

"Oh." She laughed. "It's alright, Eli," she said, her usually high-pitched voice soft and scratchy, like she had a case of laryngitis.

"You sound different. Need a drink of water or something?"

"No, silly. I plan to be plenty wet for you 'cause I'm the highest bidder on that there auction page."

"There isn't going to be an auction."

"Don't play coy, Eli."

He'd always considered Prudence, with her thin frame and flat chestnut hair, to be a quiet slip of a woman. Her older brother, Dosier, and Eli had been classmates back in the day. But in bad cliché fashion, he'd lost touch when he left for college. Coming home on the holidays didn't leave much time to kindle relationships from his youth. Eventually, his visits had slowed to a trickle. Cara had shunned small-town living after one visit, so the trickle evaporated to a once-a-day text message to start the day and a Sunday afternoon phone call. Tobias and Noah, especially Noah, had joked about him abandoning them to entertain all the single ladies in town. His parents had kept up pretenses for his sake, but his actions had hurt them all. Guilt still ate at him that he'd allowed a woman to separate him from his family. But he'd still received a hero's welcome when he had returned with all his belongings in the back of his pickup truck.

"Believe you me, I'm not. Just sorry you wasted your money, Prudence."

"Oh, don't be sorry, honey biscuit. Be ready." She winked and sashayed off like she had actually conducted a reasonable conversation with him. Honey. Biscuit. Eli shuddered at the visual. He needed to talk with his brothers before this foolishness got worse.

"You Calvarys got all the primo land...now you corralling the women." That comment came from Benjamin Buchanan. He scowled at Eli from his wallflower perch, a dark alcove near the unisex restroom.

"Not true, Bucky. Doing the best I can for my family. Getting a woman on my arm has got nothing to do with it."

"That picture of you in the paper says different," he rasped, stepping from the shadows. "And, uh, I don't like it. Not one bit."

Long and lanky in faded denims and a white T-shirt sagging with dirt stains, Bucky lived off the grid, preferring well water and kerosene heat to modern amenities. The men in that family courted their firearms more than the ladies. Frequent run-ins with the law for assault, trespassing, and disorderly conduct kept them off the streets most days.

Eli stood his ground. "I said my piece."

His concave body retreated, but not before his tinny voice reached Eli's ears. "Folks don't take too kindly to you uptown types taking our women. But the way I hear it, in thirty days, the Pendletons will own you lock, stock, and waterfront view. I already signed up for the work crew," he cackled, as if he visualized the bulldozers ripping through Calvary land. "They fixing to build a fancy Landing Falls–style resort where your cabin used to be."

Eli stiffened. So the Pendletons already had a plan in place if he failed.

"Bucky, don't count on that paycheck," Eli gritted out, rattled by the mention of the predatory Pendleton family, more than his frustration at the nagging toothache the auction announcement had caused. "I'm done with this conversation and talk of the Pendletons. You?"

"I'm guessing so . . . for now," he added.

"For—" Eli stopped himself from saying more. Wasting his time on a man who saw what he wanted was futile. The Pendletons had been a thorn in his father's side. With Levi Calvary gone, they had a target on him. Eli walked off, scanning the tables for the Calvary men, more committed than ever to preserving their lands for future generations. The Pendletons' plan for the resort raised the stakes. The time to tell his brothers the sordid details had arrived.

He found the face he was looking for. Tobias sat alone at one of the square tables farthest from the action. He never understood why his brother limited his contact with people. Underneath all that caution tape was a man of deep principle and thought.

Eli took the chair next to his brother, spinning it backward before taking his seat. "What's up, brother?"

"Gas prices." Tobias grimaced. "Cost me an eighth of a tank to drive to the station for a fill-up." Eli amended his previous musings that Service had everything he needed. On the docket for the next council meeting was the reopening of a medical clinic along with a gas station that didn't require a twenty-minute drive south into Landing Falls.

"Yeah," Eli sighed, "I know." Minimum wage had increased a few years back. In theory, it felt like a win for most of the folks trying to squeeze a living out of a town without any manufacturing plants or federal agencies close by. Retirees moving from high-cost surrounding states—Ohio, Pennsylvania, and Maryland—drove the housing prices beyond the reach of most locals. To afford the monthly mortgage on the single-family homes going up in nearby Whynot, it would take triple the wages for half the square footage. Unbeknownst to his mother, he'd done some recognizance just in case he couldn't sort out the mess with the bank.

"Saw you talking with Bucky." Tobias waited for Eli to pick up the conversation. He didn't. Instead, he sipped his beer, letting the chilly liquid spread through his mounting to-do list, ice crystals freezing the mass in place, a brief reprieve from the avalanche aimed at him.

"So," Tobias gazed over at him, "how'd it go with Amarie?"

"Worse than I could ever imagine," Eli said, studying his mug.

"Oh yeah?" Tobias's voice rose a bit. "She was that bad?"

"Nope," Eli said, shifting his ball cap further back on his head. "That good. And now Mom's thinking she's right about this bachelor auction."

And that's when he heard it. Amarie's laughter. And why did his pulse rev like a V12 engine? Must be indigestion. Eli watched his mother and Amarie socializing with the people he'd known since birth, having a good time. Everybody in town had come to meet the new girl with the BMW he had yet to see.

"Look at them."

Tobias glanced over his shoulder, the corner of his mouth lifted into a smile. The sound of his mother's laughter eased the pressure around his heart, too. He was sure Tobias felt the same. With his father gone, they worried about her alone in that big house. It was one of the reasons at least one of them joined her for breakfast every morning.

"I see their inflated heads floating from here." Eli smirked.

"Hmm." Tobias sighed, taking another swallow of beer.

"It was impressive what Amarie did with Adele. Dad used to call that 'having the touch.'"

"Oh, you missed the best of it. She actually won over Mrs. Kline this morning."

"No fooling?"

"It gets better," Eli chuckled. "She managed to get all the ladies who usually wander into the office to squeeze my butt to pay for the pleasure."

"Mom and Amarie. Sounds like you got yourself a dynamic duo."

"Huh, guess I do," he chuckled, but then the laughter stuck in Eli's throat drier than a week-old dog biscuit. "But I don't want a partner." Not anymore.

"Wow. At least Amarie is working toward your goals. She's not one of Mom's plants trying to get you down the aisle."

Tobias was right. Amarie wouldn't spend a cent on him. Dang it, that irritating thought made him think about the auction. On that, he wouldn't budge.

"It's not 'wow' in the least," he said, rapping his knuckles on the scarred wood table. "Would you just look at those two soaking up all this attention?"

"Not all of it." Tobias faced Eli, his brows bunched. "Naomi, the day shift dispatch operator, turned the siren on when I walked in the ambulance bay this morning. She waved one of Mom's pink flyers in my face, and then demanded I strut my stuff."

"See," Eli barked. "That's my point. Me, you, and Noah, we're laughingstocks."

Tobias took a huge gulp from his half-empty mug. "Trust me when I tell you, Naomi wasn't laughing. In fact, she growled at me twice before lunch."

"What did you do?"

"Ate in my truck with the doors locked."

"Smart man. Now, about Amarie."

"I can see why you had your doubts. But is it really that bad, Eli? Having somebody on the staff who can maybe help share the load? She actually added to the bottom line."

"Who do we know with a BMW and Louise Vuitton luggage, T? A woman like her won't stick around." His wife hadn't.

"It's Louis, not Louise. And yeah, you're right about our lack of an affluent social network. But you know how Mrs. Kline gossips. It could be fake news."

"Yeah, but she's not that inventive." Amarie was as polished and creative as she presented.

"You ain't never lied." Tobias polished off his beer, signaling the waitress for a second round.

"Exactly. And she mentioned some guy named Prince."

"Think that's her boyfriend?"

Eli studied his mug once more. "I don't know who he is, but I already know she deserves better."

"Do you now?" Tobias quizzed, not moving from the pointed question.

"Yep."

"Got anybody in mind?"

And just like that, Noah came strolling up, beer bottle to his lips. He swallowed before asking, "What did I miss?"

The chair scraped against the rough plank floors, the sound jarring even in the chaos.

"Amarie's a big hit in town," Tobias whispered.

"A pretty little thang like that is bound to be taken soon. I know she said she wanted to have a talk with me, so I'm gonna mosey on over and—"

"Sit down," Eli interjected. "I need to talk with you both."

Noah dropped in the chair opposite Tobias. "Okay, big brother. What is it that you want to say? Make it quick. I don't like to keep the ladies waiting."

"First, don't get close to Amarie. Neither of you. She won't be here long."

"Since when is that a problem?" Noah quizzed.

"The last time I trusted a woman I just met, I ended up divorced and I'm pretty sure close to destitute."

"Yeah, but Amarie made you money from the women interested in the bachelor auction," Tobias reminded.

"That's cause enough to light my fire." Noah grinned.

"It's not," Eli snapped.

"Can't say I'd be complaining. It's probably good for business to have a pretty woman around."

"Really, keeping her around because she's cute? Do you ever get tired of bad ideas, Noah?"

"Sometimes, it's good to be confronted with your bad ideas on a daily basis, Eli. It improves a man's disposition."

"There's a lesson to be learned in there, somewhere," Tobias nodded.

"Yep. Don't take relationship advice from a bull walrus." Eli swore his baby brother had lust on the brain twenty-four seven.

"Hey," Noah chided. "Quit with the vet metaphors neither one of us understands."

"Walruses grab the attention of several females at once by making lots of noise."

Noah shrugged, nonplussed by the comparison. "Want to be seen, got to be heard. Since when do you care who I talk with?"

"Since all your talking ends with pillow talk." There was more bark than he intended. Why that was, he decided not to ponder.

"Did you see that smile she aimed my way yesterday? Dazzling."

Noah grinned to himself like a man thinking his luck might hold for a chance to get to know Amarie better. Not going to happen on Eli's watch.

"Listen to me." Eli pronounced each word with emphasis. "She had no idea what she was agreeing to when she said she would talk with you later. This is Service. She doesn't speak our language."

"How do you know that?" Noah winked, leaning back in chair. "You don't."

Eli blew out a frustrated breath. "I worked with the woman. She's nice. A little hyperactive, but in a sweet, busy bee kind of way. Trust me, she's not the dine-and-dash type."

"Hey, you're the one who said city women are the best kind of corruption a man can experience. I'm willing to take one for the team."

"Keep talking," Eli warned. "I'm gonna take you to the mat."

"If you're going to bark every time a man shows interest in your new employee, you might want to invest in a muzzle. I heard talk all day about our bachelor auction and your new lady. News has traveled to both sides of the mountain, past Whynot last I checked."

"You mean Lois Kline drove that beater of hers to the food market, spewing blue-haired gossip to every cashier within hearing distance with a smartphone." No wonder Prudence had approached him with an indecent proposal.

Noah wiped foam from his lip with the back of his hand. "Probably has reached Landing Falls by now. Overheard Austin say he might stop by the clinic to give Amarie a good old-fashioned Service welcome."

"You tell Mayor Austin don't bother. The last thing I need is women and local politicians clogging up my waiting room."

"Gracie Lou said Mrs. Kline told her Amarie had you on the computer?"

"Did not."

"You gotta keep her, Eli. She's a natural with people. Plus, she has a head for business. Does she have any idea how tight we Service folks can squeeze a penny?"

"She has no idea. Just asks for what she wants. People respond to her." Eli did, too, his anatomy in particular, even though he kept his distance. "Can't slow her down, either. Changing this. Rearranging that."

"Amarie can handle herself with your frisky clientele. Why not let Mom have her fun with the bachelor auction?"

"That's different." Noah had experience with puppy love back in high school. He had no concept of a male ego blown to bits by heartache. Where women were concerned, old insecurities nipped at Eli's confidence. Noah had never risked his heart, so how could he understand what it felt like when someone he trusted crushed every hope and dream?

"How is that not the same?" Noah quizzed. "Either way, they're paying for service. This way you two might get dinner and a couple of kisses. With a wagonload of luck, maybe some long night conversations with a few ladies."

"How many times do I have to tell you to shut up?" Eli barked. "Everything is not about getting in a woman's underpants!"

"Don't have to get into hers when she can get into mine, big brother. You need to get out more."

"Look, Amarie's a good worker, and," he paused before spitting out the next part, "she has a fella. Name's Prince, probably British. He drove her here."

Noah burst out laughing.

"What's so funny?" Eli scowled and Tobias waited for the punch line.

"There's a purple BMW on the side of the road leading into town."

The muscles along Eli's back went rigid. "So, her and the boyfriend are going to be here in town?"

"No, Inspector Not-A-Clue. The car has District of Columbia plates."

"Already know she's from the city."

"Yeah, but what you don't know is the car's custom plates bear the name PRINCE."

"So, the woman's car quit on her, and she didn't think to mention that? That's plum fool crazy."

"You ain't never lied," Tobias said. "Why not ask for help?"

Probably the same reason Eli refused to admit he appreciated her allowing him to rest last night. Pride. Eli grabbed his phone, texting Kanaan. "I'll take care of her car."

His cousin, the town sheriff, had spent his life in Service, keeping the town's auto repair shop up and running after his folks moved into a south Florida retirement village. His aunt had never been much for the West Virginia winters and Uncle Josiah couldn't refuse her anything. Eli had been the same with Cara, only he didn't get a lifetime of forevers. Less than a year of marriage... He abandoned his train of thought. It was water under the bridge, nasty water that left a foul taste he couldn't rid from his system.

Tobias nodded in agreement. "Kannan?" he asked, gesturing to the phone Eli held.

"Yep. He can take a look under the hood. Give me an estimate."

"Huh." Noah tipped his chair back, balancing on the two

rear legs. "I see what you're doing. Barking at me to stay away while you fix her car and share her biscuit," he accused.

"That's not the reason why I want all of us to not fall prey to her pretty dimples."

"It's just one. The left cheek." Noah grinned. "Are you going to hire her outright?"

"You should already. She's good at everything you need," Tobias chimed in.

"If I do decide to bring her on full-time, permanent, we can't afford to mess things up by thinking with the little head."

"Speak for yourself." Noah jabbed at his arm in jest.

"I'm not joking," Eli muttered. "There's a chance we could lose the house and the land."

Noah jerked upright. The chair's legs slammed against the wood floor. An ear-splitting scrape of metal on wood had Eli wincing. Patrons in the vicinity glared in their direction.

"Say that again?" Tobias gulped.

"We need more money flowing into the clinic to stave off a foreclosure. The house. Clinic. Our cabins. The land."

"Since when?" Noah demanded.

"I've been making partial payments since Dad—Dad died." Eli swallowed the rising bile, a bitter reminder of his struggle to accept the loss. "With me still carrying the mortgage on the house Cara and I built and the decrease in income, I can't get the loan refinanced."

There. He'd gotten it all out.

"Why are we just hearing this, Eli?" He didn't miss the accusation in Noah's voice.

"How bad is it?" Tobias asked. "Does Mom know?"

"Bad, and yeah, she does," he sighed, scrubbing a hand over his face.

"Are we too low in the ranking order to be trusted with family business?" Noah snapped.

His brother's accusation rubbed. Eli deserved it and more. Tobias had inherited Mom's academic excellence. Noah, a former high school jock, had crushed their father's records on the football field and aced his fire science curriculum. Eli, well, straddled the middle of the road with books and balls.

"Noah...come on. I've been putting off telling you this not because I don't trust you. It's a responsibility Dad wanted me to handle." Eli had been a good son, reliable. He never gave his folks a reason to worry. Then he'd met Cara. Learned something new about himself: he wanted to be the best husband to one woman. Follow in his father's footsteps, leave a legacy for his wife and children. He'd failed at one. Now his brothers knew he was about to lose the other. Huh, what a fool.

"Whatever you need, Eli." Tobias nodded. "You got it from me."

"Yeah." Noah took another draw from the long neck. "Whatever."

Eli scrubbed a chilled hand over his face. Steeling his pride, he uttered the monetary figure of his failure. "I need eighteen thousand dollars or the Pendletons are going to take the land."

"Pendletons." Noah choked and sputtered. "Well, ain't that a kerosene can in a five-alarm fire."

Tobias grimaced, his expression drawn in concern. "You ain't never lied. That family..." He stopped himself when the waitress deposited a frosted mug of amber brew in front of him.

"Any more buzzkill news, Eli?" Noah's question penetrated his skin, biting through their kinship, daring him to confess another secret.

"That's it."

"We don't have that kind of money." A confession Eli knew without Noah offering.

"Ain't that the truth," Tobias lamented. "One question for you, though. If Dad had money troubles, why did he give you the down payment for a house?"

Eli willed his body to remain relaxed. This question was one he never wanted to answer. A man's pride, like an army battalion, could withstand repeated attacks, but none crippled as much as not being capable of providing for those under your care. Eli couldn't meet his brother's intense scrutiny.

"Guess he wanted to sow a seed in my future." Eli managed to push the words around the rise of bile at the rush of memories, the betrayal.

"Paying for your education. My emergency medical services training. Noah's fire science degree. Pop did his best for the three of us," Tobias defended. But Eli didn't need a reminder of the man his father had been. If ever a son idolized a father, he did.

"I agree." Eli cleared his throat. "Dad thought different."

Noah bounced one finger against his beer bottle. "We about as worthless as two left shoes in a greyhound race, Eli."

"Never, little brother." Eli had limited options, but bottomless hope. He refused to let life take his father's dream for their land.

"Oh, I like that grin on your face." Noah relaxed, some of the anger seeping from his face. "What are you thinking?"

"We need another plan besides this cockamamie bachelor auction to raise the money. You in?"

"When has Noah Calvary ever walked away from a challenge?" his baby brother asked in a loud voice. To which everyone in the Black Bear shouted, "Never!"

"Count me in, big brother."

"Me too," Tobias offered.

They all agreed, raising their mugs in solidarity. Eli downed his beer and ordered another round. Between the three of them, they would come up with a plan that didn't involve dating and other disasters that would be sure to follow if it depended on him keeping a woman happy who called him honey and biscuit in the same sentence.

Chapter Seven

Enlightening. THAT ONE word described Amarie's field trip to the post office. Every man, woman, and child had greeted Leah, and by extension her, with a genuine smile. Located in the Town Mall, the mail window shared the equivalent of a studio apartment with the mayor, the sheriff, and the utilities company. Compared to one block in the nation's capital, downtown Service equated to the square footage of a weekend farmer's market. The stroll, which was the only way to describe the pace of Service, ended with the two of them sharing this quaint table in a rustic pub.

An L-shaped bar that serviced the patrons just interested in a drink was in the front. Couples holding hands, men in T-shirts and work boots, and groups of women chair dancing to tunes wafting through wall speakers filled rough-hewn square tables in the back. They had chosen a table in between the two sections closest to an empty stage, more of a single raised platform with a drum set and a microphone.

"So, you excited for tomorrow's farm visit?" Leah asked, interlacing her fingers resting on the tabletop.

"Yes...I think." She draped her crossbody bag over the chair back.

"I'm proud of you. Jumping into the fire from day one. Eli would say the same if he wasn't a stubborn ox." The way Leah looked away, Amarie sensed even a loving mom found Eli's grumpy demeanor less endearing.

"I think Eli was more impressed with the money than me." His features—well, the tension lines bracketing his eyes—had softened for the briefest of moments. Amarie found non-grumpy Eli rather handsome.

"He's like his father, maybe like all men. Thinking he has to carry the weight of the world every waking moment. But we know differently," she chuckled to herself. "They walk on water, but we," she whispered, "we hold the hose."

"Do we?" Amarie chuckled under her breath, thinking about all the times she'd heard Russell taking credit for one of her ideas. Without her running the office, he would've had a cashbox and a sticky pad stack, too.

"Oh, sweetheart. It's one of our many superpowers. So, what do you want to eat?" asked Leah.

"They wouldn't happen to have any biscuits, would they?"

Leah smiled; it was soft, rueful. "I'm afraid not. No one out-bakes a Calvary."

Amarie could have taken it as vanity. But she really believed Leah was telling the truth. "Right. What do you recommend?"

"It's Tuesday, so our choices are pepperoni rolls. Or rolls with pepperoni."

"But the sign out front says barbeque and things?"

"Tuesdays are the *things*." Leah made air quotes. "Options."

"Weird." That explained the lack of menus on the table. Refreshing really, to not have to stress over multiple choices.

"It's a taste of West Virginia history. Dates back to the

Italians who migrated to our area to work the coal mines at the beginning of the twentieth century."

"In that case, bring on the meat and bread." Amarie beamed.

The waitress came over, an older woman with coal-black strands pulled into a messy topknot.

"Good to see you, Leah." She smiled, her blue eyes garaged under sweeping false lashes.

"You too, Delores. This is Amarie, our new hire."

"Oh, I already know. Mrs. Lois came through on her way downtown. Told us that you're the one driving that purple BMW out by the road."

"Actually, it's not all that drivable right now. It started spewing hot guts on the way up the mountain."

"That sounds just awful." Delores clucked. "Not to worry though. My oldest, Rocky, real name Sylvester, is just sitting around the house. He'd be happy to swing by and take a look."

"No. No," Leah chimed in. "Eli will take care of it for her."

Delores shrugged. "Alrighty then. So, two coalminer sandwiches, hot or cold?"

Leah nodded. "We like our meat hot. Thanks, Dee."

"Just like your boys, eh? I been hearing about the auction. Couple of Buchanans were worked up about the whole thing. Speak of the devil, did you hear that Kanaan released Bucky this morning? That man is a menace to this town. Poor Ruth." Delores sucked air between her teeth, making a *tsk* sound. "Can't understand why she stays. I wouldn't—"

"Ah, Delores, our orders," Leah prompted. "We'll be sure to steer clear of Bucky. But I'd appreciate you talking up the auction."

Mental note, there was a bad Bucky on the loose. Of course, Adele had been labeled a fierce feline who had become a plush pussycat for Amarie. She decided not to prejudge. It had been unbearable to be under the microscope of others. It hurt. Now, for this car business. First and foremost, Prince was her responsibility. She hadn't asked for help, and she wouldn't beg her boss's help, even if his mother volun-told him.

"Sure thing, Leah. Food's coming right up."

"Leah, I can't ask Eli to help with Prince."

"Prince," Delores repeated. "Your car has a name. Isn't that the cutest thang?" Amarie startled. Their waitress had joined the conversation...again. "Eli's been a big ol' bear to everyone in town. Ask his mama, she'll tell ya. He just can't seem to help himself since—"

Leah chimed in before Delores could say anything else. "That's Eli's story to tell. We're not ones to gossip. Are we, Dee?"

"You won't hear me repeating gossip. 'Cause I say it loud enough the first time." She laughed. "I forgot to ask what you two ladies are drinking?"

"I'll take a cup of coffee. Decaf," Leah said.

"Pepsi, light ice."

"Oh, my goodness. This is Jack Daniels and Jim Beam country, honey. Everything on the top shelf goes down easy with Coke."

"Ah, okay, no new-generation products. What about tea?"

"Tea, we got. Unsweetened, hot or cold?"

"Sweet," Amarie said, affronted. "I'm a Southern girl through and through. Florida born. We take our tea sweet or not at all."

"This is Service. So that's two coalminers. One coffee, no thrills. And a lemonade 'cause the city girl with Southern roots needs her sugar fix."

"Let the lady make her own choices, Delores," her

insta-bestie said in defense. "Is the lemonade okay, Amarie? You can order something stronger if you like. No judgment."

Leah waited, not in a rush for Amarie to decide.

"I'll try it." Amarie nodded.

Leah raised her finger, pointing as if remembering something important. "Two creamers on the side, too. Thanks."

Amarie swayed to the music, an upbeat country tune she remembered from the radio, until she lost the words and herself in the rolling notes.

Delores came back and placed the food in front of them, six thick-cut pinwheels of meat, gooey white cheese, and bread. And the fragrance of high-fat meat cured with smoky spices was absolutely soul stirring. Amarie's mouth watered and she was ready to dig in until Leah bowed her head. Amarie lowered her fork, closed her fingers around Leah's hand, and gave thanks. She'd set off from D.C. without a destination or a tune-up, but she'd arrived in Service and secured a job. Created an opportunity for herself and for that she had to be grateful.

"Do you like it?" Leah asked, while Amarie shoveled another forkful of stringy melted cheese and warm baked bread into her mouth. She would never insult her taste buds with another frozen facsimile of pepperoni rolls ever again.

"You can't tell by the lack of responses?"

"Guess you couldn't answer that without disturbing your fine dining experience."

"No complaints from this girl." Amarie laughed.

"I think we're a good team, you and me."

"Me too," Amarie agreed.

"Next thing on the list. You can help me convince Eli the bachelor auction is a great idea."

"You want me to do what?"

"Talk to Eli about the bachelor auction. I mean, you got those women to pay what they owe. It's probably my fault that he's too much of a gentleman to get into a row with a woman over money. After Cara and the divorce, it only got worse."

Married? Eli "Grumpy Pants" Calvary?

"But look." Leah thrust her phone at Amarie. She reached for it, scanning the online site, auctionluvbuzz.com.

Five pictures on a simple landing page: Eli, Tobias, and Noah, all in uniform. HERE COMES THE CALVARY'S BACHELOR AUCTION in large script above their profile pictures. The bids totaled just shy of eleven hundred dollars. Not bad for less than forty-eight hours.

"Huh, Eli's wife…the marriage, what happened?" Amarie asked, injecting casual into her tone, handing the phone over.

"What didn't?" Leah sighed. "Wasn't much matrimony in a marriage of nine months. That woman was too superficial, selfish—but my baby was in love for the first time. So, we did our best to celebrate the good times and love him through the bad. He came home four months ago." Leah swallowed. "After I lost my Levi."

"Oh, Leah. I'm so sorry. How awful."

"It still is. It's hard to see your child hurting and unhappy. You spend most of your life protecting your babies from the big hurts, nursing them through the bumps and bruises. The instinct is still there even when he wears size thirteen boots and stands head and shoulders above you."

The loss of a husband, a daughter-in-law, dwarfed Amarie's problems. Perspective changed things. "Wow, size thirteen you say?"

"Is that all you heard?"

"Well no, there's that part about you being an awesome mom. And Cara something or other hurting your baby."

Leah smiled. "Anybody ever tell you, you have a way with words?"

"I have quite the history with saying all the wrong ones."

"Eh, being perfect is overrated. I like you just the way you came to us, bold and ready for an adventure."

"Thank you, Leah. Not that you've sold me. But which part do you want me to convince him to buy?"

"It is that obvious that he's totally against the idea?"

"Yes," she laughed. "Eli turns raspberry red every time he sees pink, or a woman mentions the auction."

"That's the one. Maybe you could ease him into giving the idea some serious consideration."

"Most men appreciate subtlety. Not Eli. He literally hates it. And from what I've seen, he's not very fond of feminine attention."

"He wasn't always so gruff. And the clinic could use the money."

Amarie had noticed the revenue had taken a sharp decrease in the last five years.

"Uh, can I think on it?"

"Absolutely, how about you sleep on it."

"Ah, so," Amarie lowered her voice, "I haven't had a chance to look for a hotel."

"Oh, that's easy. There isn't one."

"Oh . . . what—what about a bed-and-breakfast?"

"Not one of those, either." Amarie'd had no idea there were actually towns without guest accommodations.

"So, where do visitors stay?"

"Well," Leah chuckled, "when there is one, they stay with family or friends. I'll get one of the boy's rooms ready for you."

"Leah," Amarie paused. "I can't pay you until . . . well, I'm short on cash and options at the moment. But—but I'll pay you back, promise."

"That's the thing about friends, Amarie. There's no charge. We're just here for one another when needed. You're good company. And," she sniffled, "it's nice not to be alone."

Amarie sighed, overwhelmed with gratitude. "I don't know what to say. Thank you seems...not enough." She tilted her head back, searching for words to express the growing sense of peace after a day heaped with turmoil.

Leah stood. "That's good enough for me. You ready to head back?"

"Sure."

"Hey, Amarie." She turned at the sound of her name. It was the woman behind the bar. Leah had mentioned she'd inherited the business after her grandmother's passing.

"Yes?"

"You have to rub your hands over the bear pelt on your way out the door. It's a newcomer tradition. Tells everybody you're one of us."

Wow. A jolt of dopamine flooded Amarie with warm pleasure. It was juvenile, but today felt like the best field trip. The ones were the cool kids invited her to share their bench seat on the bus. And she got to share their cool-kid lunch. She couldn't stop her emotions from tangling her frayed heart around today and holding on.

"You sure?"

"A friend of Leah's is a friend of mine."

She sniffled, on the verge of leaky tears again. "Okay." She nodded.

Pinned to the wall was a large animal hide, rich chocolate in color with individual hairs reaching for her before she touched it. She'd never been much of a hunter-gatherer type, but there was a sense of joining a community, like she had her very own pack after years of being a lone she-wolf. Her fingers trembled as they sank into the plush fibers.

Gracie Lou raised a frosted mug. "This is Service."

A cheer rang out and Amarie smiled at having been included. Once outside, Leah threw an arm around her shoulders.

"I'm okay." Amarie reassured to hide the swell of emotion flooding her like a dam breaking at high tide.

"I know you are, but sometimes it's nice to get a hug after a bad breakup."

"How did you know?"

"Oh dear, Levi and I were married all my adult life. Love's like a cast-iron skillet, sometimes it cooks perfectly." She shook her head. "Other times it's a scorched mess. I know what a woman looks like after a man has hurt her heart. Believe me, you want to run as fast and hard as you can to put distance between you and that kind of pain."

The tears did fall then. Amarie couldn't seem to stop them. "I don't understand how he could throw me away," she hiccupped, "like I never meant anything to him."

They stopped on the bridge, listening to the trickle of water over rocks. More and more, the pain flooded her heart. Amarie gave in, pushed against the dam she'd built year after year. Her body vibrated with the sheer magnitude of all she'd endured at love's illusion.

"It's not fair, you know," she turned her face to Leah, "that he stopped loving me. I know that sounds weird... crazy. But I imagine that whenever I left his sight, Russell, that's the ex, he crammed all of me into this too-small box, so tiny that all the wonderful parts of us got buried, forgotten. Just a subtle flirt from another woman and...he forgot that he loved me. That I mattered to him. His one." She kind of laugh-snorted at her description of six years of late-night conversations, family holidays, their birthdays.

"Some men are slow to learn the value of a good woman by their side. Some are too selfish with their grand plans to make room in their lives for real love. And some are just stupid. You ran into one of the stupids."

"Oh, gosh, that's funny." The crying continued, but with intermittent fits of hearty laughter. Her mother would've been horrified at Amarie's breakdown. She would've given Amarie a firm shake, dried her eyes, and lifted her chin. "You must think I'm a crazy person. Crying. Laughing. I'm a mess. I'm-I'm so sorry, Leah. Look at me, carrying on."

Leah stopped. "I am looking at you. And you're entitled to be angry, disappointed, impulsive, and unsure, Amarie. I'm angry with my husband."

Amarie's breath hitched in surprise. No, that couldn't be right. "For dying?"

"No." She inhaled, and then let her eyes drift closed. "Because nothing in life prepares you for death. The way we moved around each other—laughing, loving, worrying, raising three hard heads for thirty-five years—it just stops. No more memories. No more moments. We think heartbreak prepares us, but...there's a second chance at love if we allow it." She released a choppy exhale, looking over at Amarie. "I'm mad that he loved me completely for who I am. Spoiled me." She smiled, a sadness weighing it down. "I miss sharing the insignificant details of my day with him. When I first lost him, it hurt to breathe. The air in my lungs mocked me because if I could, I would have given it to him. What was I without him?" she trailed off.

"And now?" Amarie asked, wanting the answer to the question she asked herself.

Leah shifted in her direction, their shoulders bumping. "Like you, I've decided to do more than survive. I want to thrive in this next chapter of my life. My Levi is a string from a kite that never soars far from me, though. But, some-days, I give myself permission to fall apart."

When did going to pieces become an option? Women had to be strong, bold, and put together. Amarie had to be every woman, but not a real person with feelings and emo-tions. How could she admit she wanted to punch, kick, and scream at the world? Why did she have to pretend she didn't need help, when she did … a lot? Confusing, it all was.

"You think so? Really? That it's okay to feel lost and fall apart?"

"With all these gray hairs under this color, I'm sure of it."

"Okay, I would hate for you to think badly of me."

Leah chuckled. "So what if I did? How others feel about you ain't worth a pillar of wet salt. My grandmother used to say that. And you know what?"

"Is this a challenge question? Because I'm terrible with coming up with the right answer when under pressure," Amarie said, in all seriousness. At her age, she felt as if her understanding of the world amounted to Swiss cheese with a touch of mold.

"She was always right. Now, come on, let's get home before one of these menfolk think we need a ride."

"What's wrong with that?"

"Oh, you have a lot to learn about small-town dating. Riding in a man's truck, that's as good as going steady in Service."

"Really?" She gasped in awe.

"I wouldn't lie to you."

"No," she whispered. "You wouldn't." Too many people she trusted in the past had. Leah also didn't judge, whereas others had been verbose in their assessment of her short-comings. And wasn't that the best feeling, freedom to be imperfect?

So Amarie walked back up the mountain, with tears in her eyes and Leah by her side. This was the conversation she wanted to have with her own mother. Slim chance of that happening, but she guessed it was okay to cry with a member of the pack. Leah's advice didn't bruise or punish. It soothed with the healing strength of an age-old salve passed down through generations.

"Um...I'll have to think about my strategy if I talk about the auction with Eli."

"It's your decision," Leah patted her hand, "and we have time."

"Oh, what should I do with the mail?" Amarie asked, reaching for her purse.

"You're the office manager now. Open the clinic mail and sort it. Eli detests paperwork." Leah's giggle seemed more related to the past than the present. "So like his father."

Amarie sighed in relief. "No problem."

A day piled high with worry over cars, jobs, food, and a place to lay her head had ended with her surviving in the wilderness. For now, she had a home with the Calvarys. Mentally, she added it to her to-do list. First, get settled. Second, call Vali to spill the tea on today's wins. Third, call her mom, who with their past history had to be popping Xanax skittles with worry. And finally, crack the spine on the licensure exam study guide. But she wouldn't unpack because come morning, if she mentioned the auction to Eli, she'd have to find a new place to live...and work. What she needed to figure out was how to be indispensable to her new boss.

Chapter Eight

Wednesday ushered in a torrential storm, but it wasn't a weather pattern. Eli dragged his heavy limbs through the darkened clinic, squeezing his temples, hopeful the pressure added would ease the pounding downpour between his ears. No such luck. Three rounds of drinks. Not Eli's best decision. "Hey, office manager. Where are you?"

The news about the Pendletons and the mortgage had dampened the Calvary brothers' usual revelry. Like a car barreling downhill without brakes, Eli's confession, late as it was, had wrecked the flow of fellowship. Things continued to skid southward as his mind wandered to the friendly, resourceful, and generally delightful employee he never should've hired. A newcomer with no job, no vehicle, and no money. His family needed his full attention. Amarie's situation added more weight to an already-unstable load. Best to part ways before more of her problems required a solution on his part.

Eli had made arrangements for a car tow. A parting gift that meant no hard feelings. Or tears. The darn woman should've asked for help. Kanaan had agreed to meet him at Hailey's field, hitch Amarie's Prince on the back of his flatbed, and get it over to the repair shop for a diagnostic. Eli muttered under his breath. Naming a car, an absolutely unnecessary practice, yet very much an Amarie-ism. She had a lot of those, he realized. Purple dazzler. Random-idea generator. Biscuit temptress. Where was she, anyway?

"Amarie?" Maybe calling her by name would facilitate an actual reply. As a trained soldier, a skilled vet raised to follow in his father's mighty footsteps, he could manage a rural practice without a social butterfly intermediary for his customers. But right now, he struggled to keep his sandpapered eyelids from scraping his corneas.

Hiccup, seeing Eli's need, trotted ahead of him through the grooming center breezeway into the kitchen. Under normal circumstances, his pooch preferred a romp through the switchgrass before the start of a workday, so Eli appreciated the seeing eye dog assist.

"Momma? Amarie? Where's everybody?" He smelled the soothing aroma of freshly brewed coffee. Another scent, potent and dark, caught in his nostrils, burning through his haze.

"Good morning, Eli."

Not the voice he ever wanted to hear inside the Calvary home. Internally, his temperature shot from ninety-eight degrees Fahrenheit to nuclear. Lourdes Pendleton. He should've suspected. Even in high school, if she perceived a weakness, she'd scurry from the shadows to gnaw a chunk of flesh in a sneak attack. If blood could boil, his would crack the ground beneath his feet. In tune with his abrupt change in mood, Hiccup released a whine, then danced backward, his bulk colliding with Eli's shins.

"Shh. Easy, boy." He scratched the dog's head until he calmed. He grabbed a glass from the cupboard, filled it with water from the tap, then added it to Hiccup's bowl.

He ignored his unwanted guest. While Hiccup hydrated, something Eli needed to do, he scooped one cup of dry dog food into a bowl.

"Who let you in, Lourdes?" All symptoms from last night's excess burned away. He stood, facing the enemy, ready to protect and defend. She rose from the kitchen table, slithering closer on sky-high nude heels, her body undulating beneath a tailored cream suit.

"This is Service, Eli. Doors are always open, remember?"

"To friends," he replied, sliding breakfast over to Hiccup's aluminum dish.

"Tsk, tsk." She laughed, the sound more calculated than coy. "Careful. I'm here to help," she said with a sweep of a checkbook in front of his face. Taunting. Coiling. Searching for an opening in his armor in which to strike.

"You must take me for an April fool."

"I could make your money problems go poof." She puckered red-painted lips, blowing him an air kiss.

Yeah, right. Tangling with her would saddle him with a crap ton of bad baggage.

"Not interested."

"Imagine you and me together, opening a star-rated four seasons resort," she drummed polished talons on the kitchen table at her back, "right here. A dream come true for some very influential people in this town."

He came to stand in front of her and leaned in close. "Not my dream."

She sighed in mock frustration. Eli wasn't fooled by her ruse. "Same old Calvary tunnel vision. Broaden your thinking. My daddy has his eyes on this property." She stroked her checkbook down his chest, pressed the sharp point of the plastic into his ridged muscle. "And like me, he gets what he wants."

He pushed her hand away. "Then why are you here?"

"Because optics have an impact around here," she drawled. "This is business for Daddy. Personal for me."

So, the Pendletons wanted him to make them look good for trying to rob his family of their land? The more his life changed, the more some things remained unchanged.

"I'm proposing you sell me this house, the cabins, the land for, let's say"—she angled her chin as if searching the ceiling for a number—"eighteen thousand today. An additional twenty when you deliver the keys to me, in person. Play nice and I'll even convince Daddy to keep one of the cabins for Leah to visit in the offseason."

"You. Your daddy. Your checkbook. Are not welcome here. Not when my father was alive. And for damn sure, not now."

Leaning against the table at her back, she relaxed her slight weight in her palms, crossed her ankles. "Aw, you're so handsome when you're mad. Always have been, but you're powerless against the inevitable. Why just this morning I overheard Daddy fielding bids to tear down this." She grinned smug superiority as she looked down her nose at the scarred floors carved with fond childhood memories, the faded picture of a gap-toothed Tobias riding his father's shoulders.

"Answer's no." What in green hell delayed the woman who'd promised promptness? "We've got work to do. Amarie," Eli bellowed, "get in here."

"Hold your mule," she yelled. Footsteps sounded above his head. A door opened. Closed. Opened again. Like a genie from a decorative bottle, Amarie appeared on the landing.

"I was in the shower, Mr. Grumpy Pants. I had just started the mail prep when you roared again."

She trounced down the back steps, buttoning up a vibrant lavender-and-purple half top with a flash of midriff showing. He allowed his gaze to travel up to her ample chest, plum-glossed lips, and matching eye color. When the smoke cleared in his brain, Eli licked his lips.

Wait, why was she upstairs? Never mind, that mystery would unravel after the Lady Pendleton hoofed it out the door. And that's when a plan materialized. The Pendletons thought him out of options, but he smiled up at Amarie, the *unknown* unknown, his secret weapon of ideas. His new mysterious investment partner, at least for the next five minutes, with no known connections in Service except for what he created.

"There you are, partner," he beamed.

The crazy woman actually spun around and looked behind her before stuffing a fistful of crumpled envelopes, probably more bills, into a purse slung over one shoulder before crossing arms beneath her attention-grabbing chest. Which only pushed the plush pillows higher in his line of sight. Like a puppy unleashed, his libido shot out the gate, running full steam into the danger zone.

"Who, me?"

"Yeah, you." He bounded up the remaining steps to escort her down. "Meet Lourdes Pendleton. Her family owns and operates the local bank. Now that you've arrived from Washington, D.C., I can formally announce your recent partnership with Calvary Veterinary Clinic."

"Hello, Lourdes. A pleasure to meet you." She smiled.

Money exempted the Pendletons from common courtesies, so Lourdes raised her sharp chin, ignoring Amarie's greeting.

Amarie looked up at him, brows drawn. "Is partnership a metaphor for full time? I'm confused."

Good for her, refusing to stoop to Lourdes's level. Taking her hand, he pulled until she stood beside him. Her hair smelled of apples in summer rain, juicy and sweet on the tongue. His mouth watered and a few things tightened, making him hate this predicament even more. "Quit joking. Lourdes might get the wrong idea."

"Her? I've been elevated to partner overnight."

He gave her shoulders a little shake. "Exactly. Why do you smell like a fruit salad?"

She looked at him, smirking. "Stop sniffing and explain. Slowly, please. I'm pre-caffeine infusion."

Hiccup ambled closer, rubbing his dark nose along her capris. With her eyes staying on Eli, she rubbed the dog's golden coat, ruffling his ears till he flopped, a happy puddle of playful puppy at her feet. Attention hog.

"Yes, help me to understand, too," Lourdes added.

Eli cleared his throat, announcing too loud, "Lourdes and her family want to buy Calvary land. I stated clearly that it's not for sale as we, that includes you, are partnering in a new lucrative venture."

"Oh, I see." Amarie nodded. "You need me now. I think I'm going to grab some coffee, then we can negotiate my terms and benefits." She shifted her weight, as if to walk away.

"No ma'am. You stay put." Amarie's toes peaked at him…again. She had a checkerboard pattern, lavender crisscross lines through the solid purple of yesterday. When did she find the time?

"Please stop this community theater," Lourdes snapped, crossing her arms. "Really, Eli? I know she's just some vagrant you hired off the streets."

Amarie stiffened. He paused, having never seen this blank chill on her face. Concern shifted from him to her. "Hey, you okay?"

"Fine," she gritted out.

She was so in canine attack mode. Lourdes had triggered Amarie's beast. Eli found himself intrigued.

"I am not a trespasser to be overlooked or underestimated, Miss Pendleton," she rasped, spine rigid, tone clipped. "As Eli told you, I'm his full-time partner in Calvary Veterinary Clinic, effective immediately. We are working together to restructure the practice with the bachelor auction being the first of several planned community outreach initiatives to increase brand awareness and revenue."

"Now wait a minute," Eli started. "The auction—"

"Did I mention you can't afford my closing fee without the estimated revenue stream?" she whispered. "Perhaps I'll take my coffee in the clinic and leave you here...with the she-devil."

He couldn't have that, so Eli wrapped his arm around Amarie's shoulders and hauled her closer. Well, hell. She'd come to his rescue, transitioned to a full-time employee, and hog-tied him to the bachelor auction. He held her in front of him like a shield.

"We'll discuss fees later," he whispered. "Focus on the problem in the room."

"Your problem, so why am I the one in striking distance?"

"Handled her better than I did. I got your back." A very nice backside, too. Amarie's soft curves against his body felt natural. Like a warm blanket he'd curled up with for his whole life. Which was crazy thinking in the current heat wave. Nevertheless, he didn't let go. All else faded away as his senses savored Amarie's scent. If happiness had a fragrance, it would be hers, warm, soft, and sweet.

A harsh scoff intruded on Eli's very pleasant daydream.

"Helluva tale." Lourdes's narrowed blue eyes flashed in warning. "But I'll be watching and waiting. Eli, my offer leaves when I do."

"Oh," Amarie reared back, "that sounds so *Gangs of New York*. Bye-bye now."

Eli couldn't help but chuckle at Amarie's bite.

"Whatever, you—you fake. I don't believe any of this, not one bit. Nobody at the Black Bear said anything about you having an investor. It doesn't matter. In fact, I'm going to make sure this bachelor auction of yours fails. You'll beg for me before this is over, Eli. Mark my words. Beg for my help to save this itty-bitty practice, Eli." Lourdes pointed a finger at his head, like a sniper rifle.

He bristled. "That sounds like a threat."

"Oh, you can bet your sweet patootie it is, Eli Calvary."

But, with Amarie's body pressed against his, Eli's outrage dimmed as he struggled to remember why he'd been hunting for her in the first place. Oh yeah, her vehicle needed servicing. The longer he held her, the more his body remembered the length of time between his last horizontal tune-up.

"That's 'honey dumpling.'" Amarie spun to face him, grinning.

Eli took her by the hand, leading her past Lourdes. "You heard my partner. Now see yourself out."

Lourdes kept spewing hate and discontent as her heels ricocheted with each strike, *crack, crack* out the door onto the front porch, going, going, gone.

"She's really angry."

"You going to offer her a biscuit?" Eli, both relieved and bereft at the distance between them, busied his hands with the coffee maker.

Amarie laughed. "Nope. I don't like her."

"Smart woman," he said, pouring two cups of joe into oversized mugs. He took a gulp, balked at the scalding heat, and then exhaled. He'd fended off the first of the pack circling the Calvary legacy.

"I'd like to believe so and," she paused, "that's why I need you to clarify what was real in that grand performance and what wasn't." She shrugged, that confident bravado she'd displayed for Lourdes wilting. "Just to be clear on what I heard. I'm now a full-time Calvary employee, with benefits to include meals. That's real." She ticked off on one finger. "And I have complete autonomy of administrative duties. Real." She raised another finger. "And," trigger finger three, "you will commit to behaving to the best of your abilities for the bachelor auction of which all photographic likenesses are up for grabs for promotional purposes. Real. But I'm a fake partner with money to invest in the clinic because the Pendletons want to buy you out, but you're not for sale?"

"You're rambling." He handed her a cup of coffee. "Drink up."

"True." She took a cautious sip. "But am I accurate?" She blew on the steamy liquid in the cup.

"Yes. They need to believe I have options other than their offer. Now let's go." He snagged the mug from her hand. "Time's a-wasting." Eli tilted both containers; chocolate adrenaline flowed down the drain with a gurgle.

"Hey, I wasn't done."

"Take quicker showers." He took her hand in his and headed back through the clinic.

"Are we off to the farm?" Amarie asked, with Hiccup on her heels. "I have my Crocs in my purse."

"First, we take care of your car."

"Seriously?" Her voice squeaked. But her wide-open expression registered shock. "But I didn't ask for your help. And what about breakfast?" she asked, gazing at the kitchen with longing.

"'Course I'm serious. Food can wait. What's in the mail?"

"Give me a sec," she said, pulling an open letter from the

sequined bag hanging at her hip. "Oh, I have an incoming text message." She held the mail and her phone in one hand, reading both.

"Put something down before you fall."

"Eli, I'm old enough to walk and chew gum. And furthermore—"

She began to stammer, then she tripped. Eli stopped, gripping her elbow to steady her.

"What's wrong?"

Amarie wouldn't meet his eyes. "I don't think you have to worry about Lourdes."

She handed the mail to him. There it was in bright red print. The ceiling fan overhead spun; childhood memories flashed in his head, faster, faster, then disappeared one after the other, being erased, resetting the Polaroid for the next family. The blades slowed, each whirl slicing the air, a propeller headed for his jugular in slow motion. Around his neck, the shirt collar shrank, abrading his skin. Even as he stood frozen, he felt the sucking pull of quicksand beneath his feet. The notice of default shook in Eli's big grip.

The biggest mountain range, daunting and intimating, suddenly surrounded him. Hiccup's bark sounded at first like a bullet train roaring between his ears, then he heard nothing, not even his own breath leaving his body. His saving grace: Amarie's hand in his, her reassuring squeeze to his trembling fingers.

"Ah...God." Eli rubbed his brow. "I-I thought I had more time."

Amarie brushed his side and Eli stitched himself to this stranger who'd entered his life, leaning on her strength to keep him on his feet. He looked at her. Her eyes dimmed in a defeat he felt on a visceral level.

"Hey, this doesn't change anything, Eli," Amarie soothed.

You'll do the auction. I'll design our social media campaign. We're partners. Sink or swim, we do this together, right?"

Eli was where he never wanted to be again: his family's future teetering on a needlepoint of uncertainty and imminent collapse, while he was at the mercy of a purple-sparkle fake business partner with secrets he hadn't begun to sniff out. Heaven help him, he was in a tail of a mess.

Chapter Nine

AMARIE HAD SEIZED an opportunity to increase her worth to her boss. Hadn't she wished for this tiny miracle? But that was before she knew the truth of Eli's instability. If not for the absolute pandemonium breaking loose in her skull and the spiraling cartoon loops blurring her vision, her knees would be knocking in celebration rather than hysteria. Thirty days to pay eighteen thousand individual dollars or default. She'd never accumulated that many zeroes separate from Russell's shared account. Everything Amarie owned didn't equate to five figures. Poor Eli. And by default, poor Amarie. Jobless. Penniless. Manless. Carless. She literally had run out of lesses. Her grandmother's proverbial "Into every life some rain must fall" came to mind, but this—this bordered on a Category 5 hurricane, the one-hundred-and-sixty-mile winds ripping the floor from beneath her feet while an F3 tornado sucked the roof and meager contents from her straw house. A band constricted her chest, like when she squeezed into a medium-sized spandex blouse in the department dressing room knowing full well her breasts screamed extra-large. She didn't have a word to describe her riotous thoughts, so she made up one. This was Spanx-ing terrible. She was being emotionally Spanx-ed for daring to believe she could succeed on her own.

Her mother's warning squeezed into her crowded thoughts like a foul, sweaty jogger forcing open the elevator doors and wedging the stench of impending doom inside her head.

Amarie, don't be foolish and stupid. Keep yourself a man.

The realization of Eli's dire financial situation had her considering, for half a nanosecond, Russell's recent text message.

If you're ready to behave like an adult, I'm ready to consider your apology. What's the password to my TikTok account?

Not happening, Dr. Feldman. Why give him the chance to offer his basement apartment so she could nanny his off-spring? It had been a part of the plan for her and Russell to have children. This way she wouldn't have to bother with morning sickness and more stretch marks on her thighs. That was one plus in the nanny column. But then she'd have to subtract for pain, suffering, and the humiliation Russell would inflict if she returned, totally at his mercy. The man had none. And knowing him, she'd have to fend off his sneak attacks to lick her chocolate cherry on the down-low. Not how she wanted to be wanted. Delete message.

Eli squeezed her hand. "You're not moving."

"Oh, sorry for the deer-in-the-headlights. I tend to slip into a catatonic state when I'm, ah, scared. You know, just...the money, car, job thing. Whew." She did a twirly maneuver with one finger pointed at her temple. "Thoughts are nightmarish in here. You?"

He said nothing. Just stood there. Big. Brooding. Staring at her. Then it occurred to her, she'd made the possible fore-closure all about her.

Amarie Walker, you are a horrible person for thinking of

yourself. Real peril could befall the Calvary family. And she, in a crisis of emotion, had painted herself as a possible savior?! Jeezuz. And why? Because Lourdes Pendleton had called her a vagrant. A woman who, like Russell, sought to exploit Eli's financial vulnerability. Amarie detested bullies. So, she'd uncorked her Black girl magic, spinning a thread into Eli's tangled web. Yes, Amarie had helped Russell grow his client roster, thereby increasing revenue, but never under the financial deadline Eli faced. Had she oversold herself?

Could Amarie's digital marketing and IT skills improve the Calvarys' predicament? How must Eli feel? She'd witnessed how he, as the eldest, pulled at his chain to guard his family from the threat Lourdes posed. Tobias and Noah, both capable and skilled in their chosen professions, would manage if they lost the property, but what would happen to Leah?

A memory surfaced of Amarie's mother, dull brown eyes milky from premature worry, flowing onyx strands with graying roots that looked misplaced on such a young woman. The mask of homeless desperation, hope depleted, clung to Bethany Walker's face, an old cheap blanket that deposited unsightly fuzz fibers that everyone noticed. An impossible-to-brush-off reminder of how dependent she and her daughter were on her husband's benevolence. Amarie couldn't bear to think of Leah suffering the humiliation her mom had endured.

Either way, she had to decide. Stick it out in Service as Eli's fake business partner and work her hot cross buns off to raise the money with Leah's bachelor auction idea. Or she could return to D.C., move in with Vali, and live with a daily reminder of how effortlessly her career-minded bestie scaled the corporate structure and loved Amarie too much to mention she had been hurled, rather unmercifully, back to square *none*. The thought of limping back to the city to sleep on Vali's kidney bean–shaped sofa had her back muscles spasming in protest.

But if she abandoned the Calvarys without trying to help, could she stomach her cowardice? Should she cut her losses, continue her current messy broke status, but away from Service? Or possibly exceed historic data where her efforts resulted in a negative correlation with success?

Run away and hide.

Stay and face possible failure . . . again.

Her choices summed up to a laxative or an enema. Either way she dosed it, things could get messy. Oh, this rapid beating of her heart felt wrong, so very wrong. Eli stepped in front of her, his excessive height looming over her. He tracked his broad fingers through the thick nestle of curls framing his forehead, making the ends a tad bit spiky. Expression lines sprouted from the corners of his alert gaze, which she thought gave him a distinguished look.

"Amarie, what are you doing?"

Tilting her head back, she looked up into vivid green eyes. *Hmm, he's handsomer, or more handsome, in multiples.* The sky began to spin off its axis. The sky didn't have an axis, but she got the image of the metaphor.

"Trying to decide if I'm hyperventilating. Do you feel Spanx-ed?"

"Spanked? How much of those polish fumes are you inhaling?"

"It's shapewear. Does wonders to smooth bulges."

"Where are you going with this? You're making me nervous."

That made two of them. If she were going to have a meltdown, it should start now. She used her free hand to blot the perspiration gathering under her chin.

"Your meltdown has to be a traveling show. The clock's ticking on the mechanic."

"You don't understand, I'm not equipped to handle red notices. I'm falling apart. Look at me."

Hiccup, his loveable dog, lifted his round face, piercing Amarie with his black eyes, and let out a hearty woof.

"Thank you, boy. Least you're concerned for my health."

"Amarie." Eli sighed. "You're not hyperventilating. You're talking. You're in shock. Scared about the future." He placed his large hands on her shoulders. Amarie jerked in response. "Relax."

"Are you sure?" she panted.

"I'm a doctor."

Inside, she cringed at the use of his title. "Ew." She shrugged his hands off, slamming her eyes shut.

The doctor she'd worked for had berated her for needing tutors when he excelled academically without assistance. Or for spending extra hours in the library rewriting her class notes. Connections between textbook and her clinical practice improved when she wrote by hand. It was the reason she loved her lists so much. She waited for the soul-crushing stones to hit their target, the invisible bruises to form. But…nothing happened. She ventured a peek, one lid open, the other bracing for impact.

"That's it?" No name-calling. No disappointed side-eye. She recalled the tension in her muscles, releasing a shaky sigh.

Eli shrugged. "I got nothing. Can we go now?"

"Oh, right. Sorry." And off they went, through the breezeway that Amarie knew connected the house and clinic, except then they exited through a small door leading to the backyard. "This house is a labyrinth."

"My dad built it. Added on as the family grew. I can't lose…" He trailed off.

"Eli," Amarie said, her tone more curious than accusational, "why didn't you tell me the clinic was in trouble?"

"Can you say you wanted to know I'm this close," he formed a tiny gap between his thumb and forefinger, raising it for her to see, "to losing the life my father left for me to safeguard?"

Amarie couldn't imagine her father entrusting her with his pulmonary practice. Her mother had been a patient instructor, teaching Amarie how to best augment her father's staff by nurturing her love of information technology. In the end, both of them had been ignored as a daily habit. After he'd hired a young brunette with tight abs and loose bra straps, both she and her mother were promptly dismissed.

"Since we're confessing, you going to explain why you didn't take care of the business with your vehicle?"

"You first. I'm still recovering from my meltdown. Self-care is an important part of the healing process."

"Fine, I'll tell all...unless you're quitting on me?"

Rather than answer, she stated the obvious. "I'm here."

Eli scoffed. "You don't have a car, Amarie."

"Wrong, my car is indisposed for the moment. Now are you going to tell me why you would tell anyone we're partners, especially a woman like Lourdes? People like her, blue-eyed with five-hundred-dollar platinum dye jobs, mean-girl women like me. Why antagonize her?" When power players noticed her, she sucked down her plate of appetizers and vacated the room.

"She's a Pendleton."

"Means nothing to me."

"They're the country Kennedys. Her father owns the bank, literally. There's history between my father and old man Pendleton."

"Lourdes doesn't seem to care about that. Maybe you can

dust off your charm. She wants you to wiggle your patootie. Might get you a big payout."

"This is me being charming," he rasped. "Besides…I meant every word of not being for sale. This notice doesn't change my stance. She's offering a meal ticket when all I need is the means to earn my way. If I wanted to be rode like a rented mule, I'd hire on with the circus."

"Call me a capitalist, but I need money just about any way I can get it. I was serious about my closing fees." She had dropped enough hints for him to know her cooperation came with dollars and cents, so she didn't consider her directness crass. Because, unlike his high moral standards, she could be bought, rather, purchased, for a contractually limited amount of time. "I understand why you spun a preposterous story. Why did Lourdes believe you?"

"Now, wait a minute. Is it unbelievable that you and I could be partners?"

"That's unlikely because—"

"So, you're saying a decent, hardworking vet committed to taking care of his mother isn't worth the investment. Too risky for you?" Eli muttered under his breath, holding the door open for her.

"I would never say that about anyone, certainly not my boss. Really, you jump to the oddest conclusions. You did the same thing the morning when I arrived. Do you do that with everyone or just me?"

"Everyone. Now come on, business partner."

"More like a busy partner these last couple of days."

"What's that supposed to mean?"

"Well, you've been difficult since I arrived. I've done my best to be a support, yet you haven't been the most trusting of bosses. And now you want me to pretend we're equal partners to save face with the cute girl."

"Not a cute girl. A Pendleton. And you're right. Before you start rambling, I apologize."

"I'm allowed. Stop policing me. This is your first and last warning if we are to be partners. If I have to tell you again, your pretty boy chin catches these hands," she teased, doing a classic Muhammad Ali rope-a-dope two-step.

Eli chuckled. "Don't hurt yourself. This handsome devil is tougher than he looks."

Amarie believed him. Even now, she could see those sun lines at the corners of his eyes were more pronounced. He didn't want her to worry. She was a stranger he'd just met, but as his employee, she, well, her livelihood depended on Calvary Vet increasing its value proposition and its revenue. His sense of duty and responsibility included her now.

"Why aren't you panicking about the notice?"

"Because I don't have the luxury of falling apart. My father believed I could care for our family. He had faith in me."

"Must be nice." She wished her parents could trust her to make the best choices for her life and career.

"It's no walk in the meadow, Amarie. Some days I want someone else to make the decisions. Trust me, if I had any other way to come up with the money besides the auction, I would take it."

Amarie wiggled her brows. "Think of it as an ego booster. Lourdes did come with her checkbook."

"No amount of money is worth that woman sinking her fangs into this family. I can smell her kind from miles away."

"Well, at least you know there's a market for grumpy men?" Too late to snatch back the insult. Amarie winced. "Sorry, I shouldn't have said that aloud."

"Sure you are."

The apology was genuine, everyone deserved to be somebody's "one."

"I am," she pleaded. "It's just, you make women out to be apex predators lying in wait to pounce on defenseless men while they graze on the open plains. Save the dude-in-distress performance. I wouldn't need this job or any money from the auction if my fiancé had paid me for all the work I did to grow his medical practice. Don't get me started on how he left me high and dry—"

Well that wasn't exactly how she'd ended up in Service. She'd been the one to punch the gas, but Russell had ensured she had little-to-no resources to rebuild a life without his wallet.

"Okay, that explains a lot. Look, I'm a man of my word. You mentioned closing costs. How about in exchange for your partner—"

"Fake partnership," she interrupted. "I will not be held liable for grumpy pants dustups."

"Noted, sunshine. As I was saying, for your social media magic, you get a percentage of the auction's net proceeds?"

"Make that gross revenue." She winked. "And in writing."

Eli shook his head. "I'll honor our agreement with or without a written contract. Now, can we get going if you want your car looked at this week?"

"As in seven days?" She balked.

"Town's got one certified mechanic who also happens to be the sheriff. Trust me, you don't want these shade tree tinkerers underneath your hood if he's busy on the job. Been there. Regret that."

Amarie walked ahead of him in the parking lot where a rather beastly hunter-green GMC Sierra with massive tires and running boards awaited them. Two quick chirps sounded before the locks disengaged with an airy *thunk* sound. How out of character for this beast of an automobile.

An elephant's trumpeting seemed more appropriate. "Wh-what is this?

"Your steel chariot." Eli held the door open, stepping back for her to climb aboard. "Now light a fire, and let's git." Eli beamed, his face alight with schoolboy glee. It might as well have been the Empire State Building on wheels. Forget a step stool, she needed a ladder.

"What are you waiting on?"

As if she required a demonstration, Hiccup bounded off the chrome-polished running board, landing on the passenger seat.

"Next time pay for an elevator install," she said, reaching for the doorframe to hoist herself up.

"Ah, I'll help."

"Uh, okay. Yes." Amarie offered her hand. "Yes, thank you."

Instead, Eli planted one hand on each side of her waist and lifted her off her lavender NOBULL adjustable slides with rose-gold buckles.

"Uh, oh, okay, a nice display of upper body strength and er, ah, raw masculine power. Didn't see that coming. It's impressive—"

Too much. Too soon, Amarie. Her father called her a handful. Which Eli seemed to lift without a single sign of overexertion. Maybe he enjoyed handling curvy packages? Hmm, handfuls, mouthfuls. Briefly, her gaze dropped to his mouth. Mistake. Quickly she directed her attention up. He was watching her.

Eli met her eyes. "You're being weird again."

"I just remembered something," Amarie said.

"What's that?"

"I don't like you."

"But you'll take my money?" His lips lifted into a lop-sided grin which looked more attractive up close. In fact, she inhaled. He smelled…nice. Mountain air and fresh pine. "That makes us partners."

"Not really. Only that I'll act as yours. And you should've asked me first. I don't like men assuming they know what's best for me. I make my own decisions."

He frowned, those thick, dark brows drawing together like a little caterpillar. No, that wasn't right. Eli was too big for insect metaphors. His brows, rich in color above long dark lashes, looked mink-y. Yeah, that description rang with more accuracy. She noticed other things—like his strong nose, and full mouth. Amarie angled her head and her gaze fixed on his corded forearms and broad fingers with short-trimmed nails. Totally uncomfortable with her teenage girl ogling, she cleared her throat, swallowing her jitters.

"You were wrong to take my choice away." There was a little breath-holding on her part. Ideally, he'd spit out whatever was on his mind before her oxygen-deprived brain rendered her unconscious. Would he fire her if she refused?

He nodded, took the seat belt, and buckled her in. "Fair enough, but I got nothing left to offer you, Amarie. The job, it's yours. The money, it's yours. Noticed you haven't left Calvary land since you arrived. You've been living with us."

"Leah invited—"

He held up a hand and pressed a finger to his lips. "No explanation needed. Momma's happy. That's what matters most to me. Now as partners, there should be shared risks and benefits. So, I'm willing to guarantee that if you help with the bachelor auction regardless of the final outcome, I'll cover the deposit on a place of your own, the cost to fix the car, and pay you a bonus."

"Eli, what if the auction falls short? You could lose the everything!"

"The way I see it, we both have something to win. Right, partner?"

Amarie had walked into her relationship with Russell with no guarantees. Quickly, she had learned he preferred the customer service version of Amarie, where his needs took priority over hers, her role centered on making his life better.

"Yes, we do." Could she fake being Eli's partner and build a foundation for the authentic woman she needed to be for herself? Heavens, she hoped so.

Chapter Ten

THEY EXITED THE Calvary property and turned left. Quiet
and efficient, Eli's monster vehicle climbed the hill. An oval
lake came into view, a picturesque steeple on the far bank
with a four-post open gazebo. Amarie gasped at the serene
beauty, her heart cresting and falling as they drove by.

"It's even prettier in the fall when it's wrapped in lights,"
Eli whispered.

"I can imagine." Amarie let her mind drift to a future
where she surrounded herself with beauty, family...com-
munity. If—no, when—they earned the money from the
auction, she would rent an apartment, or one of the single-
story ranch houses she'd viewed from Main Street. Amarie Walker, resident of Service, West Virginia. *Yeah*, she
thought. Sounded perfect for her new beginning.

They turned right at a bend in the road. Amarie felt an
audible pop in her ears from the change in altitude. Down
the mountain they went, the drive much longer than she'd
appreciated when she'd walked across one of the shorter
Cattail Creek bridges with Leah. Roads widened in this
area, and she'd spotted replica gas-lamp posts that would

light the way in the darkness. Service had a shabby-chic elegance she liked.

"I answered your question about the clinic's finances. It's your turn to tell why you neglected to mention you lack transportation."

"Honestly, you can't help yourself," she said, exasperated. "Do you see what you did? We were having a moment until you put a spoon in the peanut butter jar."

Eli raised a brow, his forehead furrowed in confusion. "What?"

"You're stuck. Get it... spoon in chunky butter. Let it go, Eli."

"Not happening. So spill."

"Ugh, why do you care?" She exhaled. "Fine. The job... your job was the only one listed in the bulletin. At first, I thought for sure I had it, then our masculine energies collided."

"Say what kind of energy? How is this remotely related to your car?"

"Masculine. You know," she explained, quite animated with her hands, "your grinch. My gremlin. I was nervous, and hungry. I just didn't want to upset the power balance."

"Energies and power shifts, you speak like a business executive."

"Haha," she scoffed. "You made a joke. Nothing executive about me. I'm just a graduate nurse with an exam to pass. I submitted a dozen job applications for entry-level nursing positions."

He frowned at her. "I wasn't joking, but... why not come clean at the end of the first day? And, this time, leave out the grinch and gremlin. What really stopped you from asking for help?"

"Embarrassment. Failure fatigue. I'm two years shy of

thirty and my eighteen-year-old car died four hours into my fresh start. Everything I try fails. Is that what you wanted me to tell you? Is that what you needed to hear when I walked through your door at seven o'clock in the morning?"

"Cars break down, Amarie."

She hung her head. "You don't get it. I know that cars break down, but...timing matters. I needed to win on Monday. And meeting you, Leah, your brothers; corralling Adele; using my nursing skills in the clinic. It felt like I did something right, you know?" Amarie gave a humorless laugh. "It's probably hard to comprehend, but getting hired, it felt monumental."

"Not one bit."

She'd been so proud to get a job without her parents vouching for her or her boyfriend bringing her on staff. Still, she felt the surge of dopamine at the operational improvements she'd introduced in the office. Personal accomplishment. How could she lose it after one taste? She hadn't felt good about herself in years. Fighting to hold onto it came naturally. Admitting her desperate state would've crushed her.

"I'm in an on-again, off-again dance with heartache of my own making. Monday couldn't be one of those days." She didn't want to be plagued by ANTS—automatic negative thoughts—every time she tried something new, but that was the pattern she'd devolved into. "I'm tired of losing."

"Tell me about it, partner."

"I just did. Are you listening?" Amarie sobered, not wanting to release the emotion she'd packaged away for years on Eli.

"Do you ever run out of one-liners?" He chuckled.

"No. Never. Suppose that's something we have in common, boss."

"Oh, that must be painful for—what did Mrs. Kline call you?—Saint Amarie." His chest actually shook with laughter.

"Picking on your employees now?"

"Nope," he said, rubbing at his eyes. "Commiserating with someone who understands. Your car going kaput sounds much worse than my default notice."

"It is for me. I don't have your responsibilities, but I don't have your support system either. It's just me."

The muscles in his face slackened. "You're serious?"

"As a paycheck." She nodded. Without a family to rely on, she only had herself. Actually, she may be in worse shape than the Calvarys. While they had a countdown, she'd run out of time. "My parents, especially my father, would never approve."

"That's…it's…I don't have any experience with my family not being on my side."

"I know. You're lucky."

"I suppose I am."

"Happy now? I'm carless, penniless, and manless." She stopped short of blurting out *homeless*. "I spilled the tea. My pitiful story of how I ended up on your step."

"To answer the one question jumbled up in all those words: yes, I'm happy you told me. I'll take truth over peace, every day of the year."

"I'm not used to people reacting with kindness when I've needed assistance in the past. I expect less. Not more."

"Don't lump me in." He chuckled at her growl. "I'll be here if you need me. It's gonna take some convincing for folks around here to believe we're partners. You didn't speak or look my way at the Black Bear the other night."

So, he'd noticed. And why did that revelation cause a twinkle in her toes?

"News flash. You're a little prickly for after-hours pleas-antries, but I'm open to negotiation." She paused. "With a caveat. Nothing can interfere with my evening study time. Passing my licensure exam is priority. Oh," she pointed, "that's my car over there."

"Woman, I can see."

"Rule number one, use your partner voice. And here's a hint, that was not it."

They parked on the rocky shoulder.

"Hiccup, stay put. Amarie, let's go."

"So bossy," she muttered.

Amarie walked over to Prince. As if he was still in need of rest, pollen had settled on the hood, a soft blanket thick enough for her to write her name in it. And of course every-thing was as she left it; even the three goats were still there.

"Oh my gosh. Billie, Jean, and Diana. Good morning." Her old friends bleated in greeting. Playful, they romped closer, the white frosting on their short-haired black coats gleaming against the backdrop of a green meadow.

"They don't have names, Amarie."

"Well, they do now."

"You're actually talking to the goats."

"Look, it was two o'clock in the morning. It was either talk to them or Blair-Witch cry."

Because for years, guilt had eaten away at her confidence, and it had become easier not to share her hopes and dreams with other humans.

Eli lowered his head before releasing a long sigh. "Don't spring a leak. If folks see you crying, they're going to lash out at me for hurting your feelings."

"I'm not that sensitive."

"Sure you aren't," he drawled.

"Stop being ornery. I'm going to say good morning to the

goats as they caused me no trouble during my night vigil. Then, as your partner, I will stand back and observe your interaction. Always willing to learn from an expert in animal psychology."

Eli said nothing.

"Hello? Partner? Communicating is fundamental to establishing healthy relationships."

"So I've been told. Get on with it," he rasped.

To the trio she squatted low and whispered, "I know it's been days since our last chat, but I've been busy crossing items off my to-do list. I was a little nervous about how I was gonna make it in this town. But guess what, I got a job and a partner, of sorts. Eli," she called, "come on over here and meet the ladies."

"I see a pair of door knockers. Pretty sure one of the kids is male."

"The devil is a liar" came her immediate retort. "They are entirely too level-headed with superb listening skills to possess Y chromosomes. And don't call them children."

Eli pinched the bridge of his nose. "Okay, city girl. Here's a quick lesson. Young goats are called kids, both male and female. These are Nigerian Dwarf goats, a companionable, milk-producing breed. A group of kids is a tribe."

"Thanks for that. Now go ahead," she prompted. "Introduce yourself to the *kids*. And don't be mean. They know my history with the opposite sex, and frankly, they were pretty judgy of my recent choices. And remember, partner voice. Not that barky thing you usually do."

Talking with animals had always been easier than the complex psychology of human behavior. Telling Billie, Jean, and Diana her fears and dreams avoided all the side-eye glances and eyerolls from her family and friends (not Vali of course) counting her failures as justification for her to remain in a loveless arrangement. What she had with Russell never reached the "loving relationship" ideal. Six years saddled, yet single.

Eli raised one booted foot, propping it on the wooden fence separating the field from the shoulder of the road "What's up, goats?"

"OMG, stop it. Just act normal."

"You're the one under the influence of farm animals, and I'm abnormal?"

The sound of someone clearing their voice had them both turning. "Morning, Eli."

"Kanaan." Eli dipped his head in greeting to the clean-shaven giant sporting a lush raven man bun, a khaki-colored T-shirt with the word *Sheriff* embroidered on the right breast pocket, and oil-stained denim. She had to applaud the uniform. The look worked for both roles. Next to Kanaan, trotting on short legs, was a sleek black-coat dachshund mix with floppy ears wearing what appeared to be a zippered vest filled with socket wrenches. Amarie had seen plenty of domesticated dogs with smart bow ties and frilly tutus, but never had she ever spotted a pooch that looked as if he had full-time benefits.

"And you must be—"

"Amarie," she interjected, extending her hand in greeting while staring at Kanaan's working canine, "the business partner to this beastly vet." She hooked a thumb in Eli's direction. "He tells me you're also the sheriff here in Service, so why is your dog dressed like a roadside construction worker?"

Kanaan threw back his head and laughed, the sound hearty and filled with vitality.

"It's true I'm the local sheriff. But seeing as I'm here in my capacity as a mechanic and this guy's first cousin, Cocktail here," he pointed to the pooch who'd wandered over to Eli's truck and was now engaged in a barking conversation with Hiccup, "is my experienced assistant."

"Cousins?" Amarie gave Eli a quizzical look. "My partner forgot to mention that detail, and Cocktail." He'd recruited more of his family to help her. What a nice Mr. Grumpy Pants. Not that she planned to tell him.

"He forgot more than that." Kanaan shook his head. "Eli never partnered with anybody growing up."

"Dang it, Kanaan. You're supposed to be on my side."

The dog's name piqued her interest. "Why did you name him Cocktail?"

He smiled, showing off a perfect set of white teeth. "He is a she." He angled his chin in Eli's vicinity. "A, ah, mix of different breeds. 'Cocktail' seemed fitting when Eli gave her to me. It was after I returned from serving in Afghanistan." He shrugged. "My head was pretty messed up back then."

Wow, Kanaan was a war hero. Before Amarie could thank him for his service, Eli cut in.

"Quit milking her for sympathy, K."

"Oh, I see what's happening. You want all her attention for yourself," Kanaan teased. "Piano. Shot-putter. Javelineer. He did everything solo, Amarie. I'm only telling ya this because a nice lady like yourself should know what she's getting into with Eli Calvary. But I swear I learn something undiscovered every time we get together, Eli."

Kanaan still held her hand. And Eli, well, he looked… unwell.

"You do attract the prettiest ladies in town," he said, proffering his corded forearm. "Hold on to that, pretty lady. Wouldn't want to tumble." He grinned. To Eli he said, "If you're finished messing with the goats, I'll hitch up Amarie's beamer."

"Oh, the perfect gentleman in denim." Amarie smiled. No suits. Normally, she liked a man in a well-tailored suit, but she rather enjoyed the rugged masculine display of clingy cotton T-shirts and snug jeans on the men of Service.

Behind her Eli grunted, but she paid him no mind. Starting this evening, she would launch everything in her arsenal to make their bachelor auction a success. For now, she basked in the male attention. "Thank you for the warning on my partner, Sheriff."

"Kanaan. The car. And Amarie, get over here. Stand by your partner," Eli grumbled.

"Don't worry. I'm not easily deterred."

"Right."

At the doubt echoing in his words, she turned, angling her head over her shoulder and up. Eli gave her a look that said he really did have some worry that Kanaan's opinion would change her mind. Whereas in the loyalty department, Amarie did not. The Russells and Lourdeses of the world couldn't win every battle. Not to toot her own tatas, but Amarie had six of years practice in loyalty. He could trust her, but could she trust herself not to mess things up?

Chapter Eleven

THEY'D ARRIVED AT Matt Johnson's place, a two-story A-frame house with a red metal roof, thirty minutes late. Military men arrived early and stayed past quitting time. Never in reverse. Eli parked in front of the free-standing two-car canopy beside a faded blue Corolla, Ruth Buchannan's beater.

Now that Eli had resigned himself to participating in the bachelor auction, he put it out of his mind, ready to focus on his job. That's what paid the bills. At least for the next thirty days. Once again, Amarie had surprised him with the circumstances of her arrival in Service. Assuming she would fast-feet back to civilization at the first sign of real trouble was an unfair assessment of his new partner's fortitude. When she'd learned of the possible foreclosure, her fear had erupted, raw and brutal, and not just on her face. Eli could feel the tangible ropes burning through Amarie's constructed persona, strangling the light that shone from every fiber of her being. How could he ignore the darkness clouding her expressive eyes? Yes, she was intrusive in his business practices, borderline insubordinate, and incredibly flashy, but she was also brave. Which is why he peered through the open passenger window, imploring his fake partner to keep her curious, city-girl eagerness confined to his truck.

"This is a working farm. Not a petting zoo, Amarie."

"And I want to see it, you big bully. Move," Amarie glowered. "You can't keep me locked in here."

She planted her right shoulder against the door, pushing. Eli leaned more of his weight into the frame.

"Not until you agree to abide by the safety rules."

"I lived in D.C., Eli. I know when to run away." She tossed the words as if she'd had a lot of practice at retreating. Eli knew how hard toughing it out could be on the psyche.

Hiccup, an old pro on the farm, leaped through the open window and headed for the waterfall that bordered the Calvary and Johnson properties.

"Where's he off to?" Amarie protested.

"To play. You're on the payroll. He's not."

"You're either bossing me around or being a pit bull."

"Either listen up or no OJT vet assisting for you, young lady." Eli knew the threat of suspending her on-the-job training would work. Amarie Walker craved knowledge.

"Fine. What are they, spoilsport?" she huffed, rolling her eyes.

"First, keep your hands to yourself. Second, stay out of my way. Third, the manure is plentiful, the smell is powerful. If you get sick, take it behind the barn."

"You don't have to worry about me upchucking. I told you I'm a graduate nurse. I've seen all types of blood and gore, the human kind."

"You say that. The stench of farm animals is hot asphalt thick. Singes the nose hairs."

"Oh, that's actually funny. And thanks to you, I'm looking forward to the burn." She crinkled her nose in jest. Cute.

"I've never had the opportunity to visit a 'working farm,'" she said, making air quotes. "I enjoy adventure."

"You would, wouldn't you?"

"As long as there's a return trip home?"

"Why wouldn't there be?" Odd comment. Did she think he'd abandon her? Eli reminded himself what she'd said about her fiancé. Darn shame for a man to treat woman he professed to love with such malice. His father would've taken him and his brothers to the mat if he had ever caught wind of them mistreating a woman. Eli still recalled the ear blistering his dad had laid on an eighteen-year-old Noah.

"I-I...of course there would be. Sorry, that was stupid. I should've kept my mouth shut. Sometimes, I say too much when I'm hungry—"

"Amarie," he interrupted before a diarrheal monologue began. "Talk all you want. Just do it while working."

She breathed in, then exhaled. "Let's start again. Here's what I wanted to say. I like learning and seeing new things. Routine is good, but once I discover something, I get excited. That's how I got sucked into search engines. Thirsting for more in-depth knowledge. Last night, I studied for my exam, then I read more about veterinary medicine and...online auctions."

Eli groaned at that last part.

"I read about the difference between a companion-animal veterinarian who cares for domesticated small animals like cats and dogs, and what you do as a mixed-animal vet trained in livestock and large animals. But I want to see you in action. Touch what you touch."

"See, I knew it. That gleam in your eye. You're planning to be a nuisance."

"I'm not. Promise," she grumbled. "I won't be any trouble."

"I'ma hold you to it."

She gave him a two-finger salute. "Where do we start, captain?"

"The first thing you need to do is take off your shoes."

"Oh, we get to frolic in the woods?"

He pointed to the green field behind the house. "Do not enter. That's corn. And no frolicking in the fields in bare feet. There's corn fleas, beetles, rootworms, and rodents among the stalks. I'm pretty sure you don't want the bugs trampolining on your sparkle toes."

"Urgh." She shivered, face contorted in horror. "Point made. I'm ready."

"Not yet. I have a second pair of work boots in the back of the truck."

Amarie glared up at him, searching. "You want me to wear your shoes?"

"It's either that or you stay in the truck."

"Not going to happen."

"Don't say I didn't warn you," Eli huffed, opening her door.

Amarie followed him around the back of the truck, where he pulled out a pair of steel-toed leathers and a pair of clean socks. He kept spare everything in the flatbed.

He took the shoes and crammed a roll of black athletic socks with the UA logo into the toe. "They're a little too big."

"Try four inches. With your size thirteen foot, right? They'll look like clown shoes on me."

"How do you know my shoe size?"

"Your mother." She shrugged.

"What has that woman not told you?"

"Hmm, not sure yet," Amarie answered. "I'll let you know."

"Not funny. Here," he said, lowering the truck's tailgate. "Take a seat."

Amarie tried an awkward hop-jump thing that made all her lady curves jiggle. A satisfying sight Eli tried to ignore and failed. Did she realize how her curves stretched those hip seams? Deciding it best to stop his agony, Eli grabbed her around the waist, plopping her onto the warm metal. The humidity had climbed with the temperature. And on cue, he glanced up and saw her shirt clinging to her full rack, a generous helping of feminine bounty even for Eli's massive paws. This was torture. He dropped to one knee before her.

"Oh, how chivalrous," she teased.

"Give me your foot." He gripped her delicate arch, easing her toes into the shoe, wiggling the boot into place. "Is that okay?"

"Yes." She angled her one foot, presumably for aesthetic evaluation. "Cute. Got any food to go with this footwear?"

He wouldn't mind a taste of something sweet. A wildly inappropriate image, sexual in nature, flashed in his dirty mind. Annoyed by his reaction, Eli bristled, an exaggerated response for a physical awareness he didn't want to feel.

He didn't get to answer because Matt Johnson picked that moment to round the corner, holding the reins on a reddish-brown gelding with a longish black forelock shielding his eyes. Eli still had his hand wrapped around Amarie's shapely calf, her foot supported on his thigh.

"Morning, Eli." A straw stalk hung limp at the corner of the farmer's mouth. Eli had never acquired the taste of farmer's gum. He'd take his gluten in a cereal bowl with milk. Matt ran his fingers through his loose, mixed-gray waves, pushing the shoulder-length strands back to reveal dark-amber, intelligent eyes. "This why you late—playing footsie with your lady?"

He wore a clean white T-shirt, denim jeans, and cowboy

boots older than Eli. Tanned skin, the color smooth as calf leather, peeked out from the neckline and sleeves of his shirt.

"Nope. Had to get her car taken care of."

"Yep, I heard a little something about that."

"Hi, I'm Amarie." Matt accepted the hand she offered.

"The cat whisperer I heard so much about." He gave a lopsided grin, engulfing her hand in his weathered mitt. "Matthew Johnson, ma'am. Call me Matt. And this here is Harry."

Eli kept his eyes trained on the animal. Harry's head bobbed in greeting, but then his nostrils widened. Apparently, another male had caught Amarie's scent. Didn't she know she couldn't come around animals smelling like a treat? The horse danced in place, but Eli noticed Matt tighten his hold on the reins. And his curious busy bee of a partner had hopped down, and with her hand raised, was reaching for Harry the hair-grabbing horse.

Eli snagged Amarie around the waist, his heart rate jumping the second her body collided with his. "Already forgot our conversation?"

A string of indistinguishable objections fell from her lips, cursing his name. "You're asking for trouble you don't want from me, Eli Calvary," she huffed, trying to stomp her foot, but his big boots flopped around her slender ankle.

Matt stood there chuckling at the both of them. "He's right, ma'am. You smell sweeter than fresh-picked apples. I'm afraid El's valid in saving you from an entanglement with this fella."

"Oh," she said, looking up at him. "You could've just said that."

"I did." Eli smirked, releasing her. "Remember the 'don't be a nuisance' comment? Harry's a therapy horse like the goats you're so fond of," Eli added. "The women and children that sometimes reside on the property like his company more than people. He's frisky when it comes to ladies who smell like you do."

Like Harry, Eli found himself needing to add a foot of space between Amarie's lush curves before he started chomping at the bit for a taste of her, too.

"Equine-facilitated therapy," Amarie echoed. "I've read about it being used for those experiencing significant traumatic change."

Impressed, Matt beamed. Eli could have smiled, but he didn't want to.

"My late wife, God rest her soul, had a soft spot for women and children fallen on hard times. When she died, I couldn't bring myself to stop her good work."

Eli shook his head. "Noticed Ruth is here again."

"Oh, Ruth. Is that your daughter?"

"No ma'am. Ruth is Bucky Buchannan's wife. I keep the cabin at the back of the property as a women's shelter. We," he rubbed Harry's back, "offer chaperoned horse rides to those in residence."

No need to say more. The town knew Bucky and Ruth had a troubled marriage. Hard drinking and a soft ego made a man difficult to befriend. As for Ruth, well, she loved the boy she'd fallen hard for after high school.

"Aw, wow, you're my hero, Mr. Johnson," Amarie whispered, and walking over, she threw her arms wide, embracing Matt in a bear hug. She might have even hummed. What was with this woman hugging strangers? "Anybody tell you, with that thick mane and silver mustache you look like Sam Elliott in *Roadhouse* circa 1989?"

Red burned across the widower's cheeks. Eli, well, he rolled his eyes at the lie. If old Matt was a hot bouncer in a roadside bar by Amarie's calculations, he had to be Tony Bellew.

"Did I mention I took early social security? Ask anybody, I'm the best country line dancer in town, and I got a prescription for the little blue pill."

"Hey. Hey," Eli bellowed. "TMI. Too much information."

"Well now hold on, Eli. You ain't interested in having a beautiful lady on your arm on Friday night, but I am. With my movie-star looks."

"Good heavens, Matt. Knock it off before I have to Brillo-pad my eyeballs to erase things, I'm too young to think about needing blue pills and such."

"Matthew Johnson, you've already been in traction once this decade," Eli's mother called, her sneakers making a crunching sound on the loose gravel driveway.

"That's 'cause a fool stallion threw me. This time," he winked at Amarie, "I'm trusting I'll be in good hands."

"Momma, what are you doing here?"

"Just resting a spell before I finish my morning walk back down the hill."

Matt frowned then, studying his mom. "Doing that a lot lately, Leah? You feelin' okay?"

"Fine. Nothing a hearty breakfast and more water can't cure." Leah laughed it off. "These fifty-four-year-old knees hurt more than they used to on these uphill climbs."

Back in the day, his momma could outrace him up the mountain. Tobias had mentioned a medical follow up more than once. Maybe his brother had a point about making the twenty-mile drive to the general practice doctor in Whynot. Eli had trouble recalling the last time his mom had completed an annual exam. His father's health had deteriorated within a two-year span. Knowing his momma like he did, she would've focused on meeting his dad's needs over her own.

"I can drive you back home, Momma."

She shook her head in protest. "Nope. Do your work."

"Ah, Leah, I have a favor to ask," Matt said, pulling a red bandanna from his back pocket to wipe the sweat from his forehead. Today would be a scorcher.

Eli stiffened. Was Matt sniffing around his momma? He hoped Matt didn't think to mark territory now that his father had passed. The men had been the best of friends. Eli hadn't wrapped his head around his mom taking a fancy to other men.

"RJ's promised to come home soon." A proud papa grin split Matt's lips in a genuine smile. "When she does, you tell Noah I said he'd best be ready to apologize for how he mishandled the situation."

Eli gave his mother a glance. An equally concerned gaze met his. Noah had been his usual cavalier self with Rachel Johnson's feelings ever since their senior year of high school. She'd driven out of Service the day after the graduation celebration in the town's pavilion, returning home only once for her mom's memorial. The farmer's daughter hadn't spoken one word to his brother in more than a decade.

"Sure thing," Leah whispered.

A surefire way to get Noah fighting mad, mentioning RJ Johnson's name. Eli was fairly confident his brother's anger was directed inward. They'd been best friends, but she'd left Service. Most folks steered clear of how things had gone bad between them.

"Well, ah," Eli said, rubbing his beard, "I better check on Belle, that foal's due any day now."

"She's my favorite mare. I'm glad she'll have a young one to care for," Matt said, ambling toward the barn at the rear of the property with Harry.

"That's my cue to vacate the premises. Traded birthing

babes for shampoo sinks and blow-drying stalls. You never realize how beautiful pets are till they get a good grooming." His momma pivoted on her Skechers to leave. Eli thought the same applied to people. A snip here, a tuck there. He applied that to attitude and perspective, not outer attributes. "Oh Eli, Lois Kline is out for blood. Peter Pendleton accused her of spreading bad gossip after Lourdes told him that Amarie is your new business partner."

Eli stomped his boot against the sparse grass in frustration. "How is it possible news spreads faster than poop through a goose around here?"

"This is Service." His mom laughed. "Apparently Lois Kline's neighbor phoned Kanaan with a complaint about Adele tracking paw prints on his car roof. Showed up with Amarie's BMW in tow. Well, that got Lois talking about Amarie working the front desk at the clinic. But then Kanaan informed Lois that Amarie was just learning the clinic routine on her first day. She's really a wealthy investor from the nation's capital. Lois is mad at herself for believing your misinformation, even after she spotted the fancy car and the designer luggage."

"Wow." Amarie laughed. "Mind blown. No one has ever been this interested in the details of my life."

"And how do you know all this?" Eli demanded.

His mom pulled her cell phone from the front pocket of her joggers. "Delores called me from the Black Bear to corroborate the story. You know she values her reputation as the best of the town gossips, too."

"Ugh, sometimes this town is too small for its own good."

"Technically, it's not gossip if it's true," Matt added.

"Exactly." Leah winked and started down the hill. "Have fun, you two. I expect details about your overnight partnership during dinner."

"Have a good grooming day at the clinic, Leah." Amarie waved.

"Wait up, Matt. We'll walk with you," but, the farmer and his hoofed friend had vanished. Eli followed his nose into the barn, the scent of freshly laid straw greeting him.

"This place is huge," Amarie said beside him, with her smartphone camera at arm's length, recording absolutely nothing.

"One of the largest in the county." Two rows of stalls with slide doors hugged the walls. Harry hung his head through the open stall window in greeting.

"Hey boy." Amarie hummed behind him. He wasn't sure why, but he liked the sound of her voice. Excitement coursed through him at having a woman actually interested in what he did every day. She angled her phone, snapped a few pictures, including him in the shot.

Caring for animals was in his blood and he enjoyed sharing his passion with others. Some said he had an addiction when it came to promoting animal health and wellness.

They reached a rear stall on the right, the width and depth larger than the others, maybe sixteen by sixteen feet. Inside was the beautiful chestnut Halflinger, her flaxen mane shiny and full. But she was panting, her nostrils wide with distress. Eli's expression sobered.

"She been kicking at her belly this morning." That came from Ruth. Her daughter, Phoebe, clung to her leg, peeking up at Eli with wide eyes, a face too jaded to be that of an innocent.

"Howdy, Ruth. Hey there, smart girl," he said to the five-year-old, careful not to crowd them. He'd made that error the first time he'd run across them on Matt's farm.

"Say hello to Doc Calvary and his friend," Ruth prompted her daughter. Like her mom, Phoebe had long brown hair and soft brown eyes filled with cautious optimism. The world and a few folks had been less than supportive of Ruth's choice to honor her marriage vows. Heaven knew, these two had spent a fair amount of time on the worse side of until death do us part. A lot of the local women stayed clear of Ruth on account of her last name, Buchanan, and her troublemaking husband.

"Hi," Phoebe whispered. "I like your purse."

"Thank you," Amarie gushed, bending low to meet the little girl's eyes. "It's nice to meet you, Ruth." Hesitant at first, Ruth extended her dirty hand. Amarie, in what he quickly was discovering was classic Amarie fashion, grabbed the offering with gusto. "Nice to meet you. What a cool job you have. This place is awesome."

"Yeah." Ruth gave a soft smile. "I think so, too. We love it here."

"I want to stay here forever, b-but my kitty has babies in her belly and Daddy said I can't see them if we don't come back home."

Amarie's breath hitched. Ruth stilled, face glowing with a blotchy redness. The way Ruth seemed to shrink in front of them, her heart had to be broken to hear the pain in her daughter's voice. Bucky needed his hind parts kicked for manipulating his daughter against Ruth's responsibility as a protective parent. Eli didn't fault mothers who stuck it out in an awful marriage until their children were old enough to leave the house. Men like Bucky stunk worse than manure on a hot day.

"Kids," she said, as her fingers twisted her shirttail in a knot. Tears swelled in her eyes. "Say the darndest things."

"Well, Phoebe, if I run across any kittens, you can play with them as much as you want right here on the farm," Eli said.

Phoebe took one step away from the protection of her mother's leg for the first time. "For reals, Doc?"

He nodded. "Yep. As long as it's okay with your mom."

Amarie stayed quiet at his side, visibly upset with the subject matter. No one on the outside looking in could speak with authority about what happened between a husband and wife, but in a situation where Ruth and Phoebe stayed at Matt's more than their own home, the problems in the marriage were broadcast loud and clear. Bucky did a piss-poor job of caring for a wife who loved him.

"Thanks, Doc. We'd love that."

Behind them, a thunderous boom echoed. Inside Belle's stall the sidewall vibrated. Belle had delivered a powerful hoof kick, obviously anxious at her physical status. Both Ruth and Phoebe startled. Eli hated to disrupt the moment, but an anxious mare could hurt herself or others.

"How long has Belle been like this, Ruth?"

"I came in to muck her stall about thirty minutes ago."

Eli nodded, glad he'd arrived to assist Belle with her first. A mare with experience in foaling would have delivered in that time. "The foal may be breach. If so, I have to rotate it to ease the birthing."

"Huh, she seemed okay before now." Matt leaned on the stall door. "Do you think she's gonna lose it?"

"It's her maiden foal. Hopefully, with help, they both will be fine. Let me get my jumper on." Eli turned, looking at Amarie's grim expression. "This may take a while. The first foaling can be unpredictable. If you want to leave, I can walk back down the mountain so that you can take the truck back to the clinic. Grab the keys from the overhead visor. Then take my truck and head into the office."

"I wouldn't miss a baby being born for anything."

"I'm telling you, Amarie, it can get messy and smelly."

"And I'm telling you not to worry about me."

Ruth became visibly uneasy, and Eli immediately regretted his tone. The woman had to live on the edge with who she was married to. "Well, Phoebe and I have work to do in the house. See y'all at the wedding. Nice meeting you, Amarie."

"You too," Amarie called to Ruth's retreating back. "What wedding?"

Eli chose to ignore the question, instead focusing on the job in front of him. He hadn't decided if he wanted to parade his new fake partner around at Caleb and Gracie Lou's wedding. Marriage should be sacred, no place for pretending, even if he wasn't the groom at the altar.

"I'll check her canal. Make sure the foal is turned in the right direction. Then Mom can do the rest. Amarie, you and your camera stay back."

Eli slipped on a pair of gloves that went up above his elbows. When Matt helped to ease Belle down onto her side, the horse tried to protest, lifting up a little bit, but Matt dropped his weight onto her, talking in a low voice and soothing her.

*   *   *

Two hours slipped by after the repositioning. Amarie never complained about the unique scent of birthing foals or the dirt floor. But Eli noticed she'd fallen quiet. Her shoulders rounded as if a growing mass curled her spine.

"Need anything?"

"I'm hungry," she said in a small voice.

"Matt," Eli called. "If it's okay with you, can Amarie slip into the house and maybe fix us up something to eat?"

"Whatever you bring, I'll eat. My missus trained me to

eat what's put in front of me. I got a couple of drinks in a cooler on the back porch."

Amarie sprang to her feet. "No problem, I'll be right back."

"Eli, I think you might've upgraded. This one is actually a keeper."

Amarie returned with a warped wicker serving tray and a plastic grocer's bag hanging off one shoulder. There were sandwiches piled high with ham and turkey. She had a couple of pickle spears, chips. Heck, she had whipped up a tossed salad for them.

"I wasn't sure what you liked," she breathed. "I brought a little bit of everything that I could find. There's a couple of apples and bananas. A salad."

Eli was so tired, he went over to the hose at the front of the barn.

"I'll help," she said, dropping all the fixings. Amarie sprayed off his arms. "Turn them over and I'll make sure they're clear of goo."

"Thanks for this," he rasped.

"You're welcome. I don't mind, I like being useful."

And she was being helpful. When he sat down next to her, resting his back against a hay bale, he sighed in relief, his muscles tense.

"Here." Amarie placed a sandwich in his grip.

Eli inhaled the first one.

Amarie laughed. "You have a big appetite."

"I didn't plan on being out here all day. Might have to push the other visit to another day."

"Okay. Here, take another one." Amarie tossed him a cellophane-wrapped bundle.

"You made us two?"

"Yep, two apiece. We missed breakfast today. There're

enough calories to get us through dinner. Never make the same mistake twice."

"Ain't that the truth." He gave her a thumbs-up for thinking ahead. Preplanning seemed second nature to the way her brain worked. Not that he told her, but he appreciated her seeing to needs that he'd overlooked. A feminine yin to his increasingly aroused male yang. She sat next to him on the barn's dirt floor, not the least bit irritated by his armpit twang or the dirt covering both of them.

"You are amazing to watch, Eli." She kept her eyes forward, avoiding his gaze. For which he thanked the heavens. It gave him a chance to observe her. She counted her chips before squirreling away half of them in a cloth napkin. Eli caught himself smiling, then he frowned when he realized he found her utterly fascinating.

"I recorded several videos of you helping Belle. Bringing a new life into the world is one of the things I loved about working in labor and delivery when I did my clinical rotation. I loved spending time seeing moms with their new babies. The attention they paid to them. How they just couldn't take their eyes off this little person. It's beautiful."

Eli knew exactly how she felt because he was having a hard time keeping his eyes off her. Tension, low but building, entered the stall with them. Which was bad. Very bad for a fake partner. This was that awkward silence of first dates that he had no idea how to break. He looked down at his work boots on her feet, chuckling. They looked like clown shoes. When she noticed him staring, she laughed, too.

"I know . . . they look crazy."

"Actually, it's kind of cute. You wearing my stuff."

She pushed his shoulder, playful. "That's what partners do."

"That would be a first."

"So can I ask you something about Ruth and Phoebe?"

"Sure."

"Service is pretty small, with limited resources. Are... are they going to be okay? What about food, gas for the car, school clothes. Or if Phoebe gets sick and needs medical care? I mean, they can't stay at the farm forever."

Amarie looked to him, compassion for a woman and child she didn't know written in the softening lines of her face. "Her husband, Bucky—"

"Your mom pointed him out to me at the Bear the other night."

"Don't go near him," Eli reiterated. "When he gets to drinking, which is often," Eli said through tight lips, "he kicks Ruth and their five-year-old out of his trailer. Flirts with other women. As far as I know, he and Ruth manage to patch things up every time."

"That's awful. Why would she do that?" Amarie's expression tightened, closing off.

Belle's whinny interrupted their conversation. Eli hopped back to his feet. "I think it's time."

Matt had gone into the house to take a rest. Eli knew the old man had to be exhausted running the farm without family to help out, and lonely. He had noticed the sadness darkening his eyes every year Rachel stayed away. Eli had hoped the farmer would've shared lunch with them, but when he'd mentioned he was too old to take his meals on the floor, he realized an invitation to his momma's table would be best.

Amarie rose. "I'll help."

"You always this volunteer-y?"

"That's why I chose nursing. You can help people without them feeling weak or guilty about asking for it. Patients respect their nurses, don't see them as easy targets for genuinely enjoying serving others. It's a win-win. They live to see another day. And I earn a paycheck for doing what I'm passionate about."

Interesting perspective. One he hadn't considered. He had grown up with brothers and both parents, they'd helped each other all the time. Weakness wasn't a word he'd apply to any of them.

"What can I do to help you, boss?"

"Stay out of the way of Belle's hoofs, I don't want you hurt in case she kicks. By her head is the safest place. If she tries to get up, don't let her."

"Aye, aye, captain."

"You're so extra," Eli murmured. "I actually think your face started to glow."

Amarie got down on her knees and lifted the mare's head into her lap, stroking her forehead. "Oh, that's just my halo." She laughed. "You'll need Ray-Bans if you want to stay my partner."

"It's not an act, is it? You love helping people."

"If I needed help, I would want people to rally in support. You know." She shrugged. "Maybe it'll pay forward when I really need it."

Eli thought it naïve. Depending on people meant disappointment and anticipating the worst because that's how life worked. Folks who gave got taken—usually to the cleaners. Or in his case, to the brink of bankruptcy.

She hummed while she worked. He wondered if she even noticed that she added her own music to everything.

"What's that you're singing?"

"'Diamonds and Pearls' by Prince. It's a song about a man giving the woman he loves the world, but all she wants is his love."

"Sounds like a sap song. Women say they only want a

good man, but that's a fairy tale. In my story, the unsuspecting prince gets mauled by a pack of wild dogs she released when he wasn't looking."

"Sounds like you need a therapy horse ride yourself. I mean, you sound so jaded. You don't believe in romance because one woman hurt your feelings."

He'd felt more than hurt, try gutted with dirty talons. Amarie continued her armchair psychology while Belle pushed and Eli pulled, and the whole time the smartphone, propped on the half wall, recorded their at times heated debate. Twenty minutes later a beautiful foal wobbled on her legs for the first time, then stood beside her mother.

"Grab some towels out of that cabinet on the back wall." Eli pointed. Amarie did as he instructed. She came back with an armful of old cloths. Together they dried off the foal.

"Oh my gosh, if Vali—that's my *friend girl* back in the city—if she could see me now, she would be so jealous. Wait till I tell her I gave birth to a horse."

"Yeah, can't wait to hear her response to that."

"Stop it, Eli. You know what I mean. Now smile pretty for the camera."

"Nope." It would be well past quitting time when they climbed back in the truck, but Eli was proud of a hard day's work. Amarie seemed to share his joy. Cara would have had a meltdown the first hour stuck out here on a dusty old farm waiting for a horse to give birth. Eli let loose a long whistle, Hiccup's signal to move in his direction if he wanted to hitch a ride back to the cabin.

To Amarie, he said, "You did good work today. Time to head down the mountain."

Her smile faltered. Slowly she lowered the camera. "About me sleeping in your old room."

"She put you in my room?" he repeated, shaking his head. "I swear. Momma can't help herself. You know she's matchmaking?"

Amarie looked at him through long sable lashes, uncertainty stamped on her face.

"Ah, no, I don't. And if it bothers you, I guess I could look for maybe someplace else in a town close by."

"It's good that you're there with her. She needs the company. Momma doesn't say it and she doesn't complain... but I know the house has to feel empty with Dad gone. Besides, she likes you."

"I really like your mom," she sighed, and then shrugged. "You ready to head home?"

Eli didn't know why that sounded so right to him, but he wasn't going to question it. They'd had a good day together, working as partners. As for her staying at the house with his mom, he was happy that she'd told him the truth about everything today, that she hadn't held it back. He did wonder how a woman as talented and generous as Amarie Walker ended up on a dirt road, alone with a broken-down car and no money to speak of. Whoever her ex-fiancé was, he was pretty sure he didn't like the man. He stroked Belle's baby one last time. The distinct click of a camera shutter sounded. Eli grimaced.

"What are you doing, Amarie?"

"Uploading videos to the Calvary Clinic's new TikTok account. My account, PerkyLateBloomer, has over fifty thousand followers. They'll help us spread the word."

"About what?"

"We going to harness the power of social media to spread the word about the bachelor auction to raise the eighteen thousand dollars you need to save the clinic. This video has the kind of fresh content that can go viral. Hmm..." she pondered aloud, walking out of the barn as if she owned the place. Guess she had earned her place in Matt's heart. "You need a hashtag."

What Eli needed was a hot shower and a cold beer. He was almost tempted to invite Amarie to share both... almost.

Chapter Twelve

Twenty-four hours later, Eli sat across from his business partner with an icy beer in hand, a platter of buttermilk-dipped chicken fingers, fresh-cut fries, and homemade pickles between them. Amarie had managed to get him in the Black Bear under the guise of social research. Basically, she wanted to hear the gossip being passed about him and his brothers around town. According to her, he needed a target audience. A converted warehouse with exposed wood beams, the Black Bear smelled of hickory smoke, hops, and roasted nuts. As per usual, bodies poured through the front door. Before long, Dierks Bentley's tune pumping through the four-corner mounted speakers drowned out conversations. The scuff of cowboy boots roaring in unison across a dimly light dance floor created the ambience.

"The sign hanging out front says barbeque and things. Is barbeque ever on the menu?" Amarie yelled. She sliced the tip off the crispy strip, dipped it in hot honey, and popped the juicy bite in her mouth.

"Before Caleb took the job at the fire station, he kept the smoker out back in operating order. It's too busy in the summertime for Gracie Lou to run the smoker and the bar."

"Ah," she nodded, "makes sense. Oh my gosh," she moaned, and the croony sound echoed with sugar and spice. Watching the woman eat warmed his insides. And those *ooh*s and *aah*s made his thoughts sticky like molasses on steamy pancakes. "This chicken, these pickles are addictive."

"I thought you hated them," he joked, as Amarie devoured her portion and started in on his.

"Ha ha. You made a funny. Social media catnip. Funny sells."

With her quick changes of ideas and subject, Eli had started to adjust to her stream of consciousness.

He tipped his bottle in tribute. "To the queen of one-liners."

"Well, we can't all be supervets, can we, Dr. Calvary."

"You did pretty darn good today."

Her eyes seemed to glow at his compliment. Amarie's vibrant floral top exposed smooth brown shoulders that drew his eyes to a delicate cleft between her breasts. The top was paired with relaxed pink pants that hugged elegant curves, and everything about her contrasted with his T-shirt and denim attire.

"Thank you, Eli."

As he palmed his icy mug, Eli's soul, a coal lump where Amarie's shone diamond bright, the part of him he thought dead, stirred. Not good. He had little to offer a woman like her. Hadn't he learned that lesson?

"Welcome." He nodded. Yep, he broke eye contact, afraid he might stare a second longer than a platonic partnership allowed. He found himself plum dwelling on her laughter, her smile, her curves. She'd talked to every farmhand who'd answer her questions this morning. They'd had a stressful day, out at the dairy farm between Service and the town of Whynot. Amarie had been a big help in saving a dairy cow postdelivery. They'd had a new mother who had just delivered her calf and hadn't been able to get back on her feet. It had been a race against time. The cow's body weight on the legs could've caused permanent nerve damage within twelve hours if they hadn't gotten her back on her feet.

Amarie had been instrumental in Eli's ability to act quickly. With efficient hands, she'd prepared the calcium infusion to stabilize her after delivery. By the time they'd packed up their supplies, the owner was in tears. And the dam was on her feet with the new calf at her teat.

Eli was more exhausted than he had time to admit. Having Amarie as a partner was a force multiplier, a term the military applied to both people and processes that boosted productivity.

His mom and dad had worked in a similar fashion, harnessing the power of two versus one. Maybe Kanaan had been right. Flying solo wasn't always the best way. But Eli had tried a partnership with his marriage. It had failed. So had he by degree. Failure had a way of souring a man on trying the same for a second time.

"So," she swallowed, "about our social media campaign."

Oh, shoot. There went his great mood. "Let's call it a night," he said, downing the last of his beer.

But then Timmy Ramsey came running in with her little boy Ezra in tow, his red face covered in tears. She plopped one of those little round automated vacuum cleaners in front of Eli. "We need your help."

Not sure what to make of this request, Eli twisted to look at the other bewildered patrons. "Timmy, I'd love to help, but I might not be the best person to repair your vacuum cleaner."

Erza released a heart-wrenching sob, his little shoulders shaking. "Please, please, Mr. Eli. My gerbil, Gery, is stuck inside it."

"What?" Amarie blurted before slapping a palm over her mouth. The music slowed. Couples, hand in hand, broke off from the line dancing to zero in on the commotion at his table.

Unfortunately for hamsters and gerbils, the average household posed a multitude of dangers when pocket pets were uncaged.

Seconds passed while Timmy communicated the scenario.

"We let Gery out of his cage." Eli opened his mouth, but Timmy waved him off. "I know what you told us, but I had the vacuum cleaner going before, and this had never happened, Eli. We heard a squeak, but then it was too late. He got sucked up."

"Oh, poor little Gery," Amarie mouthed.

"Please, help him, Dr. Eli." Ezra sniffled. "I promise I'll keep him safe. Cross my heart." The little boy reached for his mother's hand. "Won't we, Mom?"

Timmy bent to kiss her son's trembling fingers. "Yes, baby."

Gosh, Eli heard sniffles from within the crowd.

Amarie, being Amarie, lowered to her knees. "Hi, Ezra. I'm Amarie, Dr. Eli's partner and first assistant. He's going to need help to perform a delicate extraction procedure for Gery. Do you think you can help him by bringing him a cup of water and a stack of paper towels?"

"Is Dr. Eli gonna rescue Gery?" Erza asked, his voice low and shaky with emotion.

How in the world could she answer with any honesty? Eli had no idea what he would find inside the suction apparatus. He pulled his pocketknife and all-purpose folded tool from his belt-loop holster.

"Timmy, you should go with him. Ms. Gracie Lou might have a cup of chocolate milk for my brave assistant."

"Do you promise Gery will be okay?"

"I can't make any promises, buddy, but I'll do the best that I can."

His mom hugged her little boy and led him away.

"Good gracious, Amarie. You sent an eight-year-old off for field delivery supplies?"

"Sorry, labor and delivery popped into my head." She shrugged.

"Don't apologize. It was quick thinking to get them both away."

"I'm kind of nervous," she whispered, while layering extra dinner napkins on the tabletop as a makeshift surgical area. "You?"

Flipping the disc upside down, he studied the back panel. Maybe Gery, or parts from Gery, would be visible. No such luck. Several onlookers had gathered around the table.

He lowered his ear to the metal backplate, listening. A soft squeaking, barely audible, came from inside. Gerbils tended to thump their hind legs when stressed. With the tight inner circuitry, perhaps that wasn't possible.

"The last thing I need is blood and guts all over the table." With the use of the multipurpose tool, he began the task of disassembling the vacuum, careful to minimize jostling. He released each screw, listening for movement. He heard nothing. Beneath his fingers, not the slightest vibration. A collective silence stilled the air like rust settled in a hinge. Eli began to sweat. Breath held, he removed the backing. Out popped an onyx-eyed rodent, his yellow coat dusted and powdered in Founding Fathers' white puffs. His lungs reinflated as he completed a rapid assessment on a wiggling, nose-twitching Gery. Cheers went up.

"Yay, Eli and his girlfriend saved the gerbil," someone out of sight offered up to the gossip mill.

"Oh boy," Timmy pushed through the crowd to embrace Amarie. "I'm sorry to ruin your first date."

"Not my girlfriend," Eli corrected, handing the pet to a wide-eyed, exuberant Ezra. "My business partner." His temptation.

"Don't be, Timmy." Amarie rolled her eyes in his direction. "Eli and I fight like cats in water. You just be sure to bring Gery by the clinic for a full examination."

Amarie had worked in the bottom line. Noah was right. The woman had a head for business ownership.

"Huh, you sure about the not dating him?" Timmy's brows pinched. "'Cause Matt Johnson told Lois Kline you and Eli were pretty cozy up at the farm. And you are sharing chicken fingers on Hoedown Thursday. Looks like romance to me. Both my older boys were born nine months after my Luke won the pie-eating contest at the fall festival."

"Intriguing," Amarie replied in regard to the disclosure, "but no."

Prudence from the other night sashayed over in a short blue denim skirt with matching silver-studded boots. "Why should I keep bidding on you if you're already Lady-and-the-Tramp spaghetti-kissing over a chicken finger basket, Eli Calvary?"

"That's our cue," Timmy said, waving farewell while ushering Erza, Gery, and her deconstructed robot vac away. "Welcome to Service, Amarie."

"Lady and the…is that supposed to make sense, Prudence?" Eli sighed, pinching the bridge of his nose. "Amarie said we're not an item." But he thought they got along better than two cats in a bag or whatever ill-reference she'd used to describe their relationship.

Prudence watched him for a second, as if weighing the truth of the matter.

"Well, in that case," she slapped him on the shoulder, "I'll put another twenty dollars on you come my paycheck, honey dumpling."

"Prud," Eli started, irritation coloring his words, "you have got to stop calling me honey. Biscuit. And dumpling. Eli serves me right fine."

"Okay, sugar." She winked. "I mean Eli."

Jimmy, one of the firefighters who worked with Noah and Caleb, strutted over from the bar where a pack of guys watched from afar. "If she's your business partner, Eli, can I take the new lady for a Watermelon Crawl on the dance floor?"

"Sorry, Jimmy. You'll have to find your own partner. I promised to teach her the ropes."

"Will you?" Amarie whispered, as if she doubted his word.

Eli took her by the hand, leading them onto the dance floor.

"You're wonderful, Eli. What you did for Erza." She looked up at him, those soulful brown eyes soft in wonder, and for a heartbeat he saw himself through her eyes. Pride, real and tangible, swept through him.

He pulled her into his arms. "Thanks." He swallowed against the urge to whisk her away to the cool grass outside his cabin, feel the night air sweep along soft curves warmed by his hands. "Let's dance."

"Yes, sir. But I don't know the song or the steps."

"This dance is the Crawl. I'll teach you. The Git Up. Cotton-Eyed Joe."

"Oh, sounds fun." She laughed, spinning in a full circle. The woman became one with the rhythm. Learning the choreography before the chorus. "What's this song?"

"Big and Rich's 'Save a Horse (Ride a Cowboy),'" Eli drawled, saddling up close to her curves.

"Is that an option?" she yelled above the jukebox.

Heck yeah, Eli thought, but bit his tongue to avoid an answer.

Two songs later, when Amarie relaxed in his arms and rested her head against his chest, Eli sang along with the words as they swayed hip to hip. Yeah, today was a good day to have a great partner.

Chapter Thirteen

Two days after their visit to Matt Johnson's farm, Amarie gathered her dream team, Leah, Tobias, Noah, and Eli, around the Calvary kitchen table. Dinner had been served, the scent of simmering spices clung to the air. The time to discuss strategy had arrived. Rain had cooled the afternoon temperature to the mid-eighties but not the stream of new clients interested in the Calvary brothers. Seems the possibility of the three men finding love gave the town plenty to talk about. The bidding wars had begun.

From her position at the head of the table, Amarie opened her tablet, pointing to the first in a series of computerized graphics she'd created with their target goal, daily minimums, and online content calendar template. "We have twenty-six days to raise eighteen thousand dollars."

"Not anymore." Next to her, Leah held up her phone; a digital thermometer had the bottom fully shaded in blue. "Ha, will you look at dem apples. We've raised over twenty-five hundred dollars in four days. Told you, boys. Mama knows best when it comes to love. I'll get all three of you down the aisle sooner rather than later."

The mention of future nuptials reminded Amarie that in nine days Gracie Lou and Caleb would host their wedding, the Saturday after next. She'd been invited by the bride, the groom, and the pet owners who visited the clinic—but not by her *partner*. Her brain reminded her that she and Eli had a business arrangement, but it still sucked that he chose to attend without her. Especially after last night's dinner and dancing. Since he hadn't mentioned the heat tangoing between their two-step, she wouldn't, either.

Eli jumped in. "Nobody's talking love and marriage with this bachelor auction, Momma. That's just crazy. Now onto saner topics. I've been thinking, to be on the safe side, we need a minimum of twenty-five grand to clear all our debts."

His voice carried from the far end of the table, which was littered with empty food platters. Amarie spared a glance at the last of the green beans, having devoured two slices of meatloaf smothered in homemade mushroom gravy, two biscuits, and all the glazed carrots on her plate. Be strong, gurl. To resist the compulsion to finish off the leftovers, she actually sat on one of her hands.

Wait a tick. What had he said? When had he decided to up the ante above eighteen thousand? And why had he waited till this meeting to announce it before discussing it with her?

"Whew, that's a lofty price tag." Tobias sighed, pushing the remnants of mashed potatoes around his plate with his fork.

"I'll say." Amarie's pulse began to race. Eighteen big ones would be a stretch with the compressed timeline. Now, Eli expected her to help him raise one thousand dollars per day. Did he not understand women only liked good surprises? The natural flow of conversation continued across the Calvary dinner table, the occupants oblivious to her struggles—the stress of having to generate four figures in bids every day and her insatiable appetite. Working the farms these last three days, she'd underestimated her caloric burn. No wonder Eli had the toned musculature of a gym junkie.

"Why so high above what we need, bro?" Noah said through a mouthful of homemade chocolate pudding.

Prior to dinner, Amarie had joined Leah in the kitchen, for comradery rather than actually being an assistant. As a reward, Lead had held out a wooden spoon to Amarie after swirling it through the bain-marie filled with cocoa powder, sugar, and milk from the dairy farm they'd visited earlier that day. It had been years since she'd met a cook who still owned a double boiler like her grandma Claudia. Amarie'd licked the spoon clean. Unfortunately, they'd gotten so carried away that Eli had walked in on them dancing to BTS, a Korean pop group she streamed via SoundCloud, and she'd grabbed his hand and pulled him into the house party. Apparently, dancing before dinner was an approved company policy. He'd actually given her a hint of smile. She wished he would do that more, smiling. When he did, her silly heart fluttered and her lady parts joined in the fun, too.

"Yeah, Eli. Why are you changing the goal on me?" she demanded, irritated that charts they'd worked on before the meeting needed adjustments.

"This isn't personal, Amarie. But the mortgage on the house in Warrenton still has to be paid until it sells."

"Now why didn't I know that you had additional debts? I had no idea you lived in the D.C. suburbs with your wife."

"We never lived there. No one has. The marriage ended before the contract closed."

"That's pretty darn sad." For a man who valued loyalty and commitment, divorce had to bruise Eli's ego. If the person who swore to love her up and abandoned their life together, she would have trust issues, too. When relationships go wrong, more than a heart gets broken. Seems Amarie and Eli could both attest to the fallout of left-behind lovers.

"Not for long. It's on the market again; the first realtor couldn't get the property off my hands."

"Huh, that sucks. The housing market is on fire. It's a seller's market."

"So the media keeps telling me. But I'm the one stuck with a twenty-nine-hundred-dollar mortgage payment. Unfortunately for me, the house has what the realtor calls 'ugly bones.' That's code for an eccentric floor plan."

"Doesn't sound like code to me." Amarie shrugged. "You built a butt-ugly house."

"Thanks for that, Saint Amarie." Eli pushed back from the table to put his plate in the sink. "Seems most growing families prefer spacious bedrooms and luxury kitchens, not Cara's ten-by-ten sardine can–sized rooms and efficient hotel-style kitchen."

"Sounds like Edward's room in that *Twilight* vampire movie, more for entertainment than sleep."

Eli paced the length of the table, gathering the empty bowls—and the green beans. "Never seen the movie, but the place is sucking me dry."

The distinct sound of disposal blades at work grated, and then they were gone. Amarie may have whimpered at the wasted food. At least she could unleash her toasty hand from beneath her bum before her fingers went numb.

"The last one hundred and twenty days have been slow. I'm gonna need extra cash, maybe throw in a home warranty?"

"On a brand-new house?" she quizzed.

"It's been sitting empty for six months. I might have to bankroll the closing cost."

"I'll look at your listing. Jazzing up the page will generate more activity on the multiple listing sites so it stands out from comparable properties."

"Never seen a bedazzled sales page."

"Funny, hehe. You jazz it up by showing potential buyers how the house can meet their needs. Then you create a sense of urgency."

"How do you know so much about sales?" Tobias asked, lowering his fork to the plate.

"I learned most of what I know from watching my mom. My dad is a doctor in Florida, the land of cotton-tipped retirees. There's a lot of competition in the medical market. My mom worked with him full-time, she created all of Dad's marketing material. I guess she planted the seed."

"Why do you know so much about how to sell, though?" he continued, genuine in his interest. The Calvarys had an authentic quality that many found refreshing.

"I spent a lot of time on the internet as a kid reading blog articles. Listened to few podcasts. I picked up a few things to help my ex with his business. There's a science to marketing. Hook your audience's attention and bam, you have two point five seconds to sell them on your product."

"What's our product, then?" Leah asked.

"You are. The Calvary family."

Leah folded her hands in front of her face, gushing. "Like the Kardashians."

"Oh my gosh, you watch Kris, too?"

"We're small-town folks, not barbarians," Eli remarked, lips tight.

"So your ex-wife doesn't want the house?"

"No. She lost interest early in the process. Dad got really

sick about a month after we broke ground, and I got distracted. My family needed me. Cara was doing her ananda balasana with Sven by then."

Amarie looked to Leah, confused. "An *anna* what?"

"It's a back-lying yoga pose. The fella she ran off with gave private evening lessons, if you know what I'm saying," jumped in Noah.

Tobias turned to his left and punched Noah in the arm. "We all know what you're saying."

"Ouch, you hit like an EMT." Noah grinned, but he held his deltoid, massaging the muscle.

"Boys." Leah looked to Amarie. "What do you need us to do, Amarie?"

"Be yourselves. Just do it online for an audience."

"I've been myself my whole life. Ain't nobody given me twenty-five thousand dollars."

"You ain't never lied." Tobias nodded.

Amarie had to convince them the inherent good a lot of people working together could do. Even strangers rallying to the aid of a family trying to save their home and business.

"You'd be amazed at how generous people can be for a good cause. We're going to show them how valuable the Calvary family is to this community. It's started already with the pictures I took of Eli helping Belle deliver her colt."

"A colt is a young male horse, by the way." Eli took a seat, this time closest to her. Okay, partner. This she liked. "Belle's foal is female."

"See." Amarie beamed. "You taught me something I didn't know. That's the content that your TikTok followers can use. Now back to Leah's question. Each of you has created an individual TikTok account, yes?"

Eli crossed those tanned arms over defined pecs. "Not me."

"We know," everyone said in unison.

"We'll use each account to drive traffic to the Calvary Veterinary Clinic account and promote the bachelor auction. Except for Eli because he's too stubborn to change his anti-establishment ways."

"Worked for the establishment as a soldier in uniform. There's nothing anti about miliary service."

"I know, grumpy pants. It's what we civilians call a joke." Amarie patted his hand. "The military and the federal government are dinosaurs when it comes to information technology. Let's move on, shall we? Now what are your TikTok handles? I'll follow each of you. Call them out."

"MamaCalvary."

"NoahTomCat."

Tobias sighed. "SimplyTobias."

"And you, Amarie?" Leah asked.

"I'm PerkyLateBloomer."

They all paused. "That doesn't seem right," Noah said.

"She is perky." Eli smirked.

Flattered by their appreciation of her skills, she said, "It's totally true. If you really knew me, you'd get it. Trust me, my best friend, Vali, and I have battled, like *Ready Player One*, to annihilation about my handle. We have agreed to disagree. So, we just need a thirst trap."

"A what?" Eli asked, her online persona forgotten.

"A thirst trap is a choreographed or deliberate attempt to entice or seduce the viewer to watch a segment of digital content till completion."

Eli threw up his hands. "Why are we doing this? Why do we need all of this?"

Frankly, they didn't have time to waste. "Quit barking already." Amarie huffed. "It's gonna—Oh geesh, I sound like you now." She started again, without the West Virginia dialect. "It will take more than the women and men in Service and the surrounding counties to come up with the kind of money that we—I mean you—need to stop the foreclosure process and pay my fee."

"You're charging him?" Noah asked.

"A percent of the proceeds," she proudly confessed.

"Good for you." Leah beamed. "Don't let them get the milk before buying the cow."

"Yes," Amarie said, "whatever that means. No free tit pulls."

"You mean teat."

"I do?" Amarie questioned.

"Yeah, you do." Tobias chuckled.

"You go around saying tits, all the guys are going to know you're either from the city or think you're offering something." Noah waggled his brows.

"Amarie's pretending to be my investment partner to stop the Pendletons circling and running all our customers off—"

"And bidders," Leah added. "Lourdes might stir up trouble for you boys with the ladies. Especially now with so many of the mountain folks dropping in on their way into town."

"That, too." Eli nodded. "Maybe a few public business meetings will keep the people focused on the clinic's value, so we can concentrate on work."

"I'm good with the added attention," Noah said, rubbing his palms together.

Of course he would be. The news of Rachel Johnson's imminent return didn't deter the mischievous light stirring in his prism eyes.

"Maybe," Noah nudged Tobias with his shoulder, "Mom's auction will help you find a lady of your own."

Tobias crossed thick arms behind his head. "Let's see if I got my facts straight. Older brother's divorced with a fake business partner. Younger one's porking any puddin' he can get his paws on." His face contorted in displeasure. "Nope. I'm good."

"You waiting on some special pudding?" Noah chided.

"A modicum of restraint and the woman you really want would still be in town," Tobias deadpanned.

"How about I send you to the Whynot ER in your own ambulance?" Noah bristled.

"What?" Tobias glared. "It's the truth. The first one was the right one. And you blew it."

That struck Amarie as odd. Noah had his love life, rather sex life, on full public display, but apparently he had a protective streak for Rachel Johnson to rival Eli's overbearing brutish behavior. This was the first time she'd heard of Noah having a hairpin trigger about the farmer's daughter. When Rachel Johnson returned, she would have a cowboy willing to buck off a few broncos to take his place at her side.

"Boys," Leah warned. "No more pudding talk unless it's mine."

Eli sighed. "I'm officially a traumatized child. Please can we change the subject before another dessert is ruined for me?"

"The local women see you two together and think you're in a real relationship, Eli. You and Amarie balance one another. The honey to your bee."

"Momma, don't get it twisted. The only thing buzzin' is a partnership. Me and Amarie are a business transaction, nothing more."

"The more folks see, the more they're gonna speculate. This is Service. Love has blossomed from less, so be ready."

"This one won't."

Well, Eli didn't have to sound so sure of himself. Yes, they'd started as business associates, but he could do worse than her. Sounds like he already had. Amarie placed her tablet on the table to get everyone back on track.

"Eli, we'll drive traffic to the clinic page. I'll invite my fifty thousand followers to follow each of you. I'm still thinking of a hashtag. Hopefully we can get the clinic's TikTok page trending. If we're really lucky, we can go viral."

"And you really think it'll work?"

"We're all pushing in the same direction. Tomorrow night is Fun Friday at the Black Bear. Most of the town will be there. We can promote—"

"You want to announce about our pages, don't you?" Eli muttered under his breath.

"Smart one you are, boss. If they can talk and have internet access, invite them to follow us on TikTok."

"Will that be enough publicity?" Tobias quizzed, taking notes in his smartphone. *Impressive*, Amarie thought.

"It will if we keep Leah's county bulletin ad updated with our progress and pay for a TikTok ad campaign."

"How much is that going to cost?" Eli grumbled.

Amarie released a surprise she'd been holding all day. "We have the seed money." She beamed. "Matt Johnson gave the clinic a two-hundred-and-fifty-dollar donation."

"When did that happen?"

"I called to follow up on Belle and the baby before I left the office."

"You did?" Eli's voice held a note of shock, and maybe pride. Hard to tell with him.

"Yes, and to say hello to Ruth and Phoebe." Amarie had thought of them most of the night. She'd thought of her mother. They'd spoken once since her arrival in Service. Wondered if her father had deployed psychological abuse tactics similar to Bucky all those years ago. Had her pet, Princess, been given away to force her and her mother to return home?

Leah clapped her hands, anchoring Amarie to the present.

"Oh my goodness, you're already the best at the business. We've never even charged Matt to care for the therapy animals. This is a special surprise."

"Special, my foot." Eli stood again. The motion was so abrupt, the entire table shifted sideways. "Amarie's got him wrapped around her ring finger, too. He invited her dancing two seconds after meeting her."

"Is this jealousy I hear?" Amarie taunted.

That comment brought a military halt to his rant. Eli grabbed the chair, swung it backward, then straddled the seat. "What next?" he demanded.

"Take as many pictures as you can of your everyday jobs. I'll get shots of Eli at work. You all can take selfies and do the same thing to post on your pages. Include your coworkers if they are okay with their images on social media. The key to social media is to be your most authentic self."

"Do you want me to take my shirt off?" Noah asked.

"Not at this moment."

"After the meeting then." He winked.

"Listen here, Noah, Amarie may be my fake partner, but she is still my employee. Stop flirting with her."

Amarie picked up her phone. "I like a growling, possessive animal doctor. That's good. Keep it up, the ladies online adore protective men."

"Y'all sure this pretend thing is a good idea?" Tobias inquired.

"It's fine," Amarie and Eli said at the same time.

Leah smiled.

Tobias looked worried.

"Amarie," Noah asked, smiling, "tell me more about this thirst trap."

"Oh yes. Let's do a demonstration. Stand up, Eli." He did as he was told, at first. "Take your cap off. Walk to the door. That's good…" Amarie trailed off watching his butt work the heck out of his jeans. "Yeah, now spin to face me."

Eli skull and crossboned his arms. "No. Nope. Stop the camera."

"Ooh, ooh, get that pout." Leah hopped up. "I loved that face when he was a baby."

"Mom, the dang blasted video is still going."

"This is great footage. Keep going," Amarie cheered.

"I'll do the auction. What I'm not going to do is sexy model photos to put online."

"Not sexy. Thirsty. There's a difference. This is how we're going to boost your engagement."

"I don't want more engagement. What I want is to be left alone."

"Not true." Amarie needed to remind him what he stood to lose. "You want to save your family house and your father's business. This is a vehicle to reach your goals."

"Come on, bro." Noah grabbed Eli by his shoulders. "Give us just a little pout. Think of the children."

"How about a black-and-blue eye."

"Boys. Boys," Leah called. "We will do our part to follow Amarie's lead."

"Wow, I'm in charge?"

"Of course, dear. And I think we should announce the winners of the bachelor auction at the Founder's Day Festival. Everyone will be there. It'll be a great time to show off more of the Service spirit. Shephardstown maybe the oldest city, but Service, we're the beat in the heart of West Virginia."

"Well, the fifteen-second clips of Eli delivering Mr. Johnson's foal have gotten a lot of comments. Once we reach one thousand TikTok followers, the algorithm will allow us to add a direct link to the auctionluvbuzz.com site as well as a donation button."

Tobias nodded. A signal Amarie translated as plan approval. "You've got a one-track mind when it comes to money."

"And food," Eli piggybacked on his brother's comment.

Amarie's smile slipped. "No, I don't like missing meals."

Eli looked at her, frowning. She would have to do better at hiding her visceral reaction to hunger. During her time at Howard, she'd seen a therapist more than once to address her irrational fear with food instability. The psychiatric nurse practitioner had suggested Amarie carry a light snack with her at all times, like a pack of peanut butter crackers, and eat healthy snacks in between meals if needed.

Once she'd embarrassed her father at a company holiday party by adding a second warm roll to her bread plate before everyone else at the table. It was shortly after she and her mother had returned to his home. Through the years, she'd trained herself not to fidget or reach for the last scrap of meat when an efficient server cleared the table.

"Who needs help making their first video? Then we'll repost all the video content from the clinic's TikTok page on your personal pages."

"Oh." Noah whistled. "I'm going to love this. Do you see the way these ladies are dressed on here?"

"You mean undressed on here," Eli rasped, glaring over Noah's shoulder. "I don't get why anyone would pay money for this."

"Because we'll show them the value that the Calvary family and the clinic adds to the community. All the good work the Calvarys are doing here in Service. People really do want a reason to do good and help one another, Eli."

"You really believe that?" Eli asked, his brow furrowed.

"Yes, I do. Call me crazy, but I do believe in happily ever after." She reached up, grabbing his hand. "And my partner."

More subconscious than an actual steady force, she curled her fingers around Eli's, sealing their connection. The feel of his roughened hand on hers felt amazing. Something electric jolted deep in her belly. Warmth spread like orange blossom honey in her veins.

Everyone fell quiet.

Alarmed, Amarie studied their faces. "Did I say something wrong?"

She turned to Eli for an answer. His mouth thinned, but he still held her hand. Amarie felt a little awkward. She didn't know what to say next. Luckily, she was saved by the bell. The chime sounded a second time.

"Is someone at the door?" Tobias stood.

Noah lowered his phone. "Why didn't they come in?"

That's when they heard it. High-pitched cries. More than one.

"What in the world is that?" Leah asked.

When they all got up to investigate, Amarie extricated her hand from said growly partner. The men's heavy footfalls followed, tactical in movement like they had an unspoken pre-arrangement of how to defend their home.

Eli reached for the screen door, then stopped. "Stay back. There's something moving on the porch."

Using his sinewy forearm for balance, Amarie peeked under Eli's extended arm. It's a sack."

"Why is it moving?" Tobias walked around her. Opening the door, he nudged the bag with his foot. And then the sack contents started to meow. "Someone dropped off a bag of kittens."

Amarie pointed. "Look, there's a note."

"I'm sure this is Bucky's idea of a joke," Eli growled. "He confronted me at the Black Bear accusing me of targeting the women."

"And Phoebe's cat was pregnant." Amarie frowned. How could a father be intentionally cruel to his flesh and blood? Phoebe was a sweet little girl.

Eli snapped up the cloth sack. First he scanned the note, then read it aloud.

Since you Calvarys like to cat around with every woman in town, here's some kittens to keep you busy.

"What a crap thing to do." Tobias shook his head in obvious disgust.

Eli fished in the bag. One. Two. Three. Four. Five kittens clawed his shirt. One orange striped. A dove-white one with blue eyes. A little cream-colored cutie with a big noggin. And a pair of twin grays with wild staticky hair and glowing green eyes that made Amarie think of Eli. Rather, his captivating stare when he pinned her with one of his looks, like he was doing now. It was unnerving, the flutters in her belly.

"How's Buchanan calling us tomcats?" Noah moved to stand in the fading light of day. "That's rich. And dumping a bunch of kittens..." He rubbed at his clean-shaven face.

"A kindle. Not a bunch," Eli corrected, smiling at the kindle of furry tadpoles making their way up his shoulder. They looked adorable climbing his mountain of male muscle. Aw, even the normally harsh angles of his face softened. Stupid butterflies, batting their wings in absolute glee at the spectacular view and masculine might made gentle. She should probably find her Spanx waister tamer, that would strangle those pesky butterflies. Taking a fancy to her boss, her grumpy, "not interested in anyone more than in a temporary arrangement" boss, would cost her more emotional mileage than she had at the moment.

"I'm too old to have a house full of kittens under my feet, boys. You don't want your momma slowed down with a broken hip."

"They can come home with me. I have pet supplies in my cabin anyways," replied Eli.

Was Amarie the only one that wanted to hug Eli? Yeah, no one else seemed moved by his compassion. She found herself wishing he belonged to her. Eli Calvary was the type of fairy-tale hero women fantasized about. She certainly did. What woman could refuse a generous, protective man with battleship-sized biceps who knew how to stroke a kitty?

"That's it," Amarie blurted out, all at once, super excited. "I have an idea."

Someone gently tugged a lock of her hair. "About the thirst trap or the kittens?"

Of course. Noah. Ever the playful playboy with a heart of gold, fixated on the thirst trap.

"Both," she said, swatting his hand in jest. "If Bucky is unhappy about our bachelor auction, I can't wait to see what shows up on the doorstep when we get our TikTok page up and running with the hashtag SexyKittyVet."

"I am a sexy kitty?" Eli's roar sent a jolt through everybody, even the kitties; their soft mews rang out a distress catcall—*meow, meow, meow.*

"You will be," she promised, smartphone in hand. "You will be."

He most certainly was not fuzzy or cuddly at this moment, but to their target audience, his cowboy swagger would be irresistible catnip.

Chapter Fourteen

AMARIE HAD SAID she believed in him. Why had her quiet confession pleased him so? Considering how they bickered with and jabbed at each other during the day, when Eli had briefly held her hand tonight in comfortable companionship, he'd found the innocent gesture rather pleasurable. And now she was in his home. Helping him with kittens.

He'd only invited a few women over to his cabin. His wife had been the last woman, other than his momma, to visit in the past four years. Cara had been unimpressed with the small, two-bedroom log cabin that sat at the base of the Landing Falls waterfall. He had worked with his father and brothers to build all three of the cabins. He and his brothers had taken pride in their work. Each place had its own little touch, speaking to the owner. Maybe not the owner, but the occupant, at least. Having Amarie, the city girl, visit for the first time, Eli found himself retracing his steps. He gave the air a sniff test, making sure the living room didn't smell of rank gym socks, day-old nachos, and puppy. Nope, but he cranked the Glade PlugIn to high output. Toilet seat down, check. Dishes in the cabinets, check.

Yeah.

Even though she was his employee, the man that he walled off wanted to impress her. Well, he wanted his pretend partner to appreciate the rare quality in his home on the mountain. She should value what they fought to save. He told himself that was why he wanted her to enjoy the space as much as he did.

"I appreciate you helping me with the kittens."

"No problem. I like being useful." Amarie smiled, placing the orange-and-white striped kitten, Raspberry, in a towel-lined cardboard box. Eli had used the hose out front to fill a plastic washbasin with treatment solution. Having inspected each of the kittens, he found them dirty, fleas hopping undeterred in their fur, but otherwise in good health. Without his asking, Amarie had shed her backpack and shoes. On her knees beside him, she dried as he washed between tiny toes and gently scrubbed away grime.

"How else am I going to get a look at your place?" Amarie produced her smartphone, the bane of his existence. "#SexyKittyVet."

"Can I tell you I hate that name?"

"Sure you can, gorgeous. But it's not going to change anything."

"Sounds cliché. Sexy kitty."

"For a woman, yes. A vet with real kittens to care for is sexy."

"I guess." Guessed she was wrong. Of the three brothers, women liked Eli because of his follow-through, not his sex appeal.

He toweled off another meowing fur ball. Amarie plucked from his hands a spike-haired kitty she'd named Formerly, the feline he'd previously known as *the cream-colored one.* 'Cause let's face it, Eli didn't have a creative cell in his genetic petri dish. Color him grateful that Amarie had a constant stream of ideas. Even better, she had check-lists and action steps to actually get things accomplished. In military terms, the woman was a stellar performer. Dr. Russell Feldman's loss, Eli's gain.

"Well, you could always be a sexy beast. Either way, sex really does sell. Some would consider you handsome. Take advantage before your beauty fades, grumpy pants."

"I still don't like it." Beauty had sold him on Cara. His tongue had started wagging the first time he'd laid eyes on the government contractor assigned to Fort Meade in Maryland's Anne Arundel County. He'd pursued her—hard. Mowed her lawn. He'd volunteered to paint her spare bedroom, the one she used as her private yoga studio, just to stay close to her. If Cara wanted, he stood ready to provide. Too blinded by what he wanted to give in a relationship, he failed to notice how little his wife reciprocated his affec-tion. Well, that wasn't entirely true. He'd kept working at their marriage, hopeful that his wife would grow to love and appreciate his commitment to marriage. In the end, it had provided her with more time to rob, pillage, and sour him on happily ever after for good.

"I get it. It sucks starting over, even more than when the ends barely meet. But, hey," she shrugged, "fake it till you make it. I mean, it's worth the sacrifice to live in a place like this. Under the stars. I can't believe you live here."

She'd said as much since he'd pulled alongside the cabin, the view of the water visible through the windshield. One Wonder Woman twirl in the yard and she'd pulled up the MLS listing on his house on her phone, determined to rid him of the albatross because she thought his log cabin was heaven. Perfection. That's the word she'd used.

During her tour of the inside, she'd run her fingers along

the walls with framed pictures of his family and him in uniform. Afterward, Eli had excused himself to change out of his stiff jeans. He'd kept the door to his bedroom cracked so he could see where she wandered. If she looked at his mail or peeked into his medicine cabinet. But she hadn't. She'd headed straight for the ceiling-to-floor windows. There were six of them. They gave the place a spacious feel, even though it was only about 1500 square feet. The kitchen and the family room were just a big open square in the middle of the cabin with a river rock fireplace against one wall. The two bedrooms down the hallway on the left were the same size with a shared bathroom in between.

He grabbed a beer from the fridge for himself and a bottle of water for her. "Break time, partner. I relax on the porch. You can join or not."

"Thanks. I think." She took the water bottle and followed him.

Once outside, Amarie spun around on his porch. That Wonder Woman thing again. The overhead light washed her partially in warm light.

"This is the most amazing view—the trees, the water, the mountain, the stars."

He chuckled. "I see this every day when I open my eyes."

Though not visible to one another, the three cabins formed an arc with a central area at the base of the waterfall. They'd agreed to use the common area as a picnic spot where they had laid out pavers, a fire pit, and a built-in stone bench. And they each had their own Adirondack chair that they relaxed in sometimes while they divided up a six-pack at the end of the week.

"I can't imagine living like this in the city. This is like a one-million-dollar view, you know? No, it's a three- or four-million-dollar oasis, because of the water. That's a part of its beauty. But there's so much more. There's no way you can lose this."

Looking at her, Eli had to agree. She'd made tonight so much more for him. By being here. Something as mundane as bathing kittens seemed magical with Amarie sharing the labor.

"The only water that I can afford is coming down from the sky. Eli, I don't think I could imagine a more beautiful place to come home to after work. I can't wait to get my own place. It's something I didn't realize how badly I wanted until now. I thought that I would live with someone else forever. But I think I do want my own home, you know? So I can decorate it the way I want. I have all these pictures on my Pinterest board. It's like a vision board, but it's online. Anyway, it's just fab. So, I had these visions of what I want my home to look like. All the way down to, like, my shower curtain. And the rugs on the floor and the pictures on the wall. Even my loungewear. Like I just want to be in my own space."

"I can understand that. You'll have it one day, Amarie."

"You think I will?"

"Don't sound surprised. You make things happen. Of course you will, sweetheart."

She gave him a sideways glance. "Eli, how many of those beers have you had? You're the first person to actually say those words to me. And then tack on an endearment?"

"I said what I meant. Don't start a nervous ramble over it. Just accept it." He certainly had.

"I am... I did. But not even my best friend says I make things happen, and that's kind of a requirement of the job. Things, bad usually, happen to me..." she trailed off.

Eli wanted her to have her heart's desire. He could see her creating the life she envisioned. After all, the woman was fearless, innovative, and adventurous. She would leave him and build a life outside of Service.

"Your luck's changing, Amarie." Eli's had since he'd taken a gamble on her. He cleared his throat against the clog in his chest. "Ah, I'm going to set the kittens up in the second bedroom."

"Oh, they'll be lonely in there."

"What are you suggesting, Mama Bear?"

"They arrived in a sack. At least let them roam."

The woman proceeded to take the freshly washed kittens out of the basket, depositing them on the wood decking. Of course, they found Hiccup's hind legs and started exploring.

"I mean, your family home is beautiful, but I never imagined a waterfall on the property."

"Home has always been the most beautiful place on earth."

"Woof. Woof. You lucky dog."

"Another zingy one-liner."

"I know, right? And you get all this mental and manual labor for free."

He laughed, but Amarie deserved more than he could pay her in one lifetime. In a small town like Service, catching up on the day's events was a favorite pastime. The Black Bear, the Coffee Bean Barn, and when Ophelia allowed it, the Dog-Eared Page bookstore were the social gathering sites. It was common practice if folks saw each other in the parking lot of the general store or the Coffee Bean Barn that three hours later they'd still be in the same spot catching up on old times. Since Amarie's arrival, the Calvary Clinic had become the impromptu watering hole. Eli knew Amarie had been the difference maker.

"When I was a boy, we lived downtown. My father

would walk this very land with me on his shoulders. There was nothing more than an old, dilapidated barn long abandoned by his family. He told me that one day, our forever home would be here. Tobias doesn't remember it, but I do. Noah was still in Mom's belly. I thought my dad was invincible back then. Every promise he'd ever made to me, he followed through. I wanna do the same for him."

"Eli, please don't sound so grim. Together we can do this."

"Why are you so optimistic about life when it was obvious to me that you were on the verge of a panic attack the day I hired you?"

"I haven't always been the eleven-dollars-an-hour high-wage earner you see before you."

"Used to better?"

"No," she trailed off, taking a seat in the rocker next to his. "Worse. Much worse."

"Since you've decided to hang around," he sighed, "things may get way worse before there's something other than a runaway train speeding toward us at the end of the tracks."

"Can you please pick another locomotive metaphor?"

"Why? What does it matter?"

"Everything matters, Eli. I'm not a fan of bullet trains to big cities."

"I upset you."

"Not true. The train upset me. They lead to fast trouble and slow apologies."

"There's a story there."

"Yes, and it's an unpleasant one that I care not to remember."

"You don't have to."

"Of course I do. You will bear the load of my paternal trauma for your role in deteriorating my mood."

"Unload away, friend."

"That's just earned you an extra heaping at a time of my choosing."

"Noted. Now the story."

"When I was eleven years old, my mother and I left my dad. I think he had been unfaithful for a while by then."

"Whoa, that had to have been hard on you both."

"You don't want to know how bad it got for us." Amarie rubbed her palms, now sweaty, over her capris. "Anyway, we ended up back with my father after a year on our own."

"So, your parents patched things up."

"I thought they had. My first year as a Howard University Bison, my parents drove up from home, America's old city, eleven hours in a rented SUV because my father descends into hysteria if my mother accumulates more than five thousand miles per year on any vehicle bearing his name on the title. Four hours into their visit, my father announced he had a business trip in New York and had booked a trip on the Acela train because he wanted to arrive early."

Something in her tone changed. Eli understood this story wouldn't have the happy ending she seemed to crave but had never quite experienced. His life had a similar melancholy note.

"With the details provided, I Googled the conference... I wish I hadn't."

This story would sour his mood. A burn, small and irritating, spread in his gut. The mode and members in this play were different, but he recognized the storyline—lies, deception, and betrayal.

"What happened?"

"I told my mother the truth. Dad's medical conference had happened two months prior, but closer to home. One hundred miles south in Orlando. There was an online post of him pictured with a female colleague enjoying more cocktails than conference sessions. I showed her all of it."

Eli didn't have to ask what happened next because he remembered from a conversation during yesterday's breakfast that her parents had been married for close to thirty years.

"Amarie?"

"Oh." She startled. "Sorry. So, my daddy returned late the next day, and my mother said nothing about the information I'd given to her. They left together, a perfect fake marriage. Guess I learned to fake it from my parents. Neither of them returned to the campus. Not even for my graduation." There was a time when Amarie had hoped for a return of natural ease with her parents, yet the fairy tale had given way to a reality so jarring and gut-wrenching she still wept for the girl who'd learned her father wasn't a hero and she and her mother weren't his treasure.

"Huh, huh…that's heavy for a child to process. I'm sorry."

"Yeah, I did the right thing. But in the end, I got punished. Not him," she said, a little too cheery for the damage his father's selfish actions had caused to his wife and daughter's relationship. "So now you know why trains can suck it."

Though she didn't look at him, Eli could feel the tension radiating from what he knew were pliable curves that had molded against him to perfection.

"No more train talk from this cowboy."

"Much obliged." She did turn and smile at him then.

An alarm went off.

"What's that?" he asked.

"It's nine o'clock, I need to go, but I can come back in the evenings to help with the kids."

"Not kids. Kindle. And I accept. I like the idea of you

visiting every day." He pressed his hand to her shoulder, allowed it to linger. "You could stay longer."

Her breath hitched. "Whoa, partner. That's not the kind of help I volunteered for tonight."

"You seriously think I would lure you up to my cabin to take advantage of your kindness?"

"No—I don't know. Maybe." She winced. "I mean we danced, held hands, then you called me sweetheart. So yeah, I thought…" She made this weird kissy face that totally blew his high.

"I wouldn't blindside you, okay." This was just plain weird now. "Today was…nice. I thought we could prolong the moment. That was all I was asking. So, can you stay?"

This game they'd started was far from over for him, but he wouldn't rush things. The way she'd sunk into his growing erection last night on the dance floor, he knew she'd felt the claw of desire pulling them deeper into the furnace, burning hot between them.

"No. It's time for me to study for my nursing exam."

"Can it wait?"

Amarie stiffened. "No. This is important to me."

"Okay. I'll drive you back to the house.

"You don't have to. I enjoy walking."

"That's not an option. What kind of man do you take me for?"

"Would you carry my books, too?" She laughed.

"Every day." Eli's expression sobered; the humidity seemed to evaporate right out of the atmosphere, leaving him thirsty for a drink of something sweet and juicy. "Let me grab my keys."

Eli grabbed his fob, keys jiggling, and wallet from his dresser. He followed the meows through the house till he reached the front door.

His heart nearly stopped in his chest. Amarie had scooped up all five kittens in her arms. She talked to them, telling them about their new life and how beautiful they were. Eli thought to himself how beautiful she was inside and out. Standing on his porch underneath his stars with his dog at her side and, more than likely, five kittens that he'll be raising for the next fifteen years because that was their lifespan, she was one of the most beautiful stars he had ever seen, and she had lit his night with wonder.

"I have something for your next trip to the farm."

"What is it?"

He pulled a bag from behind his back, rubbing Hiccup's head when he pawed at the plastic. "Down, boy."

Nervous, Eli pulled a box free, handing it to her.

Amarie smiled, lifting the lid to sift through the noisy tissue paper. She paused and stared directly into his eyes. "A new pair of boots? You bought me boots."

He scrubbed at his beard, thinking himself a fool. She hated them. Nothing sexy about boots, Eli. "They...er, they were at the Trading Post."

Embarrassment curled around his brain as the back of his neck heated at his stupidity. If he had a cane, he'd yank his sorry excuse of a romantic gesture right off the stage. Women expected jewelry, not outdoor gear.

He opened his mouth to apologize, but Amarie lunged for him. Opening his arms, he caught her around the waist, hauling her close. When she pressed her lips to his, instinct took over. Eli knew she smelled terrific, but the taste of her was intoxicating. And he drank deep, plunging into the warmth of her mouth, hunger and starvation stretching his restraint to the limit. Inside his need crawled at him to take more, pushed them both to the breaking point. When she breathed out, moaning, he stroked her tongue with his.

Eli took full advantage, continuing his exploration, cataloging every sensation she unlocked that he'd walled off months ago. He thought he missed the caress of a woman, but then his brain registered a new revelation. He'd never experienced a connection this tangible with anyone before Amarie.

How scared should he be that her passion carried the same take-charge, adventurous energy she brought to everyday living? On a deep inhale, he grabbed hold of the last threads of his control and pulled away. Amarie, undeterred, continued to sip from his mouth, taking little nips at his parted lips. Hers were swollen from his attention, and he gave in to one last succulent taste.

"Thank you. I love them," she whispered, planting another kiss on his mouth, and then totally taking him by surprise when she bit his bottom lip.

"You bit me," he said more than questioned, sucking the tender flesh between his teeth.

"I've wanted to do that."

He raised a brow. "Draw blood?"

"Sounds so clinical when you say it that way." Her voice dipped, low, husky, sensual. "I've wanted to taste you. Take a bite of temptation."

"And your verdict?"

Her eyes sparkled like those pretty toes he spied on every morning. "You're delicious. Thank you for the gift and… indulging my new fetish."

Sliding one arm around her back and the other beneath her thighs, he lifted. Sitting in the chair she'd just vacated, he settled Amarie across his lap.

"You're welcome," he rasped, nuzzling her neck. "And from now on, you come here after work. I'll cook. You study. Then I can review the material with you, preferably in my lap. A couple of pop quizzes in between anatomy lessons. I'll even pack your snack packs for the next day. What do you think?"

"Hmm, I guess. Considering I have no clue when or where I'll find a job once I pass my exam, I might charge you for lap-sitting."

Darn it, she sounded so innocent when she talked dirty. "I'd gladly give you every nickel I have."

He buried his nose in the soft fold right above her shoulder, inhaling her fruity scent. Sighing in contentment, Eli just held her. Relishing the feel of his woman's body, listening as she breathed in and out.

Amarie's head rested on his chest. "You'd do that for me?"

"And more. It's important to you—so, it's our priority. But a word of caution. I've been accused of being a stickler for rules." Could she hear the gallop of his heart? Somehow, she'd wiggled her way under the ice-packed organ, and Eli wanted to kiss every inch of her in thanks.

"Well, I've been known to break a few." She wiggled her brows. "I accept."

And because he'd been putting off the question he should've asked days ago, he asked, "Do you want to attend Caleb and Gracie Lou's wedding with me?"

"I do" was all she said, but his chest tightened when she started to hum. With her fingers, she drew curls over his heart. "Next time, don't make me wait."

"Won't happen again." And he would honor his word. Not because of duty but because Amarie deserved better from him. Darn it, he was acting like a boyfriend, not a business partner.

Chapter Fifteen

ELI HAD SKIPPED, figuratively, down the dirt path between the clinic and his cabin. Call it what you will, but he had fallen under Amarie's spell. Last night he'd dreamed of Amarie's magic fingers wrapped around a part of him below the belt. He'd spent the workday harder than a Corso's jawbone. Could he be addicted to Amarie after one kiss?

"What do you mean someone is living in my house?" Red clouded his vision. Amarie's suggestions to his real estate listing had increased the online queries fivefold. Spotlighting the key features of the home with larger images while removing the pictures of the multiple peace gardens and the wasted square footage had boosted the viewings. But this...

"Mr. Calvary, please lower your voice, I can hear and I want to keep it that way."

This being his third agent, but the first to actually coax a buyer to return, he promptly bottled his anger, but the pressure continued to build.

"Who's in my house?"

"As I tried to explain. I went to show the house to an interested couple, and a woman answered the door."

"What woman?" Eli swallowed. Bile constricted his throat because he knew the answer.

"Your ex-wife?"

Impossible. Illogical. Then he heard her voice. Blood thundered in his ears before hell froze in his veins. Irrefutable. Cara had returned to their home. No. Never that. She had invaded his house. He was considering the likelihood that he could be addicted to Amarie after one kiss. The mention of Cara yanked him from starstruck to thunderstruck.

"Give her the phone," he snapped, biting off the curse clamoring in his head to break free.

He heard some rustling, then—

"Eli, honey."

The one voice he never wished to hear again.

"Cara, I'm not your honey. What are you doing in my house?"

"Please don't be upset. I have nowhere else to go," she sniffled.

He imagined her soft doe eyes, red-rimmed from crying. Black mascara, because she'd never be seen without her makeup, would streak down her pale cheeks.

"That was never your home. Or mine."

"Eli, why are you being so mean to me. I ran into a hiccup—"

"Keep my dog's name out of your mouth."

"Oh," she sighed, "you still have our dog."

"He was never our dog. He came after you left."

"Okay," she drawled. "I can see you're still your same old grumpy self."

"Cara, what is it that you want?"

"I need to stay in the house for a few months. Nine at the most, until I can get my life together."

"Nope." His response struck his own ears like a bullet,

tearing through any sympathy he would feel for anyone else in Cara's predicament. "It's on the market. It will stay on the market until it's sold."

"Eli," she whined. In the past, he would've softened like fresh apple butter on warm toast. Not anymore. "I don't have anywhere to go."

"Not my problem. You stole my savings knowing my father bankrolled it, liquidated my retirement account. Spend that."

"It's gone," she sobbed. "Seriously, how many times are you going throw that in my face? You were owed that money."

Eli's fury erupted. "Don't ever say that again."

"Fine, I'll keep your family secret. But the truth of it, whether you want to admit it, is we were married. Which made me family. The judge sided with me, remember? As your wife I had every right to that money."

"My father—" He swallowed. "It was a gift from father to son." A gift he had foolishly squandered on an ugly house and an even uglier divorce.

"Not really... and it's gone. Your father would've moved on by now," she retorted.

Eli sobered.

"And so is our marriage. I'll give you until the morning to get out of my house. If you're there tomorrow, the police will escort you off my property." He rarely lost control. And Cara... everything about her was reckless. Loving her had led him down the same destructive path. Fault lay with him for trusting her with information he'd never shared with his family. His father had taken the family's history with the Pendletons, the money situation to his grave. Eli should've done the same.

"Eli," she whispered, "where would you have me go?"

"Cara," he sighed, "you are no longer my responsibility."

"You didn't feel that way a few months ago. You made a promise to always provide for me."

"As your husband. As a man who loved you. I'm neither of those anymore."

"B-but, Eli."

"Be gone in the morning, Cara."

He was done talking to his past. The memories of what could have been were too painful to confront after a grueling day in the clinic. "Put the realtor back on the line."

"Hi, Mr. Calvary. What would you like to do about your, ah, ex-wife? The family is considering other properties." The realtor's tone was too chirper for the situation. Eli knew the woman probably felt uncomfortable having heard all his business, but it couldn't be helped. Reality had kicked him in the teeth when Cara had packed up and left. He had no reason to spare her the bruising he still felt.

"You let that family know that the house is still on the market. Have the locks changed. And," Eli paused, "whatever you do, do not give that woman a key."

He wanted Cara locked out of everything that was important to him, including that awful house. She would never possess the power to hurt him again.

"Understood Mr. Calvary. Thank you," she sighed. "Thank you so much."

He hung up the phone, more upset than he'd been in months. A part of him said that he didn't have to be mean to Cara, but he vibrated, his anger and disappointment a dog whistle on his eardrums. How dare she come back to him. How dare she ruin everything he had planned for their future. How dare she think his heart was still open and available to her.

Eli would be a fool to ever make himself that vulnerable.

That's when he remembered Amarie was on her way over to study with him for the upcoming licensure exam. As complementary as they were, he reminded himself not to get in too deep. Their attraction, though undeniable, required boundaries. He respected her and appreciated her business savvy. With Amarie he would never be in danger of having his heart broken. She was pretending, just like him and he would be wise to remember that in all their interactions… even when kissing was involved. Especially if kissing happened at the wedding.

Chapter Sixteen

THE DAY OF Caleb and Gracie Lou's wedding, Amarie just about bit her tongue at the delicious sensation that zinged through all her lady parts at the sight of Eli standing next to the white stallion in the floral-strewn bridal aisle. He was clad in a black leather, pinch-front, wide-brim Stetson, had a bolo tie with a gleaming cabochon onyx stone at his throat, and his powerful long legs were displayed in fitted black jeans. Amarie smoothed her free hand down her puff-sleeved champagne maxi dress, nervous. She'd taken extra care with her hair and makeup for the wedding. Eli, used to her in her signature purple and with her glittery toes, had yet to comment on her makeover.

Today she hoped to wow him. She'd purchased the designer outfit with Russell's credit card before the split. The Nordstrom sales associate had paired it with a chunky brushed-gold cuff bracelet and glass slipper wedge heels. She reapplied flavored nude gloss to her lips, readying her tastebuds to sop up Eli's ice-cream kisses, not wanting to miss a single drop of his creamy goodness when it happened. If he kissed her again, which she hoped he would, she would literally melt, like gummy-bear-goo-on-the-pavement melt. The thrill of attraction buzzing between them had been interesting, in a perplexing way. Mere weeks. She'd studied at his place, he'd fed her, quizzed her, but not kissed her like that first evening at his cabin. *Distant* wasn't the best word to describe his hesitancy, more like restrained, as if he might burst something if they locked lips again. Amarie wanted his kisses, and this formfitting number would help her bring Eli Calvary to his knees.

Mentally she counted to sixty-nine, a distraction technique from the riotous emotions of attending a wedding while trying not to think about her own. Her phone rang. She paused what she was doing to fumble in the grassy bed where she'd dropped it. Oh great, her mom was calling again. Amarie punched the megaphone icon, engaging the phone's audio speaker function.

"When you going to come to your senses?"

"Geez, thanks, Mom. Happy Saturday to you, too. Oh me, yeah I'm fine." Their most recent conversation had degraded faster than a hot turd in a chemical toilet. Nasty business it had been. Though Amarie had assured her mother every night, providing updates on the job, sprinkling a few details about the Calvarys, her mom worried.

"Where are you? What's all that noise in the background?"

"Gracie Lou's wedding reception starts in thirty minutes. Remember the goats I told you about—"

"Ah, yes," she chuckled. "The ones that kept vigil until Vali arrived in Service?"

"Yep, Billy, now spelled with a *y* instead *ie*, Jean, and Diana. Well, they were in the wedding party. I'm adjusting floral wreaths for the photos. Their necks are so short." She grinned, happy to work alongside the other women putting the finishing touches on the wedding venue for the final photos.

"Huh, sounds like a reel from America's funniest videos. Perfect, I reached you at just the right time. Russell's been calling your father, he's quite serious."

"I hope the two will be happy together, Mom."

"Amarie Walker, you know better. I swear you have a new attitude."

"I'm sorry, but how many times do I have to tell you, I don't wanna hear what Russell has to say."

"Well, I'm your mother and you need to listen. The man wants you back. Do you know how rarely this happens? That a woman can walk out on a man, and he'll take her back. Thank your lucky star."

"Luck? I spent years with a man who didn't love me, Mom. Not out of luck. I was scared." With Russell, Amarie was too scared to take a risk. Now, she was afraid not to.

"Amarie, baby," she sighed, a tightrope of exasperation strangling her concern. "Russell admitted he can't do without you."

"I can certainly do without him. I love my new life."

"Is that so, Miss Independent? Well, do you have a running car? No. Do you have your own place? No. Have you passed your exam yet? No."

Finished with the animals, Amarie snatched up her phone, pressing the receiver to her ear. "I can't, Mom."

They both stayed silent, listening to the other's ragged breaths. Waiting for the next stabbing counterattack.

"This man is offering you an opportunity to have all of those things, yet you're settling to attend some other woman's wedding instead of dancing at your own. Stop being foolish and stupid. You could be Mrs. Doctor Russell Feldman."

"And when he cheats," Amarie shot back, "you and I both know from experience he won't stop. When his next mistress is pregnant with his second child—what then, Mom?"

"Some men wander. It's not the end of the world."

"For you," Amarie announced. "I have decided there are certain footsteps I refuse to follow. A revolving door of partners plucking my husband when he's too restless to honor his vows to me is one of them." She raised her voice on the last part. Billy froze, his little body rigid as stone. Perfect, Amarie was frightening the wedding guests. "A revolving-door marriage is not good enough for me, Mom. You know what I would become if I accepted what Russell is offering?" Which wasn't much at all. "I'd be Mrs. Doctor Feldman and company. Russell is never going to stop cheating on me, don't you know that?"

Her mom fell silent for a moment, but then asked, "Is that such a high price to pay for your own house, your own car, and access to money?"

"Do you have your own home, or do you live in Dad's house? You've owned one car with your name on the title, and Dad hounded you until you gave that up." Thank goodness she had saved enough money to buy Prince before her mother abandoned him to a dusty used-car lot. "I want a husband who loves and respects me."

"Tell me, Amarie. Can you buy whatever you want?"

"Can you?" she snapped. A tense silence followed.

"I-I wanted you to have a better life, Amarie. If the day comes when you have the honor of being a mother, you'll grow to understand that your children may not understand your choices, your sacrifices. Love and respect didn't keep you fed. Love and respect didn't pay your college tuition."

"And I would rather starve than swallow my self-respect." An audible gasp from the other end of the line sliced Amarie's heart open. But she couldn't bring herself to rescind the words.

"When I left, did your father come looking for me? No."

Her mother's voice cracked. Amarie's throat constricted. The old pain and fears tried to snake around her resolve, weaken her conviction. "Do you think Dr. Reid Walker called your grandmother over me? No. You know Russell has called Vali. Did your father call one of my friends? No. Look at all the effort, honey, Russell is putting into getting you back. You're special to him."

"Not special. Useful. There's a difference."

"What's so wrong with being needed?" There was a hollow longing in her mother's voice, the echo of years of pouring into a broken marriage without being refilled. Amarie didn't feel the same way about Russell anymore. She didn't feel the same way about herself. Whatever they'd shared, he'd destroyed with lies and betrayal.

"Mom, I know you're worried, but don't be."

"A mother never stops worrying about her children."

"That's what Leah says."

"Leah is a wise woman. This is the last time I'll bring it up, but just consider what I'm saying. Not that you have to do what I'm suggesting. Just think about your future. I know how quick you are to put everyone before yourself. You're attached to this shiny new place, but will you really throw away six years of time invested with Russell for a month of happiness?"

When her mom put it that way...Amarie looked to find Eli's attention focused on her. When their gazes locked, his lips curled up into a broad smile, for *her*. Call her a hopeless romantic. Call her goofy. None of it could overshadow the charge of energy arcing between them. "Mom, we both have a lot to consider. I have to go. Happiness is waiting for me."

She beckoned him forward. And guess what, after days of questions about his intentions for their partnership turning into a courtship, watching him take long, determined strides to reach her, her pulse raced. Please let him have come to his senses.

"It's about time you got your gluteus maximus over here," she called, when he was within hearing range.

"Name the other two muscles that comprise the buttocks and I'll treat you to a spin on the dance floor."

Eli took his licensure review duties seriously. During work he'd recite the questions they'd studied the night before and wait for her to answer before moving on to the next body system. She had to admit his random pop quizzes had alleviated some, if not all, of her test anxiety. Educating came as natural to him as breathing. Their online followers often commented on his instructional abilities, too. She hadn't shared this with him, but she'd discovered another of Eli's passions.

"Urgh," she lamented in jest. "The medius and minimus," she answered with hesitation. "Now can a girl get one day off from learning?"

He looped her arm in his. "Not when there's so much I want to teach you."

Oh, her body heated at the idea of instructing her in ways to wring out every ounce of his pent-up passion. But she'd keep the conversation PG-13 ... for now.

"You and Hiccup looked rather dashing in the ceremony. Why didn't you tell me that Hiccup would be in the wedding?"

"I wanted you to be surprised when you saw Hiccup in his finest, gussied up in his tuxedo vest. I hope you took a picture for our followers. Jessie McGillacutty's golden poodle caught his scent during the processional. He's probably behind the barn with Cocktail's work vest unzipped. Jessie's pup never stood a chance."

"Stop it. Hiccup knows how to let a lady down without causing hurt feelings." Or leaving her confused. Eli's recent withdrawal had definitely left her frustrated... and needy, in a hot-under-the-pearls way. Really, what kind of lunatic kissed a woman crazy and then went cold turkey. Or in her overheated state, cold shower.

"Thank you." He wrapped her in his arms. "I have the most beautiful girl in the world smiling up at me," he whispered in her ear.

Amarie's legs went weak. Clearly the dress had worked its spell because she melted into Eli's strong body.

"Don't let the bride hear you." She giggled. Eli rewarded her with one of his rare smiles again.

"I won't tell if you don't," he teased, glancing down at the empty basket he held. "Kinda like you didn't tell me five kittens equaled your plus-one."

"The kittens were for Phoebe to play with. Her father wasn't going to keep her from them. Not on my watch." Amarie had returned to the farm Friday morning, excited to share her furry bundle with Phoebe. Matt had met her at the door, scowl in place, expression grim. Ruth had taken Phoebe back home. Amarie had returned to the clinic, crestfallen. By midday, Eli and Leah had comforted her and helped to solve her problem. On account of their attending high school together, Gracie Lou had made sure to include Ruth, and Phoebe, in the wedding party. She suspected several of the ladies, Leah, Gracie Lou, Lois Kline, and Matt had created small ways to keep their eyes on the mother-daughter pair. Amarie loved them all the more for their care and concern.

Eli took her hand in his, squeezing. "Come on, superwoman. Let's go show them how it's done on the dance floor before I take you home."

Normally she would refute the compliment with a string of examples of how ordinary she was. But witnessing the light brighten in Phoebe's eyes, the whispered thank-you when Ruth had hugged her—the joy was unmatched. Except maybe by Eli's lips on hers.

"My hero," she preened, running her hand along his hard bicep to rest in the crook of his elbow. "And so handsome in your cowboy couture."

"It's not the clothes. It's called swagger, sweetheart," he said, placing a quick peck on her cheek. Okay, a warm-up kiss. Now, if he would just slide east to her lips.

* * *

Once the newlyweds toasted their happily ever after, Amarie inhaled two slices of the delicious apple butter pinwheel wedding cake then reapplied her nude lip gloss. Let the kissing commence. She would swirl around him like buttercream icing on sweet bread fresh from a hot oven. Gooey, sugary, lickable goodness.

Large plywood sheets had been fastened to a lattice of four-by-fours to create a dance floor overlooking Cattail Creek. Cords of lighted globes strung in a tic-tac-toe pattern hung above them, the warm glow adding to the magic of matrimony. Chucky McDaniels, who she suspected got mistaken for the famous Charlie Daniels, approached the microphone. He ran his bow across his fiddle. A dark, eerie note cut the air. He paused a beat, and then his fellow musician fired up the electric guitar, followed by the drums with a toe-tapping, soulful blend of sound.

Leah and Mr. Johnson dipped and spun beside them. "Show the city girl how the cowboys boogie, Eli," Matt grinned, giving Amarie's a suggestive wink.

Leah waved. "Amarie might teach you a new step, son. You two just have fun."

"You remember the Watermelon Crawl line dance?" Eli called, his hand a heated mass at the small of her back. Turned out Eli had a knack for rhythm. He'd twirled her on the dance floor with fluid grace. Plenty of spins, dips, and two-steps happened that night. And she softened like chocolate fondue whenever he stepped close.

"How could I forget? That's the night I discovered homemade pickles and Gery the gerbil prelaunched our TikTok campaign." The Black Bear regulars had been enthusiastic in their support of the bachelor auction and spreading the word. They already had over five thousand new followers. The daily bid totals had increased, too. She and Eli were one step closer to achieving their mutually beneficial goal. But a little voice in her brain asked a question she had refused to answer: Could she leave Service if her career called for a relocation when so much of what she held dear resided right here in this tiny mountain town?

"Yes. Lead the way."

"Daddy, no. Please don't take them."

That was Phoebe's tiny voice. Amarie stilled in Eli's arms. The music faded. The compulsion to defend and help those in need, especially a child, superseded personal happiness. After growing up in a home watching her mother bullied day after day, her self-preservation skills were honed. She wanted to protect Phoebe for the eleven-year-old little girl who had needed a champion. If she could save Phoebe, just maybe she was on the path to saving herself. Amarie's entire body shook. Or maybe it was her courage roaring to life after a long hibernation. Before she registered the next action step, her feet carried her in the direction of the growing chaos taking place on the wooden bleachers.

Eli bellowed to her. "Amarie. Slow down."

She ignored him, just like the father ignoring the sobs of his wife and daughter. Memories of the little girl she'd been, the one without a savior, armed her for this battle. Time stopped for no one, but she could stop this tragedy from happening for this one child. The scene unfolding before the wedding party and town folks rocked Amarie to her core.

"No. No," Phoebe cried, clutching Formerly to her chest.

"Give me that kitten, you hear me, girl?"

"Bucky, please don't do this," Ruth pleaded, her hand grappling with her husband and the kitty he held aloft. "She's your daughter. Just let her play with them."

Eli grabbed Amarie from behind, pulling her to a stop. "Let me handle this."

"But—"

Eli's thinned his lips. "I got this."

"Fine," she huffed. "But I will bite him."

He chuckled. "Got it, Mama Bear."

They approached the Buchanans, with the others standing by to assist.

"Put the kittens in the basket, Bucky."

The man spun on his heel to face Eli, swaying, but he didn't fall. He held Raspberry, Graffiti, Artist, and Formerly in his grimy hands, thick dirt under his nails. Amarie frowned as the stench of days-old musk and corn liquor assaulted her delicate nose. Which said a lot since she worked in an animal clinic. The kittens didn't seem to appreciate escalating tension, meowing, *Help me, help me, please*. Well, that was a bit of a dramatic interpretation on her part. But either way, they clawed at their captor's brutish forehead with gusto.

"Wh-what are you gon-na do ta stop me, Eli?" Bucky

drew his words out at odd intervals, the syllables swerving off-road before crashing in a slur of extra *sss* and *ii*s. "You a lover and a fighter, now?"

Eli towered over Bucky. Did the man seriously want this to get physical? Noah had opted out of the wedding, choosing to attend the bachelor party only. Tobias, well, he'd decided to work so the others could enjoy the festivities. Even without his brothers, by the stern expression of the other men flanking the family, including the minister, Eli had a calvary if it came to blows.

Eli released an audible sigh. "Ruth, you and Phoebe come over here."

Bucky spit a glob of tobacco at Eli's boots. A string of tinted saliva dribbled down his chin.

"You and the brat stay put, Ruth," he snarled, a clear and present threat in his tone.

Eli didn't say a word. He clamped one hand on Bucky's shoulder. The other man winced but said nothing. When he tried to wiggle free, Eli's knuckles visibly blanched.

"Put the kittens in the basket," Eli enunciated, thrusting the grass-woven carrier at Bucky.

Reluctant but compliant, he deposited each kitten in the carrier. "This ain't right, you interfering between a husband and wife."

Eli gave him a rag doll shake. "What ain't right is you believing Ruth and Phoebe don't have options. Our door. Matt's door is always open to them. The woman loves you. I respect that. But she has options if she ever wants to leave your hind parts in the rearview mirror."

"Sure does," Amarie said, walking right up to Ruth and wrapping her in a big hug. Several of the wedding attendees affirmed Eli's statement with a concert choir of *Yep. Ain't that the truth. We got your back, Ruth!*

"Give the basket to your daughter, Bucky." Eli's tone made it clear that if Bucky made the wrong decision, he'd suffer the consequences.

Stiff and shaky, the father handed the basket to Phoebe. "Here you go, kid."

Phoebe added a wide-eyed Formerly to the bunch before taking the gift.

"Thank you, Daddy."

Amarie pushed back tears. How could a father intentionally hurt the family who loved him this much? Gosh, Eli could have humiliated the man. Instead, he chose to lead him to the right answer. Be a better man for his family. Hopefully, years from now, Phoebe would remember the good parts, that her father had chosen her happiness over his selfish need to punish them.

Matt came forward, taking Bucky by the arm.

"I'll make sure this fella gets home safe and sound. You and your woman go on back to having fun." Eli nodded and released his grip. Bucky sagged in relief.

"Come here, my fearless girlfriend."

And oh boy, her, fearless? And did he say *girlfriend* aloud? She hoped that was a prophetic word. Like really, speak a new Amarie into existence.

Eli gestured, crooking his finger in Amarie's direction, but before she could comply, he entered her atmosphere, tall, dark, solid, a mountain protecting her from any storm. Amarie felt Eli everywhere. Their minds melded, their bodies blended into one of those sensual man-woman sculptures of soft curves, hand and hand, hip to hip, impossible to distinguish a beginning or an end, infinite.

"You were amazing," she mouthed, inhaling him in. His warmth soaked beneath her skin bringing with it rich notes of churned earth and mountain breeze over cool waters.

"The whole 'put the kittens in the basket,' so gangsta. I still have goose bumps."

"Stop talking," he whispered, lifting his fingers to push one of her errant curls behind her ear. "You're like a shield-maiden of women and children. But when your boyfriend says he's got you, I got you. No more charging into battle without me."

"Hmm, as a shield-maiden—your words, not mine— I make no promises. You'll just have to stay ready," she quipped, meeting his eyes. A gasp escaped her parted lips at what she saw there. Protection. Promises. Passion.

"Duly noted," he whispered, and then he pressed his lips to hers.

"Finally," she sighed into his mouth. His taste exploded on her tongue, dark, rich, and spiced. Whistles and "put a ring on it" catcalls seemed to spur Eli on. With one hand, he angled her head, and with the other, he gave her bottom a quick squeeze.

If she described their first kiss as thorough, this one moved mountains. Yes, insides liquefied, rivers overflowed, and she moaned in satisfaction. As Eli deepened the kiss, caressing her tongue with his, Amarie wanted to rip her own panties off. Really, why even wear the things when she wanted to cavewoman cub him and drag him back to her lair?

"Amarie," someone called, "heads up." When she broke away from Eli, dazed and swimming in a dopamine fog, a bouquet of golden sunflowers separated by white and yellow daisies was about to hit her in the head. Geesh, who's ill-timed idea was this? Gracie Lou's of course. Though she appreciated the sentiment, she'd much rather keep kissing her prince. Her first instinct was to back up, but then she stepped forward, both arms extended. Spreading her fingers wide, she reached for the symbol of good things to come. The satin ribbon hooked on her thumb.

"Yay," the women cheered. "Amarie and Eli sitting in a tree, k-i-s-s—"

She looked at Eli, smiling, and he didn't turn away. Reminiscent of *The Lion King*, Amarie raised the fragrant bundle high, balanced in both hands. "I-be-a-winner," she sang aloud in the *Circle of Life* cadence.

Caleb, the happy groom, called to all the party people from beneath the white satin-wrapped pavilion. Once he had their attention, he raised a full mug in toast. "Come on, folks; it'll take more than one Bucky to break up our good time. Y'all, just look at the cat-that-ate-the-canary-grin on Eli." Caleb drank from his mug before continuing. "You saved us from having to take Bucky behind the barn to put him out of his misery. It's me and Gracie's wedding day, and we're putting our money on Eli's city girl to win his hand in the bachelor auction."

That would be a miracle considering Amarie wasn't a registered bidder in the auction. How fair would it be if his pretend partner won the auction instead of a woman Eli might genuinely be interested in for the long-term? Their arrangement had a finite date, sort of, indirectly. Though she had to admit, this fake partnership involved real feelings. And she wasn't alone in a breach of their agreed-upon policy.

A chorus of *heck yeah*s, *hee haw*s, and *me too*s rang out. Next thing she knew, she and the flowers were in Eli's arms. Warm and, dare she think it, desired.

"That's enough singing," he whispered in her ear, swaying as the band started up with a slow dance song of lovers and turned-down lights. "We've got more kissing to do."

Indeed, they did.

Chapter Seventeen

MIDWEEK HAD ARRIVED with a surge of post-wedding business for Calvary Vet. Amarie's heroics on Ruth and Phoebe's behalf had spread beyond Service. News of her investment partnership took on a new life. The added attention boosted the Calvary brothers' bachelor auction bids, too. Donations poured in and the appointments slots filled as fast as Amarie opened the booking portal. Seemed folks wanted their pets examined by the Sexy Kitty Vet and his fierce assistant. He'd expanded their daily operations to include half-day Saturday clinics, and of course, more TikTok videos. They were saving Calvary Clinic, together.

Spending his day with Amarie made work easier. The nights with her under his roof, studying anatomy and textbooks, not each other, had morphed into cruel and unusual punishment. As her licensure exam date approached, Eli noticed she'd begun to second-guess her responses to questions she'd answered with ease weeks prior. Also, she'd polished her toenails twice in two hours, trading a French violet for a brighter heliotrope with pale-purple polka dots. While he'd mistaken it for vanity early on, he now understood she used self-care as a method to control anxiety.

They arrived home after six o'clock. He fed the animals and started dinner, while she sat cross-legged on his couch, her purple gel-ink pen perched over her notebook. Yep, notes by hand. Everything else, she became a computer cyborg who only spoke SEO optimization and keyword metadata, but notes needed to be old-school.

"How about R&B with dinner tonight?" Eli asked, popping a grape tomato in his mouth. He scrolled through his phone's playlist, searching for a song to set the mood. Needing Amarie to feel wanted and relaxed in his space had grown in importance. It pleased him to do little things that brought a smile to her face—keeping Pepsi on ice for needed caffeine bursts, adding a cotton-ball dispenser and nail polish remover pads to his bathroom toiletries, and of course, a steady supply of his momma's biscuits. Just for kicks, he'd tried to replicate the recipe a few times.

"I need to study."

"Let's do both. What are the three smallest bones in the body and their location?"

When Amarie didn't answer, he kicked the refrigerator door closed with his foot. "A woman who does not respond doesn't eat."

"I'm number crunching, duh. Mere mortal, that's you, will have to wait."

"Your exam doesn't accept excuses. Neither do I. The answer, please." He added that last bit to soften the not-so-gentle nudge.

"The malleus, incus, and the stapes. All three are located in the middle ear." She stuck out her tongue at him. "Happy now?"

"Actually, I'm kinda turned on."

She rolled her eyes, but then she laughed. "You are a horndog."

"Guilty as charged."

"Stop distracting me," she whined. "The auction has eight hundred and twenty-two financial supporters."

Amarie had constructed a stepladder approach to get her started each day, reproducible patterns that, once engrained, she acted upon in an automated sequence. Intelligent and innovative, she'd developed a system for analyzing their social media campaign effectiveness with efficiency.

"Thanks to your social media prowess." He dialed the stove back to a simmer under his pots.

"Oh," she cooed, "talk dirty to me, Dr. Sexy Kitty."

Pulling the baking dish from the oven, he placed the hot pan on a trivet. The caramelized sugar on his apple crisp smelled almost as sweet as Amarie—nah, not even close. "Keep that up and somebody's not getting dessert."

"Aw, no fair. The punishment doesn't fit my crime. Oh, let me check our insights before I upload the video of you explaining some of the hidden dangers of pet food marketed as organic."

He'd rediscovered his passion for teaching. Providing accurate animal care advice required research. Like Amarie, he found himself back in the books, crafting evidence-based medicine in everyday language. And educating against the ever-growing body of misinformation and at times danger-ous trends circulating on social media.

"When it comes to calling me out of my name—I'm the judge and jury."

"Meh." She shrugged. "Would you change your mind if I told you..." She scribbled something on her pad. "Eli," she paused, "the video of you at the wedding with the bas-ket of kittens went viral," she screamed. "We just broke the fifteen-thousand-dollar mark."

Eli stilled, not quite believing his hearing. "Say that again."

"We. Have. Received. Over. Fifteen thousand dollars from online donations and auction bids." Amarie jumped to her feet, dancing, shouting, chanting, "We're famous!" in her pretend megaphone. "And there's more."

"Stop holding out on me, woman." There was a double meaning there. Eli would broach the subject of her spending the night, every night, in his arms, after dinner.

"#KittyKibbles cat food is following our page. The vice president of branding sent a private message. They want a meeting with the president of Calvary Veterinary Clinic. I'm adding them to the list."

"And that is better than fifteen thousand dollars, why?"

"Companies pay social media influencers—that's you, well, Dr. Sexy Kitty Vet—to promote their product. This could be a bigger payday than we ever imagined."

"Okay then. Let's celebrate." As the exam date approached, Amarie had put their one-on-one on a timer. Her nine o'clock alarm would signal her to pack up her books, hand them to him, and he, with a petrified yule log in his pants, would walk his girlfriend home in silent agony. It couldn't happen. Not tonight. They had a future that required a new notebook, not just for the business, either. Tonight, he had a plan that would satisfy both their needs, especially the one clawing at them to answer the call of the wild, naked and horizontal.

"It's already more than I hoped for." Working side by side with Amarie, learning from her, had awakened a desire in him beyond the roadmap his father had left for him to follow. Eli didn't necessarily enjoy the daily social media engagement demands, but he didn't hate it, either. He was sharing himself in ways he'd never expected. And Service had embraced the vision, supporting him and Amarie as they worked together. She was one of them.

"People I've never met comment on videos like we're

best friends." Finding the ballad playlist, he punched the play icon. Soft notes written over piano chords filled the kitchen.

"Hey, I grew up an only child with questionable social skills. Until I met Vali, my online community were my friends."

He loved that she shared this side of herself—the vulnerable woman who had to work hard to excel, who devised plans to reach her goals, even social ones. Most of his life, he'd emulated his father, but when he looked at Amarie, he wanted to be the man she would choose to spend her life with.

"You know, I feel like you are two different people. The way you describe yourself isn't how I see you."

"Thank the stars, you got this awesome version of me."

"I do, you know, thank heaven for you, Amarie." The added publicity saw the Calvary bank balance increasing at a steady trajectory. His chest had swelled with pride when payday arrived for his Amarie, his mom, and yeah, he even paid himself a little something this week.

"Explains the shirtless cooking." She grinned, a blatant attempt at skirting the conversation about their relationship moving to the next level.

Tomorrow they'd be in his truck headed to the testing center in Morgantown for her licensure exam. Bursts of animated conversation separated by long stretches of silence, the second clue that nerves had walked home with them. Passing the test weighed heavy on her mind, but he thought her feelings for him might be tangled in the equation. Their kiss—scratch that, their kisses—over breakfast, in the office, on the farm, heck, Hiccup had taken to smooching the kittens, had become more urgent, demanding a deeper exploration of their attraction. So, this evening he set the mood for seduction. Two logs crackled in the fireplace, the pop of kindling akin to the spark arcing between them. Autumn had reached the mountain early, bringing a blanket of orange and gold hues to the woodlands and cooler nights. The felines, intrigued by the dancing flames, used Hiccup's hind legs to ladder up his spine, their fixed gazes following the shadows like a bouncing ball.

"What if Kitty Kibbles wants to cross-promote with us? Or host a live stream. If you do, the women will go crazy for you, Eli."

"Will you?" He had his mind set on seeing one woman laid out naked in his bed.

"I adore you, Dr. Sexy Kitty. I venture to claim the title as your best fan," she said, but failed to elaborate on his true question. How did she think of him, Eli Calvary?

What he knew: she liked kissing him. Touching him. But there were questions she left unanswered. "Look at how much your account has grown in three weeks. This could be the push we need to reach our goals, Eli."

"Nope. Not going live. Besides, the TikTokers see everything I do, every single day."

"But imagine if you talked with them. Not about animal care or the practice. Have you seen Tobias's videos? His followers adore how he shares his feelings after the emergency callouts."

"Good for him. The answer's still no, but we have a bunch of reasons to celebrate. The auction, your exam in the morning, and that you finally listened to me and hit the submit button for a graduate nurse job."

"I'm still nervous."

He tossed chopped onions and mushrooms into the pan with the butter. When they hit the hot skillet, fragrant steam hit his nose.

"Woman, you know everything there is about patient safety and health maintenance."

"Yum." She inhaled. "Smells delicious over there."

"Dinner's almost ready."

She closed her notebook. "I think you should offer Ruth a part-time job in the clinic." Not the first time she'd suggested he hire her replacement.

He paused. "We run the clinic together."

"I know. But I'm also done with the operating manual. It'll give us more time to live stream content and interact with the followers. One more paycheck, I can get Prince out of the repair shop. I could showcase more of Noah's work. There's only so many shirtless poses he can share."

He chuckled. "There's no rush for your car. Has it been that bad riding shotgun with me?"

"No, but…you know. I'll have to drive to my nursing job. When I get it," she muttered, but he heard her loud and clear.

Work that didn't involve him seeing her every day. What if she wanted to move off Calvary land? He'd encouraged her to apply for jobs in the neighboring Landing Falls. The tourists had transformed the once-quiet mountain town into rows of souvenir shops, eclectic coffee houses, and fancy eateries with menu items his college-educated vocabulary struggled to pronounce.

"Noticed you had more followers on PerkyLateBloomer, too."

"Yeah," she said absently. "When I added my CashApp handle, I never considered people would donate to my account."

Seems their followers speculated that PerkyLateBloomer and #SexyKittyVet had a thing going on. They would be right. Many of his female followers had placed bids under an account created in Amarie's name. At first, they'd laughed it off. But each week the bids for her to win grew. Folks wanted to see them together after the auction, even if she didn't. Eli would donate to her account... if she wanted to keep him, forever.

He plated their pork chops and ladled a generous helping of mushroom and onion gravy on top before pulling the potatoes from the oven. "Spend the night with me."

"Hmm, I thought we were talking about our final week's campaign?"

He understood her hesitancy.

"We can do some naked studying."

"Are you suggesting both activities together or separately?"

"Not picky. As long as you're naked."

"That takes the pressure off." She smiled, but those deep brown eyes he got lost in every time she looked at him clouded with emotion.

"Does it?"

"No, I'm expected to excel at two unrelated sports, man."

"What's the probability of you allowing me to lead this hands-on demonstration?"

"Is this Dr. Sexy Kitty dirty talk?"

"Not dirty. Serious."

"Eli." She sighed. Uh, that wasn't good. "I dream of seeing you naked. Really, I do. I mean with your big feet. My imagination, I just, whew. I have huge, with a capital H, expectations..." she trailed off. "But what about tomorrow? Remember, I'm the dopey romantic who wants the morning after to be the first day of forever, not a pill."

"Let's see where this leads tonight."

"You said the same thing to the Black Bear when people asked if I was your girlfriend."

He pulled a wine glass from the cabinet for her and a beer from the fridge for himself.

"My feelings, real. My care and concern for you, real. Me wanting to start every day with you by my side, real. The decision, the question you have to answer, is what you feel for me, and I know it's more than money that keeps you here. Is what you feel for me real enough to take this next step with me?"

"Eli—"

He interjected, not sure he could bear the rejection before spilling his feelings like a puppy stepping in his water bowl and turning the whole thing over. This could get messy.

"I'm not the suit-and-tie kind of man"—he crossed the room handing her a glass of West Virginia's finest Marechal Foch—"that you're accustomed to."

Amarie palmed his cheek with one hand, accepting the fruity wine in the other. "You're better," she whispered. "You're the best man I've ever known, Eli Calvary. Brave, compassionate, dedicated, faithful. And the absolute best kisser I've had the pleasure of smooching on a regular basis."

He leaned in for a kiss. "How about a permanent basis? Stay the night. Every night."

"After," she said with a smile.

He nodded, but not in agreement, before returning to the kitchen. "What? We'll both explode in sexual frustration. We're burning hot for each other."

"You'll be my treat after I finish the exam."

"That's your plan. Using me as an after-dinner mint?"

"Never, Eli Calvary. You are a full-course meal with an appetizer, dessert, and hot coffee. But if we're going to mess up the best real relationship I've ever had, I'd rather have my exam behind me. There's no ugly-cry exemption."

She sank her teeth in her bottom lip, the hold punishing. The filtered water he poured splashed over the tumbler, spilling onto the stone counter.

"You think I'll break your heart?" He took long strides to reach her and plucked her off the couch. She came up on her toes, wrapping her arms around his neck. Eli met her halfway.

"Don't think that way, okay," she pleaded more with those wide expressive eyes. "The way you make me feel, it's like a windstorm wrapping all around me and just when I think it might tear me apart, I'm floating. Instead of being torn apart, I'm being reassembled, all the little pieces of me that were scattered and I thought were lost have drifted back to me on the sweetest breeze. And it's so warm and comforting that I feel like I can't do without it. And because of that, I'm terrified that if I mess up, this leash that has us tangled up together, this sweet current that blew you into my life, will snatch you away just as fast as you swept in. I'll be scattered in so many directions that I'll never find myself again."

"You, my brave shield-maiden of endless possibilities, have never been lost. The men in your life were too blinded by their own roadblocks to appreciate all of you. When you look at me, you make me wanna soar, to reach for stars that I never saw before you pointed them out to me. I'm more sure of myself than I've ever been with you by my side. We're better together and, I—I don't want to be apart anymore. We've built a foundation. Let's keep going together, real in every way that's important to you and me. I'm scared, too, of breaking us. Of failing you. But, if I ever did, I promise you I'll fight for us. You are the best thing that ever wandered into my life. The last guy let you get away. I won't, Amarie."

"Now I'm the one with my tongue wagging. What am I supposed to say to that?"

"Tell me that I've met with success in seducing your mind. That I've earned the pleasure of touching every part of your body."

"Wow."

Amarie stared at him, her eyes softened with wonder and awe. She had never been properly seduced. An injustice he would remedy if she gave herself over, trusted him with her pleasure.

Eli chuckled. "Give more than that, sweetheart. All you have to do is say yes…or no." He cupped her bottom and squeezed. "If you're afraid you can't handle my Great Dane, I could just eat your appetizer tonight?"

Her breath hitched.

"You, sir, are no gentleman." She nipped his bottom lip, then soothed the ache with her tongue. "I like it," she whispered.

"You have no idea." He gave a lopsided grin, spinning her in his arms.

"What are you doing?"

"This is one of my favorite songs." A new song started on the Alexa. He placed her hand on his shoulder, and the other at his waist. She narrowed the space between them. "Dance with me."

They started to sway in rhythm to the beat.

"The thing is, I don't have a good track record with men. Being in a relationship for six years with a man who was cheating wrecks your confidence. I mean, maybe I was doing something wrong."

He tightened his hold in reassurance. "You're doing everything right with me. No one outside of this room matters." He moved his face next to Amarie's. "For you, I'd give a lifetime of stability, anything you want of me…" he whispered the lyrics in her ear.

"I would be lying to say that you don't make me happy, the happiest I've ever been in my adult life. Happiness is an emotion that I've never been able to trust. But I trust you with my happiness. Honestly, it would crush me if you broke my heart."

"Same here, sweetheart." He hummed, placing his chin on the top of her head. Eli's heartbeat took off, a gazelle at top speed. Gosh, his body was strung tight, ready to release. His erection stood at attention. Everything else lined up, eyes forward, ready to run an Olympic heat.

"Eli, I have to be number one. I've played second in my own life for years. There's no way I'm going backward. Not even for you. So, it has to be about you and me—then we build our relationship on respect and placing each other first."

"I agree, sweetheart. And honesty."

"And one more thing, if we start this, dinner will get cold," Amarie whispered.

He lowered his forehead until it rested against hers. "I can heat it up."

"You already have." She swallowed, then lifted her eyes to his.

"In that case, let me take your temperature." He lowered his head and covered her mouth with his. This time he kissed her long and deep, savoring the flavor of sweet brewed black tea on her tongue. When he picked her up off her feet, her legs came up and wrapped around him. The heat at her center seared him, obliterating past wounds. With Amarie he had a new start, one she'd groomed him to perfection to embrace.

"You make me hungry for more," she gasped.

He threaded his fingers through her hair, angling her head. "Then let me feed you, sweetheart." And then he reclaimed her mouth, not breaking contact when he carried her into his bedroom.

Chapter Eighteen

ELI'S BODY WAS chiseled from marble. Three words. Delicious. Thick. Cut. Not only was his jaw cut, but so were his pecs, his abs, and his thighs—good lawd—his calves could support her weight for days. Absolute magnificence. She'd seen parts of his body, but looking at the total package, Amarie panted, literally, like a canine in heat. He would ruin her for other body types. His body was a poetic specimen of male anatomy, and his pecs a detailed chapter she could study for hours.

"Tell me. What do you want to happen first?"

It was a question that no man had ever asked her before. She'd expected him to tell her what she had to do to satisfy him. Eli wanted her to share in their lovemaking, but she didn't know where to start.

"Surprise me," she said, reclining on his bed.

A wolfish smile spread across his face. "Great answer."

The gleam in his eyes was utter devastation to her senses. She was already halfway to full power from pure attraction. Would he feel the same about her body? Was there such a thing as self–slut shaming before she actually got to the act of slutting?

"Hey," he called. Amarie looked up and the way he drank in her full curves erased her fears.

"All you have to do is say yes…or no. Grab the headboard with both hands." Oh yes, he took the decision right out of her *hands*.

"Yes," she whispered.

He chuckled. "Are you toying with me?"

"Absolutely not. I love being swept off my feet and…and you do it so often. Promise you won't stop after you get the kitty cat."

"Kitty cat?"

"You know…the one with the warm center." She raised one brow, before using her tongue in a slow sweep of her lips.

Eli eye's sparkled with mischief. "Will this kitty purr?"

"Depends? If you lick her just right," she said, not shy at all with her soon-to-be lover.

When he kissed a slow trail from her ankle, the sensitive crease at her knee, alternating the firmness of his mouth with the nip of his teeth, she shivered.

Eli took his time caressing every curve. Kisses rained down, drenching her from the inside out. He found unchartered territory on her body, exposed sensitive areas, and exploited others. One by one, he felled her defenses, each touch demanding her surrender. How he loved her—words couldn't describe the tenderness of his caresses. She felt his gaze, a tangible cord binding them together.

Warmth spread over her breast before he covered it with his tongue. He moved on to the next. She whimpered at the momentary absence of his mouth. Her breath quickened when he made a lazy sweep with his tongue down her abdomen. Her belly quivered. The more he teased and tasted, the higher her need for all of him raged beyond her control.

"Eli, please."

"Can I kiss you?"

Amarie sucked in a breath and lifted her head. She offered her mouth.

"Not there, sweetheart."

At the brush of his warm breath against her inner thigh, she gasped.

"Yes," she moaned.

The slow rumble that sounded in his chest seemed to vibrate through her. He feasted again and again until her body could hold back no longer.

Just as her pleasure burst forth, so did her voice.

"Eli," she screamed, a hoarse cry until she lay wordless, weightless, hopelessly against love's allure.

When Eli entered her sometime later, safe and protected, it was unlike anything she had ever felt before. The initial controlled thrust, the stretch, the sensation of complete fullness. The emptiness that clung to her, ever present, vanished. He lowered his head, inhaled her scent, before pressing a kiss to her cheek.

"Breathe, my love."

And she obeyed. He rewarded her with a slow roll of his hips. Amarie started to move with him. Their rhythm came so naturally. It felt like the sweetest song, an original tune that they wrote with the music of their bodies conducting the beats, as they learned the harmony together.

"You're beautiful, Amarie."

"Tell me that again," she demanded.

"You feel perfect for me."

"Yes." The words washed over her. Warm water covering her head, her heart. She plunged deeper, and deeper still.

"It's true," he whispered. "I don't ever want us to end."

Wave after wave pushed her farther yet somehow drew

her closer to him. Instead of drowning, Amarie floated, stroked in the direction of the building current pulling her body into a depth unknown before Eli. For the first time in her life, she knew what it meant to be worshipped. Poems rewrote themselves. She understood the great sonnets anew. The sound of love echoed in her voice, powerful, transformative, reborn. She felt the beauty of being connected to another life outside of her own. Eli groaned. Her pleasure had fueled his. It gave her confidence. Amarie, after years of hiding what she wanted, took what she needed. She knew that if she lost herself in the darkest of oceans, he would find her because he marked every trembling inch of her flesh. And Eli, well, he thanked her, over, and over, and over again.

Chapter Nineteen

ELI WISHED HE'D lit the corner fireplace in his bedroom. Amarie didn't seem to mind the cooler nights, but he wanted her to feel safe and warm in his arms. He'd lived a life of control. Controlled by rules, first his father's, then the military's. As the oldest son, he had a duty of responsibility to his family, to his community, and to the Calvary legacy. But with Amarie, he felt the rush of his blood, could taste the hunger to claim her on his tongue.

Amarie required nothing of him. Freedom came in many forms. After hours spent in her company, she'd taught him the beauty of giving—educating others, answering questions from strangers wanting to care for their beloved pets, quizzing her about the nursing process every night—not out of duty, but for the joy of helping the next person.

He was simply Eli, not a son, not a brother, not a business owner. Amarie gave of herself. And Eli, he wanted to share with her everything he hid from the rest of world, his fears, his doubts, and his heart. With her, he could be a man loving his woman.

"You make me happy. I more than need you, I—I want you, Amarie."

With his confession, a window he'd sealed away after the divorce opened.

With Amarie, he had it all. Family. Career. The support of a compassionate and capable woman. For the first time, his life and his love were focused in the same direction, the direction that led to Amarie. No longer did he have to do life alone. Amarie shared his values. Heck, she'd given him a new vision for his future. And it included her.

Amarie shared his vision. Heck, she'd shaped his vision. Their minds synced, and now, their bodies hummed. With his body, Eli tried to show Amarie how much she mattered, how she completed him.

He pushed himself harder. She dug her nails into his back, spurring him. He loved her enthusiasm in and out of bed.

"Is this what you want?" he asked.

It was a loaded question not just for him but for her.

"Yes." The softest yes hit him the hardest, a hammer to his heart. Eli absorbed the blow and used it to power them closer to completion. The added roll of her hips had Eli biting into his lip in ecstasy.

"I want to be with you."

"Thank you," he breathed. He lowered his head, inhaled their comingled scent. The combination of sweet and spice heightened his arousal.

"For what?" she breathed.

"Being uniquely you always."

Interlocking his fingers with hers, he pushed them toward the pleasure they both craved. When they tumbled over the edge, light exploded out behind his eyes and he poured himself into her, feeling her muscles tighten around him.

Minutes passed, Eli lay there, drawing and repainting

the portrait of their lovemaking. Panting for air, he rolled to his back, then dropped his feet to the floor.

"Eli?" Amarie placed on hand on his back, her tongue soothing, her tone questioning. He twisted to face her.

"You're the best thing that's ever come into my life. I meant what I said, too, about us being real. This is our beginning."

She regarded him with those wide doe eyes, and then nodded.

"Me too."

He scooped her up into his arms, the sheet tangled around her feet.

"Hey," she exclaimed with a hoarse rasp to her voice. "Where are we going?"

"The next round will happen under the stars." Eli walked out his front door onto Calvary land with his woman in his arms.

* * *

Hours later, Eli collapsed onto his back, chest heaving from exertion. The night had grown cooler, the stars overhead shone brighter. Next to him, Amarie hummed another tune from her Prince playlist. He'd downloaded the artist's greatest hits compilation after their day on the farm, so he recognized the melody. But most important, he was learning when she was happy. He wondered if she was aware of the brush of her toes against his as she hummed off-key with a dizzying array of rising and falling octaves. Eli had never been much for playing footsies, but he would walk across burning sand for more nights like this one. The heat from Amarie's lush body, with all its curves free for him to enjoy, felt too far away. He reached for her, a satisfying rumble in his chest when she saddled up to his hard planes.

"Hmm," she sighed, tossing one bent leg over his. "You're hired."

He curled his arm across her shoulder. "Wasn't aware I'd auditioned."

She lifted her head from his chest, her face in shadow, but the smile parting her lips warmed his insides like a summer sun.

"The first time always is, Mr. Calvary."

"By my count, we bypassed the first of everything hours ago. You screamed *yes* half a dozen times. I'm thinking I earned myself a bonus and a raise."

"Huh, depends on if I pass my exam."

Eli grinned. "In that case, I better give you a fourth injection, clear up your doubts. Good lovin' is a miracle cure."

"Funny, hehe," she trailed off. "I know your body, but I'm still figuring out what makes Eli, the man, tick beyond saving Calvary land."

Boy, did she ever. Amarie had been as eager to explore his muscles as he'd been to taste her curves. With every lick of her tongue she'd broken him down, a wild horse tamed one well-placed love bite at a time.

"What do you want to know?" Being this amenable, vulnerable, for any woman should have terrified him, but Amarie had chosen to be in his corner from day one. He trusted her. And he realized he trusted himself in her loving embrace. Her genuine affection for living life in the moment and making others feel loved and valued had touched him. Being inside her, connected in the most intimate of ways, had transformed him.

"Tell me something about you that no one else knows. Something you entrust to me—only me," she whispered.

Eli's heart rate sped up. Amarie was asking him to trust her to be his *one*. His fears. His failures. His future—he no longer had to bear the weight alone. He'd thought about his choices, his mistakes, his dreams since Amarie had walked through his door. But the one secret he'd never shared with anyone, he did with her.

"This isn't the first time we've been in jeopardy of losing this land."

Amarie's breath hitched.

"My sophomore year of college, my dad hurt his back, couldn't work at full speed for more than a year. With the medical bills and monthly expenses, the finances underwater, including the mortgage, Dad tapped their meager retirement fund to keep the family from drowning in debts. It wasn't enough," he paused, not wanting to break a vow between father and son.

"Whoa, Leah had to be scared for your father—and the business, of course," she tacked on. Eli pulled his marshmallow heart of a woman closer. As a nurse, she would think of the person before any material possessions. Cara would've reversed the order.

"My father never told her. To this day, my family thinks I went off to college and fell in love with the city. In truth, I picked up a job at the animal shelter in addition to my work-study position. I couldn't afford to miss a day of work or studying."

Amarie placed her small hand over his heart. The small gesture touched more than his heart; it touched his mind. Here lay a compassionate woman who'd touched every aspect of his being, both physical and emotional, to the point where Eli felt safe confiding his darkest secret. One he continued to shield from his entire family.

"Your father would be proud of your dedication to the family and the land he sacrificed for. My father paid for my college tuition, all six years." She flashed a grin at him.

Hiccup, who'd ambled off the porch after the adult activities had ended, yawned and flopped down on the blanket at his feet.

"I never wanted to burden my folks. Tobias and Noah were high schoolers, the money stayed funny. The ends didn't meet for years after Dad's injury."

"You're a good son, Eli."

He snuggled her closer, driving the chill from his soul. "That's questionable. Enough 'bout me. Your turn."

"The year I turned eleven, my mom packed our suitcases in Prince's trunk, and we left my dad."

"That had to be scary."

She gazed up at him. "No. We were happy...at first. Dad criticized how Mom cooked. How she cleaned. How she dressed. No matter how hard she worked, it never pleased him."

"Okay." He nodded so she would continue. As a kid, he never would've imagined his parents would be happier apart. Amarie's home must have been horrible for a free spirit like hers. She figured life out by trial and error. A risk-taker would've made a lot of mistakes as a kid. Eli had a feeling the criticism extended beyond her mother. It pissed him off to think of a father crushing her creativity, making her afraid to try new things.

"Wait. You said Prince. The car belonged to your mother?"

"Yeah," she nodded. "Mom called him our chariot. I rode in the front seat with her. She said he was ours because she'd purchased him with her own money, not my father's."

"Sounds like serious girl power."

"Dad controlled the household finances."

"I'm assuming that's not a euphemism for managed?"

"Afraid not." She frowned. "Mom had to save from the

money he gifted her for managing his medical practice. Submitting his billing, dealing with the insurance companies, following up with patients on their lab reports. She did it all."

"Your mom sounds like a real gem." So, she'd grown up watching her mother multitask a difficult husband, a busy practice, and motherhood. No wonder she'd swooped into Service like a modern-day Wonder Woman. She'd been raised by a mother who navigated a marriage to a piece of crap.

"She was. Even bought me a dog, a short-haired beagle, Princess. But she was too young for our adventure."

Amarie sounded sad now. Instinctively, Eli knew the end of the story wouldn't have a happy ending.

"What happened?"

"Things got tough. We didn't eat some nights. Mom would distract me by painting my toes. Then she would let me do hers—any color I wanted."

The way her voice tightened as if every word strained for release, Eli got the sense that nighttime food scarcity had stretched into daylight hours, too.

"You do love your snack packs." He stroked his fingers up and down her spine, providing comfort to the little girl wrapped up in the heart in his woman. Yep, she was his now. And Eli had every intention of making more good memories, starting with tonight.

"True." She teased the fine hairs dusting his chest. "My therapist suggested healthy snacks and water to stave of hunger signals when they occur. Otherwise, the anxiety about the next meal, if and when it will come, turns me into a beastly diva. You know, like those old candy bar commercials."

Eli rolled to his side, shifting their bodies until they were face to face. "No divas allowed on my watch. I'll keep you fed."

Amarie's eyes widened in understanding and her gaze

lowered to his mouth. His double meaning came through loud and in stereo. He wanted her again. Couldn't get enough of this brave and beautiful woman.

"I bet you will," she leaned in, nipping his lower lip before sucking in her mouth and releasing.

He watched as she made a slow, wet trek across her lower lip, and then sank her teeth into the swollen flesh.

"What happened with Princess?"

"I'm pretty sure my father gave her away to punish my mother for leaving."

Eli pulled up. "That's pretty low-down for a father to do to his wife and child."

She nodded. "I felt the same gut-churning sickness when Bucky tried to deprive Phoebe of her kittens."

Eli's breath hitched. Understanding dawned. The connection he'd missed when Amarie had stormed off at the wedding ready to rescue Ruth and Phoebe from a badly behaving father. He'd tried to stop her, not realizing she'd been triggered. He wanted to hold her for a different reason then.

"Amarie—" His voice broke apart at the reverence he placed on her name.

"Yes, Eli?"

"Don't go back to Mom's place. Stay with me."

"I am, silly."

"No, I mean every night."

"You're offering me a key to your kingdom, Eli Calvary?" she asked, sliding both her arms around his neck.

"This is Service. Don't need a key, my door is always open," he rasped, and so was his nose. And Eli wanted Amarie's sweet apple aroma simmering under his roof. When Amarie giggled, he pulled her on top of his hardness and buried his face in her neck. He loved coming home.

Chapter Twenty

One week later, Amarie awoke on a makeshift palette under the large pine tree facing the water. The afternoon started with a hot cup of coffee in her hand, courtesy of Eli, grass in her locs, and her best friend's daily call. Their conversations had dwindled to fifteen minutes after Vali's night shifts but before her bedtime. Or, like today when she had seventy-two hours away from the unit, they could relax and catch up. And Amarie could delay looking up her exam results.

Vali's voice was animated telling tales of patients behaving badly, grabbing a handful of her assets on the sly, but Amarie was candy hearts and gumdrop eyes. And achy lady parts. Being plush in places had advantages. Who knew she could be conditioned for sex in the great outdoors? But she didn't regret one sore spot. *Enthusiastic* and *generous* could be used to describe Eli's lovemaking. Comparatively, Russell was downright anemic. She'd unwittingly deprived herself of amazing sex. Who knew sweaty, grabby, rolling-in-the-hay—which she was willing to try now—butt-naked sex under the pale eye of a lover's moon could transform her into a sex addict. She craved Eli's touch. Couldn't get enough of his, well, everything.

"Girl, I hate to say this, but you might have to tell Russell to stop calling me for his own safety."

"No can do."

"I'm just saying…if he continues with his annoying rob-ocall tactics, I will strangle him with his own baby's umbilical cord and dump his lifeless body in the hospital morgue," Vali cackled.

"Aw, block his number. I told my mom to do the same." Amarie sighed, not a care in the world to consider.

"Excuse me, Madam Butterfly, why do you sound like a breathy video vixen celebrating freaky Friday?"

"Well, it is Thursday. Me and my lady parts are basking in the clean mountain air." August had abandoned the mountain town but had forgotten to pack the morning humidity in the trunk case.

"Is that why I hear tweety birds singing 'Rock-In Robin'? You and Eli playing ride-the-pony in the great outdoors?"

"I can affirm there are only stallions on the property." Amarie squealed, slapping a hand over her mouth before she realized no one could hear or see her. The property was fully secluded by the woodland.

"Mari, you are officially in the bowlegged club."

"Not just legs. Ankles. Toes. I am remade," she said in her haughtiest imitation, "like Michelle in *Becoming*."

Vali hooted, cackling with laughter. "Eli got you out here talking about his bedroom game like he's the most powerful man in the world. All I can say is amen."

"Yes. I screamed that a lot, too."

"What happens next?"

"Eli wants me to move in—permanently. And…and I want to be with him, Vali."

"So, what are you saying?" Vali trailed off.

"I think it means…this is my new home."

"Is that what you want? I mean what about the exam, your career? Eli started as a fake-it-till-you-make-it situation, Mari. The bachelor auction will end, you working with Eli every day at the clinic stops at some point. Will you both feel the same when you're not in each other's faces every day?"

Amarie sobered as Vali's questions confronted old doubts and raised new fears. Ever the optimist, she believed she and Eli would find a way to stay together, even if they worked apart.

"I can see myself planting roots here. I have friends, actual real people who include me in their lives. I love—like my job." She couldn't say that she loved Eli, even though her mouth almost revealed the inner workings of her mind. Their relationship was in its infancy. Too much too soon could spell disaster. Confessing her undying love after one week in his bed could be considered premature, reckless, but that didn't stop her heart from galloping off like the cavalry waving the white flag of complete surrender. She wanted everything with Eli.

"I'm happy for you, I really am, that people include you in their life, but—"

"You're never quiet. Please don't be sad, Vali."

"Silence is not sad. But your life is no less important, girlfriend. If you stay, it means I'll have to drive five hours to see my best friend and her goats. Are they still alive? I mean, I hear they taste like chicken, a country favorite, with a biscuit, right?"

"Oh dear, I hadn't considered. Billy, Jean, and Diana have grown so much since your visit. At least a pound. It looks good on them. In pygmy goat terms. That question is at the top of my list for Eli today."

"Ah, okay," Vali stammered. "Not that I ever had high hopes for Russell, but you sound sure of your soldier boy."

"I've never been so sure of anything in my life, but I am

of Eli. I feel like he makes me better, more centered, and grounded. It's so foreign to me, but it happened here in Service. I need to explore my feelings for him, and the town."

"I get it. Maybe it is special to Service, but Mari, you've always been grounded and centered. Other people tried to force you to make them your center, that's why it felt twisted. Now that no one is telling you where you belong, what your worth is, who you have to settle for, you can appreciate the fact that you've always had the tools you need to chart your own path."

Vali was right. She had allowed her parents and Russell and all their expectations to dictate her choices. Now for the first time, she was in charge. More importantly, she had the control and confidence to make her own mistakes separate from their judgment. She'd learned since arriving in Service that she could help others without allowing them to abuse her generosity. She was free to build a future, not free of mistakes but free of self-recrimination and doubt. To need help was not the same as being helpless.

"Where is your soldier boy now?"

"He and his brothers are assembling the last vendor booth for the Founder's Day Festival on Saturday. He packed up our petting zoo, all five kittens plus Hiccup. I'm in charge of dinner tonight."

"Nice," she cooed. "I adore a man who doesn't mind getting sweaty. Are you still planning to announce the winners of the bachelor auction at the festival?"

"Sure am. Eli's nervous. All three winning bids are anonymous. He felt more comfortable with only the local ladies bidding. We've received a ton more visibility since Kitty Kibbles, that Chicago-based cat food company, the one I told you about, reposted one of our videos on their TikTok page. The possibility of dining with a strange woman off the internet raises his withers."

"Withers. Come hithers. I don't speak animal kingdom, but that's amazing, Mari."

"Oh, sorry. That's the highest part of the spine. You know, like a cat's hackles."

"Ah, no. I don't. But the fact is, you are leveling up, sister. You speak English, Country Grammar, and Zoolander."

Yeah, she had learned a lot about animal anatomy and veterinary medicine during her time in Service. Instead of stressing about her checklists, she just embraced her process. She realized that different didn't translate to dumb. Eli's patience and easy acceptance of her rather quirky methodology empowered rather than demeaned her.

"Kind of. The company sent a contract and a check offering #SexyKittyVet a paid brand ambassador opportunity."

"But?" Vali prompted, excitement lighting her voice.

"They want Eli to live stream on both pages, ours and theirs. He's stubborn as a blind mule, though. Just flat out refused. I mean, the man is a natural-born influencer. He's focused, a research nerd, and his smile could power Times Square at Christmas. And the kittens, they're old enough to be adopted, but he's so good with them. Instead of grabbing a backpack in the mornings, he scoops them up in their basket and heads to the office. It's the cutest thing, Vali. But," she sighed, "two folks, one from Landing Falls, the other from Whynot, plan to stop by the clinic this afternoon to welcome a new furry, purry addition to the family. I'm going to miss them so much."

"You could change his mind," Vali teased. "We both know how creative you are. I mean, he is #SexyKittyVet. Those kittens are technically his coworkers."

"I know, right. I think he should keep #SexyKittyVet alive even after the auction ends, but Eli envisions a different life for himself. And, well, the kittens won't be babies forever. Can you imagine, Eli and five cats in a basket?"

"Why not? Didn't some guy keep a cat in a hat? I think it's sexy and sweet that big daddy takes the kiddos to work and leaves the little lady at home to recover," Vali mused.

Amarie sighed, first at the loss of the kittens and then at probably losing the brand ambassador contract. The added money could pay for the clinic expansion, but she wouldn't manipulate Eli into a situation in which he felt uncomfortable. Amarie knew the pain of trying to be anything other than who she was. There would be more opportunities… she hoped. She felt a pang in her heart at releasing any of her kitties, but Eli had assured her that he would see to it that each of her fur babies landed in luxury.

"Vali," she breathed out. "I'm happy. Really, deeply, and truly happy with my choices. I have fun doing what I love with a great guy. I'm scared the other shoe will drop—"

"Girl, would you stop? Enjoy yourself. Can you do that?"

Amarie fell back on the pallet of sleeping bags and blankets in a fit of giggles. She could count on Vali to lighten any perceived calamity.

"Yes, I can. What can I say—I drop it like it's hot. And Eli, he's a fire god."

"Are you saying Eli is 'O' positive, as in orgasm?"

"He was double 'O' positive from the first night. And," she said in a conspiratorial whisper, "last night we hit a triple 'O' with a howl."

Vali screamed like a teenage girl at a sleepover. "I love a man who understands the assignment. Sounds like Eli knows how to keep the doors to the candy shop open."

"Have I told you how basic you are some days?"

"As if your opinion will change my predilection for carnality."

"You are absolutely wicked."

"And proud of it. But truly, us single ladies have to be

happy when another melanin poppin', educated woman finds a man worthy of her time and talent. Yet ironically, I find myself green candy apple jealous. I'm *healous*, because ain't no sex been happening in my city, if you catch my meaning. You deserve every good vibration that comes your way."

Amarie smirked, even though her friend couldn't see her expression. "Really, Vali? *Vibrations that come my way.*"

She snickered. "Caught that, did you?"

"Congratulations, Miss Walker." Amarie bolted upright at the new voice coming through the receiver. Vali's sister, Sunday, had overheard the conversation.

"Sunday," Amarie screeched. "Go to your room. Now."

"No can do, my sister from another mister," she sing-songed. "I'm taking notes. Love your #SexyKittyVet videos so hard, too. Please, ask SimplyTobias if he likes his Sunday with a shaved cherry?"

"Wh-what," Amarie sputtered, coffee dribbled off her chin. "Sunday, you are a mess. Vali, will you tell your X-rated sister to warn me before she puts shaved cherries and sexual metaphors in the same sentence? Real talk, I could have choked on this coffee. I'm blaming you for any and all future complications."

Vali came back on the line, laughing. Amarie missed their Saturday mornings on that horrid crescent-shaped couch.

"You ran her off, so there, problem solved. And since you've only mentioned *z luv doctor*, I'm assuming you haven't had a chance to visit your online portal about your exam results, hmm?"

Amarie's voice hitched. She'd zoned out on her career. On her future. "I-I'm…"

Scared. After walking out of the testing center, Eli had

kept her beneath him, on top him, beside him. Testing results had fallen off her anxiety list until today. Because the stress of the exam had ended with the final question. And once her man—she'd come to think of Eli as hers—had successfully distracted her in the most pleasurable ways.

"Don't fret. You're experiencing the six symptoms of an 'O' positive man encounter. Sore cheeks. Scratchy throat. Loss of speech. Profuse sweating. Spillage of time. Booty bruises."

Amarie felt her butt cheeks clench. How did Vali come up with this mess?

"Not to worry, my worn-out friend. When a woman encounters good D, a temporary *disruption of synaptic activity* occurs at random intervals."

"In Eli's case, that's great D," Amarie interrupted.

"I stand corrected and pleased." Vali laughed. "Getting butt naked with a sexy kitty vet isn't in my archives. The annals will be updated before the end of the day."

"Vali," Amarie rasped, nervous for the first time in days. "The results. I need to get to my computer."

Amarie grabbed a gingham throw, covered her breasts, unnecessary since she remained secluded on Eli's property, and rose to her knees, careful not to spill her mug.

"Relax, I got your back, girlfriend. I have the site pulled up. What's your password?" Amarie quickly rattled off the secure details. She had always been a nervous test taker. Not this time. The nightly study sessions with Eli quizzing her had helped her to build a system to de-escalate her stress levels during the two-day testing sessions. As the seconds ticked by, though, panic set in. The birds she heard chirping were replaced with the pounding of her own heart.

"Oh my God, Vali. What's taking so long?"

"The website needs a saline enema," Vali chided. "The spinning wheel of death has me in its grips."

At times like this, she cursed technology. What if she hadn't passed? She couldn't go on as an assistant to her boyfriend, dependent on his income, his housing, his—everything.

"Not again," she whispered, the cup shaking in her grasp. "Vali, did I get close this time?"

"Wait—wait. Something's happening on the page." She paused, mid-sentence. "Oh my god," she gasped. What did that mean? Vali didn't gasp. She didn't flinch in the face of disappointment.

"It's worse than last time, isn't it?" She'd arrived in Service with goals, dreams. Her plans hinged on passing the exam. Her new friends would learn she failed at everything.

"Honey." Vali's voice cracked.

Amarie rose to her feet, stiffening her spine. She would meet her fate head-on, standing proud. She'd done her best. Truly in her heart she'd studied, sacrificed, and learned to embrace her process. She believed herself capable of building the life she wanted.

"Say it, Vali."

"Welcome to the achy-feet club, Mari." Had she heard that right? Vali's screamed. "You not only passed, my sister, but you aced the darn thing."

"Flying colors, Amarie. You can write your own job description," Sunday screamed, reaching an operatic pitch.

Amarie jerked the phone away from her ear. Her feet left the ground. Not quite a Simone Biles leap, but enough to splash her coffee, now warm, over the rim. The blanket she held to her breast slipped from her grasp.

All the dance moves Eli had taught her—Watermelon Crawl, Cotton-Eyed Joe, Old Town Road, The Git Up—she did them, butt naked. Screaming, her voice bounced between the trees traveling across the water, up the mountain. Inside, she felt the growing wave of love, self-love. She'd succeeded in not failing herself.

"Mari. Mari. Where are you, lady?"

Amarie eased the phone back to her ear, panting from exertion. "I'm doing my dance. I'm a registered nurse. I can't believe it."

"Believe it. I never doubted you." Yes. They had done it. She and Eli, together. "Have you thought about your specialty?"

Huh, she'd spent months focused on the exam. Amarie thought about Eli's words, the shield-maiden of women and children.

"Labor and delivery. Maybe pediatrics," she finally replied.

"Whew, you had me worried you'd choose animals instead of patients for a second. Don't let go of your dreams, girl. I know you're living the best days of your life in Service, but is there a general hospital on Main Street?"

"I wish. The closest hospital is ninety miles away in Hopes Summit," Amarie replied, but her heart skipped a beat. Maybe she could help to remedy the health professional shortage in rural communities and improve patient outcomes. She'd earned her credentials. The perky late bloomer had blossomed into a nightingale. "I've got to text my mom. And Eli. He helped me study every night for weeks. I can't wait to tell him."

"Yasss," Vali drawled. "Tell him all night long."

"Would you stop talking about sex?"

"Absolutely—not. I'm happy for you," she sighed. "You found your perfect guy, Mari. Now that's some Black girl magic, right there."

"Thanks, friend."

"Don't thank me. Help me, girl. The next time you're in

that little general store, post a picture of me. Let the country boys know your friend is not only available, but I'll put in the miles for a big—"

"Bye, Vali." Amarie cut the line.

There'd been a time when her best friend was the first person she wanted to share all the big moments of her life with, not that there were many. But this time she wanted to share this with Eli even more. She would pick a special location because she needed him good and relaxed when she mentioned hiring her replacement. Eli loved Service and so did Amarie. Her having the career she'd always dreamed of wouldn't be a stumbling block for them. Together, they would find a workable solution. After all, they were a perfect match. She could still honor the promise to herself and keep her boyfriend, right?

Chapter Twenty-One

WHERE ELI'S BROTHERS tended to mind their own business, his mother had no such qualms about inquiring about his private life. Amarie had stayed overnight…again. They knew it. Being that his brothers had different philosophies when it came to women as overnight guests, Noah and Tobias had sense enough to not ask questions or comment.

"Eli, that you?" his mom called to him from the grooming center.

For the next two days the clinic would stay closed with the festival starting at midday on Saturday. The humidity had climbed above seventy while he coked and joked with Tobias and Noah under the pavilion. The work needed to make the Founder's Day Festival a success was finished, but the fellowship had lifted a burden off Eli's conscience. Seems the growing bids from the auction had filled the cracks his delay in informing his brothers of their financial situation had caused. He had another reason to thank Amarie when he returned home.

"Yes, ma'am. Got to grab more supplies for Raspberry, Dove, Formerly, Graffiti, and Artist. This will be their first festival." He'd placed calls to both families interested in cat adoption to cancel today's visit. Amarie adored the furry tripping hazards, and he couldn't help but feel like a bad pappa for considering letting them go. He'd adjusted his life to include a basket with a bow on one arm and his lady on the other. Besides, Hiccup had given up the foot of the bed to move in with the kittens in front of the fireplace.

"Don't leave, I'm done with my cleaning."

"Momma, I can clean my own clinic. You should be relaxing." The pungent scent of alcohol disinfectant hit his nose. Turning, he opened the two windows facing the patient parking lot where he'd left his pickup truck. A refreshing burst of clean yet warm air rushed in, diluting the noxious chemicals.

Leah appeared in the doorway. She tossed floppy yellow gloves in the trash. "So," she exhaled, exhaustion written in her taunt features. "You decided to keep the kitties?"

He nodded.

"Thank goodness you thought better of breaking up the band." She gestured to the new acrylic QR code display emblazoned with each of their social media handles. Posting them on the counter was another of Amarie's ideas. "Aiming to keep Amarie happy? Glad to see Momma didn't raise a fool."

He chuckled. "It's free advertising. Plus, you know the old saying. Happy woman, happy life." He made a substitution for wife. Knowing his mom would call him on it in the next few seconds, he kept flapping his gums. "Besides, it cost me a half gallon of coffee bean ice cream to convince her to remove the mandatory drug testing for the adoption application."

Not even that earned him a laugh. Eli leaned his back against the counter, crossed his legs at the ankles, and waited.

"You plan to sign the contract? Deposit that twenty-five-thousand-dollar check?"

"Momma, I'm no social media influencer. The only reason I'm doing this plum fool TikTok is to save the clinic. Do you think Dad would've been all TikToking and influencing?"

"Seems to me your daddy would've done what he could for this family. He did what he could to help people. Don't matter the how of it, Eli. I loved that about Levi."

"I know that, Momma. Not a day went by that I didn't see how much you two meant to each other. But I saw how he managed business. I want to honor him."

"If you were watching, then you know your daddy made mistakes."

Eli's breath hitched. Never had his mother criticized his father, not with him present. And certainly had never had this conversation. "Momma, whatcha getting at?"

"Levi left a lot on your shoulders with the financials the way they are. My husband, your father, wasn't always forward-thinking. He was stubborn. Hid problems from me to the last minute." She smiled, but her green eyes, the mirror of his, drifted to a far-off place. "Sometimes I had to pry the words from his mouth. But in the end, we did life together. Best of friends, we were partners."

"I believe that," Eli agreed, a faded memory of his father, the sacrifice he made for this land, the secret that Eli would take to his grave. The bond between a father and son that burned fresh enough that he remembered how stubborn his dad could be if he set his mind to something.

"I'm proud of you, Eli. You told me what was happening with the mortgage note and you tried your best to shoulder a burden that should've never been yours. Levi and I were so busy scrimping and saving for you boys' education that we didn't plan well for our old age. Some months we ate my biscuits three times a day. Levi wanted you not to have to worry about college. 'No struggling for my sons,' he would say. He was so proud when you decided to follow in his footsteps."

"I remember," Eli mumbled, swallowing back the lump in his throat.

"He wanted you back home after college, but we respected your choice to serve our great nation. Hmm, I miss my partner, Eli. He would brag about you to everyone, even the Pendletons took notice."

Eli stiffened. "I don't care anything about impressing that family. They're rotten to the core. Every last one of them."

"Thank goodness you never fell for Lourdes. Now, you and Amarie, you've found your own path. You are good with people and animals, Eli. Both know they can trust you. I know the TikTok talks and the auction are unconventional, but you made them your own. Not the Calvarys', not your father's, but yours. I know you painted on a brave face for me and your brothers. But, even in fear, you have options. Fear can lead some men to abandon everything and run. But you stepped into the unknown to save this family. You made the harder choice, to face everything, and rise."

Eli swallowed the emotion riding him. His mom believed in his abilities when he'd doubted himself. He hadn't considered how much of what he believed about his future he'd had to suspend to share his life via a daily TikTok feed. But there was more his mom had to say. Behind the praise, she saw a problem brewing. He could feel the boulder about to tear through the wall and knock him off his feet.

"There's a *but*, isn't there?"

Lips tight, eyes concerned, she asked, "Amarie stayed at your place again last night?"

"You're not even going to soften me up with a doggie treat before you have me jumping hoops to keep you out of my private life?"

"No. I'm not. I love Amarie like she's one of my own. I want to see her happy, fulfilled."

This could signal trouble. Hiccup padded over to his third favorite person. Eli felt pretty confident that Amarie had unseated him from the number one spot. His pup rubbed his head against grandma's hand, and then in a surprise move, hightailed it through the breezeway leading from the clinic into the house.

"Traitor," Eli muttered. Wiping the sweat from his brow, he placed the kitten carrier on the reception desk in the vet clinic.

"Me and Amarie, we—we're happy," he replied, a big smile on his face. His momma knew Amarie's comings and goings as well as everyone else's in town. "I plan on asking her to move in after the festival."

"Huh." Leah sighed.

Eli grinned. "Now what's that supposed to mean? You wanted me coupled up. And now that I've found the perfect woman, all you have to say is *huh*?"

"So, Amarie's decided to stay in Service regardless of how it impacts her career?"

The question sprung a nerve, one that ached like a rotten tooth. "Of course she has. We got real feelings for each other. So, if you're concerned about how we started out, don't."

"My worry is about you, Eli."

"Me?" he rasped, gobsmacked by the comment. "You just said you trusted me. Never in a hundred years did I think I'd have a chance with a woman as brilliant, capable, and fierce as Amarie. When Cara left, I believed I could never feel this way for another woman. I'm as consistent as the day is long. You know that."

"Better than anyone. That's why I'm doing a pulse check."

"Momma, you're worked up about nothing. This is the life I've always wanted. All of us, the family, the woman I lo—" He'd almost let the word slip. "—the woman I care about, working and living on Calvary land. That's what you and Dad had. That's what I have with Amarie."

His mom reached up, cradling his face in her hands. They were as soft as he remembered as a little boy. "Eli, Amarie is here now—working side by side with you. But," she sighed, "you need to prepare yourself for when she starts her own career. What's your plan for the days to come when Amarie is gone? Away from the vet clinic. Away from Service."

Away from him. He heard what she dared not say. He pulled away as if she'd stuck a hot poker in his eye. Logic evaded him as the truth of his mother's words flayed him open. Of course she would have to leave Service if she wanted to work in the nursing field. Landing Falls and Whynot, though larger than Service, were medically underserved areas. The job prospects were limited, he knew.

He supported her dreams, but that still didn't make it any easier to acknowledge that their working together would end once the exam results arrived. Amarie, brilliant, inventive woman that she was, was sure to pass the exam. He never doubted her abilities. Everything she touched, she improved. Including him. But the old fear: If she was away from him, ventured beyond the confines of the oasis of his idyllic family life, would he and Service lose their appeal? Would she look at his life, a simple veterinarian happy to come home to the same woman every night, as a failure?

While that fear still coursed through him, Eli sought to reassure his mom.

Clearly, she was worried, and he couldn't have that. "Don't worry. Amarie and I will find a way. She's happy here in Service…with us. There's time to figure this out. Neither of us is going anywhere."

Eli's mom had her pointer finger ready to fire off another shot of wisdom. He planned to dodge when he heard the large brass bell attached to the clinic's entry door jiggle. He and his mother looked toward the entrance simultaneously. There stood a man, older than Eli but younger than forty, dressed in a dark navy blazer over a polo and pressed khakis. Eli hated him on sight. All of a sudden, a gut-churning reaction to this man's sense of inherent superiority triggered Eli's defenses. He remembered having a similar feeling when he'd met Cara's yoga instructor the first time. While the Ivy League debate club captain with a smug expression surveyed the room, in walked an elegant African American woman who smelled and looked like freshly minted money.

"Hello." The woman moved around the jerk to actually speak to them. "I'm Bethany Walker. My daughter, Amarie, is living here on the property?" she asked, one arched brow lifted in soft defiance. The resemblance between mother and daughter, flawless medium-brown skin, almond-shaped eyes with watercolor-whiskey irises, and defined profiles. This woman was a portrait of his Amarie twenty years into the future.

"Oh," his mother breathed, clasping Bethany's hand between hers.

"Nice to meet you, Mrs. Walker. I'm Eli Calvary, this is my mother, Leah. And who are you?" Eli demanded of the man who failed to acknowledge any of them.

The arrogant ass strolled forward as if he had been waiting for his presence to be announced.

"I'm Amarie's fiancé, Dr. Russell Feldman. Already I

see signs that she's taken over your business with her process improvement checklists. She crippled my business and destroyed my social media presence. I've lost thousands of dollars because of her. That's why I've come here."

"For money?" Leah questioned.

"No." He smirked as if offended. "I came to take her back home, where she belongs."

The hell he will. Eli brain short-circuited on half the conversation, but he didn't miss that this man wanted to take Amarie from him. Eli took a step forward. Amarie's home was in Service, with him. His momma's hand on his forearm stopped him in his tracks, but not the growl that rumbled through his chest that shook the rafters.

Chapter Twenty-Two

Amarie floated into the Black Bear, a mixed ball of emotions. Giddy at having passed her licensure exam dominated, but uncertainty about Eli's reaction to her probable career move threatened to overshadow the heaven-on-earth moment. But that's the thing about the new her, she liked this accomplished, self-assured lady looking back at her in the mirror, and difficult decisions, like jobs and replacements, could wait until after the celebration. Her boyfriend—oh how she loved the word, and possibly the man attached to it—had surprised her with a pretty sweet bonus in last week's paycheck.

For the rest of the evening, it was all about her and Eli. She had it all planned in her head. First, naked dinner for two. Then they would spend all night under the birch trees—the pine trees poked in not-so-pleasurable places—exercising his hard-as-stone triceps with dips of her hips.

Gracie Lou passed two bags over the counter. "There's enough in food here to feed for three meals."

Amarie looped the plastic over her wrist and gripped the grease-stained paper bag in her other hand. "Smells scrumptious as usual." Amarie smiled.

"The apple butter is Caleb's grandma's recipe. The skillet cornbread and pan-fried trout are all mine. What you two celebrating?"

"I passed my nursing exam." Amarie beamed.

"Of course, you did, smarty-pants. So, why are you not down here celebrating with everybody?"

Amarie realized the possibility of the whole town celebrating one of its own was unique to Service, but for her personal accomplishment, separate from the vet clinic, to be deemed worthy floored her.

"Is that an option?" Did Gracie really view Amarie as a part of Service, in her own right? Not an extension of Eli or the business? She felt like she belonged, but she had a habit of creating the world she wanted to circulate in. For years she'd created a false reality to justify staying in a failed relationship with Russell, tolerating his shenanigans. Allowing herself this joy, Amarie refused to feel guilty that she celebrated what many would consider a small win. She hadn't gotten a job yet. She hadn't saved anyone else's life yet, besides her own, of course.

Gracie Lou grinned. "This is Service, Amarie. We celebrate big and small. And you being the one nurse in town, well, that's huge."

How could she leave a town that wanted her to be their *one*? She thought of how Matt and Eli had rallied to help Ruth and Phoebe, protect them when they were most vulnerable. How Leah had welcomed her with open arms and biscuits. How long had she searched for a place where she could work with people who appreciated, rather than exploited, her willingness to offer a helping hand? She'd wanted this kind of connection, dare she say family, her whole life.

"I mean with the way the bachelor auction is going, Eli can actually afford a round of drinks," Amarie joked.

"Oh honey, the whole town is glued to their TikTok page following #SexyKittyVet. We are so proud of how you've worked with Eli to save the family business and land. The Calvarys are country royalty in these parts. Mr. Calvary never met a stranger. That man would give anyone the shirt off the clothesline if they needed it."

"I think the term is 'off his back.'"

"This is Service. Other than Noah, any man with a woman from this town knows there's a cast-iron skillet aimed at his head if his shirt comes off for anybody except for his lady."

"I see your point."

"And I see that you've raised seventeen thousand dollars to keep our vet here in town."

"It's amazing really. I can't believe we're so close to reaching our goal."

Gracie walked around the counter and pulled Amarie into an embrace. She smelled of flour, sugar, and hot cooking oil.

"You've given that man of yours a new lease on life." Gracie Lou released her with a sigh. "I have known Eli since we were in diapers, and honestly, he was a grumpy baby. A serious toddler, and that lasted until he was about, I don't know, maybe college. He acted like a cardboard cutout of his father. Then he married whatever her name was, but she never stuck around long enough for the town to meet her. He came back home worse than when he left. We've gotten our Eli back. It's rare to find a partner in this life. What you share with Eli, it's precious."

Amarie's heart started to giddyap in her chest. When she held Eli, warm and secure in her arms, he was like that long-lost missing sock. Her mate.

"Caleb and I are thinking there's wedding bells in the future for the two of you."

"Oh my goodness, Gracie Lou, I don't think we're anywhere near picking out rings."

"You must not know our story."

"Do tell."

"Caleb and I met online, which is crazy because we live right here in the same town. I guess hiding behind our handles made it easier to get past folks' opinions about us hooking up."

"Why would folks look down on you two dating? Caleb's perfect for you."

Gracie Lou frowned, which was rare. "This is my second marriage. My first husband was a selfish ass. Took advantage of folks we both grew up with. I defended him at first, made excuses for his behavior. I knew he was wrong, but I wanted to be a supportive wife. People started avoiding us both, friends stopped calling. Trying to do right for the wrong man...it costs you a piece of yourself—"

"Gracie, honey," Caleb called from the kitchen, "you going to get yourself overheated."

A girlish grin flashed on Gracie's face. "Isn't your job to hose me down," she yelled back, not caring that Amarie was right there.

Amarie cleared her throat. "You were saying?"

"Basically, I married the wrong man. The union damaged the both of us. Caleb heard warnings from every corner of the county to stand clear of me. Plus, I've got three years of extra road dust compared to my hot young husband."

"The hottest." Caleb laughed, the loud and boisterous sound carrying to the empty dining room. It was still early for the bar crowd, just past four thirty.

"Anyhoo, I tied myself to the wrong man. And the thing about forcing a fit into a space where you don't belong—you get nicked in places you didn't realize were vital until a part of you is good and broken."

Angling her head, Amarie considered Gracie Lou's journey to love. She thought of her own timeline, six years of an ill-fit with a man who could never value her love above his own selfish desires. "Wow, that's a hardball that hit with a soft landing. I've been that shoe on the wrong foot. Felt the uncomfortable rub on all sides, but I was too scared to let go. Scared I wouldn't find a shoe that looked as pretty, I guess."

"Pretty is nice, but when a woman finds the right pair, she can go the distance, walk for miles, without pain and exhaustion. I think it's kind of cute that you and Eli make a pretty pair. Maybe meeting each other at your lowest makes the new fit all the sweeter, huh." She nodded.

"Try not to give him the boot." Caleb appeared behind the bar, a tub of ice in his hands.

"Gracie Lou, Caleb, I can't speak for Eli."

Caleb tipped the ice in the metal cooler, the cubes crashed and banged against the metal, a noisy shower of ice cascading on top of the waiting pile.

"You don't have to. Like I said, I've known him since we were in diapers. And thanks to you, he's no longer a shit."

"Hey, that's my man." The cooler door clanged with a heavy thud. Caleb waved before vanishing behind the glass wall with east-to-west liquor bottles.

"And that's why I'm only telling you. I put a little something extra in the bag. Just for you. Carbs be damned."

"Biscuits?"

"You know it. Finally talked Mrs. Leah into baking a batch for all the visitors coming through for the weekend. It'll get more folks buying food and booze."

"How did you manage to win her over?"

Gracie Lou winked. "Told her that the next fundraiser she dreams up to get those other two boys hitched up if it doesn't happen this time around, she can kick it off here at the Black Bear. Maybe even hire a techy new nurse to overhaul our website?"

"Really?" Amarie grinned.

"Me and the mister have been talking about doing online orders for a few years now. I appreciate him taking his time with most things." Gracie Lou winked. Amarie's cheeks heated and she thought about the man waiting on her at home. "After witnessing all you did to make the Calvarys TikTok sensations, I figure us womenfolk can work together and make things happen. The mayor took notice, too. Been talking with the sheriff about raising money for a police vehicle with the town seal on the door."

"Fine by me. Speaking of Kanaan, when you see him and Cocktail, let them know I want my car back."

"What in the world for?"

"Prince and I have been through tough times. I'm driving that car till it returns to ashes."

"Honey, you don't need transportation no more. From what I hear, Eli prefers to carry you around. If it makes that man feel like a king to sweep you off your feet, I say let him do it while the back's still good."

"I'll keep that in mind."

"Listen to me. And listen to me good. The way to a man's heart, it's not his stomach, it's opening your heart to his. That's what you've done. I know their last name is Cavalry, but you're the one that rode in and saved him, Amarie Walker."

"I've never really had a relationship where my friends felt confident sharing advice for a happily ever after. This is nice. I never planned on Eli happening. Us happening."

"I know, but maybe pretending to be happy gave you the freedom to get out of your own way and learn how to make it a reality. Loving a man is a learning process. Don't let nobody tell you different."

"Maybe, Gracie. I never thought of it that way."

"I know you've got options now that you've passed your exam. Service may not have a clinic or a hospital now, but I believe we can make it happen. Just like we're working to save the Calvary Vet Clinic. Folks are serious about other improvements. First the vet clinic. Then on to the next goal, together. That's what family does for family; we take care of one another."

"Wow, Gracie. Thank you for always welcoming me, like family."

And that's what Amarie was. Eli was her family now. She could count on him. He hadn't let her down even though she'd walked into his life a stranger. They had gone from enemies to friends to lovers.

"Sure Eli's looking for you by now, Amarie."

"Oh, shoot. See you tomorrow." Amarie was walking out the door when a beautiful woman collided with her.

"Oh, excuse you," the woman snapped.

Amarie was in such a good mood she didn't even get offended. She would've considered the woman attractive with her supermodel blonde hair pin straight, Cupid's bow lips tight with disapproval. But her brown eyes were narrowed, shrewd, with a condemning quality. A large designer tote hung from her shoulder, and inside was a white toy poodle. Its paws clutched over the snap closure in what Amarie imagined was a *Help me, please. My owner is a mean girl* expression.

"Have a good day." Amarie waved, food in hand. Heart above the clouds. New clients. Fresh lookout. The world beneath her feet. This is what it felt like to be on top.

"That's doubtful." She flipped her thick locks off her shoulder. "But perhaps you can be of assistance."

The woman was a prima donna type Russell would've drooled all over. Okay, she could be a butt and walk away, or she could welcome this woman the way Leah had made her feel seen and heard.

"What do you need?"

"I'm lost." She pouted as if that would work on Amarie. *Save it, girl*, she thought. Thank goodness Amarie had learned that she was made of tougher stock.

"How did that happen?" Amarie smirked.

"I'm looking for Calvary Vet Clinic. I got a little turned around when I came into town."

Amarie would not be releasing Raspberry, Formerly, Graffiti, Artist, or Dove to this hapless creature. Seemed if she broke a nail, six weeks of intensive therapy sessions would have to happen for a full recovery.

"Okay, this might work out in your favor," Amarie said. "I'm headed there now."

"On foot?" The woman scowled.

"It's back the way you drove into town past the main road and up the hill."

"That's right," she chuckled, "the uptown Calvarys." The drawl sounded rather refined but exasperated. "Oh yes, I remember the distinction. I'd forgotten all this uptown-downtown nonsense."

"I'm headed there on foot. If you want to walk, we can take the bridge across the creek and, voila, you'll arrive at your destination."

"Is my car safe here?"

Amarie literally fell speechless. Who was this knock-off princess masquerading as if she had money?

Amarie pushed past her. "My food is getting cold. Bye now."

"Wait up. I do have on high heels."

"Not my problem."

She heard muttering behind her back. No introduction. No *thank you, gentle stranger, for offering to assist me in my quest*.

The woman stomped along behind Amarie, talking more to her toy poodle than to the actual person who had offered her help. Amarie bypassed the house and decided it best to give Eli the signal that Cruella would not do for her kittens. Amarie pushed into the door of the clinic.

"Eli."

"Yep," he called, his voice harsh and none too pleasant. His footfalls came fast and rolled like thunder. And there were clicks of cultured steps on smooth tile, followed by a stride she knew without seeing his face. Amarie's mouth fell open when she saw who materialized from the staff lounge located behind Eli's office.

"Russell. Mom. What are you two doing here?"

Her ex spoke. "You made your point. Time to come home."

"He came to try and take you away," said Eli, at the same time.

Then Eli just stared at her, a ferocious scowl on his face. But then she realized he was looking right past her at Cruella.

"Cara," Eli hissed.

Amarie swung around to stare at the woman behind her.

"Who. Her?" she asked, anger surging that she'd lent a helping hand to the woman who'd hurt her boyfriend.

Eli morphed from a grumpy vet to a six-foot angry ogre. "Cara, what the hell are you doing in Service?"

"Where did you think I'd go when you locked me out of our house? I decided to come home to you, my once-loving husband."

"Husband?" Amarie's mother and Russell parroted in unison.

"You never mentioned your boyfriend was married," her mother demanded. *Drop. Drop. Splat.* Amarie said nothing as the food slipped from her hands in a slow-motion reel. The contents spilled onto the floor, leaking away just like her good mood.

Chapter Twenty-Three

Amarie hoped Eli handled his ex-wife in Service better than she tap-danced around her mother and Russell. What possessed the woman to bring trouble to her daughter?! Not that Eli should have concerns with Dr. Russell Feldman parading around town in his electric blue 2023 Range Rover Sport.

"Mama, what are you doing here?" Amarie whispered. "And why would you bring Russell?" Amarie had pointed him in the direction of the restroom, then speed-walked her mother into the front parlor with privacy. Clearly there were questions that required answers.

"Hmm, I received your text message about your exam. Congratulations," her mother said, sipping the iced lemonade Leah served them both.

"Mom, that was like... an hour ago."

"Russell showed up in Florida looking for an ally. He promised to come here with or without me, so," she shrugged her lean shoulders, "I accompanied him. Now that I've answered your question. I'm concerned about Eli's ex-wife being here."

Amarie ignored the Cara question, continuing with her

inquiry. She trusted Eli. Her ex, he had the reliability rating of cheap toilet paper.

"So, you're Russell's ally?" Amarie whisper-yelled.

"No, but," she smiled with a mischievous grin, "I did get a free car ride to come lay eyes on my baby girl. You're always so animated about new surroundings. I thought... what the heck. Service, West Virginia. Here I come."

Amarie's eyes widened in realization. While Russell thought he'd gained a bargaining chip in negotiating her surrender, Bethany had hitched a ride to carry out a private agenda.

"Heaven above," Amarie sputtered, "Mama grifted my ex."

Leah, who had been sitting quietly while she and Eli managed their individual disasters, chuckled. Not that she had voiced a distaste for Russell, but Amarie knew how welcoming Leah could be when she enjoyed the company.

"That fool of a man deserved it," her mother hissed, while Russell was out of earshot, "taking advantage of you for years. About time he got a dose of the nasty he enjoys funneling for others to swallow."

She shook her head, her relaxed curls brushing the shoulders of her tan St. John float jacket with tweed sparkle. Wait... when had her mother ever worn anything that drew attention to her presence?

"Do you know he had the nerve to bring his laptop into my house asking if I knew how to set up a WordPress website?"

"And?"

Bethany actually rolled her eyes. Amarie felt as if she were seeing her mother for the first time in, well, ever. Who was this bold and animated woman who mimicked the hiss of an angry rattlesnake and rolled eyes better than a teenager? Something miraculous had transformed the compliant, ever-seen-but-not-heard housewife who knew her husband of thirty plus years was a cheating bastard into a she-wolf.

"I played dumb just like I do with your father. My working-for-free days are over."

They all snickered, but abruptly stopped when Russell strutted into the room in starched khakis with a polo shirt beneath his Ivy League sport coat, a six-figure peacock in full plumage.

"This is a nice house," he snorted, grabbing a lemonade glass, a tea sandwich, and a slice of homemade poundcake with his fingers before walking to the fireplace mantel to strike a pose. His attempt to impress had the opposite effect. Why couldn't he enter the room and take a seat like a normal person? Who exactly was he trying to impress? "Didn't expect much from the outside."

"Ah…thank you," Leah said looking to them for direction. "I think…"

Amarie bit her lowered lip, trapping the building tide of laughter in her throat.

Russell, the pompous ass, seemed to be tallying up the value of the Calvary estate, his beady brown eyes flitting like insect wings from the antique detailing surrounding the wall sconces, to the ornate crown molding framing of the ceiling, to the wainscoting beneath the mahogany chair rail. "How much you pay for all this?"

"Oh my god, Russell." Amarie hung her head, embarrassment breathing on her neck, like the old drunk guy in the night club. Just foul. "That's just rude."

"What?" he crowed, talking with his mouth full.

Was that lettuce between his teeth? He looked like a rabbit on a feeding frenzy. How had she thought this man was out of her reach? Talk about distance shining a spotlight on perspective. This man had *rude* and *entitled* stitched into his high-waisted briefs.

First, how dare he expect her mother to pick up where Amarie had left him high and dry? Russell had profited from her labor, but he was too selfish to invest the money into building a more profitable business. Any guilt Amarie harbored at hiding his website and deleting his social handles vanished. Furthermore, Russell wasn't a fledgling or distressed businessman. Nope, he just wanted to use Amarie and Bethany because he believed he had a right to exploit their talents.

Her mother had supported her father's practice in the early years of their marriage, serving as his orientation and training manager. Amarie realized she had imitated her mother's example, the supportive and dutiful partner, but had diverted to a road less traveled when she landed in Service. No way would she ever consider returning to the life she'd had with Russell. In fact, she hadn't had any life at all. She existed to make his life easier at the expense of her own hopes and dreams.

Now he felt entitled to disrespect the one person who helped Amarie to see her worth.

Standing to her feet, Amarie released a weighted sigh. "Russell, you're done here. Time for you to leave."

"Leave?" he scoffed, dusting his palms together, depositing crumbs on Leah's polished hardwood floors.

"You're making a mess," Amarie hissed. "Where did you lose your manners?"

"It's just food, Amarie." He shrugged. "Since when did you develop discerning tastes?"

"When I left you in D.C. Where you should've stayed," she said with emphasis.

"Oh," he mocked, stepping off his invisible high horse.

"I see what's happening. You think you're something here in Who-ville and can say anything to me? We both know you can't cut it in the city, that's why you're hiding out in tiny town USA."

"You don't get to tell me who I am. If I'm the one hiding, why are you hunting for me? Did I call, text, or write sending for you?"

His mouth opened and closed with a squeak of sound.

"Exactly. I didn't send for you, so there was no need to come for me."

He chuckled, an attempt to distract from the rising color spreading from beneath the polo collar, like shark chum.

"Bethany. You need to talk to your daughter. I drove to Florida to pick you up, so you could do your job to get her back where she belongs."

Amarie opened her mouth to defend her mother, but Leah gave a subtle nod to keep quiet. Obviously, there was some nonverbal, mother-to-mother communication happening that Amarie had missed because Bethany gave a smile of approval. To have the two most important women in her life stand united at her side meant the world to Amarie.

Bethany placed her glass on a coaster before meeting this arrogant man's gaze. "I didn't ask you to come to my home."

"No," he snapped, trying to track his fingers through locks gelled within an inch of life support. "Your husband did. Because he understands you and your daughter can't come up with the right answer unless it's told to you."

Amarie released an audible gasp.

Her mother looked unmoved by Russell's hurtful comment.

"No sir," Leah rasped. "This is my house. Bethany, Amarie, say your goodbyes to this fella." To Russell she said, "I'm going to get my rolling pin. It'll be aimed in your direction.

If you don't want a knot on that inflated head, you best be gone."

"Russell," Bethany called, "we are guests in Mrs. Calvary's home. Please temper your stupidity."

"Are you threatening me with kitchenware?" Russell laughed.

Leah smiled. "Nope. I'm promising to tenderize your backside before turning you over to my boys."

Russell stiffened. Leah's gentle tone had delivered a mighty hammer. Her tone said she had the manpower to back up her words.

"Fine, but I drove the freakin' green mile to the swamps of Florida. And then around the world in eighty days to get to this hillbilly cesspool. I'm not leaving empty-handed. Amarie, here." He retrieved a small red velvet box from his front pocket and thrust it at her.

At seeing it, Amarie recoiled. "What is that?"

"It's what you wanted from the day we met. A real diamond ring. A wedding. Stop baulking. Take the stupid thing."

Oh no he didn't. Did he think he could demand her commitment? Real love shouldn't be transactional. And she valued herself above the Mrs. Russell Feldman title.

Amarie crossed her arms over her chest, defiant. "No, thank you."

"No," Russell yelled, his face flaming a horrid shade of bruised red. "You force me to come after you. To spend two grand on a new ring. All to refuse my proposal?"

"Ah, Russell," she mused, "I didn't hear a proposal." Looking at the other women in the room. "Did either of you hear in a man standing in this very room ask me, Amarie Walker, to marry him?"

"No" came the tandem reply.

"See." Amarie frowned, having fun at Russell's expense. "We didn't hear anything close to a declaration of love and commitment."

"Okay. Okay. Fine. Amarie," he huffed, "will you be my wife?" He looked downright ill, red giving way to ashen gray.

"Absolutely—"

Russel interrupted before she could finish. "Good." He re-pocketed the ring. "You and your mother pack your things. I'm leaving in ten minutes."

"My answer is absolutely *not*. And why wait?" Amarie laughed.

Bethany stood. "Why indeed."

"Oh, oh, you think you have the upper hand. I saw his ex-wife in that key fob–sized clinic, Amarie. She's beautiful, delicate, feminine. You don't stand a chance."

"And neither do you, Russell. The door is that way." She pointed.

"If I walk out that door, you're both stranded. You think your father will come to your rescue. He won't. He practically begged me to take you both off his hands."

"Russell, I'm not counting on you or my father. I got this. Bye-bye now." Amarie looked at her mother, who had tears in her eyes.

"Come here, baby girl." She hugged Amarie so tight it hurt, and it felt absolutely sublime. "I'm so proud of you. You could've been angry at the world—at me, but you, my beautiful sunshine," Bethany's voice trembled, "you saved yourself. You saved me."

Amarie raised her brow, having never heard these words from her mother. "You sure it's me you're talking about? The six-year champion. Your late bloomer."

"Don't sound surprised. When have you ever quit?"

"Well…"

"See." Her mother smiled. "You can't think of a time where a hard knock meant a hard stop. You're relentless. Something you didn't inherit from me."

"Mom," she said, thinking about Ruth and little Phoebe. "I owe you an apology—"

"Shh, baby. I had my own lessons to learn. When you're young, you're discovering who you are. But as you age you learn who you aren't. The fantasy of storybook marriages, perfect kids—heck, fairy-tale love falls away. I let your father tell me my value for years. But I never stopped to question his. He's not the man who deserves the woman I am. I know that now."

"I have a new appreciation for how brave you were to have left Dad back then. He gave Princess away to hurt you, didn't he?"

Amarie watched as her words hit their mark. Tears gathered in Bethany's eyes, but the lines bracketing her eyes and mouth seemed to recede like the ebb tide. "H-he threatened to take her to the shelter if we didn't return home at once. I knew how much you loved her, but I couldn't bear to turn around, drive us back to that beautiful prison of stucco and iron. So," Bethany stiffened her spine, "I kept going."

"Then I got sick," Amarie whispered, knowing her weakness was the reason her mother had chosen to return to a long-dead marriage.

"No. No." Bethany shook her head, adamant in her denial. "You were always resilient, strong. I knew you would heal, Amarie. But sleeping in our chariot had reached its end. And your father promised to pay for your college education if I returned and didn't leave again."

"So, you went back?"

Bethany smiled then. "After he had his lawyers put it in writing. I felt like a failure when we walked back into that house, your little face crumpled when you called for Princess, and she didn't appear, tail wagging in happiness. Your father had followed through on his threat, but I had the documents in my hand that secured your future. Then, you came home with Russell," she deadpanned.

"Forget Russell. I can't believe you kept your deal with Daddy Dearest from me."

"Hello," Russell drawled, "I'm standing right here."

"Shush, you," Amarie shooed him away. "Mom and I are talking. So rude."

Bethany cut him a withering glance before continuing.

"I wanted to protect you. Our marriage is separate from the relationship you could've had with Russell. I had hoped he would be a better father than husband. Turns out he was more interested in chasing tail." She shrugged. Again, who was this carefree woman who'd hidden away under her husband's thumb?

"What are you going to do about Dad? He's going to be furious once Russell snitches on us. How you failed to marry me off."

"Oh, I've decided to leave your father."

"What—when did this happen?"

"Just now. My daughter is a college graduate and a licensed nurse. Weren't you listening?"

"Yes, ma'am. I am."

"Now, what are you going to do about Eli's other woman?"

"Eli and I are together, Mom. Cara. Russell. There's nothing either of them can say that will matter to us."

"Hello," Russell yelled, "I'm still here."

Leah walked in, rolling pin in hand. "You don't have to worry about Amarie. My Eli knows the makeup of a good woman."

As if conjured by a sorcerer, Tobias, Noah, and Eli stormed in behind their mother, jaws tight, limbs loose.

Noah looked at the wooden rolling pin in Leah's small hand and frowned.

"Who do I need to smack into Middle Earth?" Noah announced, eyes locked on Russell's slack-jawed face fading to an increasingly pale complexion.

"You ain't never lied," Tobias added, stepping in Russell's personal space.

"Amarie. Mrs. Walker." Eli came right up to Amarie, wrapping her in his capable arms. "You okay?" he asked kissing the top of her head.

"Perfect," she whispered. "You?"

When Eli didn't respond, Amarie lifted her head from his chest and looked up at his face. The mask, hard and frozen, was back. That couldn't be good.

Chapter Twenty-Four

WITH RUSSELL GONE, and Amarie safe, it was past time for Eli to make it clear to Cara that he would never be an option for her again. Heavens, if he'd met Amarie instead of the woman hanging around his office and currently looking through his files, he would probably be a father to one, maybe two, little Calvarys.

"What in the heck are you doing?" Eli barked. Beside him Hiccup released a woof, his teeth bared in defense of their territory.

Cara jumped, banging her knee on his desk. "Ow, you scared me."

"Good. You hunting for the penny you left behind?" he prompted. The pout on her face would've had the old Eli running to soothe her pain. This time he stood, arms crossed over his chest, fury simmering close to the surface.

"Eli, you were never cruel," she said, slinking closer. "Why are you treating me this way?"

Eli backed away, not wanting to inhabit the same space. "You showing up here has a direct correlation with my foul mood. So, again. What were you searching for?"

"I don't know." She shrugged. "Some clue as to what you've been doing since we've been apart." She held a stack of his correspondence in one hand. Cara carried them unceremoniously back to his desk, where she straightened them into neat stacks. Watching her rearrange his papers, the way she'd done their futures, ignited the distrust he'd harbored for months, a cancer that could've ruined him for Amarie.

Eli rubbed at the bridge of his nose. "*Apart* implies reconciliation is a possibility. We're divorced."

"I know that we legally divorced," she said, slowly working her way around the sharp corners of the oak bookshelf against the shorter wall to stand in front of him. "But we don't have to be."

"I signed the same papers you did. We're done, legal or otherwise. I had every intention of honoring my commitment to stay as far away from you as possible. You should do the same."

"Why do you always follow the rules? I'm trying to restore something that was once beautiful."

"You know what, Cara? You and me both. I'm trying to dig out of the pile of crap you and Sven buried me under before the two of you cat-cowed into Zentopia."

"Oh Eli," she rasped, distress in her tone. She froze him with those liquid pools gathering in her eyes, on the brim of spilling down her pale cheeks. "I made a mistake, leaving you."

"I'm not falling for your games. You wanna play, try the lottery." During his marriage to Cara, he'd been her sounding board, listening when she told him how she'd been misunderstood as a teenager. Attractive by most standards, people assumed she was all beauty minus the brains or a gold digger using her physical attributes as a meal ticket. After she abandoned him, Eli had understood the duality of her personality. A chameleon of sorts, Cara was capable of more but preferred to leech what she could from others to facilitate her desire to do less. Within months of their union, she'd convinced him why she needed to stay at home, preparing for the children she never intended to give him.

"I'm serious. I should've never chosen him over you. His name wasn't even Sven," she spat. "It's Steven. He lied to me from the very beginning. It wasn't until last month that I learned he preys on his female clientele. What is the world coming to? He lures women into intimate relationships, young and old, mind you. His goal is to get them to trust him before conning them out of all their money. I wasn't his only victim, Eli. I-I read about situations like mine on the internet, but not the women like me. Just the old, lonely, and desperate."

"Sounds awful," he deadpanned, not caring one iota that Sven-Steven had stolen his ex-wife's ill-gotten gain. If she wanted sympathy, he was fresh out.

"Thank you." She wiped away a tear, flipping her straight mane off her shoulder. "I knew you would appreciate me trying to rebuild our lives after that horrible man ruined us."

"You don't have to try, Cara. I was being facetious. We are not connected in any way at all."

"I understand that but what I'm saying is I came here because I care about you and I want to try again."

"Try what?" he hissed. "To run off with all my money again? To leave me with a house that has been damn near impossible to sell?"

"That's what I'm talking about. I love that house. You don't have to sell it if we move back into it, Eli. Call the agent. Cancel the contract. Once that's done, we start over in our home."

And there it was. Her reason for coming to Service wasn't reconciliation. She wanted him to cancel the contract on the property.

"The house is on the market. Call my agent. Make a backup offer." He smirked.

"I'm not going to pay you for a house you built for me. You should give it to me."

"Are you insane? Or do you think I'm still some dumb hick that you can sucker again?" He'd given his heart, his last name, but all she wanted was a house.

She placed a manicured hand over her heart. "Eli, I've changed."

"Into what? 'Cause you were pretty vicious to begin with."

"Oh, there you are, Mister Perfect Husband. So I made a few mistakes. That doesn't mean I was all bad."

"Woman, don't try to tell me there's chocolate chips in the cat litter when I've already stepped in the shit you made of things."

"That hurt, Eli."

"Get over it. The house is mine. What you do from here on out has nothing to do with me. There is no us."

"You won't even consider what I'm offering. See," she railed, pointing at his head, "this is why I left."

"I thought you left because you lied to me. You cheated with another man. And you stole from me to bankroll your new life."

"Details. You always get so wrapped up in the little stuff. I'm offering you a future. You and me back in Virginia. Living in the house you built for me."

"Listen. It's pretty clear you want my house. Not me."

She lifted her chin. "Why shouldn't I have it? The house was my idea. I designed it for me."

"Yeah, thanks for the reminder. It was my own arrogance that led me to propose in the first place. But I've learned from my mistakes. Thinking you would somehow complete me."

"Exactly."

"Wrong again. I'm happier without you, Cara. Thank you for leaving so I didn't have to. At the time, I wouldn't have handled that well. You running off with Sven-Steven was the best thing for both of us."

"Eli, you promised to love me. We took vows and you're a man of your word."

"A husband made a promise to his wife. Neither of us are those two people anymore."

"Vows are forever. How can you be so callous when it's obvious I'm upset?"

"I don't care if you are upside-down. What you have to do is get back on the high horse you rode in here on and get out of Service. You never liked it here. Go on back to the city. Live your life."

"I could like it," she blurted. "You used to want to make me happy. If I stayed in town for a few days, gave you time to think about us. What we had..." she trailed off and moved closer. When she lifted her hand as if to touch him, Eli narrowed his eyes.

"Don't," he warned. "I don't belong to you anymore."

"We were married for almost a year, Eli. You actually think after only five months divorced that you're serious about this Amarie character?" she huffed, her tone loaded with envy and doubt.

"Don't forget about the cheating part."

"How can I? You won't allow it. Everything has to be your way, the Calvary legacy," she mocked. "How about you grow up? People cheat all the time, Eli. Move on."

"How 'bout you take your own advice?" he bellowed.

"You loved being married to me, Eli Calvary. I know it. You know it. So if you think some country wallflower is going to keep you satisfied a year from now, you've forgotten how good I am at satisfying you. How right I am for you," she crooned.

"Cara, enough. Whatever you planned, it won't work. Trust me, darling, your kitty isn't the only one that purrs. I'm going home now."

"Fine." She grabbed her designer tote bag and miniature toy poodle from the faded couch behind his desk. He didn't know if the dog had made a sound the whole time she'd been here.

"Where do you think you're going?"

"With you, duh. This town still doesn't have a hotel or a decent restaurant."

Amarie sashayed in, looking from him to Cara. "Oh, she's still here. Why?"

"I'm not the one going somewhere—well, that's not actually true. Eli and I are going home. You can lock up after we leave," Cara challenged, lifting her left hand where the one-carat diamond solitaire he'd given her gleamed even in this light. "He was my husband. I'm the first and only woman he's ever given a ring to."

"Aw." Amarie grinned. "I speak mean girl, too. Trust me, you don't want to battle to the death. I will annihilate you."

Eli grinned, shaking his head. Amarie had more surprises in store for him. She never backed down, just charged ahead without any backup. Not that he would've stood by if his old flame had tried anything.

Cara, who was not used to being confronted, took a step back. The depth of his feelings for his woman exploded.

"Sugar dumpling," Amarie cooed.

"Yea, babe?" Eli grinned.

"The Kitty Kibbles contracts, I printed them for you to review, please. Grab them before you leave. You should understand what you're turning down. And just in case you change your mind, tomorrow is the last day to sign."

"I'm on it."

Just then, Leah came strolling in with a blanket and a pillow.

"Amarie, your mom needs help settling in upstairs. She's asking for you."

"Oh, thank you."

Before she could turn to walk away, Eli pulled her back, placing a long, deep kiss on her lips.

"Hmm, that's nice," she said, pulling away. "Dumpling, be sure to empty the trash. It smells like rotten fish in here." She looked directly at Cara.

Cara gasped. "Is she talking about me?"

"Girl, you are as smart as you look," Amarie chirped.

"I'll meet you at home, sweetheart," Eli called after her.

Leah walked in, lips thinned, eyes determined. "Eli, don't keep Amarie waiting. Get the animals packed for home. I'll take care of Cara."

He bent and placed a kiss on his momma's cheek. "Don't leave any bruises," he whispered.

She patted his hand. "Go on now." She chuckled. "See to Amarie. Your brothers are helping the other doctor back to his Range Rover."

Eli noticed the slight raise in Cara's brows at the mention of Range Rover. Gosh, he'd really married a gold digger. His family had his back, clearing the way for him to make sure Amarie knew her place in his life was secure. How had Dr. Russell Feldman tricked a woman as vibrant as his Amarie into hiding her light so he could shine?

To his ex, Leah Calvary, the authoritarian matriarch of his childhood, pointed. "Cara, there's a pull-out couch right behind you. You can rest up for your drive first thing in the morning."

"You want me . . . to sleep on a couch in a vet clinic?"

Now the real showdown between his mother and Cara was about to begin. He needed to clear out before the first bomb blast. Eli kept moving, thinking about what else the kittens needed before he headed home. Then he remembered the Kitty Kibbles forms on the printer in his office. The contract could wait. He needed to get home to Amarie.

"Where did you think you were going to sleep? Certainly not in my lowly house and I know Amarie wouldn't appreciate you trying to worm your way back into his. So, which is it? Couch? Your car? Or your place of residence, wherever that may be? Because we both know you have a backup plan."

Cara stiffened, her chin raised. "Funny, when Eli and I were married, you all drowned me with how important family is. Yet you, Leah, condone my soulmate leaving me here, so he can be with another woman. I was family once."

"No, you weren't. And stop calling me your husband, your soulmate. I'm not either," Eli rasped, cat carrier on his shoulder. Hiccup growled, his ears lowered and pinned back. Cara stumbled on her heels, adding more distance. "Shh, boy. We're going home."

"You should know, Dr. Sexy Kitty Vet, that I'm bidding in the bachelor auction. The number one contributor to date, so don't think you can write me off."

Eli stopped and faced the woman who no longer held any power over him. "So Sven-Steven didn't take your money?" He shook his head. "Unbelievable, Cara. Tomorrow, you leave here. Don't come back." With that, he walked away. "Thanks again, Momma."

"You're welcome, son. Got everything you need?"

"I do." He had the woman he wanted. Eli thanked the stars above that Cara had left him. If she hadn't, he wouldn't have Amarie in his life.

Chapter Twenty-Five

CARA WAS A shrewd creature who'd crawled out of a hole to infest Amarie's happiness. Of the three people who'd arrived in Service uninvited, Amarie wanted to squash the former Mrs. Calvary like a bug. It grated that the woman had scurried into Service to bury her painted claws into Eli again.

"What a day we had, huh? Russell, my mom, and your ex-wife." Amarie just let the words hang in the air, like ratty underwear. Both their pasts had driven into town, ripping open old scars. Amarie had exterminated Russell, sending him packing, closing and locking the door on what they once had. Cara was next.

Bethany was safely tucked in at Leah's. Well, tucked in really wasn't the right word. She'd left the two ladies at the Calvary kitchen table with a half-empty bottle of red wine, watching old movies on the computer. Seems they both had a thing for grainy, shoot-'em-up movies with Clint Eastwood and Charles Bronson. But her mom looked happy and relaxed. And so did Leah. Amarie may have lost her insta-bestie to Bethany. However, she couldn't recall a time when her mother had cracked jokes or sung aloud. Her laughter held a foreign note, carefree and open to new possibilities. Whereas Eli had been quiet after their celebratory dinner of peanut-butter-and-jelly biscuits. Which was not at all bad considering the crap show in the clinic. Amarie had questions, but she hadn't quite firmed up her checklist on where to begin the conversation.

"You passing your exam could be sharable content from Calvary Vet today, huh." From Eli's position on the couch, he took another draw from the chilled IPA bottle he held in one hand. Circles, dark and defined, cast a hollowed shadow beneath his eyes. The easy smile he flashed when it was just the two of them, the one that sent her ever-present stomach butterflies in motion, stayed locked behind thinned lips. If he clenched his teeth any harder, he would need a Smile Direct Club makeover to cover the enamel stumps where his teeth used to be.

"Even a TikTok sensation is entitled to behind-the-scenes privacy."

"Agreed. Thanks for that," he said, pulling her down to his lap. "I'm so proud you, Amarie."

Hiccup yawned from his homestead, the rug in front of the flameless fireplace. Raspberry, Dove, Formerly, Graffiti, and Artist nestled along his belly, five pairs of paws, making biscuits, kneading themselves to sleep.

"Thank you, boyfriend. So," she mused, "the kitten cast is still here. Does keeping the kittens mean you've decided to accept the Kitty Kibbles offer? They did make you Tik-Tok famous." Amarie held her breath, hoping against hope that her stubborn man would recognize how good he was at his new job. Yes, it was unconventional, but he excelled at it.

"Afraid not. In two days the bachelor auction is over. Dr. Sexy Kitty will meet with a timely disappearance shortly thereafter."

Amarie shook her head. All their work, it needed to be continued. "Your five hundred thousand fans, their clients, too, will miss you. Think of the void in your absence."

"There are a billion other TikTokers, let them have it. It's not me."

"Eli, trust me. It's all you. Your authentic self made the hashtag a viral sensation. Your advice. Your personality."

He nodded. "We'll have the money we need tomorrow. Mission accomplished, Amarie."

"But—but this could be a new mission. What about helping the town raise money for a clinic? A library? Senior center?"

"Whoa. Whoa. How about we say job well done and get down to the real discussion? My ex-wife. I'm sorry you and your mother overheard the showdown with Cara. I forgot to use my boyfriend voice."

She rested her head on his very broad, and at the moment bare, shoulder. "That's because your ex-husband howl was in order."

He'd totally changed the subject. Normally she would object, but since she wanted to talk about the very same thing, why not walk through the door he'd opened?

"Sorry our celebration plans were ruined with Cara's drama. I'll make it up to you and Bethany tomorrow," Eli whispered, placing the half-empty bottle on the floor before wrapping her up in both arms.

"And Russell. Tomorrow sounds good. But after I show my mom the Johnson farm. She wants to walk the grounds where her daughter birthed a calf. We might venture further uptown to the waterfall."

Eli nipped her side. "It was a foal. And you helped. Reception is terrible that high up. I'm not sure I'll survive with you so far away. How long does she plan to be in town?"

"Fun fact. Mom has decided she's not returning to Florida. She's finally found the strength to leave my dad."

Eli frowned. "It would tear me up inside if my parents had split up."

"Huh, it had to be nice growing up with both parents who actually don't bring verbal ammunition to the breakfast table."

"Can't say I remember any weaponry served with the biscuits."

"I held it against her, you know? Staying with him. But now I know she sacrificed for me. My mom deserves happiness, a safe place to heal, to find herself. I don't want her to waste any more time in a marriage where she's disrespected and mistreated. She deserves more than what she's gotten in this life."

"Well, she has you. I think that's pretty fantastic."

Her tank top rode up, revealing nothing but smooth skin. His fingers teased, alternating beneath soft and firm caresses.

"Right you are. Did I mention how good you are at this boyfriend stuff?"

"Not today." He grinned.

"Hands down. You check all the boxes, Eli Calvary. But why are you deliberately aggravating my tickle zone?" she asked, releasing a breathy moan.

"I'm very interested in where you want me to put my hands, sweetheart." The noise that rumbled through his chest triggered an instant response in all the right places. "So, when you say words like 'zones' and 'boxes,' all husky and low, it gets me to thinking about finding new erogenous areas in the nine abdominal quadrants."

"Oh, is this dirty talk for nurses? Sign me up for more, sexy."

"Registered nurse foreplay." He laughed. "A reward for

handling today like pro." He ran his tongue along her jaw, and Amarie released another moan. Very porn star, which matched her responsive nipples.

"About that."

"Yeah," he prompted, between enjoyable kisses.

After the mental gymnastics, which she'd failed miserably at, of processing that she'd actually delivered Eli's ex to his doorstep, she wanted to reverse course, take the porcelain-skinned princess over to Matt Johnson's farm for Harry the horse to rip out her honey-colored hair by the roots.

"Why is Cara still here?" She winced at the abrupt delivery. Not the smooth transition she aimed for, but it would have to suffice.

"Apparently, her boyfriend, Sven, whose real name is Steven, took advantage of her. Tricked her out of my money." His chuckle, tight and humorless, resonated through the hand she lay on his chest. "The house in Virginia, she wants it. She claims she doesn't have a place to go."

Amarie sucked in a breath, but the memories of that year living in Prince's back seat bit and slashed through her resolve to banish Cara, with all haste, beyond the boundaries of Service.

"Hmm... are you considering it?"

"Nope. She'll be gone tomorrow. No muss. Not a fuss."

The last thing she wanted to feel toward Cara was conflicted, but here she was, that eleven-year-old girl praying that someone had thrown her and her mother a lifeline. Wasn't she the shield-maiden of women and children? A life of services to others. At her core Amarie was a giver. Should it matter that Cara had sought help from Amarie's boyfriend? Adulting—no wonder she'd delayed this journey as long as possible. She swallowed her apprehension, choosing to share the most painful year of her existence.

"The year Mom left my dad, remember I told you we were hungry sometimes?"

"Of course." Eli nodded, brushing his thumb along her cheek. "You explained the snack packs."

"We were homeless, Eli. For three of those months, we slept in that old BMW I drive. Other adults, their children called us names—bums, vagrants, trash." When he tried to sit up, she pinned him down. "Please, just let me get this out."

"Whatever you want, sweetheart."

"Don't sound so ominous. It's just, I know how desperation can tear you up inside. The reason I entered nursing school was to care for the world's rejected, the nameless faces on the streets, in the shelters, under the bridges." Even with her degree in hand, she was still that homeless little girl standing at her mother's side, desperate, begging for food, and disposable.

"That's why Lourdes's comment upset you so much."

Amarie nodded. "Yes."

"Wow. You and your mom are remarkable."

"She is. Me, meh. I developed pneumonia while we were unhoused. I'm the reason she went back to my father." Brave, but solemn, her mother had filled the gas tank with the last of their meager funds and drove them back into the lion's den. The mood in the car had been as desolate as the long stretches of I-95. Her father's other woman had vanished along with Princess—and her mother's joy.

"Don't blame yourself. The fault lay with your father. His actions created the condition that forced your mom to make a difficult choice to protect you both. Cara's situation is self-inflicted and there's not a child to consider."

"Thank goodness, that would be awful. But if Cara's telling the truth—"

"She's not. Trust me when I tell you that woman is full of tricks."

"I get that, but if she needs help..." She'd probably choke on these words later, but she was who she was. Helping people was her love language and she wouldn't be afraid to speak her truth for fear of being taken advantage of.

"You're all sparkles inside and out, Amarie Walker. You're giving me permission to help my ex."

"I want her gone, I do. But yasss," she drawled. "We needed help, and none came. This is probably a test for angel wings that I hope to pass. But who knows what will happen if we don't offer assistance. Either way, I don't want a guilty conscience. I'm conflicted about sending you into the fires of Mordor considering Cara's still wears the ring of power."

"Sweetheart, that's a mouth full of rambling." He squeezed her tight to his chest, but the tendrils of doubts lingered. "If she truly needs a place to live after I take care of the mortgage and your portion of the proceeds, I'll do what I can. As for my house, maybe it'll bring the next family some joy."

Amarie placed a peck of a kiss on his lips, more playful than passionate.

"You have nothing to worry about. Cara is not a threat to our future."

"Aw, so you're thinking how awesome I am to keep around."

He wiggled his brows. "Among other things."

"Thanks for saying that, I mean look at how we started out. She seems determined to cause trouble, and I don't know—I just want to make sure we're not fooling ourselves."

He took her hand and slid it down to his body. "There's nothing fooling here. Everything is one hundred percent real and ready."

"Don't tempt me with sex when your ex is asleep on your couch."

"Absolutely not. If you wanted that, you shouldn't be so darn irresistible. And for the record, you're the one on my couch. Cara's on Hiccup's office bed." Eli captured her chin. "Remember, you're my number one girl. Now let's go to bed."

"No." Amarie moved to straddle Eli's lap. She pulled her shirt over her head, tossing it to the floor. "Convince me."

Because in spite of Eli's reassurances, Amarie had doubts. The last time a man had had a choice between her and the other woman, she'd ended up homeless, penniless, and manless.

Chapter Twenty-Six

THE BACHELOR AUCTION site had been hacked. All the bids, all the money gone, disappeared. Watching the bid totals climb had given Eli the confidence boost to keep smiling for the camera even though he preferred a behind-the-scenes life. But this morning with Amarie out of bed before the morning humidity to complete the full hike with Bethany, he'd logged on under a red-and-gold sunrise. Immediately the day descended into the bleakest of nights. The website had posted a message.

> Dear Customer, Auction Luv Buzz has been the target of a data breach. Until further notice, all bidding accounts and monetary payouts are suspended. We are working diligently with our IT team to get every account restored in a timely fashion.

What the heck did that mean?

And Eli had spent the better part of an hour tearing up his office looking for the Kitty Kibbles contract. The dreaded option of him being beholden to a faceless behemoth company, not that Kitty Kibbles was a household brand, had become the only one to save his family.

He had maybe an hour to meet the deadline to accept their current offer. It was too late to negotiate if the terms favored their time above his practice. Cara and her pooch in a tote had vacated the premises when he arrived; he was grateful she wasn't here to witness his death spiral. No doubt she would've sold tickets. She really did have a vicious side when things didn't go her way.

He reached for another stack of papers on the bookshelf, but his brain short-circuited as he ransacked this pile of peer-reviewed journals twice. In a fit of panicked frustration, Eli shoved the tower of veterinary medicine reference textbooks. The four-tiered structure tilted away as if afraid of what he might do next. The entire weight struck the wall, releasing a volcanic boom. Loose paper scattered to the floor. Without that check, he would lose everything … again.

Hiccup pushed his head against Eli's hand, his whimper tugging at Eli's heartstrings. His best friend, the one companion who had stuck with him during the most difficult year of his life, was anxious.

"Sorry, boy." Eli gave his hand a soft stroke. "Don't mean to scare you." But Eli was terrified. Every cell in his body stretched thin, on the verge of snapping.

"Cara, I swear if you're trashing—"

Leah Calvary stormed in, ready for battle, with her rolling pin in hand. She froze. With her eyes, she roved over the cyclonic condition of his usually organized chaos of an office.

"Cara walked into town for breakfast."

His mother visibly exhaled; her hunter-green button-down accentuating eyes clouded with concern. "If it's not her causing you grief, what's wrong?"

"The auction site—it got hacked. We're not going to get the auction money in time to stop the foreclosure."

"Okay, breathe, Eli." She mimicked the gesture as if it was something she needed to demonstrate on his behalf.

"I am breathing, Momma. But what I need to do is sign that Kitty Kibbles contract," he said through gritted teeth, "and have that check deposited into the business account by Monday morning."

"If it's that off-putting to you, Eli, to continue the Tik-Tok page, just ask the Pendletons for more time. The whole town knows we have money coming."

"Momma, would you stop with the Pendletons. They are not friends to this family. Amarie told me yesterday that she printed the Kitty Kibbles contract. I can't find it."

"Slow down, honey. Take your time. If Amarie said she took care of it, then it's here."

"Why can't I find it?

"It's in the computer, right? Print out another copy."

"She handled the communication." He'd done this to himself. Relegated parts of his responsibilities to Amarie, now look at him: helpless. The single most critical piece of paper of his lifetime and it was locked away in Amarie's email account behind two-factor identification.

"Let's call her, Eli."

"Mom, I have been trying to reach her. Even called Tobias and Noah to get up the mountain after them."

"Where is she?

"Well, Bethany wanted to explore the falls. Amarie and her set out this morning on foot."

"She probably doesn't have a signal that far up the mountain."

"Okay, fine. But what am I gonna do if we miss this contract? I mean, our whole future is hanging on that check."

"Eli, calm down. That isn't so. Look, tonight is the bachelor auction. You'll know the winner by tomorrow. And you still have a day to spare until the deadline to pay the mortgage. Maybe the website will be up and running by then."

"Do you want to risk this house, my practice, Dad's legacy on a maybe? What do we know about that auction site, huh? It could all be an online scam. I should've never agreed to it in the first place."

"Okay, Eli, what is it that you want me to do?"

"I have rules in place for a reason. That's why I'm the boss. And I like sticking to my policies. Amarie came in here, and she's just changed everything. Now I'm lost without her. I can't find what I need when I need it." And there it was, his worst fear. He'd made another wrong turn and his family would suffer the consequences for his failure.

"Then wait till Amarie gets back."

"I shouldn't have to. This is my business. If she printed the contract, where is it? Without a contract they won't release the funds. Bosses don't wait on employees."

"Amarie is more than your employee, Eli. If she said it's here, then it is. We just wait until Amarie gets back."

"Mom, what is it that you don't understand about the timeline?"

"Eli Calvary, what it is that you don't understand is that you are not too big for me to swat your backside. Now I've had enough disrespect from men in this house in the last twenty-four hours."

"I'm not taking advantage of Amarie, so don't lump me in with Dr. Russell Feldman." Eli loaded every syllable with the contempt he felt for the man. "What did she ever seen in him?" he murmured.

"The way you're snapping and carrying on, I'm wondering what she sees in you. Now you get it together."

"Mom, this is it. Our ninth life. Without that contract, we're done. The house. The cabins. The land. The clinic."

"Listen to me. I knew Cara coming into town would put you on your ear. That woman had you in a perpetual bad mood for years, now it's back. You're barking, and I'm here trying to help you. We have time."

"This ain't got nothing to do with Cara. Amarie had one job and she didn't do it."

"Well, I say she did. Now focus and keep your head on straight."

"The only thing wrong with my head is I've allowed too many hands in the pot."

"Well, no work gets done with hands in pockets, Eli. It took the family working together and Amarie to get here."

"*Here* is relative. Without that money, we're all going to be homeless and unemployed."

"I'll call your brothers."

"Why?"

She hit Eli with that mother stare. "If they have found Amarie, she'll come back and take care of everything."

"And that's what I hate. I don't want her to take care of my business."

Just that moment, Cara, Russell, and Lourdes Pendleton walked into his establishment, laughing and giggling.

"Eli." Cara beamed. "Look who I bumped into at the little restaurant in town!"

Cara and Dr. Russell Feldman were still in town...and they'd found Lourdes, the great white hunter. Just what he didn't need, an attack from three sides.

"Hey Eli." Lourdes smiled. "You looked stressed? Guess you saw the demolition equipment on the side of the road this morning."

"Lourdes, go spread your venom somewhere else," Eli spat.

"Oh honey," Cara cooed, walking up to him and cupping his cheek. "She's right. You're flushing beet red."

He pushed her hand away. "Were you messing with my desk?"

Amarie and her mom walked in the door, big smiles on their faces. Tobias and Noah on their heels.

"Found Amarie," Noah called. "And the construction equipment."

Eli ignored that last part. "The Kitty Kibbles contract. Where is it, Amarie?"

"Good morning to you too, grumpy. It's on the printer." Amarie bypassed Russell and Lourdes without a word. She peeked around Cara. "It should be right—"

"Not there, sunshine," he rumbled, voice dripping with sarcasm. "I have exactly seven minutes to get the contract signed and scanned."

"I'll grab my computer. We can get it done." She turned to head for the house. "Oh, shoot."

"No. Not shoot. What?"

"My laptop is in the cabin."

"What?" Eli bellowed.

At his thunderous outburst, Amarie winced.

"Take it easy, brother." Tobias took a cautious step forward.

Dr. Russell Feldman laughed.

"Shut up, Feldman," Eli snapped.

"I tried to warn you." Russell's laugh grew louder. "She baits you, and then *chop*. Business losing money. Clientele disappearing."

"Russell, you used me as free labor for years. Don't pretend like I sabotaged you. When I packed up my unappreciated skills and talents, that's when you realized how much money I made for your business."

"I thought he abandoned you with nothing?" Eli frowned. Isn't that what she had told him?

"Lies. She dismantled my website and social media in order to ruin me, and then packed up in the middle of the night in that ancient death trap on four wheels."

"That's not actually true."

"Which part?" Eli questioned. "You sabotaged his business."

"I wouldn't do that. He's twisting everything. I built those sites. He had nothing before I came along."

"Oh please. She came with the clothes on her back and terrible eating habits. No real job experience besides working in her father's practice. No resume."

"I more than proved myself capable, Russell."

"Yeah, tell that to the next man who lets you upend his life. You did the same thing to him, didn't you, Amarie? Hmm, seems like a pattern to me. Make it impossible for the men you lure to function without you."

"Nobody lured you, slut-nuts," Amarie retorted. "I helped him. Just like I helped you."

"One more word out of you about Amarie and you're going to get a barroom brawl beating," Noah defended.

"You conveniently forgot to mention you left him high and dry. Tried to ruin his business," Eli challenged.

"This man told me he loved me. Gave me a fake diamond and a prepaid credit card, and then screwed any woman with a willing vagina under my nose and eventually in my face. Literally, I found him screwing the receptionist I hired in our house."

"So, my ex-wife comes to town to screw me over. But you beat her to it. When will I learn my lesson?" Eli was done. With all of them. "You know what? I knew it. I knew it. I knew I should have never trusted anyone else to handle this for me."

"Eli, you're overreacting. Websites get hacked. The money will be there. Whatever it is, we can figure it out together. Partners, remember?"

"I'm sick of women telling me to calm down. I don't want to calm down. I didn't want to calm down when it came to Cara. Don't want to calm down when it comes to you."

"Eli, please." Amarie pleaded with sad brown eyes. "Don't say any more."

"I was so wrong to let you come in here and change everything. And you didn't even ask me, and you should have. I mean, now you got me all hyped up on this contract. And now we can't even find it and the opportunity is gonna pass us by. So, you don't tell me what I can and cannot say. It's my name on the sign out front. I'm done listening to you. I never wanted any of this. Not the auction. Not the TikTok account. Not you. Should've never hired you. I let you talk me into Hollywood dreams with a dollar-store budget. Now I'm worse off."

"You wouldn't even have this opportunity if it wasn't for my work."

"Oh, so now you think I'm beholden to you? That I can't save my family business without you?"

"Eli, you're saying too much now." Leah's voice held more than a note of warning. "Lourdes, call your father and tell him I want a meeting. We will make arrangements for a temporary loan—"

"No," Eli snapped. "Momma, the Pendletons want this land. They bid on it before the Calvarys owned it, but the previous owners sold it to Dad instead. They've been trying to rip it out from under us for years."

"Levi never told me that."

"It's true. My sophomore year of college. The year Dad hurt his back. He got behind on the mortgage. He asked

Pendleton for help. When he refused, I used my college fund to pay off the loan, so we'd never have to worry again about them coming after us. That's why I joined the Army instead of coming back home. To pay off my student loan debt."

"You and your father kept the truth from me?"

"We wanted to protect you. Dad didn't want you to know."

"Amarie, come on, baby girl," Bethany interjected. "Let's—let's leave them alone."

"No. I need her to do her job, the job that I'm paying her to do."

"You know what, Eli Calvary. You don't pay enough for me to subject myself to an angry pit bull of a man who's too foolish to realize the one true opportunity he's about to ruin."

"I don't pay you to lecture me on what's most important to my business."

"Two things, boss. I get paid by the hour, so guess what, you're on my time, not the other way around. The other, per our contract, my share of the money comes after the auction. So, if the site is out of commission, our arrangement is done. Since you value your policies and rules above the person who believed in your vision, those are my facts. And I've decided I couldn't care less if you ever find your contract. I printed it. You were supposed to bring it home. Common sense says talk to the person who was here." Amarie jabbed an accusatory finger in Cara's direction. "Why don't you ask your ring bearer since she slept here last night?"

"Me?" Cara whined. "Eli, what would I know about any of this? She did this. Now she's blaming me? And in my condition." It was then Eli noticed her cradling her stomach.

"What condition?" he mumbled.

"Are you actually considering believing her over me, Eli? I stayed by your side, helping you."

Eli raised his chin, stubborn, angry. "I didn't say that, Amarie. Cara, what condition?"

"No, you're not saying anything to convince me that you trust me," Amarie continued, but Cara hadn't answered his question. "Eli, are you even listening to me?"

"No," He bellowed. "Cara. What condition?"

"I'm pregnant." And then his ex-wife looked at Amarie. "And the baby might be yours."

No. No. No. Eli's mind reeled. Cara and her lies.

"What?" Amarie stumbled back. "I don't need this."

"Amarie, she's lying."

"I don't care," she screamed. "I don't need a stupid, stubborn boyfriend who hates computers and helping people on the internet. Who handwrites dumb policies for one employee."

"Two employees."

"Not anymore. I have a rule of my own and I broke it for you, Eli Calvary. But not anymore. I take care of myself, and I want nothing from you."

Fury and fear twisted, sharp edges cut him open, severed the synapses in his brain. She was the one who'd messed up. How did she get to walk away from him? Like Cara. She would hurt him. Inflict a wound so deep, no amount of packing could fill it, and then she'd abandon him for dead. If she was going to walk away and ruin him forever, she would feel the pain he felt.

"Amarie, listen. I promise, Cara's baby can't be mine."

She faced him, expression formidable. "So you want me to trust you now, huh? Believe in you?"

"You leaving me now?" he asked.

Amarie lifted her chin, defiant, fierce, unafraid. "Yeah, I am."

"You're just like Cara."

"No." She shook her head. "I'll never ask to come back to you. I deserve better."

"On what planet? Honestly, Eli, I'm having a baby. You said I would always be your number one. What do you see in this girl who inserted herself into your life because she had nowhere to go?"

Cara's dismissive tone ignited Eli's fury. Before he could stop the careless words, the poison had spewed from his mouth. "Not just her. You. All of you, I don't want your help. I never did."

His regret came in an instant. Like the others, he was paralyzed. But that didn't stop him from praying. Please. Please. Please. No, he couldn't have spoken the lie aloud. But one look at Tobias's clenched jaw and Noah's tight lips and he knew the truth. Big mouths should come with warning labels because the strike of Eli's words, his fears unchecked, spread faster than venom, it poisoned what little oxygen remained in the room. Eli stood stock-still, reining in the cords of dread threatening to cut him in two. He loved his family. He loved Amarie. They were the steel reinforcements in his foundation. And he had just taken a sledge-hammer to each of them. *Stupid. Stupid.* He inhaled, lifted his head, ready to pay penance. All eyes looked to him, each conveying a different emotion. His mom, disappointment and anger. Bethany, sadness and pain. Russell, gloating. Lourdes, gleeful opportunity. And Cara, a sly grin of satis-faction. With his eyes he found the only person in the room who he never intended to hurt, Amarie. Their gazes locked just in time for him to witness her light extinguish.

"Amarie," he whispered her name, a plea that went

unanswered. She was already backing away from him, but the hurt radiated in her urgent retreat to escape him.

The worst day of Eli's life started when Amarie disappeared from sight, leaving him behind. "Everybody get out."

"Let me grab my stuff," Cara protested.

"Out," he bellowed.

Chapter Twenty-Seven

INSIDE AMARIE'S HEAD, old fears swirled like bad omens with fathomless eyes in ghostly bodies, screeching, *Eli threw you away. Eli used you.* He hadn't. He'd blamed her for the website problems. Which was semi-operational. She'd repeated the same mistake of inserting her helping hands into someone else's mess. Curse Eli Calvary for making her care about him. Who was she fooling, she'd fallen for the grump. After promising she was his number one, Eli had swayed out of the fairy-tale lane where there was love, skipping along hand and hand, to consider Cara's cockamamie off-ramp of an excuse. And Russell with his editorialized commentary. Well, Amarie had promised herself that she would not linger where she wasn't wanted. But she wouldn't pack up in the middle of the night like before. She'd wait for a decent hour to say farewell to the town and people she'd fallen in love with. The short walk across Cattail Creek, past the Black Bear and the Town Mall plastered with fall-colored posters advertising the Founder's Day Festival fed her heartbreak.

"Urgh," she huffed, sadness swooping in to replace her fury. She'd miss out on the bachelor auction winners' announcements and the apple-bobbing contest, the horse rides, and bake sale. Amarie grabbed the doorhandle for Kanaan's Auto Repair. She would not make the mistakes her mother had made. She wouldn't be the long-suffering wife, well not that she and Eli had discussed forever, but she wouldn't be that woman.

And this time she had a plan. Centara Regional in Del Ray, Virginia, one of the many applications she'd completed prior to arriving in Service, had requested a job interview. The email had hit her inbox late yesterday, but she'd been distracted with ex drama. Hers and Eli's.

"Love sucks and doesn't live here anymore," she yelled, the sound carrying through the steel rafters to bounce off the tin roof.

"She never did, ladybug," Kanaan called down from his second-story office. The garage was a cavernous space with an acoustic echo. Which was could good because Amarie needed to hear anything other than her thoughts. Each tool and piece of equipment had a home on pegboard walls and metal shelves, an atmosphere of pride and professionalism on display. She guessed all the Calvary men had the trait at birth. The faint scent of motor oil hung in the air. For once, she cheered not hearing the water, sure that a single tear would slam into her, a tsunami tearing away what little remained of her heart.

"Hi, Kanaan." Amarie schooled her features in a serene mask. Though there was nothing she could do to camouflage her puffy eyelids. "I need to pick up Prince, now." Her voice cracked on the last syllable. That car had served as a safe haven to a scared eleven-year-old Amarie. She needed that comfort once again. And Prince belonged solely to her.

Kanaan moseyed down the steps, dressed in a crisp white T-shirt and loose gray cargo pants. "This emergency request have anything to do with the Amber Alert I received from Eli? Seems he's real upset about a misplaced girlfriend?"

Amarie's pulse quickened. Eli actually released a call to action to find her? No. Her attention deficit had kicked in, distracting her once again from her goal. The one that would whisk her away from Eli's forest-green eyes and his talented mouth. This was for the best, she told herself. Happiness could not be trusted. She had money from her weekly pay, and she hadn't touched the forty-eight hundred dollars in donations in her CashApp account. She didn't need Eli's money. She'd wasted enough time expecting a man to be her meal ticket. Amarie could feed herself. She had earned her degree, passed her exam, and organized a winning social media campaign. In other words, she had options. In reality, she always had.

"It's not a request. I'm not Eli's girlfriend," she said a little too loud, her voice a shriek venturing into mild hysteria territory. "So, disconnect my vehicle from life support and hand over the keys."

She stretched out her palm, wiggling her fingers. "Gimme."

Kanaan, recognizing she would not be deterred, signaled for her to follow him. He led her to the opposite side of the garage, stopping in front of a tan canvas tarp.

"She's a good little girly car." He chuckled, grabbing the tarp and peeling it back.

Amarie gasped in surprise. "OMG." Prince's metallic purple paint job twinkled like a firefly jacket. "You—you removed the dents in the driver's door panel."

"Since it took a couple of weeks for the parts to arrive, I added a few of my own touches to make up for the delay."

"*Touches*. She looks vintage showroom ready." Amarie pressed her face against the rear window. "You polished the inside," she exclaimed, too shocked to contain her joy. "Kanaan. How did you do all this?"

"Ah, I'm not used to having luxury cars in my shop." He rubbed at the back of his neck, which turned more berry red by the second. "You wanna take her for a spin? Show off my handiwork?"

Amarie sobered. By now Lourdes Pendleton would've spread the word about the end of their partnership and the missing contract. "I don't think so. I'm going to be heading out of town later tonight."

Kanaan leaned against the door panel, crossing those fully loaded guns over his chest. The man did have his arms.

"What? But the festival starts tomorrow. You can't leave before Eli announces the bachelor auction winners."

She had to. Better to rip the bandage off before things got stickier. It would be harder to pull away if she delayed her departure.

"I've accomplished everything I set out to achieve in Service." She'd even managed to fall in love. "I passed my nursing exam."

"Heard about it at the Black Bear. Gracie Lou and Ruth are planning a surprise ladies' day at the spa in Whynot for you."

Amarie teared up. "They are?"

"Of course. You're one of us."

Amarie exhaled. She couldn't do this. "I would've loved it, but... I have enough money saved on my own to get me set up back in the city."

Kanaan nodded, his intelligent blue eyes shadowed. "What about Eli?"

"We want different things from life."

"Remember what I said about Eli doing everything solo?"

She sighed. "Right. You warned me."

"More of a preparation," Kanaan said, expression sad. "Eli sucked on his own. He's a couple kind of guy, Amarie. Whether you leave or stay, you're his other half. You make him want to be a better man."

"Thanks, Kanaan. You're a great cousin. But I have to do what's best for me now."

"Well," he said, flexing his biceps, "I'm still available since my lug nut of a relative messed up the best woman to ever happen to this family since Aunt Leah."

Amarie raised both hands. "Put those away," she chided. "I'm weaning myself off country boys."

"Geesh, that bad, huh?"

"I'm afraid so."

"I heard your mom was in town. Is that going to keep you here any longer?"

"Ah, I'm the reason she's here. As soon as I can pull myself together," she pointed to her tear-streaked face, "we're gone." Though she had no idea how many hours it required to stitch a broken heart.

"Amarie." He uncrossed his muscle forearms and offered his hand. "It's been a pleasure, meeting you. And thanks for bringing a smile to Eli's ugly mug."

"How much do I owe you for fixing Prince?"

"Oh, pretty lady. I owe you for rescuing my family. You're the real deal, Amarie Walker." He opened his arms. She walked into his embrace. "Take all the time you need," he whispered.

Amarie rose up on tiptoes and gave him a hug. "Thanks. I could kiss you."

She didn't. Her kisses belonged to Eli, even if he didn't belong to her anymore. If she left now, she could make it back to Leah's, get the luggage and her mother in the car, and reach the interstate before dark. Maybe she'd wait till everyone was at the Black Bear celebrating the end of the auction. Could she leave without a goodbye to her friends? Calvary Vet Clinic and Eli would be okay. The Auction Luv Buzz banner had reappeared on the site, as well as the number of bidders. Odd, but Tobias had garnered the most bids. Seems Noah's first bid was so high, it had knocked a lot of the local ladies out of the running. She'd follow the final tally from the road. She'd used everything in her tool kit, everything in her arsenal, to fund the life that she wanted. She'd helped her friend Leah in the process. And somewhere along the journey, she and her mom had plugged the hole in their relationship. Amarie felt proud of herself then and now. With her father and Russell out of the picture, she had a feeling that they both would continue to blossom where they were planted. Even if it wasn't Service.

"Kanaan, the keys," she prompted, patting his back.

"Sure," he said, "I'll go grab them."

She climbed in Prince's back seat, like she'd done as a kid, and immediately she exhaled, relieved to feel the familiar cool leather against her skin. She'd have to say goodbye to Leah, Billy, Jean, and Diana. Tobias, Noah, Matt Johnson, Ruth, and Phoebe. Harry the horse, though they hadn't quite bonded. She was practically the godmother to Belle's foal. Hiccup and the kittens she'd save for last because she wasn't ready to look into Eli's handsome face. But he spared her the trouble by ripping open her back door with enough force to rattle the floorboards.

Kanaan. He must have surrendered her location. She should've paid him. Then she could storm up the stairs, grab her check, and rip it into tiny pieces.

"Jeezuz." Amarie jerked. "You almost caught these hands, scaring me like that."

"Oh, I'm sorry, sweetheart. I was worried about you. Everyone is," Eli breathed, folding his big body into the back seat with her. The interior shrank to just them, and the rest of the world faded away. He cupped her face in his large hands. "I'm so sorry. Please. Please, forgive me. I'm sorry, sweetheart."

"You suck at being a boyfriend. Don't quit your day job."

He scooped her up in his arms, placing her in his lap. "I know. Never been the fastest learner."

Amarie certainly felt like she'd been in a major crash. Not only did her heart hurt, she felt drained, wrung out, and stretched to her breaking point.

"How did you find me?"

"Your story from when you were eleven," he breathed. "About feeling safe in Prince."

She nodded in understanding. Bless Kanaan. He'd protected her. Of their own volition, her hands rose and to cup Eli's face. She'd had every intention of choking him unconscious for ruining them, but her heart, the dopey eight-ounce organ, had her too devastated to act on the emotion.

"You know I respect your dedication to your father's legacy. Honestly, I can't imagine the pressure you experienced when the auction site went offline and you thought it all was at risk, but I can't dismiss what you said to me, Eli."

"I get it. The walls closed in—Cara, the website, the demolition equipment, the missing contract—it's the worst feeling, being trapped without options. I lashed out. You got hurt in the process."

"Not just me, Eli. When you blurted out what your father did with your college fund, using it to pay off the mortgage, keeping Leah in the dark about you working two jobs through college. How you must love him to protect him and your mother. Even agreeing to the auction, you've done all of this to protect his memory, but what about the living. Leah, Tobias, Noah?"

"I love my parents and my brothers. I'd do anything to protect them."

"I know you would. Why couldn't you do that for me?"

"Sweetheart, I got scared. One reminder of the old patterns in my marriage to Cara, and all the old fears took over."

"That another woman would use you, and then discard you?"

"Yeah," he admitted.

"When I look at you, I see the man that you are. Russell hurt me. My mother had to negotiate with my father to pay my college tuition, his own daughter. Two men who were supposed to love me hurt me, but I know you are not them." She swallowed. "At least I thought I did. I thought you saw more than my hardworking hands, what I could do for you. I thought you saw my heart."

"I'm sorry, Amarie." He repeated a solemn anthem to what could've been.

"Yeah, me too," she whispered, lowering her hands to her lap.

"Come back home with me?"

"I can't, Eli." She couldn't make herself more vulnerable to him. If she returned to the cabin, their cozy couch, their animals, she'd crumble. Amarie had to care for Amarie first.

Eli sighed, and then pressed his lips to her temple. "Then I'll stay where you are. For as long as you let me, I'll stay, Amarie."

Amarie looked into his green eyes, captured by their beauty. "Why? There's nothing left for me to say."

The light in his eyes dimmed. "Then I'll wait...stay by your side until you leave mine."

Amarie remained quiet. She inhaled his clean scent as she pushed images of their time together out of her mind. Sleep claimed her. As her curves softened, molded against his strength, she didn't fight his embrace. This would be the last time she held the one man for her, the one grumpy vet love had brought her...she wanted to remember everything about this farewell because she was done faking it. Everything had a place in this world. The time had arrived for Amarie to claim hers.

Chapter Twenty-Eight

ELI AND AMARIE walked into his momma's kitchen on Saturday morning rumpled and exhausted. Not because they had reconciled; rather, he was terrified to let her out of his line of sight because she'd barely said four words to him last night before she drifted into sleep. The best and worst night of sleep in his thirty-three years had happened in the back seat of a BMW 328i. Considering his years spent on an Army field cot, his muscles screamed from the unnatural position he'd twisted his back into to fit into Prince's rear seat. But she'd refused to come home with him or return to Leah's last night. His only saving grace, Amarie had let him hold her, but Eli had yet to exit the doghouse. After the heartbreak he'd witnessed in her haunted eyes, no way would he leave her. One look at Amarie's drawn features this morning, his mom was on her feet, pulling his woman into a tight bear hug.

"Oh, dear." She breathed in Amarie's visible heartache. "I missed you so much. He's a bonehead, sweetheart. I know it hurts."

Amarie choked out a sniffle. "I'm okay."

Eli's heart shattered all over again. Clearly Amarie's poker face couldn't hide how much she was torn up inside. His mom stood in the gap between him and Amarie, keeping him an arm's length away from his woman, when all he wanted to do was beg her to forgive his stupidity. The day was humid, but Eli had goosebumps from Amarie's verbal freeze out. Because he knew her, the rambling when she was anxious, her near obsession with her snack pack. Last night, she'd given him nothing. Asked for nothing. True to fashion, she hadn't been unkind, worse—she'd guarded herself against his presence. It was like she'd pulled up the drawbridge to her castle and he was on the other side of an alligator-infested moat gazing longingly up at her tower.

Leah gestured to the kitchen table, taking her seat. "Eli, you and Amarie come have a seat. Family meeting time."

"Momma, we're fresh from a shower." Albeit not together. Amarie had waited on him to finish his shave before she entered the bathroom. Then she'd closed the door and locked it. Seems the wall between them was both physical and emotional. They had dressed in silence. When he'd offered to carry her backpack, she'd pulled it closer to her chest, like a shield. "I need caffeine before we start figuring out what's next."

"Morning everybody." Amarie waved to Tobias and Noah. Hiccup released a woof, keeping watch of Amarie and the basket of kittens on her arm. She held a sentry position by the backdoor they'd used to enter. They'd left her car at his place after she'd snatched the key with Prince's likeness, the artist, not the car.

"Eli Calvary, if you tell your momma 'no' one more time, I'm going to give your backside a knot to match the one on your skull."

Noah walked over to Amarie and gave her a big hug. "Morning, lil sis. I was worried about you."

Tobias stood, pulling out a chair between him and Noah for Amarie to sit. It about broke Eli's heart when she looked relieved. He did this with his irrational fear that every woman would sabotage him, pretend to love him, and then betray him with a more polished, more moneyed replacement.

"Tobias. Noah," he groused. Neither of his brothers uttered a word.

"Bethany's on her way down. I wanted to show you all something first."

Amarie looked at him. "I want to say I'm sorry about the contract. I did print it."

Leah gave her a barely there smile. Tears gathered in her eyes. "I want to show you something."

"Momma?" Eli dropped to one knee beside her chair. "I'm so sorry for keeping the secret about the Pendletons. The college fund. All of it. I promise I'll make it up to you."

"Shh, your father made you swear not to tell me." She ruffled his hair like she did when he was a kid. "Not even heaven could save him from the earful he got from me last night about trying to control everything. We raised this family together and if he had trusted me with what the Pendletons were trying to do, you would've never been torn in two trying to protect us both. Levi is gone. So, you live your life for you, not for Levi. That's what your father would tell each of you if he were here. Whether we rise or fall, we do it together, not out of responsibility, out of love. That's the real legacy, son. Not the land. It's the love and trust of the family on this land that gives it value."

"Yes, ma'am. I've learned my lesson." He looked at

Amarie, but her eyes were focused out the window, like she didn't want to intrude on a family moment. She was his family.

"Good. You better not give me any more trouble this lifetime, Eli Calvary. I swear you got the craziest parts of both me and your father, loyal to a fault. And stubborn as a pee stain."

"Whoa," he came to his feet. Chuckles sounded from around the table.

"You ever been compared to a piss stain, Tobias?" Noah teased.

"Can't say that I have, brother."

"Guess that makes us the good sons." Noah chuckled.

"You can have it." Eli mimicked tossing a ball in the trash can. "It's impossible to hit the mark."

Their momma said nothing, just pulled a crumpled piece of paper from the side of her cowgirl boot and placed in the center of the table.

"What's this?" Eli frowned.

"It's the Kitty Kibbles contract. Amarie did exactly what she said she did. It was that snake of an ex-wife who tried to sabotage you and this family again. I found it in Cara's tote bag yesterday after you kicked your family out of the family business. Oh, and she is pregnant. Eight weeks."

"I was never worried." He had acted a plum fool with Amarie and his family, the kind of stupid that took years of practice.

"But you were rude, ungrateful, accusatory and—" That was Amarie, her voice ten octaves higher than usual.

"Yep," everyone said in unison.

"Sorry," Eli said, chagrined. He looked at Amarie. "I'd lost someone important."

She quickly looked away. Darn it. Easygoing Amarie

had been replaced with a hard nose, and she hadn't budged on allowing him back into her good graces.

"I'm glad you found the contract. Should've suspected Cara from the start. But it was too late by then anyways," Eli murmured.

Amarie's eyes shot to his. "The auction money will come through. The site is back online."

"That's great. Makes my news even better." His mom vibrated with happiness.

Eli reached for the open envelope in his mother's hand. He read the address. "Kitty Kibbles Corporation?" he questioned, reading the accepted agreement inside twice. Amarie burst up from her seat, rounding the table at Leah's other side.

"What—how?"

Leah did a little two-step in her fall festival outfit. "I signed the contract and sent it back in the computer."

"But I thought we missed the deadline?" Eli insisted.

"Nope. The parent company is in the central time zone, one hour behind us."

"Alright!" Noah and Tobias erupted from their chairs next. "We got ourselves a home and a business," they cheered, squeezing into the family circle.

"The twenty-five-thousand-dollar check can be deposited. The final documents will arrive via express delivery within three business days," Leah announced.

They'd done it. He and Amarie working together.

"I would've told you boys sooner, but Amarie had to be found and Eli got me so fighting mad acting like he didn't have the sense God gave a sheep."

"I'm sorry, Leah," said Amarie.

"I'm sorry, Momma."

Their apologies overlapped. Maybe Eli read too much

hope into them being in sync. He'd never have saved his family without Amarie. His mother was right, they were partners. And the partnership needed mending thanks to his shortcomings, not hers. Amarie was generous, loving, one of a kind. He'd damaged them with his pride, his anger, his self-doubt.

"I'm not the only one you owe an apology to." His mother angled her head in his brothers' direction.

"Sorry. I was wrong."

Noah grinned. "You sure are. You gotta stop letting the ladies push your buttons, big brother."

"Tobias," Eli prompted when he stayed quiet.

"I'll get over the secret," he offered. "Dad was wrong."

"I know that." Eli nodded. "We both were. He should've told Mom about the Pendletons and the finances. And I should've fessed up about using my college fund to pay off the loan."

"Ever since Dad took out the loan against the property, I wondered why he would do it. Now I understand he was paying you back," Tobias whispered.

"He didn't have to." In fact, Eli wished to heaven he hadn't. Thankfully, the house would be someone else's responsibility in a matter of days.

"That was his way," Noah said of their father. "I can't fault him now."

"But?" Eli prompted, because Tobias leveled him with a guilty glare.

"Cara was never good for you, Eli. A blind bat could see that woman was trouble. Amarie is the best thing that ever happened to you, and you messed it up. I'll forgive you when she does."

"Tobias, you have my word. As soon as I get this woman alone, I'll eat crow, grovel, and beg her to keep me."

"Make sure you do, Eli. 'Cause if Amarie is not smiling by the time I finish the breakfast dishes, you'll be the one in the doghouse."

"Whew," Noah said through his teeth. "And trust me, big brother, his bark is a lot bigger than yours."

"Amarie." Eli said her name as if the very syllables would break if he spoke them too loud.

"Here," she said, reaching into her backpack to hand him a purple three-ring binder.

Eli accepted it. "What's this?"

"It's a standard operations procedure manual, an SOP, like they have in the military." Her mouth lifted at one corner.

"For what, sweetheart."

"I, ah—I never intended to take over your business. Inside is all the login information for every account, social and otherwise, related to Calvary Veterinary Clinic. Though it goes against my nature, I've included the passwords and it's handwritten the way you like."

When had she done this for his business? Could Eli sink lower than a belly-slithering worm? Of course she would list everything he and her replacement would need to manage the clinic. He reached for her, pulling their bodies closer until they touched. She released a little grunt, as if in pain. Her body stiffened against his. No longer did she melt in his arms. The rejection, the loss of connection, felt like the breath had been severed from his body. He was empty without her. "Can we talk about us? How I'll do anything to fix us?"

She hesitated. But then whispered, "Anything means nothing without trust, Eli."

He bit back a curse, his body aching in response to the biting words.

"Good morning, everyone." Bethany flowed down the steps in a white button-down, a pair of fitted jeans, and cowgirl boots.

"Mom." Amarie rushed over. "What are you wearing and why?"

"I picked up some new duds at the Trading Post yesterday. Thought I might enjoy looking the part at today's festival. Oh, your father will probably call you. Tell him my answer is still no."

"Mom, we really need to talk. Like now. Excuse us, Calvary family."

Bethany, though cute, had the worst timing. Amarie obviously wanted to put more distance between them. And Mrs. Walker hadn't helped his cause. Eli walked up behind Amarie, crowding her space, missing the warmth they'd shared seconds before her mother had broken the spell. She broke from him without a glance, and he was more than a little nervous.

"Amarie, sweetheart. Can we talk?"

Amarie pulled away from him, her once-warm eyes icing over. "Nope. I asked you to stop talking yesterday. Did you listen? Cat got your lips?"

"The expression is cat got your tongue."

"Either way, you and your cat messed up."

One look at her fierce expression and Eli was no longer nervous, he was terrified.

"Listen, Amarie," he sighed, tracking his fingers through his hair. "I have to kick off the festivities. Looks like the bachelor auction is back online, and the town wants to know the winners. Remember, you're my date no matter who wins."

She nodded but didn't say a word in agreement. Eli leaned in, placing a kiss to her forehead. "I'll make this right between us, Amarie."

He'd fix this at the festival, give them a second chance at love. Eli wanted to tell her, but the timing was off. He wanted her alone and in his arms, not with an audience of his family and her mom. The music, the revelry, the friendship, maybe the jovial mood would grease the skillet, so Eli could slide back home, to Amarie's arms. The business and family would be fine, but he was back in a tail of a mess.

Chapter Twenty-Nine

AMARIE WOULDN'T ALLOW herself to think about how much she would miss Eli. How much she wanted him to be her *one*. A job interview awaited her. She had to leave now. Her very real heart barely held together with all the Calvarys rallying to comfort her.

She believed him when he said he was sorry. But she didn't trust him to put her first. And she didn't trust herself to resist him much longer. Love hurt too much and she couldn't be disappointed twice in the span of a few weeks.

Eli and his brothers with Hiccup padding behind them had driven the truck over to the pavilion. She'd led them to believe she would meet them there. It was the first time she'd lied to them.

She entered the bedroom her mother had taken over in less than forty-eight hours. All these different suitcases hung open, each with a different season of coats, shoes, and jewelry.

"It looks like Saks exploded in here." Amarie grimaced at the fashion chaos. She could actually tell her mother had left home with the intent never to return.

"Mom, why are you unpacking?"

"Because I'm staying? Oh, Russell left his sports coat. Take it with you."

Amarie collapsed on the bed. "Look, Jennifer Holliday." She raised up on her elbows, sitting up. "You don't know anyone here. And I'm not going back to Russell."

"I know Leah. One good friend is worth a dozen posers."

"Mom, language." Amarie shook her head. "Where did you learn that word, *posers*?" A slang term for imposters, had never entered Mrs. Reid Walker's vocabulary before now. Perhaps her mom had made a change. "Not at the Hat Society club."

"On TikTok." She laughed. "Keep up, darling, because your mother is picking up steam. And of course you're not going back to Russell. You're in love with Eli."

Amarie heard muffled conversations as folks walked past the house up to the festival grounds. Of course Bethany would be fine in Service.

"Lot of good that did me," Amarie grumbled.

"Love is risky business, darling. But you have to admit when it's right. It feels like sunshine on your face even when it's raining. You're a fighter, Amarie."

"A fighter who suffered a blow to the head," she huffed, standing.

Bethany stopped her fiddling, a behavior Amarie knew she did to hide her nerves. "It only takes one win at love, Amarie, and the pain of the bumps and bruises along the way vanishes."

Amarie pulled her luggage from the closet, throwing her favorite purple bolero jacket in the case. "I'm leaving."

"I won't stop you." Her mom smiled, blotting at her eyes. "I trust you to make the best decision. Though Eli makes a terrible first—and second—impression, he loves you."

"He accused me of sabotaging him," Amarie railed while raking what was left of her toiletries into her suitcase.

"We all make mistakes, especially when emotions are involved. I actually believed having your ex-lover come after you was a good thing. Russell and that awful Cara have enlightened this old woman. The sooner those two skedaddle, the better for all of us."

Service would adore her mother, the same way they'd welcomed Amarie. Gracie Lou would give her a coalminer sandwich on the house. Lois Kline would invite her for lemonade and pie. Amarie still was on the hook for a visit.

"Mom, are you sure?" she whined, they were running out of time to vamoose. "I dumped her son. They might hold you captive until you surrender my whereabouts."

Eli would forgive her abrupt departure…eventually. But she feared the heartbreak would truly be a permanent condition if she tried to build a life in his town. So, Amarie chose herself over love. *Go*, she told herself. She had a plan to keep herself in motion. The next step for her took her beyond Service's borders.

"Don't be dramatic." Bethany swapped a blue bandanna for a red. "They can just ask."

"Mom, you can't be a grifter and a snitch."

Leah walked into the bedroom. Amarie snapped the suitcase closed on the last of her books. The ones with Eli's fly-footprint handwriting scribbled in the notes. No. Don't think about him. She was doing what was best for her. She'd given her best to Russell, who she wasn't going to track down just to return his jacket, and to Eli.

"Hey, honey." Leah looked from Amarie to the spoils at her feet.

"Leah, thank you for allowing me to stay."

She nodded, her eyes sad. "I see you're packed."

"Yes," Amarie murmured, shifting her feet. Oh, this was hard. She didn't want to leave, but how could she stay?

"It would be wishful thinking on my part to ask if you're moving everything to Eli's place, wouldn't it?"

"I'm afraid so. I wouldn't want to lie to you." Amarie swallowed her tears, clearing her throat before she spoke again. "I have a job interview. It's at a Virginia hospital. This is my chance to show the world what I'm made of."

"Oh, you don't have to leave home for that. I know how talented you are. So does Eli."

Home. Service had become her home and it was breaking what was left of her heart to leave.

"I can't stay here with him. And I don't know what can make it better."

"We Calvarys owe you gratitude, Amarie. Now, what can I help you with?"

"Nothing. I have everything I need." But not the man she wanted more than her breath.

"You sure about that?" Leah gave a dubious smile before darting out of the room. "How about a goodbye kiss for your babies?" She beamed, walking back in holding out a familiar basket.

Raspberry, Dove, Formerly, Graffiti, and Artist meowed a melody that brought tears to Amarie's eyes. "Aw, Leah you don't play fair."

"'Course not. I'm a mom. We play to win."

Amarie plucked each one from the basket. "Mommy loves you. Mommy loves you," she cooed to each kitty. They clawed at her hand when she settled them back in their nest for the last time. "Be good for Daddy. And Graffiti and Artist can't eat too late at night, their poo is extra runny and smelly when they do."

"Give me those little fur balls." Bethany took the basket,

handing Leah a brown bag and travel mug Amarie hadn't noticed. "I'll put your luggage in the car. Let you two say your goodbyes in private."

"There's enough biscuits in here to get you to Alaska." Amarie took the cup from Leah's hand. "The coffee won't last as long. But it's the good kind, from the computer."

"Now how can I turn that down from one of my best friends in the world?"

"Oh, sweetie, you know we're more than friends."

Yeah, Amarie was hoping that they would be family. Leah opened her arms and Amarie walked right into them.

"The whole town is going to miss you. They'll be sad they didn't get to see you off before your big adventure."

There was a hint of remorse in Leah's tone, but Amarie steeled her spine. It would only get tougher if she stuck around. So, for the first time in forever, she scrapped her checklist. She'd have to wing it for today.

"I know. But I trust that Eli will explain it to everyone."

"And who's going to explain it to him?"

"It can't be me. I wouldn't know where to begin. Eli taught me so much about myself. I found I don't need a man to be my meal ticket, even though he fed me."

"That was true from the moment that you walked through our doors. Rattling off your credentials. Standing up to Eli with his policies and rules. Changing his life and ours for the better. We needed you, Amarie. Not the other way around, honey."

"Since you put it that way, I sound pretty awesome. I don't think I believed that when I got here. Everyone else with their accomplishments seemed so grand compared to mine. But I'm not afraid anymore to be who I am. And I know whatever it is life has in store for me, I can do it. And I'm thankful to have met you, Leah."

"Come on," she said, walking her out into the September humidity. Amarie was happy that Leah hadn't pressured her to stay. She just spoke her truth. What did surprise her was that Leah had invited her mom to stay in the house with her. The two had really hit it off.

"Mama, I'll call when I get where I'm going," Amarie said from behind the wheel.

"Absolutely. You and Prince be good to each other, okay? And guess what? If it doesn't work out, I'm gonna take a page from my daughter's book. And I will try someplace new. Now, you get on down the road before it gets too late."

"Yes, ma'am." When Amarie pulled away from the curb, Leah and her mom were hugging each other. She selected her favorite playlist, ugly crying to Prince's "When Doves Cry."

"Oh gosh," she sobbed. "I can hear my fur babies meowing for me to come back home to them." Geez, she could actually smell them. And she gagged, her tongue extending from her mouth trying to expel an imaginary fur ball.

"Lawd, take the wheel. What is that smell?"

The funk permeated the car and bored into every crevice, Amarie's eyes watered, and then her vision blurred. She swerved to the shoulder to avoid wrecking her beautifully polished car. She slammed on the brakes. Bags went flying, and out came Graffiti, paws extended, mouth open, eyes wide. A sleepy Artist right behind him, claws digging in for purchase. Rolling down the windows wasn't enough to rid her nose of the stench. She exited the car, sucking in large volumes of mountain air. Billy, Jean, and Diana looked up from their grassy feast.

Hands balanced on her knees, she spoke to her confidants. "Hello, ladies and gent. Seems I'm back where I started."

Rounding the car, Amarie snatched open the rear door to gauge the damage. There, in Russell's Louis Vuitton tote bag, was his jacket covered in clay litter. Two wide-eyed screaming kittens, claws in leather as if expecting the next avalanche, and fragrant poop balls dotted her back seat.

"Mom," Amarie screeched at the top of her lungs. Now she understood why Bethany seemed nonplussed about her departure. Amarie would not turn around, she would delay just long enough to clean up this—

"Need some help, darling?" Kanaan walked up, his tow truck blocking the one road out of town, sirens flashing.

This is Service, Amarie thought, hanging her head.

Chapter Thirty

THIS HAD TO be the largest Founder's Day Festival on record. The pie-eating station had contestants in place with hundreds of ladies cheering on their men. The kids had started earlier with the potato sack races. Tons of hay had been donated by Matt Johnson for a hayride later tonight. Outside of the New River Gorge Bridge Day celebration featuring base jumpers from all over the world, Service's festival attracted the second largest crowd, a few thousand people over the two days. Many faces in the crowd he recognized, most he didn't. A few folks had painted #SexyKittyVet on their windshields.

Eli stomped onto the stage with most of the townsfolk glaring at him for one reason or another. Tobias and Noah had his six, but he'd never felt more alone. Amarie's sad doe eyes had seared his brain, he could barely fix his mind on announcing the winners of the auction. His apology hadn't carried much weight in swaying her to give him another chance. She hadn't mentioned the money he owed her, not once. What could he offer her?

Stupid, a voice whispered in his head. Amarie was a

romantic, and she needed a grand gesture, something she wouldn't expect. But she had the creative gene. Eli, well, was Eli. Stubborn, controlled, and unyielding. But he'd bend like saltwater taffy for Amarie.

"Where's Amarie?" Gracie Lou had her hand cupped around her mouth, megaphone style. Caleb sat beside her in his pickup's tailgate waiting expectantly. Even Bucky had shown up, lingering close to Ruth and Phoebe. She'd moved back home, and according to Matt, things were headed in the right direction for the family. Of course, Matt was astride Harry's back ready to kick Bucky if he got out of line.

"I heard Amarie caught you in bed with your ex-wife," Delores added.

"What?" Eli grumbled. He grabbed the microphone. "That does not make a lick of sense." The PA system whistled, and a united groan flowed up from the sea of cars and trucks.

"Then where is she?" Lois Kline demanded from the hood of the land bus, Adele at her hip, sharpening her claws on the metal bars of her cage.

"I want to thank you all for showing up here today. For your contributions in support of saving Calvary Vet Clinic and our family lands."

"Yay, Amarie. Amarie. Amarie." That was Phoebe's little voice. An onslaught of cheering started. Followed by blasts from car horns, and a foghorn that had more than a few babies screaming.

"Seems the auction site is back online," Eli yelled over the noise. "So, it's time to name some winners."

Hoots and hollers sounded from the ladies, but Eli didn't miss the groans. He held the phone in his grip, which shook when he saw who was in the lead for him. With the site being hacked, the website had added an additional day of bidding with a countdown clock ticking backward, with two minutes of the clock.

TigerTamer1000, Lourdes Pendleton's online handle, flashed red underneath his picture. She winked at him from the crowd. Please, let Amarie rescue him. But he knew she hadn't placed a single bid, too honest to shortchange the other ladies from a possible match with him and his brothers. But Eli knew the truth, she was his one.

Cara strutted up on stage, smiling at him. She had no idea they'd uncovered her treachery.

"Hi," she said into the mic. "I'm Eli's wife."

Gosh, why did she keep popping up like foot fungus. Cara had claimed him as her husband more in the past twenty-four hours than during their entire marriage. He wished her the best, but away from Service and Amarie.

"Boo, ex-wife, Get off the stage. Better still, get out of our town" came an anonymous heckler from the crowd. "Where's Amarie?"

"Anyway," Cara chirped, flipping her hair off her shoulder with an extra flourish. "I want to make a final contribution right here and now. Twenty-five hundred dollars to save our Calvary Family Clinic. And that puts me, @SecondChanceRomance, in the lead for Eli."

A few cheers went on, but not many. The friends of the family knew better than to fall for Cara's faked generosity.

Eli practically growled at Cara. "You aren't going to stop, are you?"

"Why should I? With her gone, you're basically community property. And we both know you're a family man." She rubbed her belly, reminding him she'd soon be a mother with a child dependent on her for guidance.

Eli covered the mic with his palm. "I don't want your money. Save it for your child."

"Oh. That's my secret, Eli. It's not my money, it's yours. I'm just giving a little bit of it back. We can talk about the rest over dinner since I'm your highest bidder."

Before Cara could get more boos, Tobias rushed her from the stage. Eli felt rather grateful for his brother. He nodded in thanks. Tobias gave him a stern thumbs-up, taking his place next to Noah.

Mrs. Kline's car horn cut through the noise. "Eli Calvary, you haven't answered our questions. Now Amarie literally saved you three boys from your gigolo ways. I got one thousand dollars for Eli's City Girl to win his hand. Who's with me?"

Slowly, hands went up and dollar bills were passed forwarded. With ten seconds left on the clock, inspiration struck. Eli pulled the check from his pocket and handed it over to Noah. "Put all of it on my city girl to win."

Eli felt hope soar in his chest for the first time in two days. "Okay folks, that's it. All bids are in."

"The first lucky lady is," he entered the administrative keys to reveal the identities of the winners, "the farmer's daughter, Rachel Johnson. Noah Calvary is all yours."

Noah snatched the mic. "Elle, babe. You're finally back home. Where are you, Rachel 'Elle' Johnson?"

His brother shaded his eyes, the crowd mumbling Rachel's name. Matt Johnson came forward, Harry whinnying at the attention. "She's not here, Noah. I'm sorry."

"So, she hooks me again and disappears." Noah stormed off, shoving onlookers out of his way.

"Hey folks." Tobias waved. "@BookLoveWednesday won me." He gave a lopsided grin. "She's not here, either, but I know where to find her."

"That leaves you, Eli." Mrs. Kline stated matter-of-factly. "Now we all know Amarie is a part of this town. If you've messed that up, I'm tempted to let Adele out of her cage right now so she can rip your grumpy heart right out of your chest."

Eli waved them off. "Calm down everybody. Amarie and I hit a rough patch 'cause I let my past get in the way."

"'Fraid not, Eli. Prudence said she saw Kanaan had Amarie cornered on the road heading out of town."

Eli jumped down off the stage and ran for his truck. His mother and Bethany burst through the crowd. "Kanaan called. He said Amarie just about had the spill cleaned up."

"A spill," Eli bellowed. "Everyone get out of the way. Amarie needs me."

Amarie's mom chimed in. "I don't know how far she got. I left a little surprise in the car that might slow her down."

"You sabotaged her car?"

"No, Eli. Honestly, your mind takes you to the strangest of places. I added a couple of extra passengers to keep her company on the road."

"You're blocked in," Matt yelled to him. "Here, take Harry. It'll be faster."

"Oh, how romantic." Bethany practically swooned on her feet.

Matt Johnson offered her his hand. "That's the way we menfolk treat our ladies in these parts."

"Guess I'm glad I'm sticking around to learn all I can about the local traditions." Bethany batted her lashes, and Eli saw how Amarie won everyone over. Her mother was extra, too.

"What's happening?" someone in the crowd called.

"Eli's going after Amarie," Tobias announced.

"What?" came from another direction.

"Amarie took a spill and Eli's running off to save her," Gracie Lou called. "I'm going with Eli. Spread the word."

Eli didn't wait to see who followed on horseback, three-wheelers, or on foot. He had a future to catch.

"Me too."

"Me three."

"We're coming."

Eli didn't stop to answer any questions or correct assumptions. "Ya," Eli spurred his mount into a full gallop in the direction of his future, his love, his Amarie.

Eli galloped at full speed, jerking Harry's reins to slow the horse down when Prince came into view.

"Kanaan, you can't keep me here," he heard Amarie yelling to his cousin.

Eli dismounted from Harry's back, his chest heaving. "No, he can't. But I'm praying I can." He handed over his phone and the horse to his family.

Chapter Thirty-One

AMARIE SPUN ON him. If eyes could slice, Eli would be chunky dog food stewing in his own gravy.

"What are you doing here, Eli Calvary?" Eli had dismounted in a rush, landing wrong on his ankle. He winced with each step, but he kept moving closer to Amarie, praying she didn't get the notion to run away on foot. Not that he wouldn't give chase, but it would hurt like a son of a gun in the morning.

Her appearance caught him off guard. Rolled wads of white paper napkin protruded from each nostril like walrus tusks.

"I-I came for you," sweetheart," he stammered, trying to catch his breath, shifting weight, without a lick of grace, to his good ankle.

"Is that so?" she challenged, stubborn little chin jutted forward. She glanced at his ankle. "Did you hurt yourself with the Hidalgo race around the lake?"

He caught the reference to Frank Hopkin's mustang, Hidalgo, who'd won an endurance race against pure-bred Arabians in 1891. Well, Eli's love for the woman in front of him was pure and undeniable.

"It'll heal. Will you?" When she didn't answer, he started with the obvious. He'd ease them into the harder conversation. "What happened to your nose? Are you hurt?"

He took in the car angled precariously close to the ditch at the side of the road. Billy, Jean, and Diana had wandered out of their enclosure and were now in the middle of the road. Had she gotten in an accident? When Kanaan had mentioned a spill, he assumed with the car, not in the car.

"My mom," she bellowed, but then the sound of horns and shouts in the distance grew louder, drowning out her high-pitched shrieks.

Eli deciphered two words. *Kitten. Poop.*

"So, that was Bethany's grand plan." Eli chuckled, pulling Amarie into his arms.

"My own mother," she half sobbed. "She could've toilet-papered my car. Now it's too funky to drive."

He held her tighter. Seconds passed before he felt the weight of her arms surrounding his torso.

"I love you, Amarie Walker. I can live without the vet clinic. I can live away from my family. But I can't live without you." Her breath hitched but she didn't respond. Eli wouldn't stop. Now that he had her back in his arms, he knew he wouldn't last a day without her in his life. "I'm begging you for another chance."

"I love you, too, but I'm scared. Scared you'll disappoint me. Scared you'll promise me the impossible."

He sighed, stroking one hand over her loose coils. "I guarantee..." She stiffened in his arms. "Shh, listen to me. I guarantee I will disappoint you, but I'll always love you, sweetheart."

She lifted her head to regard him, her warm brown eyes hopeful, but a little less cautious. "You promise?"

"On my honor," he whispered.

"And a soldier always keeps his word?"

"I will for you. You're the woman I want." He started to sway with her in his arms, sharing the music in his heart. "You don't have to be beautiful, but you are. I love your body, but I want to make love to your mind, touch your soul like you do mine, build my home in your heart." Of course, Amarie picked up the melody to Prince's "Kiss" and started to hum in cadence with his declaration. When she turned her face up to look at him, those soft chocolate eyes liquefied the last vestiges of ice. "You don't have to be rich to be my number one girl. You don't have to be cool, but you're pretty darn awesome to me, Amarie. I want all your extra time, for the rest of our lives, and a lifetime of your kisses."

"Hmm." She grinned, melting into him. "Did you just rewrite 'Kiss' for me?"

"Sure did. Straight from the hip, too. Come on, sweetheart," he coaxed, intertwining their fingers. "No one else can love me like you do. Make this grumpy, rule-following, handwritten-policy-writing, TikTok sensation of a veterinarian a one-woman man."

When she still hesitated, he added. "I'll make you unlimited snack packs. Pack your lunch for work. And rub your feet, for starters."

"Even after a twelve-hour shift?" she quizzed.

"Definitely."

"If you don't want him, Amarie. Caleb and I could use him at the Black Bear," Gracie Lou said. "Been talking about adding a massage chair."

"Okay, this had better be real, and not just to get me back, Eli Calvary."

"Oh, it is." He chuckled. "Show her, Kanaan."

"Yep," he said, holding up Eli's phone. "Got the whole

thing live streaming on your TikTok page, more than one million likes and climbing."

"Aw," Amarie cooed. "You went live for me?"

"I'd do anything for you. Including placing twenty-five-thousand dollars under your name to win me."

Amarie's voice hitched, and Eli grinned. "What say you, sweetheart? You're my one. So are you claiming your prize or do I need to climb back up on the auction block?"

"I wanna be your lover, friend, and partner, Eli."

"Starting now?" he asked, holding his breath.

"Yes."

"You ready to head back home?" he asked.

"Nope." Amarie grinned. "We have to celebrate my winning the auction at the festival."

"Now?" Eli exclaimed, thinking him professing his love would change her mind. He should've known his Amarie would surprise him.

"Since you came to your senses and realized I'm the best thing to happen to you ever. We have to share the good news before we leave for my job interview."

"I'd prefer to take you home," Eli whispered.

"No can do, grumpy pants. I'm driving us back. You got shotgun," she said, stroking his cheek.

"No way. I want to test what Kanaan put under Prince's hood." He chuckled. "This is Service. My ankle would have to be broken, and I still might try to take the keys."

"Well, you own the keys to my heart, Eli Calvary." Amarie kissed him and they didn't stop when the hoots and horns started.

Epilogue

14 months later

ELI LIFTED HER phone, reading the social media post. Thanks to Amarie, he'd not only preserved his father's legacy, he'd expanded it to include the entire family and the town of Service. Mortgage payments, foreclosure notices, and empty appointment slots no longer plagued his dreams. Last year the house he never lived in had sold. The Calvary Family Trust owned the deed to their land and property. Before long, he would need another staff veterinarian. Now, Eli focused on the happier days ahead of him. He read the post again.

> Calvary Clinic is closed for the engagement party of #SexyKittyVet and #PerkyLateBloomer; however, you can still get groomed with Ruth and Phoebe B. The picnic and cat adoption cafe sponsored by #KittyKibbles will be live-streamed via TikTok and the KittyKibbles YouTube account from the Service town pavilion.

"Amarie, get down here, woman. We're on the clock," Eli bellowed from the Calvary kitchen table.

"Hold your mule, Eli. I did work a twelve-hour shift last night." And he had kept her awake most of the morning planting kisses in special places reserved for him.

"You could just work for our company." He smirked. Seems #SexyKittyVet kept paying dividends. Eli spent more days editing their video clips and fielding public speaking events than Amarie these days. He did enjoy interacting with his TikTok fans. The educational clips that he shared helped pet owners confidently care for their animals. He took pride in the service he provided. The town had benefited from the added publicity as well. A few real estate developers and home improvement chains had volunteered supplies to support their next fundraiser—a local clinic. Seems his momma had known what was best for him and the town when she'd signed them up for the bachelor auction.

Amarie appeared at the top of the steps. "I could, but Ruth handles everything just fine without me."

Brown eyes met green, and they stayed locked like that for several seconds. Her hair, longer now, cascaded over bare shoulders into a waterfall of thick ringlets. He watched the smile spreading across her lips as she drew near. His heart filled with desire, respect—awe. He loved everything about Amarie Walker.

Eli reached for her. "Maybe your fiancé doesn't like to be away from you."

Actually, he couldn't keep his hands to himself anymore. The primary care practice over in Whynot had been eager to hire a local celebrity. Seems patients made up excuses to meet the city girl who had saved a whole mountain town from being foreclosed on by big business, as the rumors had it.

"Well," she cooed, taking a seat in his lap, her toenails

polished with purple glitter heart emojis, "when we get the fundraiser for the clinic off the ground, we can discuss it."

Eli pointed to the camera. "I'm working on it, Sparkles. I'm working on it."

Amarie kissed his cheek. "I know, grumpy pants."

"Sixty seconds till we're live, family."

His momma, Tobias, and Noah strode in from the living room, taking their places behind him and Amarie around the Calvary family table. Bethany and Matt, both red-cheeked and a little disheveled, rushed in from the clinic, Hiccup on their heels, all five cats in a huge basket from their Kitty Kibbles sponsor.

"In three, two, one," Eli counted. "Go."

"Happy Holidays, TikTok!" they shouted in unison.

"Amarie and I, and the rest of the Calvarys, want to wish you a very happy holiday season. Words can't express how much each of you have come to mean to our family and the town of Service." Eli kissed Amarie on the cheek, proud to show the world how he adored his woman.

"Tell them the rest, Eli."

She wiggled her bottom in anticipation, and his body responded with need.

"Yes, ma'am." He cleared his throat. "Following the expansion of Calvary Vet Clinic, our veterinary technician training program will launch under our Calvary–Kitty Kibbles Partnership. Single mothers and the unhoused have priority placement and scholarship assistance with housing and tuition."

Yep, he and his wife-to-be had dreamed up a way to marry their dreams and follow their passions. The vet training program kept him teaching and working with animals, while Amarie expanded her commitment to working with women and children in need of a helping hand.

Then Noah took over. "TikTok, get ready for some fun 'cause yours truly, @TomCatNoah, is in charge of Eli's online bachelor party. And don't worry about work on Monday, @SimplyTobias has a video series coming on oral hydration to get you back on your feet. And P.S. @farmersdaughter, if you don't come home, the next bachelor party might be mine." He winked.

"Noah," Leah chided, "be good."

"Oh, trust me, Mom, I have been." He winked.

This was the family Eli had always envisioned. His momma, Tobias, Noah, and his soon-to-be-his wife, on Calvary land. Eli thanked his father for giving him a vision, but he praised heaven for sending his Saint Amarie, to help him find his own way.

Acknowledgments

To the Alpha and the Omega, all that I possess is because You have given me favor among men.

For the ladies of the lamp, my fellow nurses, you continue to inspire me to tell our stories.

To my sisters of the pen who lit the way for Eli and Amarie's story to flow from me onto the page—LaQuette, Taisha Demay, M. J. Granberry, T. B. Bond, Jacki Renee, Michele Ingrid, and the Chesapeake Romance Writers—you are my suncatchers. You believed in me and the Calvary brothers from day one, thank you.

To the women who continue to polish and refine my prose—my literary agent, Latoya Smith, and my editor, Kirsiah Depp—this is the beginning of our remarkable journey together.

To Mr. Awesome, my family, and dear friends, you are the wind in my sails, my light in the darkness, the beat of my heart.

To my readers, you challenge me to hone my craft and pursue my passions every day. I write to chronicle our stories, lift our voices, and tell our truths. We are worthy and deserving of the opportunity to hope, love, and thrive.

About the Author

SIERA LONDON is the *USA Today* bestselling and award-winning author of contemporary and paranormal romance, romantic suspense, and crime fiction. She crafts stories of diverse characters navigating the challenges and triumphs to finding lasting love. Intelligence, wit, emotion, drama, and romance are between the covers of every Siera London novel. Siera lives in Virginia with her husband and a color patch tabby named Frie. Also, Siera is a writer mentor for Romance Writers of America.